I0574863

Without Borders

Alcides Vargas Echegaray

Table of Contents

*"Not all of us can do great things.
But we can do small things with great love."*

Mother Teresa

*"Globalization and universality do not go hand in
hand; there would be, at first, an autonomy of one over
the other. Globalization is related to technocrats, trade,
tourism, information. Universality is concerned with
values, human rights, freedoms, culture, and democracy."*

Jean Baudrillard,
French philosopher and sociologist (1929-2007)

Chapter 1
The Water War

I heard the dogs barking and knew that they were glad of our arrival. The streetlights barely illuminated the walls of the adobe houses. Earlier we had passed through a path bordered by stone walls and luxurious bushes. In the street we saw, leaning on one of the posts, a man who appeared to be drunk.

"Friend, where can we stay for the night?" I asked him. The man did not seem to understand the question. However, he pointed with the finger of his bandaged hand to a two-story dwelling.

I knocked on the door, taking advantage of a loose stone on the ground. After a brief time, the door was opened by a disheveled and sleepy looking man who demanded payment before leading us up the stairs to a room on the second floor of the house. Upon entering the room, we saw others already asleep on mattresses placed directly on the wooden floor. They slept under ponchos made of llama wool with chunks of fat stuck to them.

In the semi-darkness we searched for a space between the sleeping bodies. I sensed that the last free spaces would be attached to the wall being used as a urinal. In my delirium I felt nauseous when I imagined the putrid humidity of the adobe; even so, I lay down without thinking about all the possible contagions in the infected fluids. Nor did I think about poisonous bugs slithering along the plaster molding of the wall. Despite my apprehensions, I had no choice: I had to spend the night in that place that had once been a potato tuber warehouse. I had no choice after a twelve-hour hike along a path of weeds and stones that snaked through the mountains; ascending and descending a rough road created by years of water erosion. For me, arriving at this village of adobe houses with tin roofs awakened a sensation similar to that of finding a caravanserai in Central Asia.

I was sure I would fall asleep immediately, despite the muscle aches I felt in my legs and the tingling that ran through my skin. Nothing could prevent me from sleeping, not the musky smell of the room, not the lice I felt moving around my body, not the murmur of the bats' wings and not even the pain of walking with my back hunched over, could prevent me from sleeping. Tiredness was a soporific that would take effect immediately.

I remember having a nightmare in which some strangers tried to give me a black liquid to drink. I the dream I wanted to refuse even though I knew that such a gesture would offend them. I was afraid that these people were trying to poison or bewitch me. What I did not understand was why they had chosen me to carry out that fateful ritual, although I supposed it could be because I was the only stranger in that place. They seemed to be chanting or whispering something; perhaps it was part of a black mass or an incantation ceremony against a subject they were to eliminate. Just before drinking the dark potion, I awoke to my own intemperate screams that clearly scared the other guests in the room. Then I realized that it was all a delirium produced by fatigue; a raving in which the damp urinal wall, the unpleasant smell of too many bodies and the fever that afflicted me due to sunstroke had all mixed together. Finally, silence returned, broken only by the snoring of the men and the humming of insects outside the window.

Seconds later I realized that the dark liquid in the wooden container, just like the people who wanted to poison or bewitch me, was a faded memory, or perhaps it was part of a delirious invention. I noticed that I was drenched in sweat, which I attributed to the heat of the environment or to a sunstroke. I was afraid that I had been infected, and I even thought that I was suffering from those fevers that alter the brain. I got the idea that it could be a disease caused by a tick bite. I even thought of a degenerative disease like Parkinson's or a disorder of the mental faculties due to the inclusion of Lewy bodies; alterations that begin with the same symptoms, hallucinations and delirium, followed by tremors in the hands and drool escaping from the corners of the mouth, and ending with the inability to walk and dementia.

With my eyes wide open, while my gaze was lost in the earwigs on the ceiling, which were visible despite the darkness, I tried to escape my sadness and convinced myself that the nightmare was not due to a rare disease, but rather the product of my recent experience, lived in the last two weeks, on a plateau inhabited by strange human beings of small size and atavistic customs.

I was sure that the scenery of the encounter was of a similar beauty to other places, with lagoons originated by the thaw, with a blue mirror that reflected the sky and the mountains permanently covered in snow. I imagined the same escarpments and identical gorges furrowed by sonorous streams, the beauty of many lagoons and forests of dwarf shrubs. The spaces had not changed; only my perception had changed with respect to my previous visits to similar places. Perhaps I was beginning to feel fear or apprehension. It could be that the hollows of life had taken their toll on my enthusiasm. "Nothing can last forever," I said to myself, thinking that my adventurous time had passed. I had ceased to be the traveler who climbed the mountain and then descended into the jungle to penetrate wild and inhospitable places.

"What happened, boss? Last night you scared me with your screams," Medina asked me.

"A nightmare, Medina. An unimportant nightmare," I told my assistant.

I had seen the dark liquid contained in a wooden container years before during the healing of a colonist who was bitten by a viper. The sick man's relatives opened his mouth while a healer forced him to drink. The attire of the man who officiated as healer was most original: he had a plume of red feathers tied to his crown by a hand-woven headband; from his nose hung a crescent-shaped ornament that seemed to be a copper earring because of the reddish color of the polished areas and the green tone of the cuprous oxide in the rough areas. The man was wiry and of medium size, he was an older man for his ethnic group whose life expectancy is between thirty and forty years. He kept his eyes closed as he danced, barely moving from his place, as if trying to guess the irregularities of the floor and the location of the people attending the ceremony. The fact of having his eyes closed showed in the man a distant and superior attitude to those attending the ritual.

The potion had been prepared with the juice of a black berry, similar to the huayruro seed. The poisoned person seemed to be in a stuporous phase prior to a deep coma. He was shaking his head as if he had a bug inside him that was causing him great pain or as if an aneurysm was about to burst while he was moving on top of blankets spread out on the floor. A relative explained to me that the patient had been bitten by a venomous snake in the upper part of his right thigh. From the color of the skin around the wound, which the healer had opened to expose the muscle, and from the stench it gave off, I imagined that it had been infected by the anaerobic bacteria that colonized the slime from the snake's jaws. And I thought that the alteration in consciousness was a product of the toxin from the venom of the ophidian and the septicemia caused by the anaerobes. I had to admit that this healer had the necessary knowledge to know that it was essential to penetrate the lesion so that the air would prevent the proliferation of bacteria. I assumed that the black liquid would have some effect on the toxin; perhaps it was an antidote or a buffer that acted on the protein of the poison, an enzyme that would modify the molecule or neutralize it.

After watching the ceremony, which concluded with the swallowing of the potion, I retired to rest on a hammock under a mosquito net in the dwelling that the settlers had prepared to accommodate me. I was not accustomed to sleeping on a fabric that swings in the air; however, I was able to arrange my body in such a way that my lower limbs hung over the sides. The problem was that the mosquito net only partially fulfilled its function as a protection against bites.

In the early morning of the following day, before showering, I went to the hut where the healing took place. There I came across the mourners, silent and grieving, surrounding the still-warm corpse. The bad smell continued and the belly had swollen to the point where it looked like it was about to burst. I then looked for the healer, but he was not among those present. I assumed that, before passing away, the man had been burning with fever as the back of his neck had stiffened and his body was arched. I asked no questions. It seemed imprudent at the time to make any inquiry. Somehow I felt ashamed that I had not brought some vial of antibiotic or antitoxin or antiophidic serum. I felt as if I had been condemned to be a mere spectator at the ceremony. Maybe it was that I assumed that the liquid might have some healing effect or I just didn't want to interfere. I don't know why I felt an immense sorrow, as if I shared the pain of the relatives.

Still today, after so many years, I relived that awful night in my nightmare. I remember trips through the lowland jungle bordering the basin of the great tributary rivers of the Amazon, through the African savannah, the Russian taiga and the marshes of the Caribbean. In each of them, a unique experience, yet some scenes seem to repeat themselves. Perhaps this is due to the schemes we have engraved in our minds, which simulate the reproduction of stereotyped images.

"Did you find out anything about the porters, Medina?" I had instructed him to inquire about the whereabouts of the attendants among the lodgers and the innkeeper of the hostel.

"Yes, boss" he replied, "The man says they passed through here a fortnight or so ago. He even told me that they stayed in the tambo. He says that one of them was sick or maybe blind, because they had to lead him by the arm. They were belligerent and got into a fight with the miners; there were injuries on both sides."

At that moment I was presented with details of this place, which was reached after a long walk along a path of rubble and thorns that penetrated the cloud forest where weeds were replaced by the roots of huge trees whose tops could not be distinguished in the dense fog. I had once imagined places above the clouds; castles of avenging kings, a kind of refuge for those persecuted for their religion or their ideas or for practicing unusual rites that their harassers would stigmatize as heresies.

That massif, where human beings lived, was unimaginable; basalt monoliths with cavities that communicated as if they were galleries excavated in a soft mass, and not in volcanic rocks. These caves could be the product of erosion by meltwater or perhaps the consequence of earthquakes where solid masses of rocks were moved like rivers by the force of telluric phenomena. In some of them you could even see stalactites and stalagmites covered by lichens and phosphorescent algae that gave a colorful luminosity to the space. There lived those human beings to whom we had turned for support. Then to my mind came the vision of a group of people with distinct characteristics, with ancestral customs and a peculiar history.

We must have hiked thirty to forty kilometers through the shortcuts and mule trails. Climbing and then descending the mountain ranges, looking down from the summit over the entire mountain range and the valleys with their green hues. From there you could see the sparkles of distant storms that illuminated the dark clouds in the sky and reflected in the snow and the clouds that covered the forests where the vines hung from the Monkey Puzzles and other trees.

As we passed through the misty jungle, butterflies clung to the pools of water and formed a shimmering cover on the weeds and tree ferns, while a pack of howler monkeys moved through the branches in chorus with blue and yellow plumed macaws. Climbing the slope, we reached a place of dwarf bushes and yellow grasses. Then we entered a ravine, with a creek at the intersection of two high hills, where spiky reddish plants grew.

I felt my muscles cramp due to the long walk, perspiration stuck to my back, and my spine, hurt thanks to the dyspnea caused by the effort and the lack of oxygen typical of the altitude. Despite the fatigue and the lactic acid, we had to continue to avoid the darkness of the night, which would prevent us from navigating our path safely and potentially lead to falling down the mountain side. From a distance we could make out the glow of the glaciers illuminated by the moonlight. Perhaps, because of their majesty, people named each peak after their tutelary gods. Or maybe it was the other way around: the tutelary gods were named after the mountains. Looking at the elevations it seemed more difficult to descend than to climb the slopes, or at least as difficult, because during the descent the feet would seek to adhere to the boulder floor so as not to slip down the slope or land on the thorns. In the end, toenails would be lifted out of their beds by subungual hematomas. Ankles would suffer contusions as a result of tripping over the sheared rocks on the edges of the mountain. This is where we hiked during the hours before finding lodging in this town in its gently sloping gully through which a sonorous stream ran.

There lived an Indigenous community in a village of scattered mud huts and thatched roofs. In the mountains we could see hollows from where their sentries watched us. I thought the lookouts might have some kind of throwing weapon. Our guides, who also carried the medicines, insecticides, and testing kits, which we placed in backpacks, were just as strange to the inhabitants of those villages. The community patrols would consider them as suspicious as they did us. They had requested our presence so for that reason, I was unable to understand their suspicion. No one had come on their own initiative to get to know the place or its inhabitants. They had asked for our help in dealing with a calamity that had claimed several lives in recent weeks.

During part of the outward journey, the porters guided us along a goat path until we reached a hill where there was an abandoned shack. I sat on a stone slab placed in front of what had once been a rest hut or dining room for travelers. From that place I could see the water pipes coming from the thaw that went down the ravine, as well as the vegetation, with areas of flowers and others of dense forest. I could not distinguish trails or landmarks that could guide us; I thought of chullpas – watchtowers or simple burial mounds.

"What do we do? We can't even go forward without knowing the way," I commented with dismay, not having imagined this scenario.

"It's up to you," Medina replied.

Suddenly, in the distance, a hundred or two hundred meters away, we saw a man, between the escarpment of rocks and bushes, waving to us. I presumed that he was the person in charge of the people who were waiting for us to serve as our guide. So, driven by the security of returning to the trail, we resumed our march.

The shortcut stuck to a sonorous creek with foaming waters and slippery edges. Several times I fell and landed on boulders thankfully covered by moss and straw, to the delight and derision of my companions.

As we advanced, I discovered that they were watching us from the top of the mountain. I used the binoculars to check my suspicions.

"Medina, have you noticed that we are being watched from the caves?" I asked my assistant, who was a rural nurse.

"Don't say that, boss," he said with fear on his face, "Do you think they will attack us?" His eyes were wide and his skin was pale and shiny.

"I don't know. I don't think that's their purpose," I tried to reassure him.

"I'm scared, boss. In these circumstances you never know."

"Try to master your fear, Medina. You know that they pick up the smell of fear," I answered. I did not want to comment that I assumed that the local patrols had weapons, even arrows with poisoned tips. "Try to calm down, Medina!" I stressed, even though I too was experiencing an episode of poorly concealed panic.

I conjectured that their faces would be painted white with a vegetable resin on a black background due to the tar that gushed from the fissure of a geographic fault. Similarly, I imagined that the men would have orange hair due to depigmentation caused by deficiencies in their diet, as well as skeletal limbs and distended bellies. The children would have brachycephalic skulls and red, parched cheeks, like the little ones in the Andean villages, who played with bugs and poultry.

That time we arrived at nightfall. In the half-light we could barely make out the silhouettes of the bodies nor the limits defined by the stones of the platforms. We could only guess the shapes of the camelids, which must be alpacas, llamas or guanacos, distinguished by the whiteness of their wool. And in no way we could appreciate the grim gesture or the forced smile of the locals. In my mind I recreated the village, possibly composed of a group of isolated mud huts with thatched roofs and accesses of caked earth and weeds.

Someone led us to a shack with adobe walls, which was illuminated from the within by a petroleum lamp that emitted a bluish light; we were left here. Medina was placed in the center of the room and me at the back, next to the wall. The man was not alone. In the darkness I could sense the fear of others, there was a nauseating stench clinging to their skin. I couldn't tell if it was stale sweat or if it was due to the concoctions with which they smeared their bodies. What struck me as odd was the way the stench had gone unnoticed in the forest. Now in the village it was pervasive, repulsive, unbearable.

Then I imagined the silhouettes of those men, thin arms, swollen bellies and too skinny lower limbs. And I could make out the features of the man who led us into the hut. He had an angular face and a sparse, unkempt beard. His age was unguessable.

As soon as I lay down, I fell fast asleep. Despite a deep sleep, it was fitful. My dreams presented me with scenes of landslides and climbing escarpments; in some of them I saw myself in a mess and I could not distinguish whether it was a police raid or a settling of scores for a pending matter from the past. In the mess I could distinguish several faces of angry people. The atmosphere was unfamiliar to me. I could only feel my lower limbs slacken, as if I had no strength or the floor turned out to be the slime of a gastropod. Then I had a jolt, as if I had rolled off a cliff at the edge of the road.

When I awoke from the nightmare I was assaulted by gloomy thoughts that provoked a persistent insomnia. I tried to go back to sleep to regain the energy I had lost during the hike up the mountain, but it was impossible.

The next day, after we had washed our faces with melt water in a stone hollow, we went out into the open field between the huts. The men watched us in silence. Then I dared to ask,

"Who can we talk to?" What I really would have liked to ask was, 'with whom we should coordinate?'

"They don't seem to understand us," Medina replied.

Meanwhile, our people, the porters, remained silent. As they did not respond, we limited ourselves to comply with the protocol that, we thought, was part of our mission.

We were taken to a hut, where some of the sick people were staying. We examined them, uncovered their chests and abdomens, observed their eyes, mouths and palates. In most of them we found stigmata of an old disease that appears from time to time causing many deaths, as in the case of the supernumerary elephants of the African savannah or the rats that kill themselves by throwing themselves into the sea in the fjords of Norway.

Our assessment revealed blackish spots on the chest. When we pressed on them with gloved fingers, their reluctance was noticeable; they were blood globules or something similar: pink exanthema evolving into watery blisters. Nothing we could do. I reasoned that these globules would have spread all over the body:

on the surface of the brain mass, in the capsule covering the liver, on the kidneys and adrenals; even on the corneas, where they were slightly smaller. The blisters absorb blood until the individual becomes anemic: it raises their temperature, and consumes them from the inside, drives them mad or demented; they struggle with fevers, delirium and tremors until they fall into a coma and, finally, die. However, these people have lived for centuries with this endemic disease that appears from time to time. It kills them by the dozen, but many survive and manage to reproduce. Thus, their race and its progeny has been perpetuated.

The disease appeared every twenty or sixty years, like the visits of Halley's comet; perhaps together with Halley's comet. I would have liked to explain to them the reason for cyclical phenomena in endemic diseases. I would have told them that the massive melting of ice caused changes in the surface of the continents. And that, in turn, glaciations wiped animal and plant species off the face of the earth.

Pandemics also have this periodic characteristic. For that reason, I would have liked also to explain that epidemics have arisen after wars or as a consequence of massive displacements of people. Perhaps they would not have understood anything. Even if I told them that bubonic plague arrived in Europe in the Middle Ages with the invading troops from Asia; or that typhus appeared in Russia after the defeat of the German troops in the Second World War. Then I remembered that the rabies that affected the Nordic steppes was due to the presence of hungry wolves, which spent a harsh winter surrounded by frozen lakes and tundra, without other small animals that hungry packs usually feed on. But they were not interested in my historical exposition, so I had to save the explanation for another time. Nor would they want to know if there are wolves, taigas or wars between countries. Perhaps, after examining the rashes and the bloody pustules of the inhabitants of this place of huts and hollows, I could get an idea of the disease and its possible cure. Perhaps when I cured the sick, they would be interested in listening to my globe-trotting tales.

I silently evaluated the signs of the disease to try to make a diagnosis. There I realized that they were watching me silently. I interpreted in that silent gaze a question, "Will you be able to do anything for us?" I trembled at the responsibility; I also feared their frustration in the event that I could not help them: the poisoned arrows, the spears with bone-sharp points, or an assault with tooth and nail. Beyond any attack, however, I would feel disenchantment as I met their distressed faces; frustration as I heard the children's moans at the catastrophe and saw the women's wild eyes. I must not fail. There was no alternative.

Some watched our extravagant group with pity; others saw us as if we were the advance guard of a horde of enemies. Those with the most wrinkles showed the lanky faces of leprosy, and the young ones boasted scars on their faces. It seemed to me that no one trusted my brown eyes or the gray hair that invaded my mustache and beard; neither did they trust Medina's large size, much less the guides or porters, who were sweating profusely after having carried medicines and instruments such as microscopes and laboratory reagents on their backs. I did not know what to say. "What a world!" I thought, and I kept quiet, sure that no one would understand me, and on the assumption that someone did understand me, he wouldn't have cared.

I had arrived believing that these people would receive us as saviors coming to rid them of plagues and rats. On the contrary, they were suspicious of us. It was the same as always: what promised to be fire turned out to be ice. Who am I to assign blame for such human behavior as fear of the unknown? The khaki suits we wore, the explorer's boots, our beards, our light skin… Everything would remind them of the invading settlers of the lowlands; the adventurous fortune hunters who had arrived in the upper part of the ravines, where the streams whose waters carried the auriferous mud were born. From the beginning, they became their enemies, because in the past they had persecuted them and stripped them of their lands.

"Are you sure it was them who asked us to come?" I asked, thinking that maybe it was another ethnic group that inhabited a different mountain or another place.

"The porters say it's them," Medina replied.

"They think we are intruders. We are not welcome."

The men in that place were extraordinarily small; I would say dwarfs. They looked like a group of pygmies from Africa or the Philippines. Their faces were ruddy and their cheeks had a dirty crust on them. The women were just as small and were thinner, as if they were all pre-pubescent girls. No one stood out in the crowd. All the faces looked the same to me. The men were hostile, defiant, and the women were hiding behind them.

At first, their hostility hid a defensive attitude, but when they gained confidence, they formed two semicircles around our group. In the first semicircle were the men, dressed in rather peculiar attire: some wore a beige wool jacket and others were covered by a poncho of intense colors between maroon and black. In the second semicircle the women were dressed in light-colored blouses. In a kind of folded shawl they carried their children or their belongings.

In addition to their size, I was struck by the long hair; in the case of the men, combed with multiple braids that went down from the roots to the back. The women had gathered their hair in two thick braids, one on each side of their heads. I assumed that they were an ethnic group different from the Uros that inhabit Lake Titicaca; different from the Queros that populate the foothills of the eastern Andes and the high jungle of the

Tahuamanu. Perhaps they were part of the Catacamara, who were known to be highway robbers, or a more peaceful group of uncontacted people, different from the ethnic groups that inhabited the surrounding area.

After I tried to communicate with them, one of the group uttered a phrase that I could not understand, although I seemed to have caught a word or two. Maybe they wanted to tell me, 'Why did you take the trouble to come and see us?' Maybe it wasn't a question, but a statement, 'You shouldn't have come here!'

At that moment I understood that any intrusion, even in good faith, would never be welcome. Even when they themselves had invited you. Then I remembered the racial discrimination in countries receiving refugees. To the natives we looked like dark skinned intruders. Maybe they thought we were going to steal their belongings or even their souls. That would surely seem more serious to them, because without a soul they could not continue living in their huts of stone and adobe, with the floor dug out to prevent the chilly wind from the mountains from freezing them; nor in the caves opened in the mountains, where they took refuge from the alluvium of the ravine. My analysis of the soul of these beings had its roots in Eastern mythology, which postulates that life surpasses death and converts our energy into a fluid entity that glides in ethereal space. According to this set of beliefs, we remain eternally in that place, as an ectoplasm without age or any other peculiar characteristic.

In their case, it was not the sidereal spaces or ascent to the clouds; it was more like caverns illuminated by phosphorescent algae. In that place rested the spirits that had occupied their bodies and from there came the death throes of the dead, and occasionally their messages, which were almost always warnings about dangers. All this in a tone similar to the howling of the wind.

Evidently, they needed us, but, at the same time, they found us unpleasant, strange and inhuman. That was the perception they had of our crew, composed of a light-skinned individual, dressed in an explorer's jacket, linen pants, boots and a skirted hat; a mestizo, shorter in stature, with the look of a late-night reveler, and several porters, with angular faces and greasy hair, similar in every way to the settlers of the lowlands who first invaded them and then cornered them until they occupied only the most inaccessible places.

I would have liked to point out that I was born in a neighborhood that smelled of farts and piss, where drunks made a racket and relieved themselves in the nooks and crannies of the alleys. That is why the stuccoed walls of the houses in the main square, including the side walls of the church, were damp and smelly. The men would fall to the ground and then sleep off the hangover. Next to the church were the steps that ascended to the upper part of the neighborhood. On them sat the addicts taking drugs and getting high.

I would also tell them that the old men in my neighborhood had the same wrinkles, the children the same boogers and the women the same charm. It was a neighborhood like so many others, with unhappy characters and desolate losers, abusers of their wives, spoiled by popular customs. There I lived the same fantasy and reality that then I had to experience with these mountain people. I saw the misery that rummaged the nooks and crannies in search of support and identical prayer for redemption. Likewise, I felt that the days led to nothing, that I had to read the same news in the same newspaper to prolong the routine. In the end I realized that there was no point in recounting the details of my life in such a situation. Besides, they only wanted to know if I was able to cure those fevers and the accompanying drowsiness.

They were not interested in whether I was better or worse than them.

The natives who followed us seemed to be part of a commission of interlocutors appointed in an assembly. Among them I distinguished a man who was less than five feet tall, with a tonsured head, as if he were a priest or altar boy in some local church. These men were the ones who guided us through the trail that visited each of the mud huts. Inside the houses we were accompanied only by the tonsured dwarf, who seemed not to be afraid of being infected; or maybe he had contracted the disease in the past and was now immune. I would have liked to explain to him that this was not always the case, that some viruses had multiple strains and were actually more lethal if they affected people who had already had something similar. The process is called amplification and is an autoaggression response on the infected cells; autoaggression attributed to cytokines and giant lymphocytes, which are called *natural killers*. The attacked cells may be part of the vascular endothelium or of the alveoli. Thus, complications include internal hemorrhages, cerebral vasculitis and hemorrhages in the alveoli, leading to severe respiratory distress.

That was the molecular explanation for dengue hemorrhagic fever and severe respiratory diseases. The little man with the tonsure had no idea about that, he walked among the sick, helped them to drink liquids from the wooden container, wiped their tears with the back of his hand and the drool with his fingers, which he then dried on his cloth pants. My guts churned and I almost threw up at the sight of it. Then it occurred to me to think of the nurses who took care of the wounded soldiers laid out on the canvas stretchers. I also remembered the white-helmeted first responders rescuing the wounded from burns caused by incendiary bombs. And I assumed that the whole planet had its own lepers, its own typhoid patients and its own aid workers.

"Medina, do you understand what he is saying?"

"It's a dialect, it sounds like ancient Quechua," he answered, "I think I understand some of the words."

"Ask him how many sick people have these symptoms. And also where our porters are."

Medina spoke in Quechua. The shaven-haired man looked him in the eye, but did not answer, as if he had not understood the language or did not know what to say. Suddenly he took Medina by the hand and led him to a place on the esplanade, where a large hut with a thatched roof burned by the sun stood. I saw them walk away, and after a while, during which they remained in the hut, I saw them return. Medina's face had turned white and he was walking with his eyes wide open; his hands were shaking. He wanted to tell me something, but he was not in a position to do so because of the trembling of his body and because the words would not come from his lips.

"He whispered," he said, his voice cracking. I interpreted that he wanted to confess something hidden. "In that hovel are our men drugged or poisoned. I don't know what they have done to them. They can't even sit down. They didn't recognize me at all, master. I'm so scared." He couldn't continue because of the gasp, which I recognized as a respiratory spasm.

"What are we going to do? I swear I'm scared shitless," he said, unable to utter another word.

"Answer me with a number on the Glasgow scale," I wanted to know their neurological response score to get an idea of the risk.

"I don't know how to measure, boss. They can't talk or sit down," said Medina.

"We're screwed, Medina!" That moment seemed to me to be one of the most difficult in my life, even though I had gone through many others just as hard. Dissimulate and take an interest in the number of dead and sick people. As if you did not give importance to the situation.

An Indigenous man, who had a sunken orbital cavity, possibly due to the enucleation of the eyeball, began to draw lines on the dirt floor, using a dry branch. As the man drew the lines, I counted them, until I reached thirty. However, I did not know if the lines referred to the number of sick or dead people. The other men around us seemed to confirm the number with a murmur.

Some of those present studied me suspiciously; others simply did not look at me. I thought they had not understood me because of the language barrier or perhaps I had not formulated the question well. They spoke, according to Medina, a dialect derived from Quechua or an archaic Quechua that my assistant could not fully interpret. Knowing the number of sick and dead people helped me to calculate morbidity and mortality, to know how lethal the disease was. It was clear to me that the lethality data was important in determining virulence and designing a plan to control the outbreak.

"We're screwed, comrade," I commented to my assistant, thinking that they wanted to blackmail us with the results.

"Do you think they will kill us, boss?" I noticed that his legs, indeed, his whole body was still trembling, as if he were shivering with intense cold.

"I don't know," I answered, although it was clear to me that it was a factual language that we and they could understand. "It will depend on the results we get," I continued, reasoning what our chances were. "The more of them that survive or are cured, the greater our chance of getting out in one piece, comrade."

After evaluating the possible differential diagnoses and the epidemic history of the region, I signaled the people accompanying me to take off their clothes. I was trying to find vector bites on their skin. In that area, one of the most common parasites was the body louse. The bug had a white abdomen and eight legs armed with tiny pincers that it used to attach itself to the skin or hair of humans.

As soon as they took off their clothes, I could see not only the traces of bites and scabs from scratching, but also multiple insects in their clothes, as if they were gathering to protect themselves or to reproduce. I immediately imagined the rat burrows and their inhabitants under the stone slabs. The diseases that these rodents had came to mind, such as black plague, hantavirus, even Rocky Mountain fever. I also remembered the epidemic exanthematous typhus that struck the troops hiding in the trenches during the First World War. The soldiers died with their bodies full of rashes, possessed by fever and the madness of stupor prior to death. That is why they had christened the disease trench fever or exanthematous typhus. After some time it was clarified that they were two diseases with a different evolution. Trench fever came with an outbreak and a fever of forty degrees, but after a few days it would suddenly disappear just as it had come. Typhus, on the other hand, was a serious disease, which had ravaged Russia and other European countries during the Bolshevik Revolution and the following years. As a result, thousands of soldiers, market workers and cleaners, train travelers, peasants on collective farms had lost their lives. Thousands, perhaps hundreds of thousands, of anonymous people died, as did famous people, such as the journalist John Reed, famous for his book *Ten Days That Shook the World*. It affected both the cities and countryside. More than two million people died, more than the number caused by the war between the Reds and the Whites or by shells from the western front, where the German troops were located.

"Medina, do you think you could ask them to bring us the boxes of medicine? I hope we have enough injectable and capsule chloramphenicol for all the sick people," I told my assistant.

We then used a catheter to give them intravenous solutions and antibiotics through that route. For some we injected the drugs intramuscularly, which left them lame for several days. It was a gamble. If we succeeded, we would be able to save everyone on the expedition. If not, we would not have many options left.

Medina had told me that our porters were narcotized by some drug that had been injected into the outer ear with a blowgun, or perhaps they had been forced to inhale a paste made from creeping plants. The hallucinogen would have taken effect immediately, preventing any reaction on their part, despite the fact that they were twice the weight and so much taller than these little men. Ours had been overpowered by the group, as in the wars between the Pygmies and their neighbors the Maasai of the lower Nile. Perhaps they used as a hypnotic inducer a crystalline liquid that also required a small dose of sleeping pill, which they would have camouflaged in the drink, taking advantage of the thirst after the exhaustion of the trek.

At that moment, ideas came to me. The variety of situations that could occur suddenly flooded my imagination: human cages built with balsa wood or chonta wood, dirty and dark rooms full of giant bedbugs, us crawling on the floor of rubble and weeds, unable to sit up. That would be revenge for their dead and their prostrate; for their frustration at having trusted us without getting results. It would encourage the expectation of another scenario. Would it be the same if we managed to heal their sick? I would never know. Injectable chloramphenicol and getting the diagnosis right were our chance to get out alive.

I evaluated the faces to be able to guess their intentions. In that moment of anguish, as in the sleepless nights, I ached for my sentimental failure, for being away from my children, for the burdening loneliness. To whom should I pray for a little bit of compassion? Who should I pray for on this occasion? I would not pray for the sick or the dead; I would pray for myself and my people. I would pray that we could return unharmed to the other side of the mountain, where the small towns of settlers and artisanal miners are. I would also ask to be able to cure their mourners and in that way I would save myself and the people under my care.

The day after our arrival, the villagers organized themselves to receive our instructions. Lines of people were formed: the children first, then the women, organized in pairs. Everyone went through the ritual of undressing to be sprinkled with grayish talcum powder with insecticide effect that we had brought in our backpacks. Then the lice and nits would be killed by soaking the clothes in boiled water. Then I would see that on the surface of the water a fatty cream forms, a whitish, caseous mass containing the cuticles of the apterae.

When I finished the work, I met with the delegates. There I suddenly heard what sounded like a murmur underneath the conversation in their dialect, as if someone was saying "What now? At first I did not believe that this question had been asked in my language; I thought I had imagined it as a result of the desire to communicate or that I was confused and I had misunderstood some phrase in their dialect. However, I couldn't let that opportunity pass me by, so I asked out loud,

"Do any of you speak Spanish?" Perhaps I should have used the term Castilian so as not to confuse them.

Suddenly from behind the group emerged a man with thinning hair, his face furrowed with wrinkles and shorter than his companions. I estimated that he might be among the oldest in the village.

"I do, Sir." He had the Manchego touch of some priest or missionary who had arrived in the vicinity many years ago, or maybe he learned it from a catechist who had been kidnapped long ago.

"That's good," I replied enthusiastically. "I can't tell you how glad I am. That's great!" I repeated.

Later I learned from him that the tonsured man was the village sorcerer, and that he had the power to paralyze the bodies of his fellow villagers by simply knotting the end of a blackened handkerchief. He told me that the man's name was Melquíades and that he had been baptized by a missionary with a white beard and cassock. The magic was an inheritance from his ancestors, who, for generations had been dedicated to witchcraft.

During the dialogue I wanted to inquire about the fate of my people.

"Where are my men?" I asked, looking him in the eye.

"They are bad men, mister," he said, as if to justify the kidnapping.

"What did they do?" I was interested, fearful that he would inform me about some kind of rampage in which they might have participated.

The man did not respond. I wanted to believe that he didn't understand me or that he didn't care about the anxiety I felt for the safety of my staff.

"Master, another man like you lives here," perhaps he lacked the words to express his wishes. "The man wants to see you."

Without waiting for my consent, the man took me by the wrist and gently dragged me along a path that disappeared in the bend of the mountain. From that spot I could see a hut at the bottom of the ravine. The roof looked like zinc or some reflective plastic.

Attached to one of the walls was a pipe with torrent water. The trail entered through a corridor of fruit trees and dwarf palms, similar to the forest of the cloud mountain. The puddles along the path were covered with blue and red butterflies, wasps with black cephalothorax and orange abdomen, green snakes and lizards with iridescent fur.

We walked for half an hour to reach the plain, where the hut, built with wooden planks, was located. Inside, barely illuminated by the chinks of the light that filtered through the planks, we could make out an individual prostrate due to some chronic illness. The man appeared to be about sixty years old. He had abundant hair, a graying beard and a bored expression, perhaps because of the pain or the discomfort of remaining in an unchanging position. The cornea of one eye was dull and the eyeball was projected out of the orbital cavity, the result of an exophthalmos that, I interpreted, was due to a corneal and nerve injury. The other eye followed my movements.

"How are you Mr...?" I realized that I didn't know his name.

"I asked him to bring you," he answered in a voice that I recognized as that of a military or veteran policeman; gruff, I would say imperative.

"Tell me, what can I do for you?" I wanted to know, trying not to lose my cool, although I could tell I was in for a surprise or two.

He was watching me closely; I suspected that the examination stemmed from a desire to get to know me and to be able to communicate some hidden thought that was somehow important to him.

"You're wondering what happened to my left eye, aren't you? And why I am in such a state of disability," he continued.

"You could say that." I answered laconically.

"Let's see, first, my vision. It's a matter linked to my tenure here. It was about twenty-five years ago. I was, at the time, a police sergeant. I had been assigned to a political-military emergency zone under the command of a captain named Huerta," he paused to think about whether to continue with his narration. Then he continued, "The captain's methods were anything but saintly. The day of the incident that caused the damage to my eye, he had tried to rape the wife of an individual, a high military commander of a column of subversives. I objected and we argued loudly. The officer got excited and, after taking out his regulation weapon, wanted to shoot me in the face. I defended myself and struggled to wrest the gun from him; in the end a shot was fired," he stopped talking to take a breath, as if the story brought him back to the scene of the events. Then he resumed the story, "The officer was in charge of a high-risk mission.

"The flash of the shot damaged my eyesight and caused me intense pain, to the point that I lost consciousness. When I regained consciousness, I was surrounded by the rest of the unit, who accused me of having killed the captain. For this reason, I was to be transferred to the nearest town to be tried by the military court.

"The lieutenant, second in command under the captain, told me, 'Martinez, I'm not going to repeat this: take out your backpack and flee to the jungle. In two hours we will come out to hunt you with the order to shoot.'"

I kept thinking about the internal wars, the codes of violence, the limits between the civilized and the savage. Then I looked at the sergeant, waiting for him to continue his story.

"I tried to stay away from my former colleagues. It became my life. During the day I walked among the rocks and at night I slept in the torrents. After weeks, exhausted by the effort, I arrived at this place, where Melquíades cured me with his leaf tea and frog soup and I was able to recover from the fright and the effort."

When he mentioned that name, I conjectured that he was referring to the little man whose head was shaved to simulate a religious man since I had already been told, he had astral powers and ancestors who had performed the same activity.

"Do you think I should continue or shall I go on to explain some matters that concern us both?"

"Whatever you wish." I was waiting for the man to continue so that, in this way, I could understand something that seemed enigmatic to me up to that moment. Was I facing a group of hospitable natives or were they hostile and dangerous?

"Well, I stayed with them all this time. I did not want to expose myself to a summary trial or to the revenge of his relatives or his comrades-in-arms. You will understand that the event could be interpreted as insubordination, which is punishable by firing squad for treason. So I had to abandon my family, my home and my work.

"The paralysis is another matter. It happened during an avalanche; I became invalid while trying to rescue those buried in the mud. I don't know how but I damaged my spine and have been paralyzed from the waist down ever since."

"I'm sorry. Sincerely, I'm sorry, Sergeant," I apologized, thinking that the paralysis could be due to a vertebral fracture with spinal cord section.

"Now to your business, doctor. I was the one who sent for you so that you could cure the men in the village. I instructed the paramedics to look for you, I wrote the letters to ask your organization to come and help us."

At that moment a woman in her thirties or early thirties entered the room, with a friendly face with a smile on her face. She was holding a tray with several bowls on it. I guessed that both the tray and the bowls were carved from balsa wood. The woman seemed to scold the sergeant and opened a window that let in sunlight. The window was protected by transparent glass or mica. Possibly, that material had been transported from some city by a relative or other person who had that facility.

"This is my partner," said the sergeant.

"Nice to meet you!" I said to the woman. When she heard my greeting, she smiled back at me.

The scene seemed to me to be similar to my visit to the organization's head office in La Paz. Waiting for us in the office was Judith, an Irish woman who was the director for the region. She served us with herbal teas, creams, pastries or whatever snacks she had on hand. The same eagerness was shown by the sergeant's companion, with the same smiling and friendly expression. I knew then that it was the woman who took care of the needs and demands of the prostrate man.

After hours of chatting about one topic or another, it occurred to me to ask, "Did you ever try to return to the city?" I wanted to know. To tell the truth, I was intrigued. I was sure that before suffering the vertebro-medullary injury the man had made not one, but several attempts to return to his hometown.

"Once, hiding my true identity, I returned home. When I arrived, everything was different. My wife had realized that I no longer existed and had taken up with a relative of hers. Imagine, with my character, it didn't take long for me to kill them both. Each one of my children lived somewhere else." He paused again. Then he continued, "I inquired about the status of the charge and was informed that it was not time-barred, so if I came forward, I was sure to end up in jail."

At that moment I understood that there are marches of no return. You can't always turn back. This was the case with the sergeant and others. I took advantage of the interview to ask him other questions I needed to know about the village and its people.

"Why do the natives live in the puna?" I was referring to the inhospitable climate, which did not allow the cultivation of varieties of plants that grew at other altitudes, and also to the livestock, which was limited to camelids.

"Because they were defeated in the water war," replied the man.

Then he told me the story of the water war, in which the defeated were the men of the village and the victors, their neighbors, the natives of the lowland jungle. The war had lasted about ten years. Martínez calculated the time according to the account of the natives, who had counted one hundred and twenty full moons. According to the sergeant, the confrontation took place some three or four hundred moons ago. The losers had to move and took refuge in the punas and in the caves of the rocky areas. In the end they discovered that there was another way to continue living.

Those who won the war took away the water from the streams coming down from the thaws, but they discovered that the mountain hid springs with clear water where they could drink without fear of being contaminated by the feces of cattle and shepherds. The water rolled down a spring between the grasses and creeping clovers, wetting the rhizomes and welcoming colorful birds and butterflies. They soon learned that dwarf yuccas and twenty-centimeter pineapples could be grown and that nearby grew cacti with leaves parasitized by a white powder that turned red when wet or squeezed. With the dye that resulted from this white powder, they gave color to the carded wool before passing it to the weavers for weaving.

I wanted to imagine the fight as a guerrilla war, with the groups scouting the enemy from the high ground and then taking advantage of any carelessness and coming down with arrows. Their puya was a xerophytic plant with fleshy, lanceolate leaves, polished to have the edge of a Swiss Army knife. In this war, once they killed the male, the female belonged to them, even if she resisted. I imagined the wives and daughters of those killed in action, sequestered in the huts of the one who had killed her husband, sleeping in the same bed, sexually assaulted during the night.

In my mind, perhaps the dead man was not the husband, but the father of an abducted women. In the same way, they would be received with the same lewd joy as if the act were superior to hatred. I imagined that in some cases the abducted women would take revenge and, after getting the murderer drunk, they would cut off his sex at the root, and then leave the victim bleeding on the dirt floor of the hut. The subject's blood would flow from his groin until he was left weak and drained of blood, unable to defend himself due to intoxication from the cane alcohol or whatever strong drug he had been tricked into drinking. The narcotic used could be chamico, ayahuasca or any hallucinogenic ivy that grew nearby.

Perhaps the man would not feel pain from the amputation, but would sink into a deeper and deeper sleep. After the castration was complete, the woman would flee to the bush to avoid the revenge of the relatives of the deceased, who upon learning of it would go out in search of her armed with machetes and axes. In their ethnic group, vengeance was an obligation because they believed that, without this punishment, the soul of the deceased would continue to wander through the caves of the mountain. Therefore, there would be no rest for the bereaved until the murderers were eliminated.

At that moment I remembered some old proverbs: 'with the yardstick you measure you will be measured', and 'he who kills with iron dies with iron'. That was the law in these parts. Of course that was the dance and the Murga must be danced to the beat of the drum.

Today I picture the war as any other confrontation of hostile forces: feathered Indigenes against men with braids in their hair. Men with faces painted with achiote against men with sallow faces who did not need to paint their faces. Corpses would appear in the rivers, washed up on the muddy banks. Scavengers such as mountain lions and ocelots would have a feast. Even animals that were not normally scavengers, such as black pigs and wild dogs would probably join in.

In some cases the excess of violence could be attributed to the moonshine made with potato peels or fermented corn, which turned them into unbridled psychotics, even with the children or women of the enemies. In other cases, the warriors outraged the bodies of the deceased, on which they danced; or urinated in the wounds of the head.

That invalid, the one-eyed sergeant filled me in on the old habits that still prevailed among these little men with ruddy cheeks. Until then I had thought that violence was confined to the outskirts of the big cities or was common among the lower-class elements of society. However, I could see that it was equally prevalent in the Andean villages, as well as in the hamlets bordering the large rivers. Then I remembered the murder of a family of landowners in a place that was three thousand five hundred meters above sea level. The limbs, torn off with an axe; the teeth, smashed with a club; the skulls, destroyed with stones.

Returning to the village, I saw the sorcerer walking in the middle of the slope. I observed him carefully and found him to be bald and paunchy. The hump had reduced him to a dwarf among dwarves. The limp could have been due to a clubfoot or a shortened consolidation fracture. However, despite his shortcomings, he was the best hope for my group; at least I could converse with him, even if there was a language barrier. I might ask him about the intoxication of my porters or the future that awaited us. However, it seemed to me that this was not the right time for it, despite my predicament. It was possible that among his feathered enemies there was a similar personage, perhaps skinny and long, with very long upper limbs, to the point where his hands almost touched his knees. He would have a wiry face, sunken cheeks and protruding cheekbones; with slanted eyes, as if hidden deep in the sockets.

After meeting the village sorcerer and comparing him with my imagined sorcerer of his adversaries, I wondered what they would say to each other if they ever met. The rendezvous could take place halfway between the two villages, on a stone slab simulating a ledge above a dolmen. The men would carry leather whips to whip each other before engaging in any dialogue. Maybe even the encounter would be friendly and, after studying the physiognomy of their opponent, they would throw coca leaves on a red poncho as if they were playing poker. This would serve to divine the will of the tutelary spirits of the mountains and invoke harmony between the two ethnic groups or, at least, a peaceful coexistence with precise limits.

I spent some time recreating the scene in my mind, mixing memories, such as the arrival at the plateau town that had welcomed us with musicians playing drums and panpipes, which gave the encounter an air of mystery and solemnity. There we encountered other sorcerers dressed in white and pink flamingo feathers, attached to their heads by means of a mitre adorned with silver inlays, bits of mirror and imitation precious stones. The dancers moved to the sound of a melody interpreted by the musicians of the town while their necks swayed and shook the plume of colored feathers, which varied with the reflections of the sun. At times orange feathers were noticeable; they seemed to have been plucked from the cock-of-the-rock bird, at others the red and blue from parrots. At times they had the dull color of salt lake palmettos.

The other men of the village wore leather shoes with miter-like inlays, as well as conch shells, which produced a sound that combined with the music of the panpipes and drums. The spectacle resembled one I had enjoyed at the Salvador de Bahia carnival, as well as the dances of the Mesopotamian carnival in the province of Misiones.

At the end of the conversation with the paralyzed sergeant I had to return to the present. He and I, alone with all the burdens. He with his stories; me with my apprehensions. We were two men with similar paranoias, with the iron will to get the potion that would cure all evil; with the desire to be judged by the honorable deeds, and not by the shadows and dastardliness. That was the moment to make our reality transparent and renounce any expectation of leadership.

"Of the ten prostrate patients, seven no longer have stupor or fever. The other three have stopped shivering; I hope they will be better tomorrow. The mildly ill and those who were at the onset of the disease, still in the stage of cold shakes, are already cured," I informed him, thinking that we were fulfilling our mission. I hoped that he would understand that on their part they had to reciprocate. So I dared to ask,

"What has become of our porters?"

"I don't understand what you mean," he replied without looking me in the eye. He seemed to be unaware that the people who had carried our equipment were being held incommunicado in a dark room in a large hut, restrained and narcotized with some kind of hallucinogenic substance.

"What I mean is that the sick people are, for the most part, cured. Besides, there have been no more cases in the last few days." For me this was as important as the healing of those who had suffered from the disease.

Before our arrival, and during the first week, more than two or three cases per day were detected. Even older men were found unconscious at the edge of the thawing pond; women lay on the grass of the platforms and children went into a sudden panic crisis, which manifested itself in screams, as if they had hallucinations with monsters and evil beings. Two weeks later, no more newly sick people were reported to us on the perimeter or on the outskirts of the site.

It was more than likely that this was due to the elimination of the vector, the louse, or the host, the black field rat. The women still had the gray dust of insecticide caked in their hair, and the children seemed to have sprouted among the stones and could be seen running up the hill. I felt relieved, as if suddenly the stench of the burrows was no longer there and the stench of the men had dissipated. Under other circumstances I would have been so pleased with my success that I would have screamed like a madman or an excited fever patient before the stupor. However, to my mind came the image of five young men in a toxic state with furtive looks and ataxia in their limbs who, from time to time, screamed in terror at their own delusions. As long as they were not with us, there was nothing to be happy about. That is why I had to ask the sergeant to convey my request to the tonsured-haired sorcerer, so that his people would have an attitude of reciprocity with us.

"We gave them what they asked for. It would be good if they gave us back our porters to return to our land," I demanded.

When Esteban, the man who spoke Manchego Spanish, who led me to Sergeant Martínez, gave the sergeant's order to

Melquíades, the sorcerer looked at me. Then he withdrew without giving me an answer.

Watching him leave, I experienced a moment of fear. I watched him with his limping walk as he approached the group that seemed to be permanently watching us. Melquíades lobbied with Esteban and with the other men with the flattened faces and flattened hair. His attitude was not friendly at all, perhaps because he was hiding some purpose or had a plan that affected our stay in the place. I was overcome with uncertainty. My legs faltered, until I sat on a round stone in the middle of the path that led to the huts.

I was thinking about the porters. I was no longer certain that they would be released, even though the sick had been cured; I was not even sure that we would be able to return home. I guessed that the sergeant had no decisive influence on our fate; the shaven-headed dwarf and his assembly were the ones who decided the fate of the group.

I was overcome with fear, as if I had suddenly realized that I had nothing to bargain with; perhaps for them it was the most natural thing in the world that the sick would heal, that no one would show the traces of the bites of the aptera, that the ravine would not give off the stench and fumes of dead rats. My shirt was wet with sweat and stuck to my body.

Then suddenly I saw Medina coming out of the wooden door of a hut we had not visited before. His skin had a yellowish tinge to it, which made me fear that he was suffering from liver disease or was chronically anemic, which I never realized. He was panting as if he had been running down the slope. I asked him what was wrong and he replied that one of the women we had thought was getting better had passed away. The news subtracted years from me, I aged in an instant and noticed that my face was wrinkling. I had not expected the event, and even less at that moment, when they were deciding our return to the other side of the mountain. I thought they already knew the news; I assumed they had heard the cries of the relatives when they saw that the woman did not react to Medina's attempts at resuscitation. Under the circumstances, I felt I had nothing to demand.

"I think we're screwed, Medina," I said, letting him know that they would make us pay dearly for failure.

"Don't scare me. I thought you were a friend of the hunchbacked-one. Didn't he tell you what they would do with us?"

Before I could respond, the men from the assembly arrived. Many had painted black lines on their cheekbones, which I interpreted as a sign of war. Some of them carried walking sticks with a blade strapped to their staffs, others carried *boleadoras* strapped to their waists. In their expression I perceived disenchantment for the dead woman. They looked menacing. Maybe they were waiting for someone from the group to take the initiative and pounce on us so they could join in with spears and *boleadoras*, with sticks and their knives, or with a kind of machete that allowed them to make their way through the dense parts of the jungle. However, no one attacked us. They only surrounded us by drawing a crescent moon. They had overcome their shyness and looked us in the face, although none of them uttered a single word. It was as if they were waiting for the sorcerer to make a decision.

The man approached us with his pendulum gait. The group made way for him to step in front of us, face to face.

"Thank you, Father!" he blurted out as if he had learned that phrase in the last few hours.

"We did what we could," I replied, explaining the woman's death in advance. Then I kept silent, although I wanted to tell her that the outcome did not depend on us, since it was possible that her lungs or brain were damaged. Besides, the drugs acted on the microbes; in this case, on the rickettsiae that caused typhus, and not on the after-effects of the disease.

I waited for Melquíades or Esteban to be the one to raise, in his half tongue, a question about our work. I prepared the answer in silence: some organs were affected; the woman's brain suffered small hemorrhages that converged in a major one that caused her death, or perhaps a clot had migrated from the veins of the lower limbs to the lungs, where it had blocked the respiratory function. Death followed.

"The men want to thank you with a garment of your choice. They want to show their affection," said Esteban.

"Tell them that we are grateful for the gift, but that we want to return to where we came from." I would have liked to explain that I was concerned about the porters, who were part of our group. Also, I had to inform them that our departure would not be immediate, but when we finished the task. "We will leave once our work is finished, which will come to an end when no new cases are presented in ten days."

I would have liked to ask him what the man with the tonsured hair thought about the woman's death, but I did not want to raise doubts about the quality of our task. I did not want to inquire. Most likely they would take the death as part of the epidemic, just like the losses prior to our arrival. I looked into the eyes of each of the men around us, trying to find answers. Then I noticed one of them, who had a palpebral palsy from some damage to the contralateral hemisphere of his brain.

The exchange of glances lasted a few minutes, during which we tried to communicate in this way. Then they turned around and went back to where the women and children were, sitting on a wall of stones joined without mortar; only with rhizomes of creeping plants in the joints and cracks. After a few minutes, which seemed eternal to me, Esteban and the sorcerer returned to our side. They motioned for us to follow them to the hut where the porters were supposed to be.

"They will be fine," Esteban clarified as he showed me the sleeping or narcotized men.

"Are they asleep or drugged?" I was interested while trying to perceive the respiratory rhythm, the trembling of hands or any other sign of alarm.

The sorcerer approached each of them and patted their backs. Then the porters began to wake up as if they had been hypnotized. At that moment I thought that the man had learned to induce sleep, or perhaps he really was born with the ability to paralyze his enemies, or those who had dared to speak ill of him, just by knotting a dirty handkerchief he wore around his waist.

The last of the men to awaken made an attempt to assault those present, including us. He had the look of the paranoid and the expression of being on the verge of an attack of contained rage. I assumed it was a psychosis resulting from intoxication; a side effect of the narcotic they had been given. Maybe his brain was not connecting with the past or he had suffered many years before from alcoholism with delirious crises.

Suddenly the sorcerer stepped forward and held the man by the neck as if he were trying to suffocate him or wanted to hypnotize him again. Our porter lay exhausted on the ground, and the others, as if commanded by an inner voice or an order that Medina and I did not hear, lifted him up and placed him in a portable hammock to carry him to the roadside camp. I was amazed: an old man no more than five feet tall had immobilized a six-foot-tall porter. Images of the fight between a hornet with an orange abdomen and a giant tarantula came to my mind. It was an unequal combat that made my hair stand on end.

"He is a very bad man," Esteban told me. He is a murderer of men.

I could not understand what he meant by making this statement. If so, he owed her an explanation as to how he joined the group.

"I summoned him from among the men who knew the area," I clarified, wishing to make him understand that I had made the mistake of not investigating his background. "I did not know his past," I apologized.

Later I was able to meet with the other porters, whom I asked if they knew anything about the guy. In this way I learned that our man was discharged from the army after having spent a period as a conscript. Possibly, he had participated actively during the fighting in those areas that had been declared an emergency by the military commanders or by the political leaders of the nation. I immediately thought of a war of lesser intensity, one of those in which the civilian population was also involved.

"He told us that he knew how to use pineapple grenades and long-range rifles," one of them told me. Then he told me what the guy had told him about a confrontation in the vicinity of a town located in the inter-Andean plateau. The macho man told us that he had killed a member of the terrorists' army. The boy was no more than thirteen or fourteen years old, but he was a strong son-of-a-bitch in the armed struggle. He, together with a sergeant of an annihilation group, had killed him by strangling him with construction wire. He explained that the wire was pulled taut at each end; the condemned man hung in the middle. As I imagined the atrocities the porter was about to narrate to me, I felt a shudder, as if I were to blame for having hired the individual.

At that moment my mind recreated a platoon of black sweaters with their faces smeared with shoe polish. They entered the village firing their guns into the air to frighten the villagers.

In one of the huts, behind a mud-brick stove, two children were hiding and crying loudly. Someone from the village told them that these children were, in fact, as dangerous as a whole column of subversives, since they had killed a governor, the unlettered judge and two neighbors.

The men learned of the crudeness of the actions through newspaper reports and were able to corroborate the facts when they went to the camp of a tribe of Asháninca who had been kidnapped by one of the columns of the seditionists. The mission was to treat the outbreak of an unknown disease among the Asháninca refugees who, due to the promiscuity and debauchery of one troop and the other, had acquired an unidentified type of viral infection that appeared to be delta hepatitis, although they also assessed the possibility that it was a lymphotropic virus disease with liver damage. "Damn wars!" they exclaimed then. Today they had a much worse concept.

The porter wanted to know how he had guessed his companion's past. "Was he really a sorcerer with extrasensory perceptions? Had he known the subject's background in an ayahuasca session or by taking another narcotic?" I recalled that the method was used by the technical police of despotic regimes to obtain information and self-incriminations. Those anesthetized for surgeries had a similar reaction; they even confessed to matters they avoided telling during wakefulness. For that reason, I presumed that the sorcerer had made them inhale a liquid, perhaps the juice of bluebells or the greenish extract resulting from grinding and squeezing the leaves of poison ivy. Perhaps he had resorted to injecting the drug into the external auditory canal, for which he had used a blowpipe made of a hollow reed that he had fired with a blow. Under the effects of narcolepsy tongues would have been loosened, recounting every detail of their lives and those of their relatives.

"Take him away!" Esteban shouted. Then he added, "We don't want him here! "

I got the message: the farther away, the better.

They could have sent him back through the territory of the Catacamara, a violent ethnic group living in the caves of a limestone rock. The tribe would have eliminated him with an arrow shot poisoned with curare, which causes an incurable narcosis in the body; while the drug takes effect, the sphincters relax and bowel movements become very intense. It would have been worse if they had tortured him, cut off his tongue, his ears, his penis, and left him bleeding to death lying on the waterlogged floor of a cave. I pitied the madness of the porter: his baleful look, the drool from the tantrum, the clenched hands and the contracted body expression; all mixed with the panicked gesture of a grown child.

"I beg you," I asked Melquíades, using Esteban as a translator, "free our people. In exchange I promise to take care of them," I promised. I wanted him to understand that he would have nothing to fear. They would not approach their women, they would not get surly with the men, much less with the children.

And although I did not say so, if Esteban, the translator, and the sorcerer Melquíades allowed it, I would send the porters away first. They would leave the village a few days before us; they would take with them the cargo we had brought, the laboratory equipment and medicines. Two or three natives could even accompany them to bring back a consignment of medicines from the central office. That way, the storekeepers and ministry bureaucrats would have the opportunity to send us more insecticides and other antibiotics against atypical bacteria. The porters would then act as couriers while transporting their sick comrade to safety in his home village, in the company of his relatives.

I do not have the power to guess a man's past just by looking into his eyes or observing some feature on his face; I am not even capable of discovering his behavior, despite having lived with him during the days of preparation and the hours of hiking in the mountains. At that moment I felt sorry for the porter, for his evasions and isolation when we were talking. He seemed to have serious fevers, with a kind of self-absorbed and taciturn thinking. I feared that the man would never fully recover and at the same time I was afraid that he would have another fit of anger that would be repelled by these little men. His mind interpreted the narcosis hangover as a kind of madness that removed his inhibitions and brought to the surface the psychopathy activated during the war. In the event that he went wild, the natives would surround him with daggers, beat him with leather and galena stone *boleadoras* and drag him by the ankles to the center of the esplanade. His eyes would turn from anger to panic when he realized that this was the end of his life. Then he would ask forgiveness from men or from a higher being. I don't know if he ever showed any compassion for his fellow man. Maybe he had developed psychopathy after drinking dog's blood mixed with gunpowder or after receiving the violent doctrine of pre-combat training.

Three days later the porters left the village. They dragged their companion along. The man had regained his mobility and some of his senses, although he seemed dazed or isolated. Someone had tied his hands with a rope that was pulled by his companions, in turn, to drag him along.

Medina and I stayed in the village until the mission objectives were achieved. We would complete the missing doses of antibiotic treatment in the new cases and follow up on the old ones. We were also going to continue with the rat extermination and elimination of vectors, including a type of gregarious mosquito that flew in white clouds. For this task we counted on the help of women and children, who washed the clothes and wool covering the camelid hides. The men were in charge of eliminating the domestic and field rats. They felt they had the right to do so because of their skill in handling blowguns, arrows, machetes and *boleadoras*.

The days went on and on until one day several dragonflies appeared flying over the top of the bushes and dwarf shrubs. I remembered that in my hometown we children interpreted the presence of insects as the announcement of news; in this case, it could be good news. It was time to leave.

I kept thinking of octagonal crystal viruses and intracellular corpuscles in the case of rickettsiae. As I looked at the toes, gangrenous from clots in the blood vessels, I thought of intravascular thrombosis generated by protobacteria of the mycoplasma type. "How much did I have to learn to perform the dance?" I said to myself silently as I moved to the beat of music that only I could hear.

I talked to the paralyzed sergeant again before leaving the village. I went to his hut to bring him a packet of pain medication. There I asked him if he had any errands he could fulfill when he returned to the city. In the end I asked him,

"Were you there during the war?"

He remained silent. I imagined the villages razed to the ground, the thatched roofs burning like torches; the surrounding area full of corpses and dogs that approached with the desire to bite them; worms crawling out of their nostrils and hundreds of carrion vultures flying over the scene.

After a silent moment, which he used to reflect, he answered me in a laconic way,

"We were the defeated ones."

He did not explain anything else. I understood that the dead and wounded had been caused by the Andean people or whatever the ethnic group to which the sorcerer and the little men with mottled faces belonged. An ethnic group with men and women with multiple braids tying their woolly hair. They were the ones who had to flee to the mountains, take refuge in the cracks of the slopes and smoke the caves to scare away the vampires. They formed caravans of transhumants, who moved along the deer trails, and herded the llamas and alpacas. They had to carry the chickens with their hairless necks in baskets. They also had to painfully drag the elderly and children along with them.

They were not the first displaced by the war; neither would they be the last. Each scene reminded me of the refugee camps; the groups that moved away in buses with baskets on the roof, where they placed mattresses, bedpans and all kinds of belongings. Perhaps they were like the caravans of gypsies moving from one place to another in carts pulled by vans converted into trailers. When I imagine the transhumant groups, I seem to be reading Lajos Zilahy's *The Wandering City*, with women in colorful coiffures and weeping children populating the wagons of a railroad traveling from one city to another. They stayed in the outskirts of one city and after a while a locomotive pulled the convoy along the railway to another city, and in this way they changed places. What did not change was the routine of sleeping on the boarded floor, sharing food prepared in a common pot and getting used to the noise of the stations, hearing the whistle of the departing trains, the sound of the bells announcing the proximity of the departure and the screeching of the wheels rubbing on the iron of the rails.

I also speculated about the exodus of the little Andean men marching through the ravines with their belongings; slipping on the wet straw because the morning dew had turned to ice. They had to camouflage themselves between the rocks and the bushes so as not to be detected by the enemies; hidden in the dark crevices of the peaks, from where they could watch the movements of their pursuers. They crossed the cloud forest and then spent the night in the pass, where they found a place with chullpas built in stone several centuries earlier to house the remains of the inhabitants of another era.

Another similar place came to my mind, also a gap between two valleys separated by a mountain range. There I found the skeletons of fortune hunters who had arrived after contracting malaria in the low jungle. That time I discovered the traces produced by diseases whose remedies were not known and ghost towns on the shores of the oceans, abandoned by the bereaved of the dead in epidemics. The sorcerer brought me the image of doctors during the previous centuries.

In those mountains you could find red or yellow flowers, turquoise butterflies the size of your palm, large and small monkeys, three-meter-long snakes that attack only when you step on their nest, and herds of piglets. Before descending to the lower lands, we had to cross the pass, at four thousand meters of altitude, where the plants did not bloom; there was only a yellowish grass where we could observe the occasional dung beetle pushing the dung of a mammal that had adapted to that altitude, perhaps a white fox or a black bear, a camelid or simply a vizcacha. At that height there were pools of yellowish water that seemed to me sulfurous or ferrous; waters that boiled with bubbles and emitted fumaroles. Then it occurred to me that I could bathe in the deepest of them, fed by two springs, with floors and walls of stone slabs joined with mortar.

I still remember the heat I felt, the erythema of my skin, my impudent nakedness. Medina's flabby fatness, with that big drinker's belly and neck and face of a different color than the rest of the skin tone. I ended up with scalded balls; just like Medina, only in my case they were not balls, but scalded ping-pong balls, because I had spent more than two hours in the pool, enjoying the temperature of the water in the middle of the cloudy mountain, with hundreds of witnesses, among dwarfs with sallow skin, monkeys and iguanas with green and spiny backs.

While I was soaking my body in the hot water, ideas came to my mind; ideas of better times, when in some town next to the road a person we did not know was waiting for us and who could be transcendent in our affective selection. This was a strange way of thinking after seeing sick people with exanthema and fevers. In connection with this, I thought that we were facing a disease that had arisen in rodents, from where it had passed to humans, as a zoonosis whose vector was the body louse. Therefore, the first victims had not been humans, but rodents. Perhaps the stench of the creek, which increased in the burrows, under the roots of the bushes, was due to the rotting of the lifeless bodies of the vermin. Then came the infestation of the natives by the bite of the apterae attached to clothing and hair, lice and nits.

No sooner had I left the village, which looked more like a dotted patchwork of huts, some here and there, lurid thoughts came to my mind, as if I had drunk a punch of blueberries mixed with snake skins and rhinoceros' tusks. The morbidity came with erotic fantasies. I thought I saw a woman from a Caribbean port. The young women in the group looked like Tropicana women to me; even the women with two children hanging from their hips were a sip of water in the desert. I experienced a horniness as if I had suddenly been released after twenty years of imprisonment without seeing a single woman, but never forgetting the crescent moons of the neighborhood girls showing their cleavage. This horniness consumed me like a malt fever or a sudden madness with an out-of-the-ordinary excitement.

Today, after so many sheepish years, I wonder if the exaggerated eroticism was a reaction to the fears of contagion or if it was due to the proximity of some enigmatic female who was going through a period of unbridled desires. At that moment it occurred to me what the lice might reek of. They gave off a smell of cattle dung or rotting rags from the hut of the seventy-year-old village priest who had ten children by different old women. I also remembered the food markets, with their flying rats, somewhere between ground rats and bats, with axillary folds that when extended are like wings and allow them to glide across the high floors. Later, when I observed the lice on the wooden rafts made of balsa wood, I could see that the parasites gave off a musky odor that made me gag and vomit.

Poor little Andean people who lived up there, on the slopes of the cloudy mountains, where the savannah begins to be tropical forest and the horseflies transform into singing cicadas, insects that have a head so disproportionate that it occupies more than seventy percent of their body; the rest are wings and an abdomen similar to that of shrimps. Poor little men with dastardly faces, chained to their fate, waiting for the settlers to arrive at some point and drive them out of the village and off the mountain. Then, once a mineral vein is discovered, the invaders will haul their front-end loaders and dredges to explore the pipe that holds gold-bearing sand. And they will arrive like an invasion of locusts, they will build barracks for their supplies and camps for their workers and their retinues, which will include women to serve their needs. Then the little men would again be displaced from their village and would be forced to gather in caravans of nomads to look for another place where they could settle.

That second time they will be more exposed to contract another disease and endure new plagues, and life will end up being a chimera. They will be a ghost people, with fantasies such as witches who travel on the backs of condors, with beliefs that imply being close to the tutelary gods. But in the end they will be nothing more than an ethnic group of losers in a millenary war.

And when I hear the airs of a flute played by the shepherds of the Maghreb or the Lapps of northern Scandinavia, I will remember them. And I will get the idea that this instrument predates the universal diaspora; even before the era in which the continents migrated to become what they are. The same flutes in the hands of the Zulus and the snake charmers in Calcutta; the same pentaphonic scales.

I had budgeted that we would leave them insecticides and a supply of chloramphenicol capsules when we left. Then? Then return with the same ones, fleeing from death. Fleeing from those little beings with whom I could not communicate in their language and whose fate I did not understand. Fleeing from myself, even though I was the one who suggested the trip, and even forced the reluctant ones, who wanted to avoid the twelve hours of walking, the wounds of the thistles, the risk of catching typhus and scabies, coming back with lice or carrying the sorrow of having been in the mountain of white snow and icy winds; to carry the melancholy of a village of stone walls with no mortar or of adobe bricks, with thatched puna roofs and earthen floors soaked with the urine of children and old people.

Both I and Medina, as well as the porters, wanted to return from the past to the future, to forget the present because it burned. We could not bear to live another day with the men of the mountain, not even with their women with braided hair or their children, who played near us. Much less did we want to explore whether the stones in the crevices were silver pyrites or shiny argentite. Nor did we want to receive the red range ponchos because we believed that everything was infected, that everything could be dangerous. Likewise, we did not want to accept the silver ornaments they used as pins to hold their shawls and skirts. My companions seemed to have traveled to hell, like Eurydice, and were ready to return to earth. Once in town, I would not see the porters again; they had already collected their money and would leave with another group that demanded less risk.

On the third day we recovered in a village of two thousand inhabitants. We stayed in a two-story house, which had a small lodging sign on it, and which must have been more like a tambo of the traders of supplies or a miner's lodge. The second floor turned out to be a single room, without partitions or divisions, in which there was no bed. The mattresses, thinned by use, had all been arranged in a row, the edge of one next to the edge of the other, on the floor.

Medina and I ended up in that shelter; there we had to blow away the bad smells of the bodies, the fleas invited by the neighbors, the snoring and the murmur of the wings of the bats that lived in the crawl space. I presume that we slept like blessed people preserved by the smell of insecticide, which would keep the parasites away from the skin and the cockroaches from the floor. I'm convinced that we both dreamed of those men with mottled cheeks. And although the obsession ended for me the following week, it continued for a long time in Medina's obsessive brain; possibly, telling his part in the adventure in a bar in his town, where he would chat with friends from the neighborhood. Surely he told them a fantasy story in which he represented himself as the hero of an epic: in this version he was the one who confronted the warriors of the tribe to rescue the members of his group. In doing so, he prevented them from being killed by the ethnic tribesmen.

Medina would culminate the narration by telling them about his bath in a pool of sulphurous, overheated water with a group of girls from the tribe. Not only that; he would tell them that the chief of the tribe had offered him one of those girls for his company, but that he refused so as not to attract the fury of his jealous wife. And, of course, that thanks to his work we saved more than a hundred human beings affected by a rare disease that caused gangrene in their toes, caused the appearance of blue patches of ecchymosis on the thorax and caused a fever of more than forty degrees, until finally, after one or another convulsion, death came.

I compared two essential moments in my life: the one I spent in that place, which is reached after crossing a pass at four thousand meters above sea level, and my experience in New York itself, in a PATH train station bound for New Jersey, where my companion Daniel Gutiérrez was working as a factory stevedore. There I witnessed a scene of two women kissing. Both were thin, skeletal. Both had an indeterminate number of earrings in their ears. Both had hair dyed an exotic, bright color, as if they were birds of paradise, varieties of quetzal or a type of moiré.

Each one had her own thing: lips painted crimson red or steel blue; open necklines over a black leather garment; long, flaming giraffe collars and skirts that reached thirty centimeters above the hips. There was something different about them. Maybe it was their brazenness or their boldness; the scent they gave off or their strong grassy look. Maybe it was all the result of my lack of connection with that world, which seemed to me a hundred times more modern and, therefore, a hundred times more real. My suit was obsolete in that environment full of guys with headbands on their foreheads and huge jackets.

Almost all the men were giants dancing in their tennis shoes. I felt in danger, as if I were walking through the masonry of one of those fifty-plus story towers; it even seemed to me that I should attempt an honorable retreat to the hotel. For those things of life, I remained on the back of a horse and let myself be carried along the predestined route. In this way, I continued to travel all the way to New Jersey.

Many of the men I encountered frowned in hostility at my presence; the young women looked to me like alien beings or mannequins in a fashion house. I was out of place, as if I were an iguana in a lingerie fashion show, with very long and very beautiful skinny women who seemed to me like angels or something similar. They had come from another solar system similar to ours and their mission was to bewitch us with their siren song as we returned by boat along the route of Ulysses.

Suddenly I caught a glimpse of other people walking along the platform. They were wearing suits similar to the ones worn by the citizens of Fifth Avenue, similar to the one I was wearing, although they had a different shine. Possibly they were from brands I had heard of, like Giorgio Armani, Hugo Boss, Louis Vuitton, Versace. I didn't have the slightest resemblance to them either, just as I didn't resemble the dystopians at the train station. They all had the same taste in clothes, the same way of walking, as if they were Hollywood actors, and would dine in Vietnamese restaurants in Chinatown or Thai restaurants on Fifth Avenue.

The same feeling of invalidity in the mountains and in the big city. Identical fear of not being able to survive the experience. So I adopted a cocky attitude, I know the same route, and I took the train like any other citizen. I sat in one of the last seats, close to the window, so I could watch the people walking along the avenues: guys coming out of the gym, wearing sleeveless polo shirts and sweatshirts; people, older, who seemed to be rushing to get to the office or a sales job; cool guys, stereotypes with a prefabricated personality and design; tattoos on shoulders and breasts with no interest in sex. I imagined how fucked up it was to play each of the roles. No one would even find out who was who.

I continued the trip, continuing to look out the same window. Others seemed to have an air of tiredness, as if they had finished their day and wanted to return to their homes. Those who had nowhere to go had to look for shelter. And on the way they would meet friends for a few beers. I remembered the little bars around the dock at the port. The same hustle and bustle, the same cheerful bustle, even if the cities were different: it didn't matter if it was the Hudson River wharf, Hamburg or Canton. The agitation of the comedians on stage would be identical. And I imagined thin, languid women, consumed by the same needs; and obese, ruddy men, sitting at the bar.

I enjoyed the solitude, even though there were hundreds of people on the transport. No one seemed to be looking at me and I had my eyes fixed on the outside. I had no desire to communicate. If I had slept it would have been the same.

When I arrived, I had several questions prepared for Gutierrez. I met him at work. He was a longshoreman in a brick-red container yard.

"Why do you live in this country?" Maybe I should have phrased it differently, 'why was he still in this city since he had lived in other cities before coming to this one?'

"Well... In the homeland I was broken," he answered, looking at the floor, as if he noticed the defects of the surface and felt the need to feel with his feet and eyes those imperfections so as not to fall.

"I don't want to discuss your decisions; it's just a loose question," I wanted to apologize for my intrusion.

"The truth is that I had no future there. My options were bad. My debts were eating me up. My children were coming to me in stained clothing and the fat lady was fucking me up." I didn't know what he meant; from my point of view, he had no future in this country either.

"What do you mean?" I continued, regretting my question immediately because I thought he would not answer me.

"No one knows more than you how my life was over there. Not even any fucking savings. In this country, sure, I work non-fucking-stop, but I've managed to have some savings. I even send money to my ex-wife and kids. I can send about five hundred dollars a month; sometimes I send up to two thousand dollars," he told me. Then he continued, "That's not all. I'm looking at the possibility of buying a house in a neighborhood near here. Maybe in Patterson. In the meantime, I have a small apartment, where I live with my current fiancée." He was giving me a detailed summary of his life, including his current financial situation. "I even have a credit card that would allow me up to fifteen thousand dollars of debt."

"Life is difficult. I think it's the same here as it is there." I didn't want to touch the subject anymore and moved on to a safer topic.

"Come on man, I want to buy you a few beers. Tell me what time you finish your work and I'll be back then. In the meantime, I'll get to know something of the city." The truth was that I didn't want to keep on talking about the same subject and I was looking for a fourth intermission.

"I can't believe it. You buying beers? I can't believe it." I'm sure he just remembered I was a teetotaler.

Then I evoked anecdotes from our childhood. A deserted beach where we used to go as youngsters escaping from National History or Physiochemistry classes. All the dog killers of the city. The little girl who accompanied us, whom we nicknamed Lolita because of the impact of a movie, who then ended up being his girlfriend and then his first wife. She had brown hair and a mischievous look. I think all of us boys, who watched her frolicking on the beach in her one-piece bathing suit, were enamored of her.

"What brought you to New Jersey?" I wanted to ask him, and then I would have questioned the choice. Maybe he got carried away by the neon lights of the great glassy towers of New York. And I remembered that we were envious of him because Lolita chose him out of the whole gaggle of lowly hooligans. In the end, time passes and there was nothing left of Gutierrez and Lolita. Everything fell apart; there were fights and insults in the street, the barracks scandals and then it was all over. No one was jealous of her anymore. Suddenly no one knew what had happened to the macho man. He disappeared like the good news and like the governments in power. The mayor had been arrested and the president was being investigated for corruption. No one believed in anyone.

The town's love triangles were as scandalous as the nation's political scandals. One guy sold some land to the governor's mother and then the state bought it at an overpriced price to build a cemetery. The same method as Artemio Cruz, who acquired agricultural land around Mexico City and after a law, approved by his political godchildren, made it developable with prices raised from one to ten thousand.

Lolita became la Gorda. Gutierrez left town and she ended up as the wife of one of her first husband's longshoreman colleagues. She seemed more real than the ads on the main avenue.

I would have also told him "Comrade, what if you tried to be a chauffeur for one of those Latin pop stars?"

He had come to the conclusion that in New York there was more money and you could have businesses on the side, since they didn't require a lot of capital. There were many issues. For example, his ex-wife became the girlfriend of a longshoreman and then realized that it was a great idea to have the guy working for her. After just a few months she was engaged to a guy half her age. Can you imagine? No one could believe that the woman could manage to get ahead on those notes. She stank of farting human bait and sweated sugarcane brandy. I wouldn't have imagined eroticism to suit her.

Gutiérrez told me about a guy we met at the port who today lived exploiting a businessman he said was his boyfriend.

"How?" I was surprised. I didn't understand if the guy's partner was a woman or a man. I assumed that for the guy in the port it was the same thing.

I was definitely out of touch. I realized that time had passed. He was still in the race, but I had fallen by the wayside.

With the new nihilism, the urban tribes were left with nothingness and living the *carpe diem* of pleasure, loving no one and wanting nothing. Some guys did contortions on the asphalt floor while others created a rap counterpoint with street songs. I didn't want to stay in any hotel in the vicinity, so I took a bus to the island of Manhattan. At that moment I was reminded of the Hong Kong ferry. The crowd was moving in one direction or another. There was a guy watching me; he seemed to be a six-foot-four transvestite with oriental features. I immediately rushed to catch the bus, almost pushing the people in front of me.

Today I remember those experiences as if I had never lived them. The confrontation between ethnic groups, between the men with braids and those with feathered plumes, sounds to me like the war in Rwanda between Hutus and Tutsis, with a death toll of hundreds of thousands.

Years later I ran into Judith and got a hell of a surprise when I saw her looking all shabby and chubby. Almost immediately I wondered what kind of visual or mental distortion I was in to have had any dirty thoughts about her. She was the regional director of the WHO Communicable Disease Program. That time I mistook kindness for seduction. I was sorry to hear that her marriage had gone to the dogs. Apparently, her husband took off his racial complexes and tried to become a fatal male for blondes. I felt sorry for her, as the guy beat her unconscious once he lost his fear of the woman's hissy fits and the ten kilos the gringa had on him. It was then that she realized that her boxer's body was an illusion. I experienced so much sadness that I waited for the guy to return home before I punched him twice in the cake-hole in front of Judith herself. Then I threatened him, "If you ever lay your hands on her again, I'll kill you!"

I don't know if he assaulted her anymore; what I do know is that the woman didn't deserve the son of a bitch. Deep down, he was just a hustler who had taken all kinds of advantages from her.

What became of Medina? I never saw him again. I remember his muffled tone of voice, as if that way he was showing his respect; I also remember his double skin color in the hot spring pool, the huge belly, the fatty mattresses on his hips and the ratty underpants that let us guess at his infantile genitals. I guess he eventually retired from the ministry and began to enjoy injectables in a topical place at his own home.

Once I was shown some watercolors by the painter Palao. In one of them I thought I could make out the portrait of the sorcerer or someone very similar to the old man. Afterwards I said to myself: "All the Collas have the same bad habits". Although I still think that the old man had his portrait taken on Good Friday, when he went down to receive the blessing of the recumbent Christ in the church of a town with two churches and four bell towers.

Perhaps if I visited the village again, the scene would be different. It is possible that the huts of stones joined without mortar and thatched roofs were no longer standing, nor were the men with braids on the back of their necks, much less the medicine man with powers. Instead I would find adobe huts with iron roofs, a little school without a teacher, a church without a priest and a few locals in leather jackets exploiting the silver mines. From time to time they would be visited by typhus and the endemic disease would also kill many villagers.

No one would remember the sorcerer. Of course, they wouldn't remember the visit of a couple of guys either; not even the oldest men with the mottled cheeks. All that makes me doubt whether the village, the disease, the old witchdoctor who officiated as healer, midwife, fortune teller and historian, and a paralyzed sergeant with the last name of Martinez ever existed. I even doubt that we had made the trip with Medina and a group of porters.

But no. I am sure that the village existed, just like the war between ethnicities; that diseases come and, after a while, go away. I am surprised that villages disappear as individuals do. I imagine the disappearances of people in a dark night. It could happen in a village in Arauca, close to the Venezuelan border, or perhaps in a puna village in the Andes, or perhaps in a hamlet in the north of the Republic of Congo. The doors would be shattered by the blows of the guns and the men would be dragged away by force while the women and children cried and screamed. In the end, they would have no news of the abductee.

Likewise, the village had gone up in smoke. Everyone I asked told me they had never heard anything about it. Everyone denied knowing of a native people living in an unnamed village. On the maps of the region there was no construction within forty kilometers of that village, whose name I do not remember and in whose tambo we spent the night when we returned from the expedition. However, I am told that the inhabitants of the region have identical characteristics: they are small in stature and their faces are dark in the cheekbones. Some of the men still wear their hair in braids and the women wear a pair of thick braids. Most of them live in stone huts; some even live in caves on the slopes, in the middle of the mountains.

"What about the Catacameras?" I wanted to know.

"Who, sir?" answered my interlocutor.

Then I remained silent, with my gaze lost at a point on the horizon.

Chapter 2
Too Late

Within the immense mix of memories, it occurs to me to land on one of Manhattan's avenues, perhaps Eighth Avenue, as a passenger in a cab to which a ribbon of small black squares, similar to a chessboard, had been added on the yellow background. The cab driver had a neck full of acne or beriberi pores, and smelled of bait and sweat, even though the weather was cool from the rain and cold coming off Hudson Bay. My complexion told the man that I could be Hispanic or South American; therefore, a victim to be assaulted in any way, either in the fare of the taximeters, manipulable by an electronic mechanism, or helped by his cronies, who were waiting for the opportunity in a mechanic shop close to the route the driver would choose.

In the end it was all a show. It seemed as if the vehicle was going to fall apart at any moment and the wreckage sounded all over the place. The driver pretended to be on the verge of hysteria and I pretended to understand that the car had to enter the workshop with passenger included. In the yard where the jacks and pulleys to disassemble the engine were supposed to be, there was a sheaf of boys with baseball caps; they had their visors over their temples on either side. Their faces showed an expression of hatred for Latinos or any asshole who might be their victim. Their intemperate shouts frightened me, so much so that I was ready to give them even my underwear and stand without a copper in the middle of the street, even without documents and without even my tennis shoes, waiting for a patrol car or the garbage truck to pick me up and take me to my hotel. I was shivering with cold and fear while the police officers and the street cleaners were laughing their asses off when they saw me naked. I got off cheap. I could have been dead. Undocumented in a shed, then naked on a stretcher in an unidentified morgue.

When the agents heard the name of my hotel, they hesitated about whether it was better to transfer me to a nut house or to take me to their station to seek information that would qualify my mental state. They chose the second option. Then I told them about the assault, but they continued to look at me as a slacker. They questioned me about my addiction to drugs or alcohol and asked me what I was doing in that neighborhood. I answered that I didn't even know the neighborhood by name. I was going to tell them that I was a professional invited by a university, but in the end I kept quiet. I didn't believe that version myself.

I asked for a lawyer or a member of my country's embassy. I gave them all the names I remembered of people I knew in the city and they wrote them down in a notebook without giving me much hope. I was wrapped in orange clothes twice my usual size. They were the same clothes they give to undocumented immigrants or suspects. The place looked like a hospital emergency room, with hundreds of people moving in one direction or another. Women talking loudly. Emaciated or obese men. Everyone had a story to tell and everyone was asking for a lawyer or a relative to get them out of trouble.

I mentioned several names of university professors. They rewrote them in the little notebook and then typed them into a computer. I imagine the computer had software with the names and addresses of the city's inhabitants. A few hours later I was informed that I had a visitor. It was Larry, the university bursar.

He was smiling his best smile, trying to hide his dislike of the place and his surprise at finding me there. He also asked me what I was doing in the area. I then explained about the wrecked car. Larry was furious with the head of the police station and when he was about to pay the bail with a card, he got madder out, assuring them that I was the victim of a robbery and not an out-of-control freak, as the head of the police station believed.

The bursar, who handled the university's finances, was a dark-haired, six-foot-nine, almost one-hundred-pound man, impeccably dressed in a Hugo Boss suit. When I was taken seriously by the stewards, I had to give a spoken portrait of my assailants before I left.

It was raining. People were running and they wanted to cross the streets. Other yellow cars with their emblematic ribbons lined the avenue. Larry took me to the hotel in the university shuttle. The driver smiled at the sight of my clothes.

When I meet Daniel Gutierrez again, the first thing I will ask him is to tell me how he came to live in New Jersey. That will be the first question I will ask the nutcase. He may change the record in response and ask me the question, "Why did you stay in South America?"

He would tell me, "First, Miami; then, New York. Finally, New Jersey. And I imagined that when I least expected it, I would be offered a permanent job and therefore a green card. It never came, neither the permanent job nor the residency. The consequence is that I am still illegal. I have a provisional permit and I'm waiting for new laws for residency, or for the lottery - I was trying to explain to myself how I got where I did."

"You have to tell me. How did you get the courage? It's not easy to make these decisions," I continued. "It's very hard for me to understand the optimism that comes with bottoming out," I thought.

It seemed to me that Gutierrez was hiding a secret like deep depression or chronic alcoholism. In the first case, he would be taking large doses of fluoxetine or some other similar antidepressant in its highest doses. On the assumption of having overcome depression, he would be going to group therapy, with Alcoholics Anonymous or a rescue group for the depressed. And at some point on Saturday he would dedicate himself to composing the lyrics and his friend Joao would set it to music. The rhythm would be similar to a Jon Secada or Marc Anthony hit.

In the end we are all Latinos, or at least that is the idea, although of course there was a gap between my buddy and the idols in terms of looks and dollars in the bank. As for the money, perhaps he had been lured by credit cards, which gave him a promising outlook; perhaps he thought he could compete in one or more television programs that were looking for talent. For example, *American Idol* and others with a set full of stars and luminaries, and multi-colored smoke effects that seemed to rise from the floor. Tremendous delirium.

In his wallet, next to his driver's license, he kept his credit cards, MasterCard, Visa, American Express. I couldn't understand how an illegal could have those benefits: credit cards and a driver's license. Later I found out that the cards were tied to the company and whatever he could earn in that job. That gave him the possibility to buy a thirty-six-inch plasma TV, a cold bar for every room in his apartment and many, many cans of beer to fill the freezer.

"It could have been Chicago or Detroit. It's all the same to me. I want to live in this great country." That was the way so many Latinos see it. After all, this is the country of opportunity for blacks, browns and yellows.

"Of course, my friend. Besides, I think your twenty-five-year-old wife is an important reason." I didn't mention that she was obese and must have weighed more than eighty kilos, even though she was no more than one meter sixty. I also didn't want to know if he had sex with her or with some slut from 42nd Street.

Most likely the fat woman was waiting for him to gorge herself on junk food along with her father, mother and four brothers and sisters with whom she had invaded the rented apartment of my old friend Daniel Gutiérrez. That was the reason why he went out every night in search of the Thai whores in Union Square or the Latinas that lurked along Fourth Avenue. Just imagine sex on the floor with an entire tribe as witnesses. A tragedy, like waiting for the family to give him a standing ovation at the end of the orgasm. Maybe he was content to watch porn movies on pay-per-view channels when all the invaders were asleep.

"She is Cuban. When I met her she was a real beauty, a stylish skinny girl. She weighed forty pounds less. If you had only seen her, compadre" Even he doesn't believe it himself. Even then the fat woman had a tremendous double chin and her waist showed two huge rolls cultivated over many years.

"I imagine," I said, although what I imagined was the opposite.

The guy was held by the balls by an entire family who had invaded his three-bedroom apartment. Not only that; they raided the territory of his privacy. He couldn't watch soccer games, not even those of the United States Soccer Federation, nor the channels that reminded him of South American soap operas, much less listen to the music he liked. Worst of all, he could not eat what he kept in the refrigerator because it had already been consumed by the group of piranhas. How could my poor buddy not be depressed?

I don't know why, but at that moment it occurred to me to think of the army's assimilated soldiers, of the strychnine-poisoned dog face of the region's army conscripts. The truth is that the image was similar in any country: the spiky hair, the corners of the lips with a whitish pasty residue. My friend looked as if he had been a reservist in the U.S. Army, a true graduate.

He had told me about his time in the army or in one of the agencies that do the dirty work in wars. He claimed he had served in the Persian Gulf War, the first war against Iraq. That seemed to me to be a farce because he was still an illegal alien and war veterans were entitled to acquire residency. The explanation could be that he was not recruited by the regular army, but by the Blackwater agency, where he worked as a mercenary. Same action movie in the deserts and the cities that rise between the Euphrates and the Tigris though. Similarly, these mercenary troops would wear khaki-colored uniforms with tobacco stains. They would use the same sunglasses and identical long-range weapons with telescopic sights, fitted with infrared beams that allowed them to see the movements of the enemies at night. "They were the vice president's troops," I said to myself, thinking of George Bush's administration and his vice president Dick Cheney.

Maybe my friend felt that my arrival had uncovered a pressure cooker. Maybe he realized that he was running out of something that, according to him, was a rehearsal and, in my opinion, the same fucking life. The Cuban woman was a gold digger who took full advantage of poor Daniel. The fat woman's mother spied on him through some crack in the bathroom when he went in to pee or defecate. Her father drank the beers and ate the junk food they ordered from a delivery service. He had to pay the bill at the end of the month. It was a disaster he couldn't escape, not even by outwitting half the world, much less by disappearing at a moment's notice.

In the end he will end up as a psychopath, one of those who suffer from various disorders in varying degrees. I imagined him walking down 42nd Street trying to spot a Latin American-looking whore. She could be a Honduran or a Mexican from the Gulf Coast, or even a Filipina with a Latin American look, although she couldn't even manage to utter a sentence in Spanish. Then he would enter a pornographic show on Fifth or Eighth Avenue. The doorman, a man of color, six feet tall and of indeterminate age, would let him in when he saw that he was carrying a gold MasterCard. In the meantime, the fat Cuban woman was hooking up with a bodega vendor who looked like a fruit bird at a Paris flea market. She might even have liked the delivery man better, since he was six-foot-four and looked like an Irish butcher or a Scottish coal miner; and she told her mother that the very presence of the giant made her wet every time they bumped into each other in the package delivery section of the crawl space. In the end, at least I assumed, the fat woman ended up being the big man's lover and buttoning up a weekly shipment of groceries.

In connection with the story of his exploits, it was clear to me that the war in the Persian Gulf was part of Daniel's alcoholic delusions, as was his experience playing in the second division with Marítimo, a team in the port that enrolled stevedores and other boys who were looking for a future in soccer. I was convinced that my friend never even got to clean the fuselage of airplanes, nor was he on the aircraft carrier John Kennedy as a Marine. The poor guy was trying to reproduce what he had heard in some pub from a veteran who had been brought in a wheelchair because he had suffered a traumatic spinal injury and disarticulation of the entire right lower limb, starting from the head of the femur, after being hit by a bazooka shell.

In the meantime, I'm sure he was still looking for something new on the East Side. He might end up hooking up with a crazy woman who would ask him for ten dollars a blowjob to support her crack fix, or he might hook up with a hysterical woman who would make a scene for him on Seventh Avenue. Both of them, skeletal: one because of the anorexia caused by the drug and the other because she had the hysterical biotype. I'll have to pray to God that neither is sick with AIDS. Assuming that is like hoping you win the lottery out of a million tickets sold. We will have to hope that women are lucky enough to have CCR5 type cell receptors, and not CD4, in their T lymphocytes, which would give them a natural immunity to the disease despite having had serotype-positive partners.

Thinking about his situation, mine, the fact of having been assaulted in that fake mechanic's shop for the wrecked cabs, and that had left me naked, was nothing compared to the kind of life he had been given. The beatings that he must have received in yards, streets, avenues, parks, night clubs, pubs, will be counted by dozens, because he is definitely not immune to the beatings in the alley, to the slaps of the black women who feel offended by a gesture of his, to the charges of the pimps who pretend to have their share in the business. Nor is he immune to the follow-up of the police officers, who must have him checked as an illegal, frequent drinker, occasional drug addict and sporadic packer of high quality cocaine.

Once inside the hotel room I pondered his fucked-up life. Knowing him, he too would reflect a lot on his fate and ponder whether things could have worked out differently for him. Each day was as bleak as the last and every hour was a game of Russian roulette or betting his dough with a bunch of Bronx hustlers. After all these meditations it seemed to me that I could not leave things like that. I still had hours left in the Big Apple, so I decided to have a serious talk with him.

"If you had a small chance," I began, "even a small chance, wouldn't you make the effort to leave all this and go back in time?" I meant back to where he had started. I wondered if he would have understood my approach.

"No. I'm fine here."

"Are you sure?" I insisted like someone throwing loaded dice on the mat.

I felt an enormous sadness when I remembered his son, Little Daniel, wearing shoes two sizes too big for his feet and with the sole replaced by a piece of cardboard. His uniform pants were patched and darned. Of course, underneath them, only skin, without underpants or socks. Not to mention the little girl who was born after my friend emigrated to North America. I also felt sorry for his wife, who dedicated herself to drinking in the canteens of the port, screwing longshoremen or any good-for-nothing bum. But most of all, I felt sorry for my friend, whom I considered wracked by alcohol, drugs and frustrations. It distressed me to know that the man didn't even realize the real situation he had gotten himself into. "Maybe," I said to myself, "if we went back ten years, if the arrival of cargo ships at another port a hundred kilometers to the south had not changed, with the liberation of import taxes, Daniel would still be the most successful stevedore. In that scenario my compadre would continue to live in the same place, a two-story house on the main avenue. His wife would have a catering business for the stevedores and thus contribute to the household economy. And the children would have boasted a television in every room and a fan for the hot summer days.

That way, the woman would have avoided the current situation: the boozing and the encounters with so-and-sos in sleazy hotels. And my friend would have a small port warehouse and a couple of forklifts, which he called ducks, to transport the bales from the container depot to the warehouse barracks. Maybe then he wouldn't have screwed up his life chasing a dream, encouraged by the lies of friends and relatives, who from time to time came from the United States telling tales of resounding triumphs in business and orgiastic adventures in incredible nightclubs. Daniel believed them at face value. He never knew fact from fiction in the dilettantes' tales.

I still remember listening to a guy who claimed to be a war hero. He claimed to be suffering from a spinal injury caused by shrapnel from a grenade. In the end he turned out to be the sufferer of a tropical spastic paraparesis caused by a virus, which had condemned him to a wheelchair. The man frequented the port canteens that Daniel used to go to. I would have liked to warn him that the guy was a mythomaniac, a schizophrenic who swore on a pedestal; if it were up to him, he would have told us that his children were born standing up and weighing more than four kilos, and Daniel would have believed it. It was as simple as that.

"It's too late, my friend, for any return to the old life," he told me resignedly. He understood that processes are irreversible.

"Maybe." I should have told him that it's never too late while you're alive, but I didn't want to insist. Then I continued with my speech, "You know that your wife and your two children are waiting for you at the port: the little girl and Little Daniel. You can start again. Maybe you will need a long treatment in some hospital, maybe several months, but sooner rather than later you will come out clean and you will be able to reinvent yourself. Then you will recover what is yours and move on. Don't you think this is your last chance? Don't you really want there to be a last chance?"

I thought about the man's addictions: alcoholism and dirty sex. It is possible that he was also dependent on drugs. An individual with compulsions that linked him to tragedy; someone who is interested in being in the world with a relationship of successive failures. Perhaps he tried to get out of that mire over and over again. He tried his hand at being a Marine in the Iraq war and applied to be a platform worker on one of the aircraft carriers. When he related to me the details of his attempt, he confessed,

"I would have liked to tie the order. I swear it was simple. I would have worked on the takeoff platform of the fighter-bombers, helping with the maintenance of the hoists that pulled the planes; preparing the hooks and cables for takeoff and landing," he said. At no time did he admit that his brain was burned out from alcohol and crack.

"I still believe that you can still get out of the mess, here or in our country. The important thing is to get organized. You may have to start by going to a rehabilitation home for addicts and alcoholics. It will take several months, after total isolation from your surroundings. You will have to overcome all the hangovers and then overcome the period of abstinence: tremors, melancholy, perspiration, anguish," I let him know that this is what my proposal consisted of. "Who knows, maybe you will not be able to bear the burden and in the end you will throw in the towel. But there is time for that.

"You have to try now; otherwise you will end up like so many others, dead under the East River bridges, mummified like the dead cats on the rooftops. If you don't achieve that resurrection, your life will be the beginning of a slow death."

I never heard from Daniel again. The last I heard, his ex-wife had married an individual who claimed to be his former partner. It was the best thing that could happen to her and the children. As for him, I think he will be wandering around Sixth Avenue, unless he died in an accident or after an overdose seizure; or trying to get off drugs, not strong enough to withstand the crisis of suppression.

Different scenes about his fate come to my mind. In one of them, the Cuban woman beats him with the supermarket vending machine or resorts to a gang of assholes who wear the same attire: polo shirts a size too big, jeans and golf caps to hide the features of his face. The gangsters fall on him like wasps on their victim, each one with its sting, until his face is a mass of flesh and blood. Then the Cuban goes to live with the giant while her parents and siblings are left with no one to fill their refrigerator with provisions.

In another image Daniel lives in a slum in the old part of Harlem, or under a bridge built over the East River. I even identify him with the old man who made the papers because he was bitten by an illegal Haitian. The old man had a mangled face, as if he had been bitten by an angry dog, so it was quite difficult to identify him. Maybe my speculations are not true and he is now earning money in abundance in some profitable business, selling betting pools or transferring money remittances, taking advantage of the need of residents to send money orders to relatives in the country of origin; or something different from the lucrative businesses that attract customers in social networks, such as importing alpaca wool from some Andean country to supply the artisans of fine wool factories. I imagined the shipment arriving in bales transported in the holds of cargo ships stowed in New Jersey and then transported in four-axle trucks to Columbia and even Montreal, to supply the weaving mills.

Sometimes in the evenings when I go for a walk in the center of a city I start to think about the fate of my old friend and fellow countryman, Daniel Gutiérrez, and I replay in my mind the last conversation we had in the pub.

"By the way, in New Jersey I told you that the return was your last chance. You didn't listen to me because you were already deaf and only read the lips of people who sent you flattering messages. You didn't pay attention to me because you were completely crazy and in your delirium you thought I was the crazy one.

"Instead of heeding my advice, you told me that I had never learned to live life to the fullest with the most extreme sensations; for example, Mardi Gras, with women flashing their tits in exchange for necklaces. You told me about new sensations, like the ecstasy of neuroleptics from having those Frenchified East Side butts around. Likewise, you gave me a hallucinatory talk about Manhattan nights, SoHo with its restaurants and buildings over fifty stories high; Little Italy and Chinatown for those who want to taste Italian or Asian food. You also told me about the walks through Central Park, Broadway or Fifth Avenue while you felt on your skin the ice of a hurricane wind coming from Newfoundland or Greenland.

"The amount of dough you make in this country contrasts with the peanuts you get in other places over a lifetime." Daniel was referring to the pittance of the absurdly small salaries workers make in countries south of the tropics. "Besides, you don't know the quality of the shows I have attended: the NBA basketball finals, the MLB baseball finals, the galas in cabarets like Café Carlyle, with almanac beauties showing their charms, a high-level jazz presentation at the Blue Note, with chords that made the souls of spectators of any cultural background vibrate. It is not a matter of geographic space, not even of time; it is the choice of a kind of life among so many kinds of life.

"I have been inclined to liquor for a long time. When I was thirteen years old, on the beaches of Punta de Tablones, after having swum to the fishing boats competing with other boys from the port, we had a bottle of pisco as a prize. The prize was a farce, because at the end, whoever had won, we shared the bottle with everyone. We were so much fun that no one could understand us with the ranting of our thoughts.

"Under the effect of liquor, the ill-fated boys would congregate in the vicinity of the brothels while the rest of us would go out to look for girls our age, who were our little schoolmates, with the aim of attempting an absurd lance."

Then I imagined girls with curls in their hair and almost flat breasts. They swam with the boys along the beach, where the first tumbles of the surf would burst. I remembered a girl of about fifteen who was called Lolita in the neighborhood because of her resemblance to a movie character. They could have called her Jodie Foster or used any other name of a teenager in a Hollywood film. The girl, whose real name was Clara, had brown hair that fell in ringlets and a mid-thigh pleated skirt. Daniel like the others, dreamed of being her lover.

In addition to teaching me how to use mint leaves to roll fish fillets, at the Vietnamese restaurant in Chinatown he wanted to explain it all to me, "The girls would let themselves be fucked for a drink or a meal in a restaurant, or for some money to buy a fashionable dress. Then with the prize already won, me and my companions would go to Doña Alicia's canteen after the day's work to play cachito and drink farm wine. Pure grape. Wine is the best aphrodisiac, buddy. We used to go crazy. We used to try to fuck Alicia's daughters, who were very nice, and if they rejected us, because they were engaged to older boys, we would ask Alicia herself, who was no longer up to that sort of thing.

"In short, compadre, we looked like madmen on the loose," he sighed deeply. Then he continued, "Buddy stop believing everything you read, thinking media that corrupts people. That's not true, I learned nothing bad in this country. I had already been burned a long time before, when I lived in our homeland." Then he stopped to think and gave me his own diagnosis. "Buddy, I am just this way. It's in my blood. I'm a firm addict; if it wasn't the drink, it would be the women. Don't you realize that I was born a failure? Nothing more; I had to fulfill a destiny that was written."

"That so?" I said, "I swear you're exaggerating." I turned the tables on him, "I'm no better than anyone else, but I'll be damned if I didn't try." It was a mistake to compare his life with mine, but I had no choice but to turn his fatalism around.

"It was hard for me to get out. I had to get used to sleepless nights in front of a book. I had to avoid friends, drinks and bad meetings. I'm sure I was labeled a geek or stupid, but I kept on going, pushing forward."

I wanted him to be clear. It wasn't a matter of bad joints or Cuban shit-eaters or whores on the East Side; it wasn't even due to frustrations in the army or war trauma. It was something simpler than that: Daniel's disease was written into his genetic makeup. The compadre had alleles that predisposed him to addictions. It was an imprint that condemned him to adventurousness, instability, depression, irritability and suicidal tendencies. I had to leave things as they were; perhaps that was the best natural reordering. But I became obsessed with one subject: genetics. The codes written on a mesh of acid, sugar and protein connections. In the end, the compulsion for some form of life.

I got to hear a version of *My way,* performed by Sid Vicious. The free fall or downhill was also a way of life. Not only addictions, bad habits, bone and joint pains, tension headaches, mixed feelings, episodic rages; all could be part of the genetic code, as much as the fat on the jowls, the nose, the way you walk and even the way you open the door of a parked car. Destiny is written. Not in a book of yellowed, parchment-like pages, but in a tangle of nucleotide fibers bound by sugars. In the end, behaviors, crises and even schizophrenia and paranoia sprouted from under the skin. "I'm that way and no shit!" That's what came to happen with Gutierrez, mistake after mistake.

"Maybe you should have stopped the hand in the first moment, when you were still studying in the Great School Unit," I opined. "You wanted to learn mathematics with integrals and logarithms. Worse, you were trying to memorize confusing names in geography: the capital of Estonia is Riga. Or maybe it was Tallinn. Then you'd come up with an interjection, 'What the fuck do I care' You just thought that in that country, Estonia, you could find the most beautiful women on Earth." In the end he realized that what he remembered was his imprint. "Since then you've been obsessed with women.

"Maybe at that time the first symptoms of paranoia appeared. Everyone was your enemy. Everyone wanted to hurt you. Everyone wanted to steal from you. You went so far as to claim that they had stolen your wallet with the papers, when these were utility bills that you had not paid. Then there was the theft of a photograph of you posing with a friend on the boulevard. I had doubts that your complaints were true.

"Then you took to looking for six-armed starfish and pearl oysters that had an iridescent tear instead of a pearl. And you would dive the cliffs off the coast or offshore islands looking for oysters and oysters of any kind."

"Don't go on, buddy. Please don't go on, don't you see that it hurts me to remember that?" he protested with shining eyes, trying to hold back tears.

When I did some background research on his psychiatric history, I came across information about his time in the emergency department of a New Jersey hospital and, later, a stay at Mount Sinai Hospital. I tried to remember if any of his relatives had suffered from mental illness or had a predisposition to dementia, and yes, his father was a dilettante, a good-for-nothing, a bum, who would go around from one woman after another to be supported. His grandfather, too, told stories in which he appeared to have sailed on a warship and fought in a battle, but he could not detail what that battle was or with whom he fought.

A delusional family of mythomaniacs. In the same way, Daniel invented good jobs; once at Mount Sinai Hospital, another time in Manhattan itself, or at Johns Hopkins Hospital in Baltimore. As a nurse's aide or as a nurse. But, in reality, he had been a patient, like any other, only that at the end of the internship he stayed to help elderly people with pyramidal and extrapyramidal signs due to tricyclic intoxication; symptoms that prevented them from fending for themselves.

And when he was discharged, Daniel narrated implausible stories typical of psychopaths, "In the psychiatric ward you could meet movie stars who couldn't kick their addictions; boxers who were famous in their time and became maniacs, who had to be restrained in safety gowns. There I met a famous writer with several *bestsellers* who lived under the East River Bridge, near the tunnel that connects to Queens. No one who saw him in that state could believe he was a famous novel author."

"Who was that writer?" I asked him then.

"I don't remember the name, but I think he published something about a deserted city after a nuclear hecatomb," he told me.

"Why didn't you have children with the Cuban?" I wanted to know.

"It's my fault. I guess a venereal disease made me sterile or the mumps I had as an adult gave me orchitis." He attributed the disability to himself, exonerating the Cuban woman, who could easily suffer from hypothyroidism with amenorrhea.

I wanted to tell him "You're screwed!", but in the end I kept quiet because deep down I knew that at any moment any of us could go one step too far and end up with a blue jumpsuit of dementia. Maybe I could have replied, "look around you, man." But that was as cruel as saying, "You're screwed, amigo." We would end up in a slippery quagmire, like a war movie in which the paratroopers of the British air force end up landing in a pigsty with a floor full of pig excrement. How many times had Gutiérrez been in that pigsty?

Suddenly I realized that it was not Gutiérrez, but a whole generation. I recalled an episode in which two women were snorting and injecting drugs. They were both dressed in black, with a tight-fitting synthetic material outlining the shape of their bodies. They were surrounded by utter losers. Some had cropped hair, half-grown beards and long mustaches hanging down to the corners of their mouths. Those in T-shirts revealed arms tattooed with unreal beings, names of people, special dates. I calculated that those tattooed could be clans of Harley-Davidson motorcyclists or adventurers, some of them dangerous because of their bizarre codes.

"A world of nausea! Or should I say, disgusting!" I thought, but immediately reconsidered. Maybe it's not that bad? The world is what it is. I felt as if I were a judge trying to penalize the sexuality of lions or acting as a moralist in the death matches of two adult silver-backed gorillas, tearing off part of their opponent's skin and muscle with each bite. That attitude of supreme judge did not suit me, like so many others in which I seemed to be making a fool of myself.

Gutiérrez was definitely not the only one, nor was he alone in that mire. The streets were populated by such specimens. You could find them in subway corridors, on superhighways, in public squares, in parks, even around Times Square. Some of them were crazy; others lacked little, like the preachers in Central Park or the schizophrenics who sought shelter on the banks of the East River, between Harlem and the Bronx. There were those who dressed in bright colors or dyed their hair with multicolored dyes, as if they intended to parade in Mardi Gras or in a South American carnival. Others had a tip of the years, like the hippie couples from the suburbs near Woodstock, in Sullivan Country, with extravagant clothing, white-rimmed, butterfly-shaped glasses and jackets in lilac, orange and pink.

They all seemed to be performing in a variety theater or in a street musicians' show, jumping on the sidewalks, blowing kisses to cab passengers, looking more butterfly-ish than ever. Somewhere there would be urban tribes with dark clothes and gelled hair reminiscent of the crests of the curassows, as well as other urban tribes: punks, goths, Rastafarians, some of them with red, yellow and green caps. The guys had half-grown bristly beards and their clothes were impregnated with the smell of marijuana cigarettes and the sweat of several days.

They were not the only inhabitants of the city. They might be notorious for their weirdness, but they were not the majority. Nearby neighborhoods were home to university professors, office workers, art students. I sought to approach academics from Columbia University; among them, Joseph Stiglitz, Nobel Laureate in Economics, who lectured on the iniquities in the economic relations of countries. I also met Mario Capecchi, Nobel Laureate in Medicine, who was presenting his work on stem cells and genetic manipulation in animal models. Undoubtedly, this society had produced scientists, economists, writers, philosophers. I had the feeling that I was watching Einstein and Gödel in the corridors of Princeton chatting about the future scope of the Turing machine. Similarly, the schools, the high schools, the universities could give rise to scientists from Cornell University, Princeton, Harvard and other members of the Ivy League. Long ago, I read Claude A. Villee's *Biology* as part of my resurrection, as the advent of a new life. There was no need to compare. I assumed that both molds were common, equally frequent, and I took as true the assertion of an economist: "The only stable thing in the modern world is instability."

Suddenly, I remembered the events of September 11, 2001, with the attack on the Twin Towers. We were in a meeting in the conference room. At that moment we heard the receptionist screaming. At first, we imagined anything: that a rat was running from one end of the lobby to the other, or that an object had fallen from the second floor. The woman could not explain anything, and from the look of her face, she seemed to be on the verge of collapse. With her finger, she was pointing at the television screen. We could see that one of the towers had been hit by a plane. Nobody knew what kind of plane it was. A few minutes passed and we all witnessed, stunned, that a second plane, a huge one, crashed into the other tower of the World Trade Center.

At that moment I thought that there were galactic beings, ancestral hatreds, invisible governments. Saturn devouring his children to prevent one of them from destroying him. Then Jupiter would banish him to Ionia. His own creation had turned against him. I wanted to believe that man is born to destroy his father, like Oedipus himself. Empires have an expiration date and there are wars that, initially, have a victor; then the defeated take their revenge. Jonathan Littell's *Las Benévolas*, staged in another place and time. The crime from the point of view of the murderer, and the victim becomes the third person. The massacres in Chile, Guatemala, Nicaragua. The Palestinian people living in the shantytowns of Gaza. At the end of the novel, the man is judged by the newborns. He could not share the action - no way! However, he could understand the causes of the fray. I had to reflect on the gripping chapters written by Hemingway, Steinbeck, Faulkner, Dos Passos and Tom Wolfe. Roads traveled by poor migrants, large numbers of displaced persons, caravans of wagons carrying all kinds of household goods. Suddenly I imagined a group of Blues musicians playing while a couple danced contorting their bodies. The whole Tower of Babel in a handkerchief, and in the middle of it, a name: Enola Gay; nothing less than the name of the plane that dropped the atomic bomb on Hiroshima.

The images shown on television that September morning were devastating. The Twin Towers were collapsing. The spectators of the catastrophe were fleeing before the cloud of dust generated by the collapse of the buildings. The debris, dust and fire looked like something out of a graphic depiction of the apocalypse. I would have liked to phone my friends in and around Manhattan. It was customary in South America; everyone was anxious to telephone their relatives.

The first person I needed to talk to was Daniel. I needed to ask him about his safety; then I would inquire about his Cuban wife and his parasitic relatives. After recovering from the surprise, I would call a professor named Littmann who had invited me to his residence in North Houston. I had talked with him about phenomenological psychology in the interpretation of human behavior while we were warming ourselves with the warmth of the fireplace in his living room decorated in a Nordic style.

"Not all human behavior can be measured by the fashionable social yardstick. The phenomenon-consciousness correlation is above any subject-object dualism," he explained to me as part of a conversation we were having about the behavior of some citizen tribes in New York and Los Angeles.

Perhaps he was referring to the Native American tribes of the Wild West and General Custer in the midst of battle against Sitting Bull, although I thought he was talking about the birth of the Calle 13 Mara, or Mara Salvatrucha, which later devastated Central America. Meanwhile, I was thinking about Daniel and his meetings with people with tattooed faces and hair dyed in unimaginable colors. But more than the faces of the people, it was their absolutely atypical behavior that I had in mind for my concept of the decadence of that group. I assumed that Gutierrez had failed in life and developed psychopathological behavior when his expectations were frustrated. However, for a moment I compared my achievements with his. We had both failed in marriage. He for his reasons and I for mine. Daniel had to leave for another country to seek a future and escape the hardships of poverty. I migrated several times for a job that did not admit partners. Were they pretexts or was it part of life itself? The point is that they left us or we left them and then… nothing. My friend was obsessive compulsive; I was chronically depressed, almost melancholic in my loneliness. His miserable life paralleled my globetrotting life. He sought pleasure in every nook and cranny and I sought the nook and cranny to find purpose in life. He would evaluate each fall and then force himself to get up. Right and left in every circumstance.

"Professor, I am realizing that the mirror has turned around and now looks at the observed, while we look at ourselves in the opaque side without perceiving our own figure as deteriorated as that of the explored." Each detail reminded me of a language full of gibberish, similar to the one Professor Littmann had attempted. We have no choice but to see ourselves in unknown facets, even if we pretend not to accept that dark side of our integral image.

The professor of quantum physics at no time pretended to explain the theories in vogue; the energy packets, as the foundation of the existence of the universe, nor the theory of everything and other topics such as entropy. That silence, emphatic, seemed to me a true demonstration of respect and affection for the interlocutor.

Suddenly he told me that he had been in a South American chef's restaurant eating chicken wings with a sweet and sour seasoning and that he licked his fingers because of how tasty it was. Later we talked about obesity in the elderly as a genetic issue. Then he asked me about the situation of the Indigenous people in the Amazon. I told him that some ethnic groups were in danger of extinction, such as certain Hottentot clans or some Papuan natives. Although it was not clear to me exactly whether these communities were disappearing or merging with other majority groups, which absorbed them for less skilled jobs in mining or fruit gathering.

Littmann had introduced me to his Finnish wife, who struck me as a woman of unquestionable dignity and a most friendly manner. She joined us for dinner, the main course of which was a barbecued porterhouse steak with the aroma of a Nordic hut. We chatted for hours about the food of the southern countries and the landscapes of the mountain ranges, with peaks of more than six thousand meters of altitude and beautiful lagoons produced by the thaw.

When I had to leave my friends' home, I felt the November chill. The streets were immersed in steam from the ground water and the garbage containers seemed to be on fire; meanwhile, ordinary citizens walked around in warm trench coats and overcoats. The girls resembled silhouettes outlined against a backdrop of neon-lit advertisements. We all looked like we were part of a cabaret scene from the forties or fifties of the last century, in a neighborhood near the banks of the Hudson or perhaps in the city of Chicago.

After observing the mass panic in that city, the de facto capital of the world, I would have liked to talk with Max and Matilda Littmann about the fundamentals of religious wars. The talk would have taken place in their home or in an unoccupied classroom at the university. Perhaps we could have come to interesting conclusions about the schism between Sunnis and Shiites within Islam, a rift that is now leading to crimes, internecine wars and explosions in the holy cities of the Middle East. Littmann would have made it clear to me that the schism dated back to the birth of Islam. In that conversation, which would be the summary of others with additions of reasoning on both sides, we would mention the action of the kamikazes that caused the attack on the Twin Towers of the World Trade Center and the future consequences that the attack would entail.

An imaginary conversation with Daniel kept replaying in my mind. In this case, the dialogue would take place in a SoHo or Chinatown restaurant as we sampled a salad with spicy wings sprinkled with radicchio and tomatoes. There we would have touched on substantive issues to avoid inappropriate small talk we found ourselves discussing during my visit to his home. He tried to explain his behavior while I apologized because no one has the right to judge the behavior of others, least of all me, who cannot even justify criticizing his choice.

"My father used to talk about the future as an uncertain time and the present as a blessing from the creator," Daniel commented about his father. I remembered his father's dock boy look, the shiny coat, the polished shoes and the slicked-back hair.

"I remember what he looked like. He was so elegant," I answered, alluding to his moustache that resembled that of the Cuban comedian Tres Patines, and the cigarette he always wore stuck to his lower lip like an appendage to his mouth.

We knew him as the Count. I don't know if the nickname was given to him by someone with a sense of humor or if he, in his alcoholic delirium, invented a lineage for his family. This last detail, very frequent in people from my town at the end of each hallucination, concluded with a title and even a coat of arms and a family history taken from the internet. The man lived in a bachelor apartment he had inherited from his older sister. Evil tongues said he had more than thirty children by more than ten wives. One of the children was Daniel.

The Count must have been twice as bad as my friend. You could see it in his asshole pimp attitude when he hit up women twenty years younger than him. It was also said that he would sting the mothers and would sting their daughters when they were old enough. "It was only a matter of time," he would tell me, thinking that the male seemed eternal and the females were the ones who went out of circulation.

When I met him, the Count lived in a married woman's bar. He lived with the owner of the business: a corpulent woman, the wife of an aging longshoreman Nothing new to see, the same story in two different scenarios and two different times, with a cloned character or a pair of identical characters. Yesterday it was the Count; today it is Daniel. That's the situation, the madman is not to blame. It was his genetic legacy and apprenticeship all along. Someone once remarked that just like the father, so will be the children. With such an example, it couldn't be any other note!

The only time we talked about his father, Daniel explained the following, "My father died several years ago. Regarding his last days of life, two versions circulated: the first referred to his death in a hospital for the indigent, abandoned by his children and his former wives. The second version said that he had been found on a bench in a public square. The person who informed me said in his letter, via e-mail, that the man had shrunk so much that he weighed no more than thirty kilos."

Suddenly, remembering our origin, I realized that in the city there were hundreds of individuals with the same behavior as the Count. The longshoreman himself, the husband of the Count's mistress, had his own mistress: a slim brunette in her forties who had four children by four different fathers.

"How could he behave this way?" I wanted to know. Immediately, I regretted having asked the question.

"I don't know." Maybe he would have liked to answer me, 'And what do you care?' But he kept quiet out of respect for his father's memory and not to give a bombastic answer to my impertinence. He kept quiet, although he had several options in mind.

He may have been maintained by the women and later by the children, who would contribute periodic fees for medicines and clothing. Perhaps the woman, or the women with whom he lived for prolonged periods, took care of food and lodging. Or neither. He had a most unusual occupation: he managed and collected the pensions of widows and elderly people who did not know how to prove their survival and their social rights. Some people said that he played poker with loaded dice and in that way he got the money from the other gamblers.

I instantly realized that my question was a judgment. I judged those who did not fit into my classification according to a code that had been imposed on me as that of the good citizen. I judged them with arrogance because I thought I was better than them; yet I was a scientist because I had scientist friends, and a researcher because I had researcher friends. I judged with the haughtiness of the enlightened. I was asking for explanations about how one person or another was maintained. As if he had asked a question about the way in which the catechumens, persecuted by the sicarii of the Roman Empire, were kept in the catacombs. It was like being interested in how poker players and foundlings in the slums or favelas were maintained.

I did not respect the memory, considering that during our childhood and adolescence the boys of the neighborhood, those of us who lived in the town and those who resided near the port boulevard, were fond of him and showed much respect. When we saw him pass by, we would shout in unison, "Good morning, Mr. Count!" And he would greet us with his hand and a nod. We loved him because he would prepare traditional seafood soup for us and because we loved his way of imitating the songs of the gypsy Sandro. Nowadays I think that the illness that took him away was pulmonary fibrosis caused by smoking, or tuberculosis caused by a deficient diet. Perhaps he had previously suffered from prostate cancer as a result of a viral disease spread by a woman during one of his wanderings.

I'm sure in the latter part of his life he was even more wiry and ghostly than before. He might even have painted a linear moustache over his bearded lip with mascara and put on his old fashioned suit and his little hat of worn and sticky straw. And he would have strolled the same sloping streets of the port, poking his nose into every joint. Somehow he influenced all of us. In some cases, that influence had the wind at his back and in other cases it was against his every act.

Suddenly, when I saw the explosions and the collapse of the Twin Towers, I felt that it was the beginning of the apocalypse, which would last another thousand years. Immense angels would blow immense trumpets and force us to be on the right and left of a being that appeared as an eye framed in a triangle. I could not know which side Daniel, the Count, Professor Littmann, the Salem witches, the Chelsea streetwalkers, the witch of the Andean village, the head shrinkers, the maras and their hitmen, the cartel commandos would be on. Where would I be? I thought of all the probabilities: the right or the left side of the triangle. Genotype plus environment plus triggers plus chance plus thunderbolts equals phenotype.

I assumed that we had all been fools like those in a nearby village, where children grow up to be fools. Maybe we were part of a community or a clan from the Tyrrhenian islands specialized in conjuring and tricks.

I would be at the right hand of God the Father. I do not know why. I may attribute it to a beginner's hallucination. In the end, the same loneliness, the same lack of affection. Identical walks along some boardwalk next to the sea or along a fast-flowing river in which meanders had formed along its entire course. I saw myself in a fogged mirror that reflected an altered image of huge eyelids and tiny feet. Deformed in context. Then I thought that this was the figure I projected on others, even in front of those who should judge me.

I immediately imagined the Count in an old people's home, or in a public health hospital to which he had been transferred after a raid on the destitute and mentally ill. This version of his death could be guessed: a short agony in the hospital. Or they might have found his corpse on a park bench, covered with sheets of old newspapers. A chronic lung disease, with dyspnea at rest and limitation for his minimal chores, was consuming him until he became a blue wreck. I saw him in his last hour, with definitive baldness, sunken eyes, Hippocratic fingers, nails thickened like watch glass, bluish skin tone and a cough with expectoration between gray and rusty.

In the waste of man's life, he could give rise to the sentence *errare humanum est*; for him and for so many who did not take into account the passage of time. He could remember hundreds of protagonists of the night, with painted lips and rouge on their cheeks, eyes lined with mascara and plucked eyebrows, who ended up on the sidewalk in a suburban neighborhood or as waitresses in a dingy cantina in the port. I could remember a pianist who came to play in important theaters, and after a time of English cashmere shawls and Armani suits, ended up as a soloist in a tourist restaurant, for a few pesos a night.

I firmly believed that none of the Count's children took care of him in his old age. The gave not a medicine nor a spray nor even a replacement white shirt; much less a daily plate of food to prevent him from begging in the food market. And the children justified the abandonment with a host of arguments.

Undoubtedly, they were right about the infractions, the neglect and the negligence that the man had committed. Of course, the phrase, "With the yardstick you measure by, you will be measured by" is true. That's how simple life is.

I pondered the aftermath of the Twin Towers attack. Never again would life be the same. In the parks, the cross-dressers would resemble masked terrorists. The bearded preacher could be a deranged Taliban. Brown people would be accused of practicing Islam, as if it were a stigma. Phone calls to the police would be repeated every second, with reports of suspects or myths of hysterical old men. At the same time, thousands of lines would be jammed, thousands of Twitter accounts. Lonely people could become victims of a serial killer or be investigated by the CIA or the FBI. The psychology of Big Apple residents would undergo a transformation; it would deteriorate as if it were a collective delirium. Neighbors or passersby on the street would look askance; certain vehicles parked in a neighborhood would be denounced, even if there were no elements of suspicion. New attacks would be feared, next time, on a university campus or in a high school playground. The sniper would be a boy with no prior record, but with a particular characteristic common in all cases: he would be silent, distant, self-absorbed, a fan of a TV series or a first-run movie. All paranoia! All this I said to myself, thinking that anyone could be a masked terrorist, be a psychopath who commits serial murders, or a member of the mafia.

Then I scolded myself, because it was unhealthy to think this way. Who chose me as a judge to go around instructing Gutierrez or his peers with measures of salvation? In fact, I was taking my life as a paradigm of good habits, but the truth is that many times I went through similar stupidities. How could I judge an individual who did the same as I did? Identical drunkenness, the same adventures with girls who liked to take risks and act as femme fatales. The difference was simple: he was wasted in a country that lived at a higher speed and with comparative advantages to the one of my choice; I was wasted in the daily grind.

Like Gutierrez, I left a home with children who had to wear the same shoes all year long; I restricted their school supplies and book budget. That's right; I didn't end up as a leper or a stinker. Life gave me another chance and I was forgiven in the middle of my journey. More for the merits of the Good Samaritan, which she was, than for my own, or for having shown some repentance and amendment in the future, as I learned in the catechism courses in the parish of the Benedictine priests. I returned to the sheepfold with the conceit of spoiled children.

I also had a genetic load of an eyesore, with childhood traumas, with a face full of wrinkles and a fat abdomen. At that moment I remembered a girl from high school who was my classmate in one of my equivalency classes. I remembered her youthful face, full of tenderness. She had a look of a doll or a spoiled child. She would have looked good in a little hat with the front of the brim up, as well as a bib blouse and short skirts up to a third of her thigh. She had a special charm that was also perceived by all those who hovered around her. I could picture her strolling along the boulevards with a friend. In my mind it was autumn, because the boulevard became a passage of bare trees with brown leaves on the ground, as if it were a Renoir painting.

She was walking along the path in her pleated skirt and white blouse. She looked like a character from a watercolorist's dream. That image stayed with me and always came up during periods of nostalgia, when I was far away from home and out of the country, remembering my homeland and my family. And there she was present.

Sometimes the scene I recreated was different. I was traveling in an urban transport minibus. Suddenly, a couple of dolls with transparent dresses that showed their small breasts and their colorful panties would get on the bus. They were apparitions confused with fantasy. What bodies! What beauty! No one could contradict the appreciation; on the contrary, the travelers were stunned at the sight of them. There was a joint murmur, as if they had seen an accident on the track or were commenting on a goal of their favorite soccer team. Nobody moved from their seats; nobody wanted to get off at the next stop. We all continued on the urban line as if we were hypnotized. They stood in the aisle, between the seats, as if consenting to their objectification. Indeed, as if they were conducive to ecstasy. Maybe they were laughing at our dumb satyr faces; maybe they enjoyed watching the bulging eyes and the awkward positions of the boys who were having strong reactions to their presence. They were just talking to each other, not even looking at the audience. Apparently, it was an amusing dialogue, or they simply wanted to introduce an enigmatic variant that would make the moment more fascinating.

Although I tried to be at that time and on the same day of the week in the urban minibus line of the dream, trying to match even the driver of the vehicle, getting on the bus stop, prowling the streets of the capital where they got on or off the minibus, I never saw them again, so that I was left with doubts as to whether the moment really existed or was just a daydream caused by the weather that summer.

Why did I want to meet them again? It was simple: I wanted to meet the girl from high school while I was taking the equivalencies in History, Geography, and Civics. I wanted to see her to go back to her. The same as at the *premiere* of a national film shown in one of the downtown movie theaters, when suddenly a black car with tinted windows appeared and three completely naked girls emerged from inside. Three boys in trunks ran after them in the lobby of the ticket office. On the street a tremendous commotion broke out. The girls were screaming and the boys were laughing loudly. I guessed that they were part of the cast, or maybe it was marketing.

Three minutes after they left in the vehicles with tinted windows, provincial police officers appeared and began a raid in the movie theater itself and in the adjacent streets. Some officers were asking viewers to identify themselves with their personal documents. "What's the point of asking for IDs?", I reflected then, observing the police reaction. Like the time they started shooting in the air five minutes after the robbers of a bank branch in a rural district had escaped. "Pure theater," I thought; when you can't do anything, try to do everything.

The appearance of the naked girls had the same effect on the public as the scene of the two young women who boarded the minibus in transparent dresses. A fleeting appearance to then disappear inside the car parked at the entrance, which immediately departed, quickly, down an avenue congested by traffic. I was not surprised at all. They, the girls in the minibus with transparent gauze dresses and the naked girls at the *premiere*, had dreamy faces and the bodies of models. Perhaps they were variety show actresses, runway models or escort ladies from a VIP agency. Their exhibitionism was part of a hormonal flow that drove them to adventure; or maybe it was something simpler: a matter of beauty and narcissism. When you have the assets, you must show them. If they had been university intellectuals, they would lecture; if they were watercolor painters, they would exhibit their paintings in a downtown gallery. They were beautiful, that much was obvious, and they had the most extraordinary bodies imaginable. Therefore, they would arouse whistles of admiration from a crowd of suckers and assholes. Why not show their distinct value? I rephrase this question: why should they be modest like nuns?

I admired them as one praises a work of art or contemplates the beauty of some exotic place. It could well be the Khmer temples of Angkor Wat, in Cambodia, surrounded by ficus roots set in the stones, with millions of orchids with corollas of all colors, with hundreds of earth-colored monkeys and baboons with scarlet buttocks; it could well be Machu Picchu, the lost city of the Incas, with the magic of the past and surrounded by enigmatic landscapes. That was its particular charm.

I remember her eyes lined with makeup. They seemed to have a clear iris, perhaps brownish. In any case, they invited the spell. I don't remember details of the hair, whether it was straight or fell in curls over her delicate shoulders. Most memorable was the youthful body, the slenderness of the female figure, the harmony between her small breasts and concave abdomen. In addition, there was the detail of the dress in the case of the dolls on the minibus and the lustful nudity of the girls in the anteroom of the cinema. It was all part of the show. Next was the surprise of the chance spectators, who seemed to have been hypnotized by some circus magician. Then the lewd comments and erotically charged glances, which were not erased from the astonished faces.

I return to the memory of the high school girl. She also had a dreamy face, a youthful body and the joy of innocence. When she agreed to be my friend in exchange for treating her with respect, the first thing that came to my mind was to try to pet her. Her reaction was to send me to hell and she immediately regretted making concessions without knowing me. The skirt with straps that joined under the chest, Tyrolean style, and the impeccable white shirt were the attire of the girls who walked along the boulevards and stores of the central part of the city. It was also the attire of high school students and those in the first years of college. She was my classmate in the subjects I had to take in order to validate my studies from my home country. This was a requirement for university entrance. I had to study the history of the country, with its internal wars, its leader, Juan Manuel de Rosas, and the gauchos of Güemes; the geography of Argentina, with its Mesopotamia and the provinces of Cuyo attached to the foothills of the Andes; the coast of the Paraná River and the southern provinces, with their characteristic pockets; and civic education and political economy, with the division of powers between the executive, the legislature and the judiciary, the provincial governments and the federal spheres.

She had to explain to me what I did not understand about the Mitre and Sarmiento governments, the federal and unitary war, the conflicts against Brazil and the Chaco war. She had to locate the national roads and railroads. She would also work with me to study the geographical division between provinces, departments and parties. At the same time, I would talk to her about the influence of Argentina on South America. The liberating army and the cry of Cordoba. The tango and the chacareras. She was a healthy girl and I was a spoiled brat. We still made a good couple.

I was impressed by her friendly expression, her body drawn behind her uniform blouse and a provocative candor that could be perceived from a meter away. She had dark brown hair and delicate cheekbones. I asked her for many things, like going out in the afternoons and evenings, going for a ride on the river in one of the pleasure boats, crossing the bridge on a bicycle. She accepted the first invitations and gradually became my girlfriend. But I did such shitty things to her... I cheated on her whenever I felt like it and humiliated her because I thought I was the biggest dude or the wisest of the wise. Not satisfied with so much humiliation, I repeated the dish with our children, making fun of their knock knees, or their inability to talk, without realizing that they had inherited those deformities from me. Therefore, I could not reproach the behavior of Gutiérrez, who abandoned his family to rebuild his life in the northern country. I was just like him, with some camouflage, but just as perverse. To be consistent, I would also have to enter a rehabilitation program, even if I had no faith that anything could be done with a distortion of affections.

The bad thing is that, without realizing it, the time of regret passed. "The business had failed and the store was closed." It's as simple as that. Life gives you rare opportunities and if you miss them, it's over. I was that lucky. I was given several that I didn't know how to take advantage of. In the end, someone got tired. I would have to pay for my faults by doing good, even if nothing would help me to recover what I had lost, neither crying nor beating my chest. I could go to the Persian Gulf or immolate myself in any other place. It didn't matter.

In the solitude of a room in which I installed a stereo, a computer and a personal library, I had time to chew my sorrows. Then I boarded a plane at the first opportunity. Thus, I traveled around the world: a war-torn country in the Far East, where I had to investigate the possibility of a yellow fever epidemic; a region of Africa, with the purpose of drawing a map of the spread of Ebola; the jungle of the Madeira River, in the state of Rondônia, or the high plateau, trying to guess whether the disease that had eliminated several villagers was caused by hantavirus or by the typhus rickettsia. From all the experiences I drank bittersweet drinks; sometimes pleasant and sometimes bitter, like everything in life. Among all the experiences, what marked my life the most was finding a village burned down in the middle of the Amazon jungle.

I went to the states where the Paratintines lived to support the organizations that worked to maintain their ethnicity and thus prevent their extinction. The dog with rabies ended up being a Saint Bernard with a barrel of wine around his neck. That's life, neither good nor bad: sometimes bad, sometimes good. I had to pay for all the bad things I had done. I had to value myself: I had to be good for something.

The first encounter with the natives was like a premonition of what was to come. In the state of Rondônia, I met the Akuntsu, the Tupi-Guarani and the Matis after flying over extensions of land ravaged by illegal logging by loggers. Wanting to know more about their history, I learned that the anthropologist Melo Morais Filho had spread the concept of primitivism in the native Tupi communities of the Brazilian rainforest. He postulated that the physical characteristics of the Botocudos were part of a racial degeneration of other ethnic groups. He had emphasized the prognathous face, the size of the thumb and the position of the body when walking. According to this conception, these people had the characteristics of ancestral hominids, so that they could not be included among modern hominids. Ethical theories in anthropology would appear only after the defeat of Nazism, as a movement to reject theories of racial supremacy.

We found a village consumed by fire and, among the smoldering embers, the charred bodies of human beings. This was an important event for us. Anthropologists, sociologists, staff of a non-governmental organization, a priest… and I participated in the discovery. That shocking episode forever changed our concept of justice.

I was told the story of a survivor of another tribe that had also been exterminated. I assumed that the man had a hut built with banana or oil palm leaves, with bamboo canes tied with climbing vines, and as a roof, an old ficus branch. I imagined that during the day I would walk following a circular path and at night I would dream that I would meet the last transhumants of a tribe, also decimated, which I would join to hunt or fish. Together with him, we would travel the reservation in concentric circles. After having witnessed the murder in Massaco, between the Marmelos and Madeira rivers, I came to the conclusion that the man wandering around the protected park of Rondônia was the result of an identical event, that had occurred months or years before, but just as tragic.

For how long did I suffer from insomnia or have dreams with jolts? How long did I wander through the jungle numbed by panic? Whenever I could, I would comment on the slaughter of the natives who lived between the Madeira and Marmelos basins. I would narrate the scene in great detail and emphasize the pain I felt having witnessed the massacre. I repeated over and over again the frustration I experienced for not being able to denounce at the border police headquarters or before the Criminal Prosecutor's Office in the cities near Rondônia. I was just as outraged with the massacre as I was with the authorities' refusal to accept the complaint and initiate an investigation. How many times they claimed that they were not competent to open a report when there was no evidence of a victim or proof of the crime. They sounded like characters out of an old novel I read as a boy. In the book, the protagonist goes through the offices of various branches of a state's legal organization to prove his innocence in a crime he did not commit. Nobody knows what he is accused of; the only thing they know is that he is a defendant before an enigmatic court.

I left the novel and returned to real life. In it, I could not accept the fact that there were cover-ups with equal or worse responsibility than the perpetrators, since they were given free reign, which gave the criminals the freedom to commit any ethnocide. It is clear to me that behind the murderers, whoever they were, were those who hired them to clear the area over which they wished to increase their wealth.

Back to the first scenario, New York, the big city, with its avenues and kilometer-long streets, busy with an incredible number of vehicles; with its three-hundred-meter-high buildings and soundproof windows; with its neon signs and multimedia screens that invite consumption. Snow dance shows or UFC fighter fights; previews of movies to be released in the following week. A context with robotized or idiotized humans watching the multimedia ads in Times Square and vying to attend one of the nineteen Broadway theaters.

During my trip I was amazed to visit the Lincoln Center, as well as Columbia University, with its library and all the knowledge accumulated in the archives. Gutierrez and I were impressed by the casual eroticism of the homosexual couples walking the streets of Chelsea. We could see that money, which they call *pasta*, flows in torrents as if it were part of the trick of an old, alcoholic Russian clown, who pulls coins out of the nose, ears, armpits and even the crotch of the spectators. In that bluff that I invented to fill a gap in my memory, Gutiérrez was unable to explain the amount of money he spent on his vices: alcohol, drugs and pornography. Nothing was clear, neither the origin of the crumpled banknotes that seemed to multiply in his pockets, nor the way in which he squandered the money on binges and games of chance. I imagined him with some skinny women with black tights adopting a symbiotic form of coexistence. He did the advertising and gave them protection; they got their money by fondling a perverted old man. My friend's trade had several names: pimping, pandering, procuring and finally, trafficking of women.

Maybe none of that was real and Gutierrez was just the agent of some clandestine pool being sold to Hispanics in the Bronx and Harlem. The area assigned by his managers would be the run-down area of the Bronx; not the Riverdale on the banks of the Hudson, where the prosperous families of the borough live, but the area next to the Harlem River, where the gray, shanty buildings rise up a flight of stairs from a street full of cannibalized cars, rappers immersed in a dance competition and children playing soccer or baseball.

Perhaps Daniel was interested in listening to the music of Duke Ellington and Aretha Franklin in a pub on 155th Street accompanied affectionately by two skinny women who charged him fifty dollars each. The women were always the same; one of them even introduced herself as his girlfriend. Just like when they accompanied other guys they hung out with. No, his thing couldn't be jazz or blues; it was salsa. In fact, I heard him humming old Hector Lavoe, Marc Anthony and Jon Secada songs as we walked down the avenues of Manhattan. At the same time, I felt him whistling a tune that belonged to the Sex Pistols or Led Zeppelin; a melody more in line with the musical taste of his surroundings at the time of his arrival in the country. I never thought that Gutiérrez was so syncretic in life and in his musical taste. He even told me that he had participated in a Latin American music contest, with his own songs. A Brazilian partner played and he composed the lyrics.

Every day my friend's life held a surprise in store for me that made me think that the former South American port worker was nothing like the man I had visited in New York. I had to understand that he had assimilated the habits of the longshoremen of the East River docks, who went out at night to the neighborhood pubs and then looked for their fat woman with whom to procreate. I understood then that the Cuban woman played a role in Gutierrez's life. Otherwise, he would be just another schizophrenic from the shipyards.

Supporting the woman and her relatives was a way of paying a quota or tax to get rid of loneliness and its sequel: madness.

Without her, Gutierrez would be a suburban nut, an old pimp, a broke drug dealer, a poor half-dollar-an-hour funk. In that case, I would have had to look for him on the Upper East Side, where I would have found him in a trench coat that covered two-thirds of his legs, ending about six inches below his knees, with an unkempt gray beard, graying hair and an empty memory. He would be part of a group of derelicts who warmed their bodies by burning garbage in a metal dumpster under an East River bridge or elsewhere near the river. When I met him I would realize that he had lost his memory, for he would not recognize me even if I gave him details of his youth, told him about the Count, his father, or referred to Clara, his ex-wife, and their children, Little Daniel and Clara.

Daniel, my friend, would have burned his brain cells with crack, methamphetamines and other filth. And I would repeat again, "Come on, buddy, I will take you to the homeland so you can recover. I'll take you, even if I have to drag you through the corridors of the customs registers to leave this country and enter ours. I told you not to go to extremes in your fucking life". Maybe that way he would react, and also avoid losing all his teeth and pathological fractures due to bone decalcification. He could avoid certain diseases, such as the acquired immunodeficiency that one of those girlfriends might pass on to him, and sarcoma of the skin, lung damage from *Pneumocystis* and cancer of the lymphatic system. Although it was more likely that he had acquired some disease related to the kind of crazy life he led, such as cytomegalovirus and condyloma acuminata; or blennorrhagia with recurrences every winter. And it might already be too late for any resurrection, for the man would have melted connecting rods, his mind would have darkened and his brain would have filled with small caverns resembling a gruyere cheese.

It seemed impossible to me that the uncontacted natives of Madeira and the street punks of the 70s and 80s could coexist on the face of the earth. Who is real: Melquíades, the Indian sorcerer of the Andean dwarf community, or Daniel, my alienated friend from Manhattan? I'm inclined to think Daniel, because Melquíades looked like a spirit who had descended from the sky on a condor to visit humans before returning to his Olympus on a cloudy mountain, where extraterrestrial beings also dwell.

It seems that the idea of a mountain as the dwelling place of the gods was a widespread belief across the globe. I had read the concept in Ernest Hemingway's *The Snows of Kilimanjaro* when he refers to the western summit of the mountain as "the house of God of the Maasai tribes". I wanted to remember part of the dialogue between the man with the gangrenous limb and his wife,

"Bastard birds!" He was referring to the vultures that were on the lookout for rottenness, such as the workers of the Lower Police or the body snatchers of the bombed cities.

"I won't let them hurt you, honey," she told him. I'm sure she would watch him to keep the scavenger birds away.

By association of ideas, I thought of an article by Noam Chomsky that narrated the Cuban missile crisis. The text, which appeared in the chain of newspapers with the largest international circulation, uncovered a secret order, sent at the time by President John F. Kennedy, to give the green light to a nuclear bombing of Moscow by NATO planes manned by Turkish pilots flying from Ankara. The article mentioned diplomatic means of exhausting all avenues before the event took place. The deterrence scheme was repeated in the present to try to prevent an Israeli bombing of Iran's nuclear plants, an attack that would jeopardize the world balance. What a mess!

I imagine that would result in an atomic cloud burning up the bread crops. I also suspect that the carnage would be so gruesome that the vultures would surely have to migrate to Persian territory, or they might breed in the area like the cockroaches, *Periplaneta americana*, which multiply in the cracks in the walls or under the floorboards. In this way, the black birds with hairless necks would avoid the rotting of human remains; on the other hand, the orange-collared bugs would rather be the vectors for the transmission of microbes and parasites, which would increase mortality. Likewise, in this scenario, rats would reproduce exponentially and spread leptospirosis and black plague, in addition to hantavirus. The diseases would concentrate in Mesopotamia, then spread to the Middle East. They could later affect travelers, who would carry them to Europe, India, China and North America.

At that time I imagined a hecatomb as a consequence not only of the conflagration itself, but also of the collateral damage, such as the pandemics that would affect the valleys of the Euphrates and Tigris rivers. And I felt immense sorrow for the destruction of the Sumerian vestiges of the ancient city of Ur and the step pyramids or ziggurats of Eridu and Uruk, which would be wiped off the map. In that place, ten thousand years ago, the black-headed nomads, to whom Zecharia Sitchin's theory attributes an extraterrestrial origin, founded the first known cities of mankind. The patriarch Abraham, born in Ur, set out with a caravan to the land of Canaan. This gave rise to the Abrahamic cultures and religions: Judaism, Christianity and Islam. Clearly, Western civilization has its roots in Mesopotamia. Perhaps in that same place the first nuclear hecatomb and the beginning of a destruction without precise limits will take place in the future. The same scenario for the birth and destruction of humanity.

In New York the train stations and car stops were populated by hedonists who looked like puppets in the middle of a performance. "No one is born alone," one of the characters who took refuge in the streets around Time Square, where shows on forbidden subjects were being shown, blurted out to me. A body had been found at the intersection of Tenth Avenue and 80th Avenue. He was wearing a gray overcoat and had matted hair, a bristly beard, a gibbous back due to a deformed spine and a protruding abdomen. Seeing his swollen face and the stigmata on his skin, I imagined that the man must have been one of the many alcoholics who walked around the vicinity of the shipyards or the shallows of the columns that support the embankments. The guy had fallen to the ground, possibly fulminated by a galloping pneumonia or some other cause of sudden death. Passersby had placed sheets of newspaper over the body. Then the officers of a patrol car covered him with yellow plastic sheeting and cordoned hm off with yellow tape to keep curious onlookers away. Among them was a short man who attracted my curiosity because of his resemblance to Melquíades. When he noticed me looking at him, the individual raised his middle finger and shouted, "Fuck you! " I felt embarrassed. Seconds later I disappeared into the crowd.

The individual had swollen, puffy eyelids, chubby hands and short limbs compared to the trunk. I would have liked to explain to him the reasons that induced me to observe him, as I did not intend to offend him. Although on second thought, if the subject had found out, he would not have forgiven me. It would be doubly offensive to him: not only for having mistaken him for a South American person, but also for comparing him to a dwarf. He would probably not understand my excuses. For this reason, the best thing to do was to take a cross street to avoid the presence of another rare specimen of the concrete jungle that might attack me.

The next day I left the great city of glass towers rising over three hundred meters, illuminated by neon lights; the wide avenues, darkened by the shadows of the buildings. I was leaving the capital of the world, with its diversity of neighborhoods, which at the same time formed ghettos where individuals of a certain characteristic or singular preference lived: some were fashionable; others were metrosexuals, artists, university students, politicians, rappers, punks, goths… or what do I know. They could be grouped by nationality or ethnicity: Hispanics, Chinese, African-Americans, Jews, Irish, Orientals.

At the Sixth Avenue and 42nd Street subway station, an African-American musician recalled the great performers who had passed through the Wha Café in Greenwich Village in the days of Bob Dylan and Jimi Hendrix. In Central Park, retirees rested on benches from whence they watched the passersby strolling through the green spaces. One guy was trying hard to attract attention with a mystical speech about the salvation of the world. He used as a platform a wooden crate that had once been a fruit crate from a department store. Young musicians rehearsed with electronic guitars. The streetwalkers, dressed in minimalist garments, let their buttocks and breasts show, seeking to impress the people walking along the boulevard. A new world for me. A world that gave me mixed emotions: on the one hand, I had the feeling of having charged my batteries, which allowed me to perceive the unimaginable; on the other hand, I was afraid of ending up like those brainless people who melted their neurons with some toxic substance.

Among the abandoned prospects were aging narcissists, arthritic musicians and war cripples. Daniel Gutiérrez would also have a place as an individual immersed in an immense solitude, despite being surrounded by a crowd. At that moment before leaving, I remembered the dialogue I had with his wife, the Cuban woman. She had spoken to me with a venomous tone about Daniel, whom she described as a South American shit eater. Then she told me that he was no good at all, just a hustler, a pimp. I asked her, "Why do you keep living together if you are no longer fond of him?" From the conversation I got the woman's nickname of one who plays backwards. At the same time I felt the outdated xenophobia of some people who think they are the lid of a pot without handles. Segregation in an endless chain: whites despise blacks; brown people offend Indians; North Americans, South Americans; Irish, Jews; Japanese scorn Chinese; and North Africans look down on sub-Saharan Africans.

Life repeats experiences. Walking down a New York street is much the same as walking through Hong Kong or Los Angeles. The towers of Melbourne are similar to those of London. The streets of Istanbul resemble those of Casablanca or Marrakech. In many of those nooks and crannies you can find women with gaunt features and sunken eyes. Likewise, in the Amazon jungle you can discover men with faces deformed by inlaid lips or nose wings, and in the Andes, individuals with cheeks burned by the cold. Then you seem to have already experienced the same episode with similar actors. And when you turn the corner you run into a woman you met a long time ago in a different city and you think it is the same person, without calculating that twenty years or more have passed and no one can keep the same or maintain the same expression.

I reasoned that iniquities had been going on for centuries. Therefore, tribes of young men taking over cities were not a new phenomenon. Still, it seemed to me that they had been invaded by bugs that had the body of sewer rats, six insect-like claws, a gray fuzz on their backs and two bulging bile-yellow eyes, as well as mobile antennae. To defend themselves against them, citizens built shelters in buildings and invented home delivery. Everyone feared the danger lurking on street corners and at subway entrances. Likewise, they were terrified of the gangs that plagued the neighborhoods. The sheafs were made up of people whose hair was artificially bristled thanks to a hairspray that kept it fixed in the center of the head for twenty-four hours. In other cases, they were made up of brown people with matted hair, Chinese people with bad hair or Latinos with shaved hair, all with tattooed bodies.

Meanwhile, I walked along the avenues feeling afraid of neurotics and bipolar psychotics in their hypomania. I was afraid of the assholes who went out to fish for unsuspecting passers-by and the poisonous women who, besides fleecing you like experts, could give you a sexually transmitted disease. Not to mention the drug pushers and the addicts who could turn you inside out to get the drugs. I was afraid of each and every one of them.

As I walked along, I pondered the origin of the rampage, but when I couldn't find an answer, I asked someone I didn't know, "When did the circus begin?"

That pedestrian made a gesture with his face. The expression in his eyes indicated that he didn't know the fact either.

"Maybe it was the return of the soldiers, after the war was over," he commented, calculating my reaction.

When did the war end and did he mean the Vietnam War or the Iraq War? I was intrigued. Then I imagined the ex-combatants crowding the streets of the big cities of the east and west. They became part of the mass of unemployed people walking around window-shopping and sniffing the smell of food wafting from restaurants in downtown New York or Los Angeles. They were almost always weirdos. At that moment I thought that another war was urgently needed to end the aftermath of the previous one. And I concluded with an antithesis: wars are necessary for the development of the economy and, above all, to channel the predatory vocation of human beings. I am laughing my head off at the adjective I used: human, and I repeat the term thinking of the legacy of Thomas Aquinas, Martin Heidegger and Jean-Paul Sartre.

At that point, there was so much clarity in what the Andean mountain sorcerer was saying....

"Tell me, why were your people at war with the feathered ones?" I was interested in the Andean war.

"For the water. What else is there to fight about?" he answered.

The answer, which was also a question, perplexed me by the assurance with which the old man spoke. I thought you could fight for the metals of Thrace, for the oil reserves of the Middle East, for world domination or for the preservation of a way of life. But, of course, you could also fight for water.

Some articles by Michel Foucault explaining the operators of domination came to mind. This author understood power as a commodity; in fact, he went so far as to affirm that power was at the origin and end of wars. It is power that represses; to do so, it uses the dictatorship of totalizing knowledge, which subjugates the subjugated knowledge of peoples and the ignorant.

It was now clear who the triumphant warrior was. In the end it was the mass rebellion against subjugation that was being fought. Masses of ragged men, walking through deserts like Sonora or the Golan Heights, confronted the dictatorship imposed by the holders of power. Hundreds of migrants in search of the huts that had not been plundered by the warriors, still standing in the grasslands near the borders. Villages rose up out of the desolation of the desert areas. The wind raised an earth that damaged the sclerae, so, in order not to inhale the sand, they covered their noses with handkerchiefs. This also prevented them from drowning or becoming contaminated with fungi such as histoplasmosis or coccidia. And they dragged their children along, trying to ensure the survival of the whole species.

A world of sand, dust and mushrooms that settle in the lungs of travelers. Again, sandbanks and hurricane winds. Aging boys, children with adult reasoning, women distrustful of their own offspring. That was the world I shared with others. Within that scenario were the Madeira Indians and the jíbaros who lived in the Putumayo basin. Also the emaciated people who had massacred them in an itinerant village and the bosses of the predatory companies of the Amazon. And, without a doubt, so were the prosecutors, police and judges who exonerated the perpetrators of the devastation of uncontacted native territories.

Chapter 3
Other Women

We saw a wooded mountain from a fighter plane and then realized that it was in fact a village of huts on a palisade on the side of a river. The Burmese women showed the expression produced by panic, with contracted eyelids and eyes evidencing a slight exophthalmia. Their pupils were probably mydriatic due to the effect of adrenaline. Sweat beads were visible on their foreheads; the hair looked wet and the skin had the pallor of fright.

The people in the group were panting from the effort, as they had been working for several hours. I assumed that they had had to go deep into the bush, cutting the vines and low branches of the trees to be able to move forward. Likewise, I thought they had had to mire themselves in the rotting mud bogs, trying to avoid ophidians and saurians; in this case, ochre-colored vipers and black lizards more than two meters long. Their hearts were pounding. Some of them had even wet their clothes with urine because they did not want to stop and lose time because of that need. The young women set the pace; however, they had to wait for the stragglers: older women, the elderly and small children.

I did not know how long they had been fleeing; perhaps they had been walking for several days. On many occasions they had had to endure the rains that fell like buckets of water; on others they had felt a sense of suffocation from the unbearable humidity of the jungle, with the mist rising from the pools covered by colorful butterflies and that seemed to emerge from the rhizomes that were entangled with the roots of the trees of more than thirty meters.

On their march through the jungle and swamps, they had hidden during the day so as not to be detected by their pursuers. The fog and trees protected them from the low flying planes and helicopter gunships, but not from the human heat detectors used by the army. To advance, they had taken advantage of the twilight, despite the danger of encountering large predators. The proximity of the border promised them safety, since flights were prohibited in a strip of land comprising one kilometer on each side of the dividing line, except for an unknown agreement between the governments of the two countries to contain the flow of mass migration.

At the entrance to the camps authorized by UNHCR and the Government of Thailand hung a sign announcing that there was no room for more refugees. From the UNHCR high command barracks, the sound of cannons firing their shells could be heard, even though the fighting was taking place some ten miles away.

I asked Lars Olsen, the head of the blue helmets.

"Are the women running away from that battle?" And I pointed my finger at the horizon, locating the place where the detonations were coming from.

He replied that he had no record; he did not know if they were fleeing from the bombing or from the war itself. I had to understand that fleeing a war is different. It implies being clear that there is no other option but to abandon one's home, land, country; to leave everything behind for something uncertain. Then a Bergman film came to my mind, where Indian people were lined up at the border checkpoints. Perhaps it was not a Bergman film, but a scene from a short film, where caravans of German children and elderly people were escaping from the cities on the eastern front during the final phase of World War II.

Nor did I clearly remember a border checkpoint, but rather the rubble of buildings in a bombed-out city.

"Two or three caravans of people arrive every week," Olsen said.

"I noticed the overcrowding in the refugee camp," I replied. Then I wanted to find out why most of the refugees were civilians who did not seem to belong to any group in conflict. As always, the most frequent victims seem to be those not involved in the hostilities.

"This is a mess," Olsen explained. "The fighting is between the regular army and the rebels. The thing is that there are not two clearly defined sides. On the one hand, there are the official forces and the police, which have long been overwhelmed; on the other side, groups of irregulars with different purposes: from armed gangs, who obey the warlords, to mercenaries who sell their firepower to whoever can pay for it.

"In that labyrinth we must also mention the gangs of outlaws who seek to seize the moment to gain their own advantages. Often these are roving groups of dissident rebels who leave because of disagreement with their leaders. Then he paused. Seconds later, he continued, "In short, war between families, tribes, religions and hordes of boys who have been driven mad. The latter don't need any order, not even a ringleader; they all have the chip of violence in their brains. They think this is an opportunity to make money working as mercenaries or just looting the villages," complained the boss. "Do you know what they use the money for? For crack cocaine, for pills or for whoring around."

I imagine that, when talking about pills, he was referring to methamphetamines or some other substance such as Benzedrine.

"What madness!" I exclaimed. Perhaps I should have said "Murderous thugs!" to be more expressive.

The noise was so close that I felt like I was on a roller coaster without a seat belt. People were running away from the conflagration. At that moment I cursed the bad time I arrived at this place, the border with Burma, after a long flight with stopovers in Amsterdam, Beijing and Bangkok and a trip in a van with the United Nations logo on the side. At what time had it occurred to me to enlist in this type of mission? Like the photographers in the group, and the freelance journalists, the drivers, the brigadistas trained in public health, the guides in the region, the nurses specialized in first response and other professionals, I felt my bowels moving and my legs trembling with panic. No one said anything, as if it were shameful to admit that we feared the brutality of unhinged men who see an opportunity to hurt a protected individual in the uniform of the international organization.

I had been to other similar places before, so the whistling of bullets being exchanged by armed groups or the spaced-out sound of sniper fire was familiar to me. For the most part, they tended to be very young people. They were armed to the teeth with mortars, bazookas and machine guns and rode on the hopper of open pickup trucks. I had not been to the Middle East, but I imagined the tremendous mess in desolate cities like Beirut, Baghdad, Aleppo and, more recently, Mosul.

I don't remember if I vomited from fear, but I am almost certain that I felt nauseous; that sensation that precedes vomiting and diarrhea when food contaminated by colibacilli, amoebae or any toxic substance is ingested. The dread had accompanied me not only during the day, but also when I closed my eyes. I had been sleepless for many nights now; the few nights I managed to fall asleep I suffered nightmares in which I saw myself as the victim of an attack, dead while the executioners threw shovelfuls of earth over my corpse. These nightmares repeated over and over again. In the end, I would wake up screaming like a madman, bathed in sweat like a lung patient, shivering as if I feared the dream was a premonition.

"And you, why did you come?" asked the Norwegian, even though, as commander of the organization, he knew beforehand why he was there.

"They reported five deaths and they think it could be yellow fever." I should have explained that no similar cases had been detected in the region before. Nor in the rest of the continent. This was a more common disease in Africa and South America. "My mission is to confirm that it is this disease or if it is something with similar symptoms that also presents as jaundice and hematic vomiting.

"We are talking about several types of malignant hepatitis; for example, the delta variants of hepatitis B or diseases such as leptospirosis septicemia or a very contagious type of meningitis that in its final stage causes jaundice and convulsions," I told him, reproducing the text of the mail sent to me by the mission. The organization's idea was to prevent any variant that combined jaundice with hemorrhages.

"We are here, comrade, for a matter that does not involve us, like two rabbits in a shootout typical of the American West," he opined with a smile on his lips. "We've been sent to do something that many are too scared to do," he continued, criticizing the superiors because we were the ones risking our own skins.

In wars everyone believes that they have some kind of reason. In Rwanda the Tutsis claimed that the Hutus dominated them fiercely. On the contrary, the Hutus fled from the cruelty of the Tutsis. It was a real mess. In this case, in Myanmar, formerly Burma, the persecuted ethnic groups, such as the Rohingyas and the Karen, were defending themselves against the government troops, who had declared war to the death on the armed wing of those ethnic groups of Islamic confession.

I don't believe in the polarity of good and bad, black and white. I do not believe in just and unjust, in wars. In all cases men are invaded by a madness similar to encephalitis in their period of psychomotor agitation, prior to a coma; a rage similar to the homicidal exaltation of the most serious paranoids. Like the annihilation commandos and their variant: the predation commandos. These were composed of boys who wore bullet cannons crossed over their bare chests, with their heads covered by a turban or a cap with which they pretended to pass incognito. All similar to each other and, therefore, unnoticed in the ensemble. They were like fighters in a form of hand-to-hand combat, or like a pack in search of prey. Civilians and those not involved in the war saw them as a pack of rabid baboons, like a flock of hungry eagles fresh down from the Himalayan mountains. Villagers would shake like leaves during a typhoon when they appeared near the village.

It felt like an action movie starring Sylvester Stallone or Bruce Willis, with explosions in the jungle, shells that raise dust and smoke, fire, burning huts. The screaming of women and children without the appearance of a vigilante hero. In short, an apocalyptic chaos, a chain of clashes with an undetermined end. The difference was that in this scenario there was no warrior capable of firing seven hundred and fifty bullets per minute while showing off his pecs. And no one says "Stop!" to stop the action.

In these places anyone could be hit by a projectile and die with their viscera scattered on the ground. Then I thought I had some kind of armor; something that allowed me to survive the danger. I knew that the armor was a deception, although I tried to think that the United Nations logo would act as a shield, sending a message of neutrality to be respected. In that way I tried to cajole myself not to panic when I heard the whistling sounds of shells and the thunder of bombs. And with two milligrams of clonazepam, I tried to fall into a deep sleep in one of the barracks that served as our quarters, always within the yellow zone, which was protected by the blue helmets.

Suddenly someone told us that one of our patrols had been ambushed. Then panic set in among all of us who made up the mission. "Who the hell got us into this? Of course, to find the answer we had to look in the mirror. Then the same story: "No! Nothing can happen to us, because it is written in the script of the movie", even if it was the movie of our own life.

Those involved could take us for the cover-up of the guerrillas infiltrating the refugee camps or as informants of the groups in conflict or as agents of a foreign power with its own objectives. Perhaps this last conjecture was real, although we were unaware of the strategy that moved each piece in this geopolitical chess.

In any case, it didn't matter because in the exchange we were exposed to whatever their paranoid brains believed. For them, we could be friends of the military dictatorship, of the rebels, and even friends or enemies of randomly chosen subjects (men with tattoos, cabaret dancers or drug pushers, prostitution and human trafficking networks). This without taking into account that we would be accused of being believers, agnostics, nihilists or atheists; even Islamists committed to jihadist groups. Those of Islam could claim that we were Buddhists, close to the lamas and their self-defense commandos. They might label us as Coptic Christians, with ideas of catechization. So, in one way or another, we would be truly fucked.

No one listening to me would believe that I was there just because of a disease that first attacks monkeys and then humans. No one would think that I was a researcher of epidemics caused by microscopic germs called viruses, bacteria and rickettsiae.

Worse still, no one could explain that there are diseases caused by bits of protein called prions. And that these pathogens could wipe out a county and spread across a continent and then jump to others to kill hundreds of thousands of men like a war without quarter or rules. Because you would not believe that my passion for healing the sick began as a child. For this reason, I had been to other places for the exclusive purpose of treating diseases that the doctors in the area did not know about, even if they were the most deleterious, the most risky, because they jumped from one person to another, from one community to another; even from one species to another.

Every word spoken would be dissected at the time of the final judgment, which could be at any time, without our presence and without our having the right to defend ourselves. We could be judged and then condemned to a vicious attack, from behind, by a subject infiltrated among the refugees. Perhaps our assailant would be a woman or a child under twelve years of age, who would first trick us and then poison us with arsenic or cyanide mixed with the ranch ration served in the camp.

In those circumstances, I had to send our sanitarians to fumigate the jungles, but I was afraid that my group, being Burmese, would be mistaken for soldiers or insurgents, gang members or dissidents of conflicting groups, spies and counter-spies. I was afraid that they would be ambushed in the clearings of the jungle, where they were looking for the macaques killed by zoonosis. Because after having dispatched them with bullets, they would slit their throats and throw their bodies into the river. Later, we would find the corpses in the pools, partially devoured by scavengers, or in the process of putrefaction, with hundreds of flies and maggots emerging from the flesh. If that were to happen, I would never forgive myself, because I would have exposed them to danger while we remained in the refugee camp.

The din of battle could be heard in the cloud forest of the mountains, in the dwarf bush savannah and in the rice fields that had been planted next to the village. Baboons were fleeing from the thicket to the plain and birds were flying in flight to other valleys. I was convinced that many villages had been burned and that under the rubble the corpses of their occupants awaited, a common pattern in all wars.

The Norwegian officer of the blue helmets, which were something like the United Nations security commandos, described the situation to us: the battle front had moved to the Mekong Delta on the Thai border and had therefore abandoned the mountains of the Lamas. Government troops had recaptured almost all the Karen-occupied villages. That was the description of the last movements of a war of positions, where a village can be the center of operations and, after being devastated, become the refuge of the survivors.

Olsen continued talking. I barely understood the geographical notes of the area, much less the description of sides and ethnicities. I was in the limbo that precedes tragedies. What I did gather was that people were fleeing leaving their belongings behind. No one was interested in taking something they had worked hard for. It was about saving the lives of those close to them, whether it was a child or an elderly person, the child or the father of a family already diminished by the disaster. What was the use of despair? And crying? In the end, tears do not flow, but anguished moans can still be heard.

Indeed, and although Olsen did not mention it, that cry seemed to be the howl of the wolves that inhabited the steppe, or maybe it was the shriek of the primates of the forest. At that hour of the game, who had any tears left, if they had long since been consumed?

What the Norwegian did say was that desperation did not protect us one bit. At that moment, while I was listening to the final part of his speech, I remembered the women pulling the naked children. There was a grimace on their faces, I would say a rictus of desperation and exhaustion after several days of walking. I would have to examine their feet to cure the skin lacerated by the thistles of the road and eliminate the larvae of filarias or butterflies, interdigital fungus and chiggers. These insects are similar to izangos, but with a different name, and climb from the sole of the foot to the testicles.

In my mind I also planned to check the neck, as well as the deltoids to discover if the screws, which were fly larvae that were extracted with the juice of tobacco leaves, had nested under the skin, between the muscles. Similarly, I was to examine the sclerae to see if innominate worms had nested underneath or possessed the icteric tinge of liver disease. For this reason, the next step would be to palpate the liver and spleen for splenomegaly caused by some tropical disease. Then I would do a blood test for agglutinins or immunoglobulins, and take a stool sample for parasites, rhizopods or foreign bacteria. Finally, we would auscultate the lungs and take radiographic films to rule out tuberculosis, pulmonary fungi or alveolar diseases caused by viruses.

Once all this was done, we were going to vaccinate them against the different types of hepatitis, as well as influenza, whooping cough, tetanus, typhoid, poliomyelitis and measles.

I had come for the yellow fever, but ended up as if I were a sanitary doctor just out of college. A doctor without borders. A sanitarian in white scrubs who moved to the beat of volunteer nurses. They treated me as if I were a monkey or an employee of one of the non-governmental organizations dependent on UNHCR or WHO.

I had several more talks with Olsen. We both felt it was cathartic to talk about a wide variety of topics.

"I know your country. Many years ago, when I was engaged to my first wife, we visited Machu Picchu, Cusco, Lake Titicaca, La Paz. Nice places. I loved the feast of the saints; I enjoyed the images walking around the main square. We spent a magical night in a hotel in Machu Picchu."

"I'm glad you liked my land. I was born in one of the older neighborhoods. My parents lived there for a while; then we migrated to a port in the south. My father was a language teacher."

"Some places have similarities. The Andean landscapes remind me of the valleys near the Himalayas. I don't know, maybe they are impressions with which the brain tricks us," he commented, without specifying which places and which landscapes he was comparing.

"Look what a coincidence. I recently visited a hermitage north of the Mekong and it seemed to me to be in a religious enclave near La Paz. I don't remember the exact name," I told him, although I didn't really know if it was a shrine in Cotoca or Copacabana.

"I'm sick to death of this mission. The whole thing is a mess. The crooks have moved their center of operations to Mae La." He was referring to the refugee camp in Thailand. "I was sent there when UNHCR delegates reported a massacre of women refugees who had apparently been recruited for prostitution. The police believed they were hit men from a Filipino mafia who were recruiting young women and then transporting them to Bangkok. I had to protect the survivors.

"The women knew that to get to safety they had to cross the border river. From the ages and appearances, I could guess that the children were not only the children of those who fled, but also of other women who had straggled or died in battle. It looked like a wandering orphanage or a children's school during an end-of-year excursion. At that moment I hated all wars, even the so-called just wars.

"Then I reflected on what had happened. Are there just causes for killing people? Maybe yes, when it comes to defending your life, your village or your country. For example, to survive the murderous jackals whose eyes are reddened by the splashes of innocent blood; to protect your territory from invaders, who intend to take away your belongings."

The image of the Gurkhas and the maras came to my mind, with their hair shaved on the sides and a crest in the center. The same baleful look, the same angry drool. The chest and shoulders tattooed and, on the drawings, scars of varying thickness. A sinister symbology: each scar represented a battle and dozens of dead; also the assassination of an important enemy. Perhaps each rough line was the memory of a felony that caused enormous damage to the opponent. And the same language, even if in different languages.

In the past I had witnessed atrocities that no one could imagine: children's bodies piled up in the street leading to a village, dismembered corpses of women in a vacant lot, old people dead on top of the roof of the big house in the village. Still, I was not used to the cruelty of homicidal madness. I could understand any other kind of madness, but never the murder of innocents. I would not get used to such violence. It was even worse, because after having lived through those experiences, my fear grew. From that moment on, I developed a kind of paranoid apprehension about places with a violent past. Both to those territories that had suffered a low and medium intensity war and to red light districts, areas of clashes between clans and drug cartels, port dens. In short, I was suspicious of all heavy neighborhoods.

The women's clothes were close-fitting and made of the same fabric used for religious ceremonies. They did not wear the three-part miter, in imitation of the domes of Buddhist pagodas, bathed in gold and inlaid with gems. Their faces showed the characteristics of their race: protruding cheekbones and hooded eyelids. Some were weeping silently, as evidenced by the glow in the concavity before the cheekbones. The children were being dragged by the women and the elderly were carrying wicker baskets with their belongings: colorful fabrics or worn-out clothes. I guessed that none of them even concealed a knife under their clothes, much less a low-caliber weapon for defense. They were definitely a group not involved in the war; simply people fleeing from barbarism.

I often wondered what I was doing there. Why did I have to go there and not someone else? At the head office, they knew they could count on me. It had been like that so many times, as if I was part of a list of volunteers for impossible missions. Yellow fever? They could have called someone else, an expert from Cuba or the Virgin Islands; someone with knowledge of epizootics or zoonoses, since thousands of infected monkeys and corpses rotting in the jungle had been found. A specialist in the vector, the *Aedes aegypti* mosquito, or in the causative virus, the flavivirus. What did I have to do with mosquito-infested wetlands?

Obviously, I did not find the answer. I made a decision and at that instant I regretted it. "Is it possible that I let myself get carried away by loneliness and depression? A roll off the cliff?", I pondered silently.

Before leaving for the mission we were vaccinated. Someone at the hospital asked me what yellow fever was. I began to explain that the damage caused by yellow fever affected the liver cells and the supporting or stromal cells. The disease was caused by the inclusion of the flavivirus in the cytoplasm. In short, an alteration was produced that turned the organ into a hard and elastic mass or a stony hardness, with the consequent obstruction of the biliary tract by a dry slime and the formation of clots in the vessels of the organ. The veins close, impeding circulation, and the affluent veins of the inferior cava become varicose; among them, the esophageal veins, which could burst and cause digestive hemorrhage with risk of death by exsanguination.

I also told him that human cases occurred after wandering epizootics, when affected apes migrated to avoid contagion between individuals of the same species. Many apes, especially macaques and orange-haired orangutans, died in the jungle. They had previously left the infested sites, where the bodies of sick animals decomposed before being eaten by scavenging birds.

Migration was a form of intelligence in primates and other animals, which induced them to flee from dangerous areas; in this case, from areas invaded by the virus. Wandering epizootics spread the disease, which reached human populations. Puddles, marshes and even rice fields were breeding grounds for *Aedes* mosquitoes. The humans displaced by the war could be a population at risk.

With that clarification I wanted to justify my stay in the field hospital of the refugee camp. She was looking at me behind a pair of myopic glasses, with an expression of astonishment or skepticism, or both. To break this attitude, I asked her, "And you, why are you here?" Perhaps I should have phrased the question differently: "What are we doing in this dance?" I didn't mean a veil dance. In this dance there were no women with sinuous, petite, sensual bodies. I was referring to the refugee camp, with hundreds of barracks that served as shelter for people of all ages; people who had fled the devastation caused by a medium-intensity war. I could have asked her so many questions.

Most likely, she would not answer anything, because she would not find an answer either, but only unintelligible explanations, such as "the will to serve", the mission "entrusted to each person". Evasions to avoid assuming the real motives.

Then I thought about what had happened before arriving at the border, when I still had the idea of finding dances of veils and tiaras adorning the heads of young dancers in a show in Rangoon or Bangkok. I had dreamed of exotic places crossed by rivers with mangroves and trees with aerial roots where otters and colorful birds took refuge. It all ended up down a pipe, which sent all my preconceived ideas to the cliff. In the end I had to see how the displaced people joined the first inhabitants of the Mae La shantytowns in the Thai province of Tak.

According to the office, there were more than seven hundred thousand refugees from the war. Vaccines for yellow fever had long been exhausted and a new shipment was expected to arrive the following week. Vector elimination was the most important task of the health services. Barracks made of pressed cardboard or sawdust, converted into laminate sheets that imitated wood, were grouped in the settlements, where thousands of people of different ethnicities lived in overcrowded conditions.

The camp's security manager, Lars Olsen was a Nordic man who smoked a pipe, ate dehydrated seaweed and kept his body athletic. Serious and isolated, he did not give anyone the opportunity for a closeness that could be mistaken for friendship. However, several times it was he who initiated a conversation with me. And there I realized that he was also serious and distrustful, even fearful and shy.

One afternoon, while he was smoking sitting in a canvas folding camp chair, I was trying to wipe my sweat with a silk handkerchief. I had settled next to him in a wicker chair. The heat was intense and mosquitoes landed on my forearms and bare legs. That day the conversation ran through a myriad clichés.

"I didn't know there was no yellow fever in this place. Why is it that there are no cases in Asia?" I'm sure you had to be vaccinated against the disease as a requirement for travel to this unhealthy place.

"There is no obvious explanation," I replied. "There are two unproven theories. The first is that populations endemic for dengue may be immunized for yellow fever. Maybe cross-immunity, which is rare." I could have explained that cross-immunity occurs in agents with similar structure and genetics, as in the case of flaviviruses. The second theory is even more implausible. Those who defend it claim that it is an immunity between primates, with attenuation of the virulence of the strains. Similar to the decrease of virulence in culture broths to create vaccines. This theory is rather doubtful and in the present circumstances it seems a myth to speak of a decrease in lethality. I kept quiet that virus strains often have more aggressive mutations.

"Is there any way to check or rule out that the disease is yellow fever?" He wanted to know.

"The suspicion in humans has not been proven, but in monkeys the presence of flavivirus of a wild strain has been detected in biopsies taken from the viscera of diseased specimens," I replied, fearing that he was as knowledgeable about zoonoses as any of the doctors on the mission. "Electron microscopy has shown the presence of virus crystals in the diseased cells."

"Well, we'll have to wait for other cases to be reported, doctor," he commented. Maybe he thought he had study material.

"I have a couple of questions for you," I interrupted him. "The first is that I'd like to know if you've been on another mission like this before." I didn't ask the second; I waited for him to give me the answer.

"Yes, I was in the war of independence in Bosnia and Herzegovina before. Same thing, tens of thousands of dead, genocides, mass rapes." He was sad. I assumed he remembered the cases of child victims, many raped and murdered; outraged by the psychopaths of war. He'll have remembered massacres like Srebrenica, with hundreds murdered and buried in mass graves. Ethnic cleansing as an institution. To my mind came the image of the persecution of Jews, Gypsies, Poles and Slavs in the Nazi concentration camps, and that of Christians against Muslims. The Serb army, supported by the Bosnian Serb population, at war against the Bosnian Muslims and Croats, persecuted and eliminated the Muslim population. Olsen sighed and then continued,

"At the beginning of the war, they occupied seventy percent of the territory and the displaced persons exceeded one million. This resulted in Muslims showing solidarity with their Bosnian brothers. Calls for the participation of recruits among the Islamic Revolutionary Guards and the jihadists began. Thus, battalions of international fighters against the Christian Serbs appeared." His denuded face was a sign of the horror he had lived through.

"I read that it was a detestable war." I had doubts, because the information I had consulted was not complete. I believed that during the confrontation, Islamic commandos were created.

"Psychopathy is contagious," he said. I don't know if he was referring to the Balkan war or to his recent experience in Burma. "A week ago, during the night, two men were killed in the refugee camp. There were no witnesses. No one wanted to denounce the culprits, or even testify. Their fingers had been mutilated and their faces were smashed, which prevented identification. One of the guardians told us that in the last few months they had had to report the violent deaths of more than thirty people," said Olsen. "I have to find the killer or killers.

"I presume that ethnic warfare has moved into the refugee camp, although I also think that the killers could be hitmen sent to disrupt any defense groups. Many guerrillas use the refugee camps as hideouts, camouflaging themselves among the displaced. In addition, some mafia cartels have been found to be trafficking drugs inside Mae La. This, together with the recruitment of girls for pornography and child prostitution, explains the violence."

We had our work cut out for us. The misty mountains seemed to be part of the biblical paradise; the plants bloomed in all colors and the butterflies seemed to have come out of a drawing of an expressive child. The birds competed in color and exoticism with the surroundings. However, there was something like a pervasive miasma, which made us uneasy. Maybe it was the decomposition of the macaques, or the carnivorous plants that were entangled in the ground to suffocate the bugs that crawled on the surface. I assumed that all this was the result of my persecutory manias and my fears, which put me on alert at every instant. Even though I was vaccinated against the diseases of the area, like every member of our delegation, I panicked about contracting an unnamed infection, with an unknown etiology, and running into warring parties with whom I could neither communicate nor defend myself. No one would understand that I was there to fight a threat equal to or greater than the war itself.

No high command informed us of the proximity of the war, with the rebels fleeing to the border in the face of an onslaught by the regular troops against the KNU, self-defense groups of the Rohingyas, who claimed to have reinforcements of jihadist volunteers from other countries. Therefore, our movements in search of the epicenter of the epidemic were limited to the areas close to the border with Thailand, without penetrating to places that might be close to the rebel shelters and the regulars' camps. It was obvious that losses due to yellow fever or any other epidemic disease would be confused with deaths due to malnutrition, physical exhaustion, dehydration or hepatitis. Moreover, they would swell the number of unreported deaths.

I did not know what was more important, to accompany the displaced to a shelter in a border village or to find the source of the outbreak. It could be in the jungle immediately around the Malay Peninsula or in the Mekong Delta. It was a question of attitude: to show solidarity with the refugees or to look for those sick from the epidemic. Both situations meant supporting them to the end, as Teresa of Calcutta said: 'We cannot always do great things, but we can do small things with great love.'

The slippery floor reminded me of my childhood in a small town where the workers wore the attire of English laborers at the turn of the century: wool caps, vertically striped *tweed* coats and capris. It was as if we were watching an old black and white movie, with Gary Cooper as the lead actor and Bette Davis as the star. I also remembered my adolescence at the port, with the little boys trying to woo the girls. Never in my wildest dreams would I have imagined that I would have to land in a country that was embroiled in a civil war to track down the source of a tropical disease outbreak. What's more, we weren't even sure it was yellow fever, but there was a possibility that it was another one with identical symptoms.

I seemed to be reliving the discovery of a cemetery next to a deserted beach. There I noticed that the crosses had the dates of death marked with white lead. I immediately noticed that the dates were very close in time, as if they had all died as a result of a natural disaster: an earthquake or a tsunami. Or due to an epidemic: Asian flu, cholera or any other devastating disease. Then it occurred to me to ask the local elders what had happened on that beach, which they had christened Waterfalls, even though there were no waterfalls there.

The old folks told me that when they were little it was forbidden to bathe at the beach because the waters were poisoned. Those who ventured to swim in them ended up with fevers and diarrhea that led to death. How fucked up! On that cursed beach we frolicked without even knowing what had happened more than fifty years before. Not to mention that my own life was decided there, because soon after I became an investigator of diseases and other people's ills.

I was assaulted by melancholy for remembering places that I thought were maybe invented, meetings that I had forgotten, for remembering the lead painted crosses, the steep streets of the port or the musty smelling neighborhoods of a mountain village. I felt a longing for broken shoes and shirts with ink stains in the pocket; for the smell of the perfume of a girl who agreed to accompany me to the movies, whom I hugged during the screening of an American Western movie. In the movie the hero fired more bullets than an army and killed more bandits than a troop of riflemen.

Among the young women fleeing the conflict zone, I came across one who looked just like Nobel Peace Prize winner Aung San Suu Kyi. I assumed she was still under house arrest in Rangoon. Maybe I was in for a surprise and she was part of a coalition government. The same white robe on a terse body. The same angular face, identical eyes and a broad, sloping forehead like hers. The woman seemed to be the teacher of a school or the manager of a shelter for orphaned children, because she dragged with her a group of about twenty infants between five and ten years old. The older children were in charge of the younger ones, pulling them by the hand, and she led the older ones.

When I had to question her to begin triage of the group, she explained that they came from a village immediately adjacent to the Arakan mountain range. She also told us, in broken

English, that Buddhist monks had led a civil protest in defense of human rights, which was violently repressed. The monks were persecuted and troops sodomized the lamas. Indignity versus virtue. Maybe ignorance versus talent. She did not explain to me why the Buddhist monks had to flee for their lives when they had been allies of the military government in the war against the Muslims. To tell the truth, I did not know what the root cause of the conflict was and had to process my own concept. I then assumed that the fighters were drawn together by ethnicity, tribe and even survival instinct. People took the weapons of the fallen in combat and then joined one of the active groups. Sometimes they did it out of affinity; other times, so as not to remain isolated and to protect themselves, just as zebras, gazelles, wildebeests and giraffes do from predators' attacks.

The women were talking among themselves; in fact, they seemed to be shouting as they walked through the streets of this village built on the delta of a river that was a tributary of another great watercourse: the Mekong. According to them, the attackers were not soldiers, for they were too young to cause such destruction. They were convinced that they were mercenaries who hung the scalps of the dead around their waists. In the case of the shaven monks, their killers wore the hairless hide, scalped and tanned with salt and tannin from the lanceolate leaves. In other cases, the trophy was the victim's hands or fingers, removed from the body with a curved saw or a machete that was also used to clear the jungle. Troops would receive extra payment for each trophy.

The refugees' narration reminded me of the old western movies, where the redskins scalped their dead enemies. Just like the head-shrinking tribes. The losers' snouts, reduced to the barest minimum, hanging from the waists of their killers. It seemed to me like a horror movie set in the jungle, with Marlon Brando as the protagonist playing a madman with a serious mental anomaly, only in this case it was not a movie, but life itself, and it was not Marlon Brando, but a bunch of psychopaths.

In the Burmese civil war it was not known who was financing the mercenaries. They could be regular army generals or provincial feudal lords; even the Muslim brothers of the Rohingya or Buddhist lamas. Perhaps the war was subsidized by transnational organizations involved in arms trafficking, or by drug cartels that used India and the sea to transport hashish in hundreds of sampans. In the end, a clan of warlords was created that functioned independently of the orders of the government and the leaders of the Islamic insurgency. Even the warlords traded their services to the highest bidder.

Olsen had to explain to me how the predator commandos were generated. They began by avenging their own dead. The punishment was terrible, and in some cases exceeded the perversion of the first barbarism. After that, the only thing that mattered was the accumulation of atrocities in order to achieve prestige and thus have contracts for increasingly exorbitant amounts of money. Lars Olsen explained psychopathic atrocities in this way. I compared them to major epidemics and natural catastrophes, whose chain damage was unpredictable. They start as whirlpools and turn into hurricanes.

The women had to cross the river with water up to their waists, carrying their children as if they were a transfer of cargo bundles. The woman leading the group of war displaced, whom I met crossing the border, told of other atrocities, such as the burning of non-evacuated villages, with the inhabitants burning like human torches, and the mass rapes, both of women of any age and of children, who were sodomized by the perverted mercenaries or the boys of the troop.

I assumed that she had also been raped by several warriors because she was interested in AIDS and the danger of contracting it. I explained to her that she should have a serological test in two to three months to rule out a false negative during the window period, when it is not yet detectable by any test. I also wanted to stress that any other disease she might have contracted could be as serious as AIDS. The worst were hepatitis, lymphotropic virus infection and sexually transmitted diseases. God forbid, but it could be spastic paralysis or a disease with immune damage other than AIDS. In that case, she would eventually develop non-Hodgkin's lymphoma.

While I was thinking about diagnoses, all sorts of delusional ideas came to mind. Lamas, in orange robes and shaven skulls, fleeing from their pursuers down the monastery embankments. The fat monks were collapsing from the effort, for the monasteries were built on the slopes of the mountains, from where one could see the river that ran along the lower part of the ravine. Through the stairs one ascended to the cells of the religious, built in a precarious way despite being part of the complex. The temple had domes painted in gold and a polychrome hue. In times of peace, silence reigned. At that time, the interjections of the attackers and the panting of the persecuted could be heard. Old monks were usually executed and young ones tortured. Some managed to escape and reach the Himalayas. In the villages near the monasteries, women were raped by soldiers with unhinged faces, drooling and leering.

Damn war! I cursed that and all wars of any intensity; of course, also ethnic conflicts and territorial killings. I cursed the warlike confrontations caused by ideologies and beliefs. Fights between followers of prophets and messiahs, between people who had the same physiognomy and ethnic features, who only differed in their clothing and religion. Not even that. It was even simpler: an evil, ambitious, Machiavellian mind came up with the idea of starting the war in order to accumulate wealth or avenge affronts to their ancestors. Perhaps it was a dictator or a member of the military junta. Or maybe he belonged to a wealthy family involved in the trafficking of arms, women, hashish. Then I thought that Burmese hashish was as famous as opium from the Chitral Valley in Pakistan. And I remembered the opium war in China and the cartels in Mexico today. The same experience: genocidal madness, money over any moral brake.

Then everyone fell into the game. The Arakan Muslims, the Buddhist monks, the poor who were neither Muslim nor Buddhist, the retail drug dealers, the highway robbers, the rural schoolteachers, the students. They all got into the car without thinking that they were going nowhere; well yes, to a slaughterhouse located on a cliff.

The Burmese woman continued to explain her tragedy and that of her relatives. She had already sought refuge in another village when hers was razed to the ground. Several close relatives had been killed. She was then forced to flee the second village to avoid being killed along with other relatives, including her mother. When she had no more dead to mourn, she led the orphaned children. Many had forgotten their names and those of their parents; they also did not remember the name of their village nor did they remember what had happened in their hut. Some were still very young, but others suffered from retrograde traumatic amnesia, like a tape erasure from a tape recorder that served as a psychological defense mechanism.

For those who did not remember their name, we gave them a name and a number. The younger ones were registered with only one name, because we hoped that at some point their parents, relatives or neighbors would appear and recognize them.

On the reservation there were many children, all with chubby faces and round skulls covered by little hair. It looked to me like the same child cloned a thousand times. The woman I had spoken to looked in her forties. Perhaps too thin and shabby, wrinkled and haggard. But she was clearly in her forties. She also had a slight tremor in her hands that I attributed to fatigue or vitamin B deficiency. She showed a lot of tenacity for having overcome the loss of her relatives and the humiliations she had had to endure. I thought she was sick or on the verge of chronic panic. I don't know if there is a form of permanent fear, a war psychosis. However, despite what I had experienced, I felt an enormous inner strength. I embodied the will of an entire people to overcome any misfortune and win.

Through it I could see the pagodas rebuilt with the silence of the mountains; silence that was only broken by the ringing of the bells placed on the doors of the monks' cells. Perhaps I could also distinguish the mosques with their minarets and the prayers of the faithful of Islam. That woman was the image of so many people in her village: the rural people cultivating rice in the flooded fields, the caravans of nomads arriving somewhere, the schoolteachers playing with the children. She represented the hope of thousands of refugees who fantasized that peace would soon be signed and the forces of evil would be eliminated. They wished that the predators, the victimizers, the madmen and the warlords would succumb. The most savage would fall prey to their own wrath. Because war does not last forever, even if the sale of arms is eternal and the traffic of hashish is maintained. Peace will return one day. Like diseases caused by viruses: after the crisis there remains immunity, which coexists with a type of virus that, from time to time, manifests itself by small relapses, never as serious as the debut crisis.

Even so, the Rohingya Muslim minority will continue to be persecuted by Buddhist fanatics, even if the military junta is replaced by a democratic government with Nobel Peace Prize winner Aung San Suu Kyi. I wonder if this award was given with justice or if it ended up being a fiasco, like the case of Kissinger, the strategist of the dirty war in Indochina.

As time went on, the persecution intensified and the displaced Muslims crowded the refugee camps in the region. When their numbers exceeded all estimates, they were housed in sampans and obsolete merchant ships still floating in the Bay of Bengal, as several countries refused them entry as refugees, including Thailand itself, which had previously given them asylum. Some time later, Sri Lanka denounced the situation of the persecuted Rohingyas before the United Nations Council. This led to the formation of a UN High Commissioner for Refugees in the region, based in Bangkok, whose task was to observe the reality experienced by the minorities in Myanmar.

Suddenly, my thoughts returned to the genetic changes in viruses, the injection of inherited material from one to another. The thermolabile enzymes cutting the coiled-coil strand folded into the nucleotide surrounded by the capsids to fold it end to end with another strand from another virus. Perhaps that was the explanation for the non-presence of human yellow fever in Asia. It was a virus that only affected apes and not people, as in other continents. There were such exclusivities, such as the SV40 virus, which causes cancer in hamsters and does not affect humans. This could be the case of the flavivirus causing yellow fever that affected apes in Southeast Asia.

During my stay in the Mae La refugee camp, I was able to screen hundreds of displaced persons and create an information network for them to notify me of new suspected cases. The result: not a single verifiable case. I did note the presence of other endemic diseases, such as dengue, hepatitis in all its varieties, influenza, herpesvirus, salmonella, *enterotoxic Escherichia coli*, malaria, parasitosis; but not yellow fever. I saw alterations similar to Nile encephalitis and other variants of Japanese encephalitis, and even poliomyelitis, with weakness in the muscles of the neck and thorax. Of course there were deplorable sanitary conditions, mosquito spots flying over swamps and marshes; however, not a single case that could be identified as yellow fever. My mission was about to end at the Thai-Burma border, which had been renamed Myanmar by a military junta decree, without being able to verify a single suspected case of human yellow fever.

Somehow, the field hospital staff organized a farewell ceremony. When it seemed that the tribute was over, Olsen arrived. He justified his delay by an emergency that had prevented him from being there from the start. I had thought that the commander was on a mission or meeting with the authorities of the region, at an embassy meeting. When the tribute speeches were over, to which I did not respond out of a minimum of decorum and humility, Olsen took over. For twenty minutes he told us the details of an attack against the mission's second-in-command. He mentioned that the latter had been wounded in confusing circumstances, without the perpetrator or perpetrators of the attempted murder in the refugee camp having been identified. As a result of the attack, the officer had a bullet lodged in his chest and underwent emergency surgery at a private hospital in Bangkok. The bullet was removed and a chest drain was placed to evacuate the hemopneumothorax while the alveolo-pleural fistula was closed.

Olsen went on to emphasize the dangers of missions in conflict areas. He added the following, "Our work is high-risk in places like this, where racial conflicts extend from war zones to the UN camp."

He did not rule out drug cartels operating in the Mekong jungle and the Gulf of Malacca. Nor could the presence of criminal organizations involved in the trafficking of women and children for nefarious purposes, such as prostitution and pornography in all its variants, from magazines to films, be excluded. In fact, all mission personnel had perceived a tendency towards unrestrained violence; something akin to homicidal madness.

I had heard that part of the speech in one of our evening talks. I noticed a deep breath, similar to a sigh, before he changed the subject and resumed singing my praises. He wanted to explain the significance of my stay in the territory and spoke of jobs as a microbiologist and epidemiologist and their importance to the population of the geographical region.

"Some people, including me," he continued, "considered him a madman. A madman who dedicated himself to doing autopsies of dead macaques in the jungle or chased the sick to operate on them or to do laboratory tests on them. I am the first to admit that I did not appreciate the importance of these investigations."

As Olsen made his presentation, I thought of the buboes in the axillae and the nape of the neck of the apes affected by the disease. It was clear that, at first, the target cells of the flaviviruses were T lymphocytes. Then I found the viral packet inclusions in liver Kupffer cells. Our team, which included surgeons with expertise in comparative anatomy, had performed hundreds of surgeries on live diseased monkeys, as well as biopsies by direct puncture, without cutting, or by laparoscopy of diseased primate organs. Our pathologists were able to observe lymphocyte nests around the vessels of the affected organs. They called the lymphocytes as *natural killer* (NK) cells, which were characterized by larger size and affinity for staining substances. The NKs injected their proteins into the infected cells to destroy them.

The immune reaction of the diseased organism increased the production of substances such as tumor necrosis factors (TNF), interferons and other interleukins for the purpose of sweeping the invader in and out of the target cells and ultimately destroying the diseased cells. It was the first line of combat against the virus. In some cases this form of immune defense could have up to three results: efficiency, with the healing of the organ and the patient; inefficiency, with the death of the primate; and overreaction, leading to a severe inflammatory response that attacked the diseased organs themselves, resulting in an even more intense acute disease, with immediate ominous results.

Later in the course of the disease, viral inclusions occurred in liver cells and red blood cells, leading to platelet aggregation. This caused red thrombi in the liver vessels. Its effects were also felt in Bowman's membrane, renal glomeruli and tubular necrosis. In this situation the pericardium was pulpy, with patchy hemorrhages and fatty degeneration in the myocardium. When the skull of a macaque was opened, cerebral edema and hydrocephalus could be seen, with increased ventricular spaces.

The bodies of the dead apes hung from the highest branches of the trees; some fell to the ground in moss and humus. The image reminded me of the little devils in a dance I had seen in a village near the small town I had visited some time before.

I had doubts as to whether the molecular changes had occurred in the human cells or in the virus itself. It could be recombinant DNA with RNA messages by means of reverse transcriptase, and after the genetic mutation, the possible generation of lymphocytes having the message for the synthesis of proteins that would be activated as antibodies against the antigen of the invading virus capsids and thus lysing it in the cytoplasm of the invaded target cell itself. Something similar to an ambush of the enemy troop inside our territory. Based on research into the molecular process that resulted in the absence of the disease in Asia, the possibility of creating resistance to the disease in order to eliminate it in the rest of the world, corresponded to the geniuses of Stanford, Melbourne, New Delhi, Tokyo or Beijing. In those cities were the research centers directed by Nobel Prize winners in medicine, such as Paul Berg, Cohen, Boyer, Riggs, Itakura, whom I knew by name and fame. They were responsible for the multicenter studies on the possible implications of our fieldwork on the Myanmar-Thailand border.

After the farewell lunch, Olsen invited me to chat in the front yard of the barracks that served as his office. We both sat on canvas camp chairs, which were uncomfortable for prolonged conversation. He then opened two cans of beer, one for each of us.

"I'm sorry you're leaving; I think I am losing both a friend and a good person. Anyway, there are many more people who recognize your work in the refugee camp and in the province." I just noticed something of a Nordic accent in his language.

"I feel sorry too," I replied.

"Where are you going? Is someone waiting for you?" he asked me with friendly concern.

"Maybe," I answered. Then I kept quiet.

I pondered my lonely past while thinking about Nadia. Her name had emerged from this context of loneliness. Nadia, twenty-something years younger than me. Yet perhaps she was somewhere I could find peace. Sitting in a camp chair, after a beer, my mind dazed by events, I wanted to dream of something uncertain, like a harbor in the South Seas. Nadia and I would look at each other. Then she would raise a small, friendly hand and I would run to catch up with her. The harbor would have a fishermen's dock built long ago. And I would experience the most beautiful feeling in the world: the gentle cold of the southern seas and the warmth of human affection. In the distance I would notice the sails of a small sport boat and the silhouette of several fishermen's ships. At that moment I thought I wished it was an illusion mixed with an omen.

I finished the beer and Olsen brought out two more cans. He, too, wanted to continue talking.

"Where was the second commander wounded?" This time I resumed the conversation.

"On the periphery of the camp. The circumstances are strange. He was visiting a woman and was attacked from behind." I had the feeling that he didn't understand the second-in-command's carelessness.

"Do you suspect anyone in particular?" I was interested.

"I don't know," he said, afraid to make an unverifiable statement.

I was suspicious of a group of tattooed guys I had seen hanging around in the streets, among the barracks of the Mae La camp. They could also be some guys wearing jackets with hoods, with which they covered their heads.

Olsen was silent. Perhaps he was evaluating options. Suddenly, as if awakening from a dream or a temporary absence, he commented to me, "It is in the hands of the local police. They will be in charge of identifying the attacker. Legally, we, as an organization, cannot do any parallel investigations. Worse still, even if we were to locate the direct assailant, it is possible that he is taking orders from some criminal network. My guess is someone from the outside or a covert element among the refugees. Maybe I'm wrong and it's something more domestic. Jealousy for the woman the second commander was visiting or a rivalry for her favors." He took a swig of beer and kept silent.

"What is his state of health?" I insisted, although I had an idea that the prognosis was good. However, Olsen knew that the motives for the attack made him vulnerable to further attempts. It was likely that he would order his temporary evacuation from the area under the pretext of receiving specific treatment after surgery.

In Olsen's entourage was an English journalist named Walker, who was a war correspondent for the BBC and also worked as a freelancer for several European newspapers. Occasionally we met at a place near the Cambodian border. I was trying to locate a mountain covered with ficus and fine wood trees on the cloudy slope, as that was the refuge of tribes of apes in the region. If flavivirus zoonosis existed, with thousands of dead primates, that was the place to look to find the source of the epidemic. At the same time, Walker was investigating the exodus of the last Khmer Rouge fighters. According to the journalist, the Khmer had been frustrated in their attempt to create a new man in accordance with their theory of permanent revolution, for which they had ordered the elimination of millions of Cambodians who belonged to what they called the corrupt society. Based on an agrarian policy, they forced millions of people to move from the city to the countryside.

Without adequate conditions, the displaced people died by the thousands under forced labor; in many cases, they lost their lives in mass executions by the hosts of young men who obeyed Pol Pot's thinking. When we met in a village near the city of Pakse, built on the Mekong River, close to the border between Laos and Thailand, we looked like two explorers lost in the jungle, with high boots and straw hats of the agrarian rice farmers. It felt like an imitation of the meeting between the English missionary Livingstone and the explorer Stanley at a place near Lake Tanganyika in 1902, although only in form and not in substance. Walker and I were two explorers on a mission and we could both be categorized as suffering from a compulsion.

Walker explained to me in detail the history of Cambodia after the invasion of the Vietnamese army. After several military defeats in a battle of positions, the Khmer had to abandon the capital, Phnom Penh, to take refuge in the jungle, which bordered Thailand to the north. From there, their troops launched lightning attacks on the soldiers of Hanoi.

I performed the last autopsies on the macaques, whose viscera appeared to come from young macaques. By means of this examination, I had discovered livers with a depulped surface and brown spots on the yellow background that gave it the appearance of a nutmeg, typical for zoonosis. The citrine fluid, collected from the ape's belly, plus samples from the spleen and axillary lymph nodes, would be sent to Beijing, where it would be analyzed.

In the meantime, the journalist had just visited one of the death camps. There, more than five thousand graves had been documented with thousands of skulls and bones buried under the undergrowth. Years earlier, in 2002, Walker had been able to interview one of the last commanders, referred to by the Revolutionary Guards as Brother Number Five. His name was Ta Mok and he had been the military leader of the remnants of the militias fighting for Democratic Kampuchea. After Pol Pot's death in 1998, the organization disbanded. Ta Mok, a war invalid, having lost a leg, was tried and sentenced to prison by a court; he died in prison in 2006.

During the 1990s, they had belonged to a coalition that ruled the country after the departure of Vietnamese troops. During the coalition period, the Khmer renounced their sectarian and radical practice, along with other developmentalist and conservative groups. After going through a period of legality, dissident Khmer troops who did not accept the centrist positions started a guerrilla war that subsidized their actions with illegal trafficking of timber and precious stones, in collusion with the high command of the Thai Army. Walker did not want to mention it, but it implied a link between the Khmer and the high command of the Thai Army. Of course, the arrangement was motivated by economic interests rather than ideological issues. According to Walker, political projects were never part of the Thai military's ideology and were also no longer part of the thinking of the new Khmer Rouge leaders.

It was clear to me that many of these fundamentalist leaders, regardless of what they claimed, become opportunistic peacemakers during the off hours of revolutions and political conflicts. I cannot deny that I knew little of the history of the Khmer Rouge, a history with many passionate strands. I had seen sinister photographs of extermination camps and cemeteries with hundreds of skeletons in a mass grave. What I did know was that the extreme ideology of the Khmer led to the creation of fundamentalist groups, whose radicalism reached inscrutable limits.

That afternoon of farewells, as we drank the cold beer in a tropical atmosphere, Olsen tried to evaluate the historical context of violence that had generated the migratory displacements and the devastation of large populations. In this way, he wanted to explain the implications of the attack against the second commander.

"The second commander was in Laos on a mission as an observer for the United Nations, and I imagine it was there that he fell in love with the woman who arrived from the northern border of Thailand, where the Khmer who had demobilized after the death of Pol Pot were. The last pockets of fighters, under the command of Ta Mok, a dissident of the organization, surrendered their weapons in 2002. The Khmer supporters arrived in UNHCR refugee camps and there isolated themselves from the others." He paused again to process the information he was trying to convey.

"Do you think these people, who must be over seventy years old, are active in the refugee camp?" I asked.

"I don't know. Maybe they are his children or grandchildren," he said without much conviction. "Quite a mess, don't you think?" He invited me to clink beer cans in a toast.

Although I believed that the hashish and opium cartels were involved in the acts of violence taking place in the refugee camp, there could also be something more underground that had deep roots: a political organization with fundamentalist practices. Perhaps Muslim fighters or old Khmer were continuing extremist practices.

At night you could smell the foul stench of indica marijuana. If you went out, you could find the stoners lying on the jungle floor. The women, stripped of their inhibitions, danced with their hands moving over their abdomen and chest while showing off their cleavage.

I would have liked to discuss with Olsen the stigmas of the times: wars, illegal trafficking, perversions, murders, human agglomerations caused by overcrowding. All this leads to health catastrophes with the emergence of diseases in the form of unknown epidemics.

Olsen's words stuck with me. Then I imagined a woman of oriental beauty seducing the second commander. And I thought of the loves that lead one to commit an attack or suicide. I remembered the woman driving the children to cross the border, with her skinny body and the two-piece dress, which seemed to be a peculiarity of the women of the region. Had she forgotten the vexations or was she waiting for the end of the window period to undergo several tests? Perhaps she had already felt the first symptoms: continuous diarrhea and perspiration during the night. Then I said a prayer for her, even though I had forgotten the prayers.

I drank the second can of beer before saying goodbye to Olsen. The next day I would fly to Beijing via Bangkok. In the airplane seat, I would smile at the thought of my bad luck, or my bad head for having accepted such a mission. In the end, I would leave the stage with the same nostalgia of departure. Maybe, another time, I could visit the Buddhist temples of Angkor Wat, the city of Rangoon and go up the Mekong to Nha Trang, where I would see the amaryllis and orchids cultivated by the scientist Yersin, the name by which the bacteria that caused the bubonic plague had been baptized. The wetlands would not have changed, nor the poverty of the people, and rice cultivation would spread along both banks of the great Mekong River.

Chapter 4
A Personal Story

Many years ago, in a pub near the River Thames, I got to hear a version of *My way*. The boy looked English, with blond hair falling down his back and cropped short on the sides. It was not the same version that had been played by Frank Sinatra, Elvis Presley or Sid Vicious.

The pub followed the art deco style, with Warhol influence and monochromatic portraits on metal sheets. Each verse of the song struck a sentimental chord, as I tried to decipher how my personal way was generated. In my mind appeared the images of my parents and the neighborhoods of San Blas and El Inclán, in the two cities through which my family clan moved during my childhood. Then my journey in search of a professional career; the passage from one stage to another doing what I had learned, destined anywhere regardless of borders. The boy in the beige trench coat performing the song seemed to feel every phrase; he reminded me of every space of time.

The city was Rosario, next to the Paraná River. The School of Medicine and the Centenario Hospital were built between Santa Fe and Entre Ríos avenues, with the front facing Francia Avenue. More than a thousand professors, among them Professor Assad, taught there.

His infectiology lessons remain in my memory. Perhaps because the Turk was a master in participatory education, in group dynamics to create entertaining dialogues among students and superimpose on these dialogues the anecdotes of his travels in the Middle East, Asia and the Maghreb. When we listened to him, it was as if we were visiting with him mosques with four minarets, walled cities, castles with cells for the confinement of prisoners. Then we would try to memorize the symptoms of diseases such as tubercular scrofula, which spread throughout Europe during the time of the Carolingian and Merovingian kings and was treated by the laying on of hands by thaumaturges, both magicians and priests. When Assad referred to paleopathology and its influence on the history of civilization, he was ahead of Jared Diamond and his book *Guns, Germs and Steel* in the concept of the prevalence of disease in the history of mankind. Immunity as part of the genotype turnover of societies linked by trade.

Assad told us the story of a disease that initially occurred on the Himalayan slopes and on the northern frontier of India. The Silk Road travelers called it the plague of the Himalayan Mountains. According to Assad, the disease was the bubonic plague or black plague. The epidemic spread to Europe between 1345 and 1350. It had previously decimated China, where half of its population, estimated at one hundred and fifty million, died. It arrived with the invasions of Mongolian Tartars; it was like an oil stain on the surface of a crystalline lagoon. The disease probably entered through the fields of Ukraine and then spread through Byzantium and Anatolia. It would be more appropriate to think that the invasion displaced the rural inhabitants, who, fleeing the ferocity of the conquerors, sought refuge in the outskirts of the cities. With them came the black rats of the countryside, which infected the gray rats of the sewers and docks. Thousands of dead, major cities under siege, hasty burials, cremation of corpses in public squares. Ships in quarantine, dock drafts, shelters for the survivors of the crews depleted by the disease.

As Assad spoke of the impact of the disease on the great European cities, I tried to imagine the streets of London during the plague years, with their cobblestone floors and illumination by lanterns hanging from walls and iron lampposts. Likewise, the Seine bridges in Paris, with their wrought iron gates. The cathedral of Notre Dame was just finished during the onset of the disease, in 1348. I thought too, of the little streets of Prague and Budapest, from which the bell towers of the medieval churches could be seen. My mind began to associate scenes from movies in which the actors dress in the style of the time and the streets pretended to be narrow streets with nooks and crannies. Then I focused on images of the sick, with buboes in the armpits that secreted a purulent bloody liquid that gave off a smell of corpse or putrefaction.

In other cases, the disease showed its pneumonic variant, with expectorations of lung fragments and blood. The stench spread even more than the epidemic itself, covering the cities and spreading to the countryside, even reaching the mountains of the Urals and the Alps. It was a graveyard smell mixed with cinnabar and methane.

I have in my memory the professor's wiry face, deep-set eyes and half-grown white beard, with the Hippocratic fingers caused by pulmonary fibrosis or possible bronchial carcinoma. I also remembered the hoarseness of his voice and the gasp he emitted when his lungs had gone to dust and were no longer able to cope. I remember him explaining the urlian parotitis and its relationship with diabetes mellitus due to the involvement of the pancreas and the necrosis of the beta cells of the islets of Langerhans. Possibly, he did not know that the same urlian virosis could give a type of cardiac fibrosis, after pancarditis, in which the muscular tissue was replaced by collagen.

The explanation of each variant of the disease, both its complications and the severity of the sequelae, was not understood by the scientific community until later, when molecular medicine investigated the reactions occurring on the surface and inside the target cells. Viruses changed the structural proteins and enzymatic chains of the body's cells; they could even modify some membrane glycoproteins by changing the major histocompatibility complex (MHC), so that they were recognized as antigens by the immune system: T lymphocytes, antibodies, cytosines and *natural killer*. Thus, the body attacked healthy tissues. This could also lead to the destruction of beta cells in the pancreas and endothelial cells in the heart and blood vessels.

While Assad was lecturing, I suffered an absence seizure similar to that of a petit mal epileptic, with an imaginary journey through different places and knowledge. In my delirium, I believed I was the discoverer of a molecule that would stop mitosis in cancer, that would lead me to give lectures in Sweden and England, or in an American university with more than twelve Nobel Prize winners. My imagination flew to places like Cambodia, Singapore, Indonesia, the Arab Emirates and Senegal, where I would study the behavior of various diseases that had appeared in the last decade. "Cut the crap!" the professor told me, but I didn't understand because I was disconnected from the real world.

In the middle of the disconnection, I pondered about the condition of a boy affected by Chagas-Mazza disease due to the bites of vinchucas in the *quebrachales* of the province of Chaco. The disease had left him with a bagged heart and had probably caused dilatation of the esophagus and colon. The boy gasped at the slightest movement and had a belly like an inflated balloon. His brothers would drag him on a mat, before leaving for their daily chores, to the sidewalk they had built with concrete and steel in front of their shack, near the Salado River; there they would leave him out in the open until they returned late at night. Then they would drag him back into the house.

The Turk was getting more and more excited in his dissertation, emphasizing the frequent symptoms of an infection affecting the liver and blood, caused by spirochetes. Meanwhile, I remembered the Paraguayan leader of the human settlement and, more than on her, I focused on her son, a priest of more than six feet tall and one hundred and twenty kilos who had died during the incursion of a group that had taken up arms in the federal capital, an action in which the priest had participated. As a result of the shooting, the priest was hit by more than ten bullets in the thorax, skull and abdomen. I would have liked to ask the professor why a Catholic priest ends up joining a group of subversives with a Marxist ideology. Assad would have replied that he could not understand the reason either.

The professor probably did not have a valid answer to the political questions. Perhaps he had listened to Joseph Stiglitz when he described in his lectures the inequities of economic development, which he later collected in his book *The Great Divide*. As I read the text, I was struck by the fact that one hundred rich families own fifty percent of the world's wealth and six billion human beings only have the other fifty percent. Maybe that inequality was the basis of most ideologies; maybe it was not about color, but about inequalities. The priest had bled to death on the way from the place of action to the interrogation room. Meanwhile, his mother cried her last tear and cursed the prophets of all times, political speeches, clandestine meetings, forbidden books, and even complained about religion and human injustices.

I don't know if while I was deep in my own delirium, the Turk had had the time to describe leptospirosis or another disease with a similar etiologic agent. I could not grasp how the disease entered and what the identifying signs were; much less, what tests needed to be done to prove the diagnosis. I would have to read it in Zinsser's *Microbiology*, the fifteen-hundred-page book that gripped me like a novel by García Márquez or Cortázar. Each character figured with its surface cilia, its shapes and groupings, its staining with Gram stain, the differences in the composition of its outer membranes. All the microbes had an astonishing authenticity; they could be as dangerous as the Russian Mafia allied with the Italian Cosa Nostra, with the Japanese Yacuza and the Colombian and Mexican cartels.

When I reconnected with the infectious disease class, a drizzle was threatening to turn into a tropical rain. We had to take shelter inside the cafeteria and Assad ended the class for the day. Then the students left in different directions before the inevitable downpour. I would have to postpone my analysis each case: a man with a disabling illness, a woman in leadership, a priest-turned-subversive for the night while I slept.

Perhaps the man with the heart failure and the mat on the floor had been a poor peon, like the characters of Atahualpa Yupanqui, with his matted hair and denim overalls. Almost a tango or a weeping Pampeñan. The woman had to be strong in the face of misfortune and mourning. She was used to it, perhaps because of her childhood working non-stop in a Paraguayan hacienda with Argentinean bosses and Guarani peons, where she was seduced by a much older man with no grace. With this penniless and aged man, she had crossed the border clandestinely, carrying her belongings in a blue plastic or white raffia bag so that the river water, which reached her neck, would not wet her belongings and clothes. Then she had to stay in one or another hotel full of fleas, until she found a shack in a settlement. There she gave birth to eight children, four boys and four girls, some bigger and stronger than others, some more beautiful and graceful than others.

After a few years, her old husband died and she was left alone. In an ingenious way, she had to support and educate her children. Always strong, almost always cheerful, always proud and almost always supportive. Until the real tragedy came with the death of her son, the priest, the beloved, the mystic. Then everything went into the dustbin. Nothing to think about, nothing that gave her joy: neither the newborn grandchildren nor the mischief of the little ones, nor the caresses of the girls, nor the signs of affection from her children. Neither the color television bought on Mother's Day nor the goal of the national soccer team that qualified the country for the World Cup. In that last year she had aged and her hair was the color of dirty ashes, and on her forehead, many penetrating furrows. And then she came back to life one Good Friday, after having listened to the three-hour sermon. She was able to find out where the body had been disposed of, either by burying it or sinking it in the waters. Once located, she made a pilgrimage every so often alone or accompanied by her more willing children. She carried bouquets of flowers, which she placed on top of a mound of stones that she built with her own hands. Sometimes she would throw these flowers into the sea from cliffs shaped like castles.

I don't know if the classes in a cafeteria on the corner of Francia and Santa Fe Boulevard saved my life or broke it. I don't know if all I did afterwards was to realize Assad's fantasies or senile nonsense, looking for the last disease he could not have described, because it had not yet been discovered or had been confused with another very similar one. Perhaps I followed the deliriums of a dilettante who had traveled a lot, but who also did so in dreams, in a constant slumber, lying next to a woman who dyed her gray hair so as not to give the appearance of old age because she thought that in this way she was preserving her marriage.

Sometimes it was not clear to him whether he had visited a country with little streets full of nooks and crannies and arches at the entrances. According to him, it could be Madagascar or Marrakech, even any city in the Maghreb. Even Anatolia. He spoke of wars and religious and ethnic persecutions. I never found out where he was born; I only knew that wars were chronic there. Bombings in Beirut, war in the Golan Heights, intifadas in the West Bank, massacres in Kurdish settlements in Turkey, clashes between Iran and Iraq. He never confessed to me that he belonged to a nationalist group that sent money from South America to the militias of the Palestine Liberation Organization, commanded by Yasser Arafat, nor did he mention that the Jews had, in turn, another hero named Moshe Dayan. Nor did he tell me that the Six-Day War was just one more battle in a forty-something year war that began when the United Nations created the new State of Israel by decree in November 1947. Ben-Gurion proclaimed the new state in May 1948. Then his family was expelled from southern Lebanon, because his father and uncles belonged to an Arab nationalist organization, opposed to the cession of Palestinian territories for the new Jewish State.

When he spoke of Mrs. Assad, he did it with a passion not understood in these times of kisses on the fly, sex at night, passing loves, courtships that, at the most, turn out to be ephemeral cohabitations. For him, his wife represented the union until the end of life; it did not matter that he had developed a taste for good wine and beautiful women. I got the idea that, in his way, that was love. And it was a good choice because during old age she polished his shoes, buttoned his shirts, matched the color of his suits with the color of his shirt and socks. She loved his fragility and tenderness, his caresses on her hair, his kisses on her forehead, the thorny roses, cultivated by grafting to bring out unlikely colors: black, blue, violet, crimson, yellow with pink jasper, which he then turned into bouquets of freshly opened blossoms and flowers that he gave her every afternoon. As if praying the last prayer of the day, squatting on a Persian carpet and looking out to the sea, where he supposed Mecca was.

The Turk told us that she combined beauty with a rare culture. When she was young, she became the executive secretary of the university rector and had two professions: law and business administration; with two postgraduate degrees: business law and finance. It was the memory that weighed on his feelings for her. He described her with the black eyes of Abyssinian women and the full lips of Lebanese women. I imagined her as a Greek actress in an old, black and white, classically beautiful movie.

At that time the professor was entering a phase of senility in which he confused reality with fantasy. He thought he remembered a gala evening when he showed up in an elegant suit, Dior or Armani; his wife wore a red Versace dress with a high neckline. Surrounded by people, he pondered whether he had actually been there or had seen it in a movie about the kings of Jordan. He thought his wife had attended an award dinner for the scientific work of a professor at the university, who was Assad himself. The award had been given for his contributions to the detection and subsequent treatment of endemic diseases in the south of the Río de la Plata. He did not remember well whether it was enterovirus encephalitis or a fever of uncertain origin. The professor himself had described the etiological agent as a cluster of rough capsid spherites resembling those of the Nile fever virus and flavivirus of tick-bite encephalitis. This, in turn, was very different from the herpesvirus encephalitis he had detected in brains during autopsy, where he noted the presence of bullous clusters resembling skin vesicles.

Until the discovery and typing of the viral agent, epidemiologists and infectiologists had maintained that the disease was caused by a rickettsia similar to Rocky Mountain fever, whose vector was ticks, and to the bacterium of exanthematous typhus, which was transmitted by the body louse. The disease tested positive for Weil-Felix agglutination precipitation tests, which could be a cross-reaction to the febrile antigens, but differed in tests for IgM and IgG immunoglobulins. This led the Turk to study the brains of those who had died of the disease. In the end, he found in the vacuolar lesions and in the softened areas of the brain cells with intracellular corpuscles that, when studied under the electron microscope, were RNA viruses, which need reverse transcriptase to replicate. Perhaps the virus was a mutation of the polio enterovirus or a strain EV25 that caused flaccid paralysis.

Neither so much nor so little. In any case, the disease was feared by the parents of children with fever. When they caught it, the infants suffered delirium, if not febrile convulsions. It was feared that some of the children would develop lifelong flaccid paralysis or require articulated plates attached to their limbs to enable them to move about after convalescence.

In his old age, after having belonged to the National Academy of Science and Technology as a life member, and after having received honorary doctorate degrees from different American and European universities, Professor Assad retired from the hospital, where he was head of the Infectious Diseases Department. However, he continued to teach his students at the Faculty of Medicine. In addition, he was called upon to give master classes to incoming students; master classes that had the virtue of mixing philosophy, history, ethical limits and ideas of vision with the description cities, seas, jungles and other places through which he had traveled during his life. He would appear with his broad forehead and gray hair crowning the upper part of his face, visible wrinkles on his face and gray mustache, as thick as ever; dressed in a white shirt and silk tie combined with a black suit of exclusive design. During the dissertation he would take off his jacket and remain in shirtsleeves. Even so, he looked very elegant.

I don't know when old age set in. He began to come in wearing different colored socks or with his moccasins over his bare feet; sometimes he wore a tie over a short-sleeved shirt and at other times he wore a somewhat shabby gray suit. Most distressing was when he would repeat the previous class as if it were a new lesson, or when he would forget a word and go blank for several seconds, until one of the students would mention the forgotten word or complete the unfinished sentence. Then I covered his residence with little signs on cardboard painted by Mrs. Assad, with names and arrows so he could find his way around. Toilet, bedroom, dining room, reading room, recreation room, and others that might even remind him of the hours of use. At seven o'clock he would go into the bathroom to defecate, at seven thirty to take a bath, at eight o'clock breakfast, at eight thirty to brush his teeth. She helped him get dressed; when he became rebellious and tried to do it on his own, sometimes he was left with his pants fly open, his socks on backwards, his shirt buttoned in disarray.

Assad marked my life, because his knowledge of infectious diseases was like an encyclopedia that remained in my memory. The narration of the trips and the places he had known allowed me to reach those places as if it were *déjà vu*, as if I had visited every corner of a city in the past or had traveled along roads that I remembered even without having traveled on them before. Likewise, he marked the lives of countless disciples and his family, including his wife and children, so that she lived with him to share every moment of his life. His two sons were professors of infectiology in London and New Delhi. His wife was so attached to him that she did not know what to do when he died suddenly, perhaps due to a massive heart attack complicated by arrhythmia and shock, or perhaps due to a pulmonary thromboembolism, which took him away without the doctors who received him in the hospital emergency room being able to do anything.

When I saw her at his wake, she gave me the impression that she would not survive long after her husband's departure. In my case, it made me believe that there was the unrealized fantasy, behind which came the applause and admiration of the people. Perhaps Assad spared me from a pariah life or a future with a fat waist and chubby cheeks while serving in some position in an office of bureaucrats. He gave salt to my life, even if the salt tasted bitter. He gave fire, even if the fire burned and caused pain. Today I recall it with the fondness I preserve for my father, a part-time English professor at my hometown university, who had previously worked as an elevator operator in a building in Chicago, years after the end of Prohibition, after Al Capone's thugs had ceased to dominate the gambling dens and liquor distribution depots in the neighborhoods near the shipyards, run by the mob.

They were different times and spaces. The teacher was an immigrant who arrived in Buenos Aires as a child. My father was a boy who wanted to study in the United States. Assad came from the war. My father had been a young man trying to survive in the Windy City, avoiding other Hispanics who drank themselves to exhaustion on the sidewalks of neighborhoods with gray buildings of suffocating uniformity. I keep the image of a boy walking through these neighborhoods. The buildings had a semi-basement that had to be accessed by stairs, with a lobby above the semi-basement, other stairs that started at the back of the lobby and elevators with double doors; one had folding doors and the other had two pieces that opened to the sides. These South Side buildings were crowded with factory workers and students from college and the University of Chicago. Young people sought to specialize in trades that were good for the times, such as baked paint for automobiles that was manufactured in neighboring Detroit, or becoming electricians to work in General Electric's appliance factories.

But there was nothing to be done because hobbies are inherited and then honed through life experiences. In my case, I inherited from my father that adventurous spirit that took him to the Windy City instead of staying moth-eaten in the city where he was born, along with his parents and his youthful friends. Although the result could have been the same: a part-time university professor. I wonder to what extent my career choice was influenced by trying to translate the *National Geographic Magazine* articles that my father bought every week from a small English-language magazine store attached to the wall of a viceregal church. It was exciting to see photographs of landscapes with ochre-colored mountains that explained the deepest canyon in the world, or fossil sites in Arizona and Mozambique.

The first surprise about my progress came from my mother, who by then was working in a wool weaving factory. I think of her tears when she learned that I had won a contest for high school students. They were tears of joy and pride, as if taking revenge against the episodes of cruelty in her life. I imagine the factory whistle sounded longer or more musical than any other day. According to her, it was worth it to have enrolled me in a religious school, which cost an arm and a leg, so that I could become that knowledgeable about minerals and other subjects. I should have made it clear to her that little natural science was taught at school and that I had learned that and other knowledge from the English magazines my father collected. Another part of my knowledge I learned when I walked along the tectonic faults of the mountains near the city, when I collected samples of rocks with different characteristics than limestone. For example, the galenas were the mineral form of lead, although because of their brightness they looked like stones with silver sparks.

The jury of the contest was composed of teachers from several schools in the city and was sponsored by the American mining company Southern Corporation. I could recognize chalcopyrite, malachite, pitchblende, uranite, azurite, oropyrite, argentite, galena; even stones with iridescent surfaces similar to aerolites that fused their minerals into a dark and glassy amalgam. In addition, I could appreciate the quality of the veins by looking at the color of the rock surfaces by means of the mineral grade. No one would imagine that the son of a foreign language teacher and a textile factory worker would have this knowledge, as if he were the offspring of a geologist or a worker in an open pit mine in the Andes.

My teachers could not believe it, nor could my classmates; neither could my parents or the parents of my classmates. I understood that vocation was superior to any pretension of effort. Maybe I would have been an excellent miner if I had continued with the hobby, or maybe a great physical anthropologist if I had met Professor Juan Comas in Mexico City. It worked with me as it could work with anyone. Then the figure of the madman Bonet came to mind, who dedicated his soul and life to the theater, until he became a skinny schizoid, with the face of a beggar in the worst need, but when it came to playing a Beckett or Wilde character there was no one who could surpass him. Once I think I saw him directing traffic on one of the busiest avenues. In reality, it may not have been Bonet, but another similar crazy person. Someone who knew him told us that he saw him riding on the back of the horse of an equestrian monument that presides over the square of one of the liberators. We all thought Bonet was lost and he believed that we had ceased to exist long ago because we did not have a minimum of fantasy.

I think Assad and Bonet had the same alienation of Louis Leakey searching south of Lake Victoria, in Olduvai, for the fossils of the first hominids with his wife Mary Leakey. They were after the fossils of extinct lines of primates no taller than a chimpanzee, with whom they shared bone structure. Their cranial capacity was above five hundred cubic centimeters, like the *Proconsul africanus* and other apes that could be in that intermediate line, between the current anthropomorphs and the current hominids, like the *Sivapithecus indicus* or the *Australopithecus afarensis*, up to the *Zinjanthropus boisei*. This one is in the line of hominids, one million seven hundred thousand years old, which was given the name of *Homo habilis* and lived at the same time as *Homo erectus*.

The Leakey couple were fanatics who made a living collecting bones and fragments of splintered bones that they found embedded in rocks blackened by oxidation. Then they would sit down to write an essay about their find on pieces of paper. Later they would try to put together a giant jigsaw puzzle by joining the pieces found with pieces made of acrylic, taking into account the possibilities or variables that could fit with the original piece. Today, the prototype of that hominid could be assembled with the help of a computer; all that would be needed would be a fragment of the lower jaw and a tooth in an arch with empty sockets. The computer would have suitable software to draw the reconstructed specimen in three dimensions. The Leakeys would have been happy with such a computer.

Evidently, a degree of fanaticism or a component of fantasy was required to be involved in an occupation without regard to profit. I remembered people like Lucho Palao trying to draw in watercolor the hardest expression on the faces of the old indigenous people who came down from their villages to the city during Holy Week to accompany in procession a recumbent Christ in his urn. And of other people, like the elementary school teacher Ingrid Bausch, who wanted to teach us some of the works of Bach, Mozart, Beethoven while we, who were still children, made fun of her work. Perhaps I had become fond of that way of living that did not yield fortune or sustained fame, not even ephemeral fame.

It was certain that in any sleeplessness I would question my way of life. During those nights, when the hours did not advance and I refused to turn on the light bulb and the TV, because I pretended to sleep, bad thoughts would cascade in. "What will be the next step on the cliff? Someone will be dealt the heavy deck". That time I was afraid of having contracted a disease that would manifest itself after twenty years of incubation; an encephalopathy, with replacement of the gray matter by myofibrils, caused by prions acquired on a trip to Africa, with signs of anthropophagy. Or perhaps an oncogenic viral infection causing lymphoma. Or, simply, the amplification of an eternal virus that caused an intensified reaction of my immune system and destroyed my pancreas and lungs.

Surely I had to be crazy to follow that path. My friend Daniel, on the opposite slope, enjoying any misfortune; me, looking for tasks so as not to slacken. The same in one or the other variant. Daniel on the Upper West Side or in Queens and me somewhere else where I was needed or presumed to be needed. Perhaps a Yunga valley in Bolivia or a stone-built village in the mountain range bordering the Atacama Desert or in the middle of the Darien jungle. Daniel would be among crazy people while I tried not to lose my mind as I observed the world upside down. He would listen to the crazy people of Central Park or the Riverside; I would listen to the witchdoctors of the indigenous villages, who prided themselves on knowing the cure for all illnesses.

I had to deal with another fundamentalist; worse, a delusional who fantasized about finding viruses in the sieves of the objective of the scanning electron microscope. At that time I was studying at the university. At that stage I was dreaming about the future. One of my wishes was to look something like the Turk. Another one was to go for a ride with Gabriela on the Paraná River on a small boat.

At that time in my life I was staying in a room with blue painted walls and a light fixture in the center of the ceiling. A bookshelf was attached to one of the walls, where I placed my study books and notebooks. It was a vibrant and exciting city, with dance clubs in the center and in the coastal areas. There were neon lights on the avenue that extends northward, to the limit of the urban nucleus. Some amber and gleaming red bulbs resemble the *doppler* shift or the psychedelic sensation of vertigo. A man with gray hair and mustache, with a grumpy look, was playing the life saver. Someone told me that he had once been the commissioner of a sector of the federal capital and that he had been responsible for a massacre of students with at least three seriously wounded, one of whom may have died in a sanatorium in the federal capital. All because of the desire to punish indiscipline bordering on terror; the students were just chanting in chorus a song with trova rhythm and protest lyrics.

The man boasted proudly of his past, as if he had scored the goals with which Argentina defeated Holland in the last FIFA Cup match. The face was accompanied by a big voice like a tango singer from the suburbs and a squinting, yet defiant look in his eyes.

Only once did Professor Assad make a marginal comment on the political situation, as if the topic did not interest him or was too hot to expose, "What do you think of the mess in the homeland?" I thought he was referring to the chaos of the night before, when firecrackers went off and shrapnel exploded. Or perhaps he was referring to the television news broadcasts that showed images of government men implicated in corruption cases.

"The truth is that it is very sad," I told him.

I was referring to the fact that they had been treated for gunshot wounds at the Centenario Hospital. I assumed that the wounded were pedestrians from the neighborhood that was the scene of the battle between police and subversives. I did not think the wounded were those who were involved. I took for granted that the insurgents would have their own clandestine sanatoriums in the basements of unsuspecting buildings or in a chalet in the countryside, where they would treat their own wounded. The same as the wounded of the police and the army would be assisted in the military hospitals.

"How is everything going in your country?" he asked me.

"The same," I answered. "A military junta governs the country with the same disastrous consequences.

The professor quickly changed the topic and referred to the situation of injustice in South Africa with the apartheid laws. He commented that the scientific community had spoken out against discriminatory, racial and social laws in the world. He then explained that Nelson Mandela had been imprisoned on Robben Island for twenty-eight years. He mentioned in passing the hurricane winds coming off the Atlantic Ocean and the biodiversity around the city, with several ecological floors and different endemic species. While he was talking about places

I didn't know about, I thought about the peacefulness of my neighborhood.

Gabriela lived in one cottage with her family; the other was occupied by three of us students. The first time I saw her body I was moved to the point of delirium. She was a Latin goddess. Tall, slim, very white, jet-black hair. How many nights she caused me to rave, how many dreams I spent in a state of sleeplessness. At times I remember the beauty, the harmony of the lines and the intense lascivious desire that I experienced, just as I remember my pillow, my books on the small table and on the floor, depending on the subject I had to delve into; the used coffee jar, that I used as an ashtray for cigarette butts, and the new jar of coffee that I was drinking at the time. And Harrison, the enormous book of internal medicine, with its hard and black cover. I was proud of this possession, as if I had contributed some article on some important subject.

Understanding each page gave me the sensation of knowing something more about the handling of an instrument. Sometimes I would go to San Telmo to gawk at a skinny, blond-haired boy with some kind of autism who played the saxophone. Or perhaps he had a misunderstood vocation that had forced him to leave home because of a conflict with his father. The boy was disconnected, not looking at passers-by, concentrating on the harmony of the instrument, inventing variations; he was improvising a melody that I recognized as a creation of an English band: Pink Floyd or maybe Led Zeppelin. Each page of the book was the equivalent of discovering an unknown or partially known world. Each page brought together what I had learned in pathology and physiopathology, until each disease was unraveled, while I felt that I was getting closer to integral knowledge.

At times I would go through Zinsser's book *Microbiology* and stop at the section that dealt with the structure of bacteria and the target cells on which antibiotics act. In the end, the professor's comprehensive explanation reminded me of the blond boy.

A few steps ahead, an older man played a tango with his accordion while a young couple danced. Years later I came across a man, in his sixties, playing the saxophone on the Seine River walkway under the bridges near Notre Dame. He looked to me like an alcoholic on tour, an individual with a Parkinson's-like tremor and an expressionless face. I thought that the young man from San Telmo and the old man from the Seine River had the same degenerative disease that turned them into dilettantes, with a communicative capacity that I envied. Both were like musicians who join together to perform a melody in Riverside or Central Park. I could never hear their voices, but I could hear the melody coming out of their instruments; a rhythm that mixed some blues, jazz, subway rock and other genres that I could not classify.

The Turk continued with the explanation of prevalent diseases and others that were not prevalent, because they appeared from time to time. "A cholera pandemic that struck the coastal populations of Egypt spread to North Africa, Asia, and South America. The mutant strain of *Vibrio cholerae* 01, the Tor, affected Pacific coastal towns from Mexico to Chile and then spread to Brazil and Argentina between 1909 and 1910."

"Look," I interrupted, "I knew a deserted cove near the port where I lived, with a small cemetery where the crosses were painted with lead paint and the dates of the deaths are all around the summer of 1910."

Maybe the Turk remembered Istanbul and the Bosphorus, the Golden Horn, the Galatas, the Hagia Sophia Cathedral or the Sultan's palace. I recreated the unpopulated cove, the swimming contests until we reached the first fishing ships and, after a rest of half an hour to catch our breath, we returned, surfing the lurches and pissing off the big waves, letting ourselves be dragged by the sea currents that first expel and then suck in the proximity of the beaches. I asked myself a hundred questions: "Had the beach been abandoned after some epidemic because it was an unhealthy place? Could it be cholera or another disease? One never knows.

Then I started thinking about Daniel and Clarita. How long had it been since that yesterday? No one could tell me if it was cholera or a viral disease; maybe black pox with hemorrhagic pustules or poliomyelitis with paralysis of respiratory muscles. Maybe it was a natural catastrophe, an earthquake on some South Pacific island and a tsunami or tsunami variant, with hundreds dead in the cove. I could never get an answer, because the answer was uncertain and because it had taken just a few years to erase the collective memory.

When I asked the older ones, they also had no idea what could have happened since it was before their time. To my question they would answer: "It seems that the sea changed its route and left the sand deserted." It had nothing to do with an emerging disease, or even that it had been an abandoned fishermen's cove long ago. I didn't say it so as not to contradict them, but I still thought something disastrous happened. The crosses on the graves with similar dates painted in white lead must have had a reason, a reasonable explanation.

Assad explained that diseases continue to plague mankind again and again, like natural phenomena. "Between 1918 and 1919 we had the Spanish flu, which killed fifty million people. Later, during 1957 and 1958, came the Asian flu, with more than four million deaths.

"Almost ten years later, between 1968 and 1969, the Hong Kong flu claimed the lives of more than two million citizens. And in 1980, cases of AIDS began to be diagnosed, with millions of deaths to date."

"Professor," I jumped up, "is it true that diseases cause more deaths than world wars?" Perhaps I should have mentioned not only world wars, but other large-scale conflicts such as the Korean and Vietnam wars.

"Of course," he replied, and then fell silent, assessing the truth of his answer.

Diseases and wars. I reasoned in the sequence war conflagration and disease. The fever of the trenches or Quintana fever, transmitted by the human louse and caused by *Bartonella quintana*, a bacterium that enters the human body by the contamination of the scabs with the excrements of the lice. Its symptoms were fever and myalgia, which produced intense pain in the lower limbs and limited movement due to muscle weakness and pain. After a period of several days, it was removed as it came: abruptly and without sequelae.

It was nothing compared to the typhus epidemic detected after the Bolshevik Revolution. Journalist John Reed, author of *Insurgent Mexico* and *Ten Days That Shook the World,* was one of its victims, along with at least a hundred thousand sick and thousands of dead. The largest and most lethal epidemic in history, the Spanish flu, emerged in the final phase of the war (1918) and lasted until the following year. It caused more than fifty million deaths, tripling the number of casualties in World War I, which claimed the lives of seventeen million individuals.

That afternoon the professor invited me to accompany him to his residence. There I was able to visit his library and reading room. I browsed through books about the artists Diego Rivera and Alfaro Siqueiros. I would have liked to read the works he owned about European museums and contemplate canvases by El Greco, Rembrandt, Velázquez, Goya, Van Gogh or Gauguin, Manet, Sorolla, Dalí, Picasso. Photos of paintings in the Prado, Louvre, Hermitage museums.

After being silent, engrossed in exploring the jewels Professor Asad had in his library, we passed into Mrs. Assad's tearoom. As she served the infusion in a variation of the Chinese tea ceremony, I regretted not having presented the lady with a crimson rose.

Professor Assad resumed his conversation with a certain anxious tone. A redundant conversation, perhaps because at that moment he was already forgetting what he was saying.

"What do you think of the country's mess?" I had heard the same question before.

"Are you referring to the political situation?" I wanted to know.

"No, I'm talking about Guimpel's suicide."

He was talking about the psychiatry professor Federico Guimpel. Professor Guimpel had committed suicide a week earlier, after he was accused by medical students of conducting experiments on human beings. In addition, he was an ex-Nazi who had belonged to the SS, the Schutzstaffel. The students claimed that he had participated in the exterminations of "inferior races" during the Holocaust. According to them, he was involved in the mass sterilization of Jewish women, Gypsies and other ethnic minorities in Auschwitz. He was also linked to genetic studies on identical twins, having worked with Nazi physician Josef Mengele's group.

In reality, there were two complaints with criminal connotations. Before the denunciation, the professor was the director of the psychiatric hospital of the city. Years before, he had presented a study on calcifications due to toxoplasmosis in children of women who were sick or carriers of *Toxoplasma gondii*, reason for which he advised *serological screening* to all pregnant women to avoid placental transmission from mother to child. In addition, he demonstrated that some schizophrenias or dementias with hydrocephalus could be attributed to the disease in patients with some type of immunosuppression. For example, cancer patients treated with immunosuppressants or patients with an autoimmune syndrome. The disease was known to be a zoonosis that initially infected cats and rats before being transmitted to humans. Guimpel described, by observing the symptoms in animals, an uncontrolled rage leading to abnormal behavior in rats. These, instead of fleeing from cats, confronted them as if they did not fear their natural enemy.

"That's a slander invented by some son of a bitch who works at the faculty," Assad said, though he gave no name.

"Do you think it's an unfounded plot drawn up by some professor or doctor in the service?" I asked him.

"I have no doubt. Guimpel was not more than twenty years old during the war. The most he could have been was a conscript in any army. By no means was he an SS officer, let alone part of the exterminators of Auschwitz," Assad said. "What makes me sick is that there are facts that the students could not know on their own.

"It has to be someone close to Guimpel. He must have given them that false information about his past."

Maybe he should have added what he thought: that the data was full of bullshit. Who knew his background? We, his friends, never heard from his mouth any participation or opinion in favor of the regime. I imagine they were referring to the Wehrmacht. The people who accused Guimpel knew what he was researching and used that information in a cowardly way to question the scientific ethics against the professor. It seemed that Assad had studied his argument in defense of Guimpel, as in his best days, when he had the lucidity of a sage and the oratory of a politician. "I don't think it's the students," added the professor with an anger I had rarely seen in him. "This is directed by Zionists against an old man who was invented as a trick."

At that moment I remembered that the Turk owed an old debt to the Israelis: the destruction of Beirut, the battles in southern Lebanon and perhaps the loss, during the Six Day War, of a close relative in the West Bank or in the Negev desert, at a place near Eilat, on the coast of the Red Sea.

I did not know what to say to him. At that moment I could not confess that I too had been outraged to learn of the complaint against Guimpel via a mimeographed print. In the pamphlet, charges were raised against research carried out on schizophrenic women who tested positive for toxoplasma. This was a time before today's tomographic studies and long before tests such as MRI. It was clear that the professor had needed to autopsy the dead suspected of toxoplasma brain damage to provide traceability for his thesis. In no other way could he have analyzed brains affected by abscess formation in the ventricles and basal ganglia. Nor could he have obtained tissue samples with tachyzoites and cysts to determine the maturation stages of the parasites, nor could he have observed the softening of the encephalic mass and the calcifications in the furrows of the cortex.

Several times I observed him staining and studying under the microscope the samples he obtained from the damaged brain tissues. He would then review with that instrument the histopathological alterations, such as intracellular rosette inclusions of some giant macrophages and the inflammatory reaction, with nests of lymphocytes around the vascular lesions. Perhaps the appropriate approach was to analyze the eyes of newborns for the chorioretinitis characteristic of congenital toxoplasmosis, which had a cobblestone-like morphology on the retina.

I understood that cadaver studies were part of the investigation of most diseases, but I was also of the opinion that they should follow a very rigid ethical control by the scientific community.

For this reason, Guimpel should have informed the Society of Neurology or the Faculty of Medicine itself. A simple notification would have sufficed without going into details. He knew that necropsies could not be performed without the authorization of the relatives of the deceased, except if the law allowed it in order to seek the diagnosis of the disease that caused the death.

My opinion was ambivalent, oscillating between the prevailing ethical reason and the scientific usefulness of studies of cadavers suspected of brain toxoplasma. The balance between what was permissible and what was useful had a very fine line that was tipped by subjective criteria. Perhaps their research served to prevent brain damage in those born to mothers with toxoplasmosis and thus avoid congenital damage such as mental retardation or early blindness. If the disease was detected in pregnant women, it was sufficient to use antibiotics, sulfadiazine and clindamycin to eliminate the parasite.

Prior to Guimpel's studies, little importance was given to infestation with the parasite because the disease was thought to affect cats and rats almost exclusively. Only a few cases had been observed in immunocompromised or senile elderly humans. The other infested individuals were healthy carriers without any symptomatology, and even without the possibility of spreading the disease to others. It was clear that these studies had a scientific and practical utility. However, I recalled that in recent years the world scientific community had challenged genetic studies carried out in humans, including those on identical twins, which would have prevented diseases or deficiencies in those who shared those genes. The 1975 Asilomar congress limited studies on the human genome with an ethical argument. Perhaps this moralistic current was splashed on Guimpel.

For some time the scientific and ethical validity of the investigations was discussed, until one cold May morning we came across another piece of news that shocked the university and medical circles of the city. That early morning, the interns and the hospital staff on duty heard a noise that sounded like a gunshot. After the shock of the sound, they feared it was an attack. The doctors and staff on duty rushed to the rooms of the medical residence used by Professor Guimpel. It was horrific. His body was on the floor, in a pool of blood, he had a shattered skull and a .22 caliber Luger pistol in his hand, which showed traces of gunpowder.

In the university community, the event caused an enormous commotion, which increased with the passing of the hours, when it was known that the bullet had shattered the brain and that the pistol used was a Luger, the regulation weapon of the Nazi SS during the war. Some, the majority, were saddened by the news; others, a minority, assumed that the event was a form of proof and repentance, or an escape route to evade responsibility as he was cornered by events. It seemed to me that the whole process was a riot promoted by young idealists and other subjects with a different motivation: envy or unscrupulous ambitions to get hold of the professor's work.

There was no complaint in court against the teacher. Everything was legal. As for his past in the SS, the Nuremberg archives and other post-war documents had to be investigated to trace names and records. Even if any incriminating information was found, I doubted that these records were available to the university's staff. I was not sure that secret Mossad information could be used in a legal act in a country that had declared its neutrality during the conflict, as was the case with Argentina. Perhaps Guimpel, if he had really belonged to a sinister genocidal organization, had taken the precaution of changing his name and even his nationality.

Professor Assad was shocked by the events, like many others, so he showed his indignation during the funeral proceedings. At the same time, I felt an enormous weight on my mind. Somehow, I had been in favor of putting Guimpel on trial, since the aim was to punish the practice of using the resources of medicine in the service of research without an ethical limit. According to the authors of the apocryphon, the aim was to penalize fascist ideology, which used handicapped individuals as guinea pigs; and this included schizophrenics, the feeble-minded and those suffering from senile dementia.

Perhaps I had been infected by the political sentiment of the time, whose most combative exponent was the students, who questioned the disappearance of people during the years of the internal war and the practice of torture on suspects of belonging to subversive groups. Perhaps I was also against any segregation of citizens considered inferior or different. That was the most sensitive part of my perception of the behavior attributed to the professor: a foreigner who sometimes felt the exclusion in his own flesh. Or perhaps I should look for others, such as the professor's solipsism, which amounted to an isolation that could be interpreted as racist arrogance or contempt for inferior individuals, with less intellectual capacity or knowledge. I presume that in that category were those of us who differed from him, such as students of other nationalities, professionals who were far from having his capacity and other people who had not been able to reach his level.

"The saddest thing is that he shot himself with a .22 caliber Luger," Assad said. "I imagine him with his hand shaking as he blew his brains out, with his finger on the trigger and the conviction of not giving up, typical of a brave individual," he stressed.

"The truth is that his death is inexplicable," I commented, experiencing a contradictory feeling, a sensation that oscillated between the pain of mourning and the relief of seeing the punishment for the transgressions.

For a German special forces officer, a shot to the temple, with a burst parietal bone, was the most consistent way to take his own life. I could expect nothing less from a man who had been rough with people and, above all, with himself. I imagined him as a member of an assault group during the battle of Stalingrad, in the uniform of the Wehrmacht. And I imagined a scene I saw in a black and white film. In it, ragged men defend the city from the uniformed military. The defenders have dirty beards and matted hair. The attackers wear steel blue uniforms. The buildings were in ruins from aerial bombardment.

Maybe that scene was the fruit of a recent memory, when I was in a bombed city in the Middle East: maybe Homs or Aleppo. Suddenly, children emerge on the stage and from a sinkhole, which is actually the basement of a dilapidated building of which only walls remain, some women emerge. The women and children are armed with PPSh-41 drum submachine guns and shoot at the attackers before being shot down by enemy machine gun fire. The battle is permanent, there is no rest, there are no truces; it is house to house, street to street. During the day the attackers advance a few blocks, during the night the defenders recover the streets and the ruined buildings. Each day is identical to the previous one. A terrifying routine is relived that plunges individuals into a sense of hopelessness.

Snipers on both fronts, stationed in selected positions on the upper floors of the workers' tenement buildings, fire at the soldiers as they attempt to advance along the rubble-strewn tracks. Guimpel was just another soldier, or perhaps a young officer of the Schutzstaffel (SS) in command of a contingent of soldiers.

After several months the situation becomes untenable for the attackers. Food reaches the besieged by the river and by air thanks to cargo planes that drop the lunch boxes in small parachutes over the ruined city. But supplies for the attackers are not getting through at all. The ground supply route has been cut off and the Luftwaffe planes are shot down in the air before they can drop their cargo. The attackers look like specters in their positions. Blue coats cover their weakened bodies, with ulcerated skin on the support sites and scabies caused by parasites that spread from one to another. After a few months, the defenders go on the counter-offensive and the attackers are cornered. The reinforcement troops have broken the front on the Don, which threatened to take over the Caucasus oil basin, and form a pincer with the groups defending the city.

The dead are piling up, this time in the German trenches. Tanks of the 4th Panzer Army are partially destroyed, as are Luftwaffe aircraft. The Wehrmacht's Operation Blue is a failure. The 6th Army is totally destroyed.

This battle is the turning point in the war. The invaders have caused seven hundred thousand dead and there are one hundred thousand prisoners. The locals also suffered casualties. It is estimated that six hundred thousand soldiers died, as well as an incalculable number of civilians among the elderly, children and women. Young men and adults participated in the war, so their casualties are counted with those of the soldiers.

Historians recorded in their chronicles that during the siege they fed on rats, cats, dogs, cockroaches and any other living thing that crawled on the ground; they may have even eaten the muscles of the deceased before cadaveric decomposition began. I was thinking of the gnawing face of the cannibals. In Berlin

Von Paulus and Von Manstein were blamed for the failure. The result was attributed to the cold and to the scorched earth policy whereby crops and dwellings were burned before being left in the hands of the enemy. In this way, the opposing troops were prevented from being able to stock up on food or take shelter from the winter ice.

After a few days, the professor's relatives disclosed a letter he had left. Some of the paragraphs were incomplete but spoke of the scientific foundations and the benefits that these studies would bring, since it would be possible to treat pregnant women prone to suffer some damage from the parasite. But in the most sensitive part, the man confessed something unusual:

> I was not part of the Schutzstaffel, I am not even German. I am a Jewish and Polish citizen. My real last name is Gimpel and I am seventy-eight years old. During the war I was part of the Polish resistance to the invasion, and after staying in the Warsaw ghetto, I had to flee, first to Hungary and then to Czechoslovakia. I was confined in a cellar in Prague with a group of persecuted people, among them several Jews. We survived thanks to the solidarity of some women, who supplied us with food through an air duct.

No one knew the veracity of the statements contained in the letter. It might have been an apocryphal missive written by a person in solidarity with Guimpel. Could it have been the work of Professor Assad or his wife? Had other professors, colleagues or disciples of Guimpel written it? Then I remembered that Assad's wife had shed thick tears during the wake. Perhaps the last part of the letter was added by her:

> With the humility of one who knows he is a man unjustly judged and who, in the future, may be exonerated

of the falsehoods that were used against me, I say goodbye with a farewell.

But there was also the possibility that what was mentioned in the letter was true and, therefore, everything that was said about him was nothing more than a slander concocted by feverish minds. Perhaps the man had defended himself against his accusers with a version that made them into fallacious schemers. Thus, his suicide was to be interpreted as a moral revenge against them. Even today I still remember the sentences written on bond paper that reproduced the original letter on thread paper, sentences written on an Olivetti typewriter. It was a forgery and had no signature, but it had evidently been copied in its entirety from the original, which was also of dubious authenticity. I kept the mimeograph copy as an emblem in my life. Whenever I could, I read it again to give me strength for every misunderstood action.

It seemed simple, he could have been a murderous son of a bitch or the soldier of a country at war who caused hundreds of deaths with his own hand. Maybe it was the opposite version: a partisan fighting against the invading forces and against the ill-fated regime, with hundreds of deaths in his catalog. From then on his life became a purgatory to atone for guilt. His own *My way*, his way of living. What was important was the coherence of the end of the plot. I could not imagine Guimpel taking barbiturates or injecting himself with potassium or insulin to end his life. A Wehrmacht officer or a Schutzstaffel captain could not kill himself with organophosphate insecticides or dog strychnine. A Spanish or French maquis, or a Yugoslav or Hungarian resistance militiaman, would have ingested cyanide or arsenic after his arrest.

Then I thought that in the final minute, in the manner of Colonel Aureliano Buendía, from *One Hundred Years of Solitude*, the professor had reviewed his life as if they were the images in a film: war battles, the march of the German prisoners, who had surrendered after the battle, the almost one hundred thousand soldiers who besieged Stalingrad, among them Guimpel. And my mind pictured the professor in the line of prisoners, walking along the roads or transferred in freight trains to be confined in the Soviet gulags, where the isolated were the perpetrators of the holocaust. "With the rod you measure you will be measured."

The prison camps had been created in the image and likeness of the already famous Auschwitz, Dachau, Lublin, with a double fence of barbed wire and barracks with sheet metal walls inside which the prisoners of the enemy powers (Germans, Austrians, Hungarians, Italians) were crammed, frozen and malnourished. Taking advantage of one of the transfers, Guimpel hid from his jailers and escaped in the open. The escape took place on a particularly dark and terrifying night, with hunting dogs chasing him. The Russian soldiers had orders to shoot. He went into the wolf-filled steppes and avoided other camps, as well as towns taken by the Red Army. Finally, he reached a port on the Adriatic, where he took a cargo liner to South America.

Life gave him a new opportunity to build a sanatorium for the insane that would serve to redeem himself. With that purpose in mind, he did not leave a peso in his savings account. He used it all to build a ten-thousand-square-meter building for a modern mental health hospital. To this end, he created therapeutic communities where the patients' relatives were integrated. The idea was to address the emerging problems of a dynamic society in which there was drug addiction and other addictions, cyclical depression and child psychiatry, which dealt with autism and infantile idiocies. There was also a place for the mental care of the elderly, offering assistance for vascular and degenerative senile dementias. In those years, between 1980 and 1990, many of these concepts were innovative in South America and were being tested and implemented in Europe.

When he pretended to have achieved success, his wife, a German émigré whom he met at the *fazenda* in Belo Horizonte, died. The woman was the daughter of a German landowner who had settled in the Southern Cone after the war, like him. Once in southern Brazil, he bought a tract of land of hundreds of acres at a price no one had ever paid before. Part of the payment was made with coins of a silver and nickel alloy that had been minted in Germany before the end of the war. In making this type of coin, Germany intended to obtain an alloy that would stand out for its metallic content rather than its monetary value.

The woman, his wife, the daughter of the landowner of Belo Horizonte, accompanied him until she passed away due to an ultra-fast cancer that made her small and emaciated. She weighed no more than thirty-odd kilos. When she passed away, Guimpel became even more silent, more isolated and more distrustful of the people around him.

She died ten years before his suicide, even though she was twenty years younger than he was. The man felt so lonely that he had to adopt a German shepherd to have some company, as he wandered like a soul in pain through the precincts of the residence. On one occasion a psychologist, concerned about his near catatonia, asked him about his life before marriage, thinking that perhaps he had been engaged to another woman. Guimpel replied, "I don't know what happened before the war. It's as if I had erased all memory. It seems to me that the whole thing was a nightmare that I refused to accept as part of my life."

He even thought he had made it up, because he was incapable of admitting to having been in those places where human beings were abhorred. Names like Lublin, Warsaw, Prague, Stalingrad and Kiev brought back bad memories. They were full of shabby human beings, wiry men with clothes too big for their squalor. They were bombed-out cities, streets turned into rubble dumps, residential buildings destroyed, windows without a single pane of glass. "Fucking life!" he blurted out to himself as he thought about the choice of method to end his existence. Perhaps earlier he would have liked to have shot the first bullet into an Ashkenazi. In the end he shot himself in the temple. He ran out of balls. He had no more time for an action of that magnitude that had not been adequately planned so as not to fail. At the moment of the attempt on his life, the tremors, thick and thin, that prevented him from putting food in his mouth ended. He believed it was Parkinson's or a parasympathetic tremor caused by some other disease.

Finally, not only Assad taught us a lesson; so did Guimpel. Whether the Turk had been an anarchist, a member of a very active cell in Ankara during the military coup of 1960, or whether he participated in the resistance against the designs of the United Nations, which demanded handing over part of Palestine to Ben-Gurion's new State of Israel, meant nothing to my assessment. Whether Guimpel was a regular soldier or an SS soldier who participated in the siege of Stalingrad was not relevant either; not even if the opposite happened and he was part of the resistance against the Nazi occupation. His influence was on other terms. His compulsion was contagious. He seemed to give off the smell of dusty books, burned by the light of the libraries: books moldy and valuable at the same time.

The two men belonged to a different world that subjugated me right off the bat. I didn't consider at all that they both had a controversial past. I did not take it into account because they were not the same times. The dice are not thrown by the character who lives what he believes to be his own story, but by someone who was not present on stage. I remembered the verses of *Los dados eternos* by César Vallejo:

> My God, and this deaf, dark night, you will no longer be able to play, because the Earth is a gnawed and already rounded die by dint of rolling to adventure, which can only stop in a hole, in the hole of immense sepulcher.

It was clear to me. There was someone else in the poker game. Someone who was not present, but who managed our fate. I remembered the London pub again. Maybe I should have remembered a Liverpool or Manchester pub. In that place a skinny guy with gelled hair, with a kind of exotic bird's crest, was singing *My Way* while trying to imitate Robbie Williams; or was it Sid Vicious? Then I thought that everyone has their own version of events, even if they are out of tune.

The matter of the accusation linking Guimpel to Mengele seemed to me to be a hoax influenced by the novel and film *The Children of Brazil,* by Ira Levin. The book was published in 1976 and the film of the same name, directed by Franklin J. Schaffner in 1978, was released a year before Mengele died in a swimming pool in São Paulo. At the same time, the indictment was based on the work of Nazi hunter Simon Wiesenthal, who brought another genocidaire, Adolf Eichmann, to trial in 1961. He was sentenced to death in 1962 for the crime of genocide. He had been kidnapped by members of Mossad on the outskirts of Buenos Aires during the course of Operation Garibaldi. I didn't believe it that time, I wouldn't have believed it now. In this case, it seemed to me that fiction surpassed reality.

I met the teachers as they were at the time. A snapshot of the moment. Two professors: one loquacious, nice, friendly; the other solitary, silent, self-absorbed. What to say: this is life itself. Neither sweet nor sour. It simply glides from day to day.

At no time is life careful not to hurt you. It doesn't even pretend to be sympathetic. Who could have put in my way the teachers who instilled in me the passion for this way of life that prioritizes the uncertain over the everyday? They infected me with their addiction to adventure, but it was also a discomforting way to feel useful. The problem is that once you start, you don't find your way back. You continue forward without thinking that you should stop to measure the risk or latent danger, because you don't know any better. It seems as if the next step has been planned in detail, as if it were a footprint that has already been laid down on the ground before you set foot on it. And then you wonder how you got here. "I don't know! But maybe it doesn't matter anymore.

For this reason, once I found my path I had to continue despite the cost. I gave up a formal home and condemned myself to become a wanderer. I had no opportunity left for evasion. Nor to analyze the danger, even knowing that I could have been infected with diseases that would later manifest themselves with cellular changes, degenerative brain damage or an increase in the proto-oncogenes that would derive in their alleles, the oncogenes, such as c-myc associated with growth in hemopoietic tissue, which evolves in different types of leukemias. Or like the oncogenes c-jun, c-myb, c-fos, c-erb A and other molecules related to different cancers. I was also thinking about kuru, or atypical Alzheimer's. Although it was more likely that somewhere in the conflict a boy mistook me for the enemy and died from a bullet in the thorax or occiput.

Perhaps my destiny was not to lose my life through illness or war, but through an accident on a dirt road that climbs from a river canyon to a plateau a thousand meters above sea level.

Then I remembered Assad and the urban guerrillas in Ankara, as well as the militias in southern Lebanon, and Guimpel, whom

I remembered with the wiry face of a Wehrmacht general. And my mind drew the atrocities of the war. The Dante-esque scenes. The battles without quarter. As if they were nightmares of a feverish mind or deliriums typical of the hangover of a drug that had previously bruised the brain of the hallucinated.

Along the way I could see the rubble of what was once a besieged city, completely destroyed from the foundations to the upper floors, with cavities where there were once windows, walls and partitions. I came across caravans of refugees fleeing the war. And with the combatants of both sides, with their faces covered to avoid being recognized or to avoid inhaling the smell of gunpowder and the stench emanating from the decomposing bodies.

Several times I had the feeling that the inhabitants of the area had gone mad. Some soldiers behaved like a pack of scavengers; others, like felines stalking their victims. They seemed part of the wind and sand. Suddenly I thought I had lost my mind too. That it was all the result of a hallucination because my frontal lobe was damaged.

And when I witnessed the discovery of the lifeless bodies of displaced Syrians in an open field in northern Turkey, I was ashamed to call myself a man. They had frozen to death in the cold of an unseasonably cold snowfall, without the food sent by humanitarian organizations, including UNHCR. When we went to check the deaths, the corpses had been covered by the woven straw blankets used as mattresses by the nomadic herders in the area. Most of the dead were children and women. The men numbered no more than half a dozen. All bore the stigmata of frostbite: black, sphacelated skin where the phlyctenas of ice burns once were, mummified and blackened musculature, and punch cuts on the pinnae of the ears.

Specialists concluded that the death occurred six to eight days before the bodies were found. They attributed it to unseasonal ice, shortage of clothing and hunger during their last few days. Worse, to avoid any accountability to the world press, they emphasized their illegal status. The geographical corridor through which they were fleeing their war-torn country was also used by drug smugglers from the valleys of Afghanistan, as well as by arms smugglers supplying the Taliban in the mountains of Afghanistan and Pakistan. Someone remarked that the same corridor had been used more than 1,500 years earlier by Silk Road traders and nomads seeking to reach the Black Sea. Today it was traveled by displaced Syrians and Iraqis fleeing the atrocities of war. To reach Europe, they first had to pass through Anatolia and reach a port from which to embark to Greece and then to Germany or France.

"Fuck!" I exclaimed then when I saw the corpses. "Fuck!" I repeated some time later, when we found the charred bodies of the natives in a precarious camp on the Madeira River slope. How many times will I have to use the same interjection? "Fuck!" Possibly so many that someday I'll stop keeping count.

At that moment I thought of my teachers again. I evoked the Turk with his gray mustache and half-grown beard. I pictured him with a short-sleeved shirt and white hair, or was it gray? Although I knew he had passed away, I felt the need to look for him; to return to the cafeteria where he taught us, even though I was convinced that nothing would ever be the same.

I also wanted to see Mrs. Assad. Perhaps she had passed away after a depression filled with memories and many silences. If this is confirmed, maybe the people living in her residence can tell me how she assisted the professor when he was sick; how she cleaned up the spilled food on his shirt and pants and then bathed him carefully, so he wouldn't scald himself, and changed his diapers every time he pooped. In the end she had to carry him in a wheelchair so he wouldn't fall because of ataxia and muscle weakness in his lower limbs. And to put him to bed, she had to carry him like a child. Those who informed me of the situation explained that she did it with great patience, singing, because she believed that her husband, the Turk, felt happy when she sang the songs that he had tried to sing with his raspy voice, a product of the irritation of his larynx due to being a compulsive smoker.

They were in the same places and in similar circumstances as the Syrian refugees. Perhaps it also snowed when they lived in a canvas tent, and they still froze to death. Maybe they sat on the edge of the Negev desert, where the sand ended and the oasis began. Maybe he wasn't Turkish, but Syrian. Or Egyptian, or both when there was the RAU, which stood for United Arab Republic. She must have met him in Paris, when she was a student at the Sorbonne or at the time when she worked in a Sanofi laboratory next to the Pasteur Institute. Perhaps she was his student or his secretary at the professorship. What I am sure of is that she was thirty years younger than him and that she fell in love with his way of being: professor with dilettante hallucinations. She also fell in love with his emptiness and his boasts. How could she not be depressed when he died? Her soul was broken. It split in two. She became nothing. So much so that all day long she talked about him to anyone who would listen.

To the students who visited her from time to time she would say, "I prayed that he would not suffer with a cancer that had been discovered two weeks earlier during a cytological study of his sputum. Today I realize that I would rather he had stayed alive, even if I had to inject him with morphine every two hours so he wouldn't feel the pain, even if I had to take care of him like a baby. He would have been alive. Life, even with the incoherent pain, is always better than no life at all. I had hoped he would be with me to the end. No, I can't bear it."

We did not know whether she was referring to her future alone or to the life of her husband, from whom she never accepted this enforced separation.

When I walked as a boy through the steep streets of the working-class district in my hometown, or when I wandered through the port neighborhood, sneaking in with the rascals of the slum along Marina Avenue, I was a boy with different dreams. I thought I could be a sailor on a merchant ship or work as a stevedore in the port, with hundreds of cranes lifting containers carrying goods from China. I also dreamed of being an emigrant from a rich country, where I had made my fortune but never of being a student at the Faculty of Health Sciences. Even less of being a student of Assad, Guimpel, Fracassi, Pagano, Tano and other professors. At that time nobody gave a penny for me. They wouldn't have cared if I had stayed in either of the two small towns where I spent my childhood and youth. With a little luck, I would have traveled to some big city, but I would have kept the imprint of the characters of my homeland. Neither small boy nor pimp any other trade, no way those. I reviewed: I was for sure a crafty man who manages to take advantage of the life he has to live.

It is that simple or that complex. Nothing is useful or useless, it is simply there. Achievements are due, ninety percent, to circumstances and failures depend, fifty percent, on the unfavorable environment. It is not the same in any way. In the failures you contribute more than in any of the achievements. In the failures, it is clear that you erred, you messed up, you were overcome by idleness or fear; finally, you were not prepared to succeed. In success it was the circumstances that paved the way: your parents or your teachers, your friends, even your enemies;

the city, the opportunities, the canned coffee, the cigarettes, the books - *War and Peace*, by Leo Tolstoy, *Crime and Punishment*, by Dostoyevsky, *One Hundred Years of Solitude*, by Gabriel García Márquez, *Frustrated Victories*, by Von Manstein, *The Trial*, by Kafka, *The Plague*, by Camus. With the passage of time, the protagonist becomes a character of Poe or Victor Hugo or ends up being one of the Karamazov brothers. It's as simple as that!

In the end I ended up being a character created by the hallucination of a Turk, or maybe I was the clear shadow of a psychiatrist half-crazy or with an impressive solipsism. Perhaps I resembled another teacher, another neuropsychiatrist, Professor Marcelo Fracassi, from a family of neuropsychiatrists, son of Teodoro Fracassi, who had become rector of the Universidad del Litoral.

My empathy was born in the neurology exam, when he asked me about the place where I was born. Then he said, "That is the most beautiful place in the world. It only compares to Angkor Wat in Cambodia, a Khmer archaeological complex built in the twelfth century."

I remembered the two mountains with the pre-Hispanic citadel hidden by vegetation and clouds. There the air was heavy, as if it were an anesthetic, ether or ozone; it put you on the verge of sedation. Thousands of years in one place. Thousands of stories in that scenario of walls surrounded by jungle, both elements, perfectly combined.

In the middle of the amphitheater, Professor Fracassi began to recite a poem by Neruda about the beauty of the citadel. I remained blank, unable to recognize a single verse, thinking that he was either half-crazy or an eccentric infected by characters like Dalí, Picasso, Gauguin, Van Gogh. Perhaps he had sporadic attacks of histrionic madness, like many psychiatrists infected by the schizoid neuroses of their patients. The same expression of astonishment was shown by the members of the jury of the subject. That expression was somewhere between stupidity and sarcasm.

> From air to air, like an empty net,
> I was going through the streets and the atmosphere, arriving and leaving...
> [...]
> So on the scale of the earth I have climbed
> among the atrocious tangle of lost forests
> to you, Machu Picchu.
> High city of scalar stones,
> at last the abode of the terrestrial
> did not hide in the sleeping garments.

I was blank. I did not know what it was about, nor did I have any idea that Neruda had written a poem about Machu Picchu. Its beauty was indisputable for any human being; even more so if this human being had the sensitivity of a poet like Neruda. Maybe Fracassi felt it like everyone else or more than everyone else. Maybe I had to learn those verses too.

The professor did not ask me anything about *The Nerve Pathways and Centers*, a book I had published after having studied nerve bundle structures and electrical conduction by means of evoked potentials, which traced the path of axon depolarizations. He did not ask me to explain the concepts of neuromuscular transmission in asthenic diseases. He did not even want to know if I knew about demyelinating alterations in multiple sclerosis or to tell him about new therapies to treat refractory epilepsies. He was more interested in the findings of skeletons showing cranial trepanations using ceremonial instruments made of copper or an alloy of copper with another metal; knives that were shaped like a crescent and their handles carved with the figure of their tutelary god. He then explained to me that the success of the interventions could be verified, insofar as there was a subsequent osteosynthesis process with growth of the internal table of the skull bone.

When describing the proto-surgery, Fracassi issued a hypothesis: they may have been warriors who, during battle, had been wounded with blunt weapons that caused bone fractures, cranial collapse and epidural hematomas and had to be evacuated to avoid death. Or perhaps the surgical intervention took place in peacetime, when neurological alterations associated with brain tumors were detected. Evidently, the professor was referring to the findings of bones in precise places, with equally precise characteristics, which showed alterations on the internal surface of the skull bones that could give the presumptive diagnosis after hundreds of years. The places where these proto-surgeries were practiced were, at the same time, religious ceremonial centers, since they were part of that archaic mixture of religion and medicine.

After the examination, which was either a study of my emotions or an attempt to understand his own impressions of the town in which I had lived, Fracassi introduced me to the studies of muscle cells with vacuolar degenerations in the fibers, a typical symptom of Erb-Duchenne disease. The vacuolar edema resulted in a pseudohypertrophy of the calf and thigh muscles of boys suffering from this genetic disorder. The result of this disease was the inability of the patients to maintain an upright position due to the weakness of the gluteal and spinal muscles. They were children who moved on all four limbs as if they were still crawling, despite their late age.

The initial explanation of the disease was that the muscular receptors of acetylcholine, located in the neuromuscular plates, were refractory to the entry of the neurotransmitter that produced depolarization. This eventually caused muscle degeneration due to lack of stimulation. Later, Fracassi and other researchers discovered that the disease was due to the presence of an altered protein, dystrophin, which did not allow the connection of actin with the basement membrane of the muscle cells, leading to the replacement of the muscle by fatty tissue. The mutation of the allele of a gene located on the X chromosome encoded the altered protein. Duchenne pseudohypertrophy was a genetic disease, predominantly in boys, but of rare occurrence in girls.

Fracassi chose me as his assistant and, little by little, we developed a friendship because of those rare decisions that cannot be explained. For a while, he took me to work at his sanatorium for elderly people with senile dementia and other degenerative and vascular diseases. After a while he invited me to exclusive clubs in Rosario and Buenos Aires to discuss travel. He told me that the Greeks knew the Dardanelles Strait as the Hellespont. I imagined a channel linking the Aegean Sea with the Sea of Marmara, which at its widest part measured three hundred kilometers. At the same time, the Bosphorus was the tongue of water that opened between the Sea of Marmara and the Black Sea. On its shores was the historic city of Istanbul, which had been the Constantinople of the Byzantine Empire until 1453, when it was taken by the Ottomans with Mehmed the Conqueror as their leader.

He also told me that he had visited Cambodia before the war. He told me about the ivory route. He regaled me with Hemingway's *The Snows of Kilimanjaro*. He then spoke of the Vietnam syndrome, understood as a national depression after the disastrous war, the symptoms of which were irritability and fury against the elders, who were blamed for having sent the young men to a war in a country so far away. I saw that same fury in soldiers returning from other wars. He shared with me his thoughts on the Cambodian genocide, which he said brought with it a disease of rootlessness that affected the boys led by Pol Pot; a tragic odyssey for having conceived of a country without old and corrupt men. That fury I saw in some rituals, when individuals were induced to drink the juice of the seeds of amaryllidaceae in a ceremony intended to eliminate anger.

Professor Fracassi's life had nothing heroic about it; perhaps something mystical and artistic, but not heroic. He was never in any battle nor did he join any political movement. He was not persecuted and neither was he imprisoned. It seemed that he was only interested in old people with dementia, the genetic study of neurological diseases and the microscopic analysis of the brain alterations shown by the destitute elderly, whose corpses were picked up from the railroad tracks while their peers wandered around like beggars dressed in rags and with their skin covered with ashes. His research focused on the degeneration of the cerebral cortex in those who drank the undistilled fermented cane sugar drink. I am convinced that he described neurofibrils and amyloid peptides earlier than other neurosurgeons during the autopsies he performed at the School of Medicine.

In this way, he anticipated the study of kuru degeneration caused by prions, which were nothing more than fragmented cell wall proteins, including neurons and neuron-supporting cells. This disease produced spongiform encephalopathy and was related to the anthropophagy practiced by the cannibalistic tribes of New Guinea, who believed that the ingestion of human remains allowed them to absorb the wisdom of the dead. The professor had also described the same alteration due to amyloidosis in the brains of elderly people with senile dementia of the Alzheimer's type.

Years after the professor had resigned from teaching I learned from mutual friends that Fracassi participated in the multicenter study conducted by the Humboldt University of Berlin to investigate the etiology of neurodegenerative diseases.

However, no one could be aseptic without commitments to the nation's circumstances. Shortly before, the Falklands War had ended. The arrogant military men who boasted of their preparation under the standards of the European school had suffered an undeniable setback. Commander Alfredo Ignacio Astiz, for example, known as the Angel of Death, was a clear case of defection. Astiz was sent to the Malvinas and there, when the situation looked bleak, he surrendered to the bombardment of British soldiers. For his role in Task Force 3.3.2, he was accused of genocide and of being behind the disappearance of prisoners of war; among them, two French nuns and a Swedish citizen, as well as three founders of the group Madres de Plaza de Mayo, whom he took to the headquarters of the Escuela Superior de Mecánica de la Armada (ESMA). Hundreds, perhaps thousands, of detainees, whose bodies have not been found, were tortured and murdered there.

Social conflicts, later covered up by the internal war against subversive groups, could no longer be concealed. The loss of the currency's purchasing power and the decrease in the average salary were evident. Corruption crimes were beginning to emerge in the big business deals of the families of the south, who had become rich with the shipments of cattle and meat to the big markets. The Swift organization was accused of monopoly, as well as of several scandals. The disappearance of people generated a movement of mothers searching for the disappeared. And the trade of children born in prisons, children of women committed to the revolution, gave rise to another similar movement: that of the grandmothers of the disappeared children.

Economic inflation, which reached three digits, impoverished society to the benefit of exporters, who took advantage of the monetary exchange rate. The slums were populated by people recently arrived from the provinces and immigrants from neighboring countries. In those human settlements a popular culture of demonstrating with their murga-dances was generated. The military junta could not stay in power any longer. The only way out was to opt for free elections, since the alternative was to leave the chimera of power in the hands of nothing to be filled by operators of domination.

Fracassi and I knew as much as the others. I had just seen *The Night of the Iguana* in a Broadway theater. In the end, Shannon seduced Maxine and then Hannah Jelkes and the rope with which they had tied the iguana ends up trapping the lovers.

On some occasion I have stated that those who danced in the *murgas* were the same people who went out to protest against the military dictatorship. The professor, from whom I had not heard any opinion about the times we were living in, commented to me, "The era of the flag and terror is over. Like all stages in the life of nations; as good times and bad times end; as the tales of fear and the most sinister times come to an end." He was referring to the fall of the military government.

"Professor, let's hope so." Perhaps he was more skeptical or more realistic.

Leopoldo Fortunato Galtieri, alias "El Borracho", who had sent the young men completing their military service to their deaths in the Malvinas Islands, was quickly replaced by a junta of military men who claimed to have the formula to cede power to civilians. The country then fell to unprecedented economic levels. GDP plummeted by 11.5%, with three and four digit inflation and an unwieldy foreign debt. The exhausted population had only memories of typical foods such as asados (local barbeque) and chimichurris (a delicious sauce), mate (traditional tea) or even the pleasure of a daily siesta. Despite the goals scored by

Mario Alberto Kempes, with which Argentina won the World Cup; despite the fact that Roberto Rimoldi Fraga, the son-in-law of General Agustín Lanusse, enthusiastically sang a tune that summed up the pride of his compatriots: *Argentino hasta la muerte* (Argentinian until death).

I was a foreigner who should not stick my nose into the internal affairs of the country, but I could not be indifferent to the events that, one after another, were shaking the nation. When talking to Fracassi I should have mentioned to him that, in a peripheral way, I was involved in a human rights organization: the Latin American Peace and Justice Service. I should have told him that I met the Nobel Prize winner who was involved in those days: Adolfo Pérez Esquivel. He was a skinny, balding man who had created a movement for the defense of human rights. I would have explained to him, with some embarrassment, that I had accompanied the Mothers of Plaza de Mayo, who went out in procession to call for their disappeared children and grandchildren once a week. Not only I participated, but we were a multitude, marching in silence. Perhaps Fracassi would have understood; he would have even disguised the broken voice and tears that he tried to avoid.

I gratefully acknowledge the professors. Just as I remember the city next to the Paraná River, its boulevards and university campuses, the National Historical Monument to the Flag. Above all, I feel sighing dyspnea when I evoke the School of Medicine, the Centenario Hospital, the riverside neighborhoods, the cafés on Córdoba Street. Also the streets of the San Telmo neighborhood in Buenos Aires, with their antiques, art and crafts fair, with the pieces spread out on tapestries on the stone cobblestone floor of that long and narrow street. I still repeat in my mind the melody of a saxophone played by a boy with autism that touched my soul.

Of the three professors, the one who gave me the most important lessons was Fracassi, perhaps because he never pretended to project his own life onto that of his student. I did not find in him the will to impress anyone. Marcelo Fracassi did not tell me that his father, Teodoro Fracassi, had been Albert Einstein's host and friend during his visit to Argentina in 1925. I found out years later, when he was no longer living there and I had no idea what had happened to the professor. It was while consulting a magazine published by Cornell University; a sort of memoir that collected the visits of great personalities to South American countries. Then I came across the photograph of Albert Einstein accompanied by Teodoro Fracassi, who had also been a professor of Neurology and Psychiatry at the Universidad del Litoral. In the picture, Professor Fracassi was posing with the physicist in the Buenos Aires neighborhood of Belgrano. I realized that he never mentioned this special moment, nor others that referred to his scientific lineage or past achievements. Much less did he tell me details about his personal life at the time, which involved a lady much younger than him; nor did he say anything about the past. I presume that his manner was due to his knowledge of Zen philosophy, or maybe it was due to a shyness that he had partially overcome.

It has been a long time since those days of classrooms, the smell of disinfectant and subjects in oral exams in the amphitheater. I don't know what became of his life. Nor do I know anything about Assad's widow. Maybe I will meet one of them in Montparnasse, at the Laboratoire Pasteur or at the Sorbonne. Although considering time passing and the wind, they may already be just a memory in the classrooms of the Centenario Hospital, just like Perez Esquivel. It is possible that I will read their names in some European or American library, since they wrote articles for medical clinics in North America and Europe, as a result of research on infectious diseases, in the case of Assad, or neurological diseases, in the case of Fracassi. They wrote one together on a neurological disease of infectious etiology. They worked on a project on brain diseases of genetic origin documented in descendants of Mediterranean emigrants, like those suffered by the children and grandchildren of those who arrived from North Africa. Above all, descendants of Sicilians and Moroccans. I am convinced that the working hypothesis of both professors would be linked to sickle cell anemia, common in North Africans and Southern Europeans, which predisposed them to cerebral infarctions due to the formation of thrombi in the arteries.

I would have been happy to meet them again in an article, even if the collaboration was posthumous and for the scientific community to recognize their contribution to medicine even if it meant seeing them more worn out and somewhat obsolete.

I also longed to walk the streets of Rosario, Francia and Oroño Boulevards, and to again see the classrooms of the Centenario Hospital. Then I imagined that I would meet them there, in their residences or in the restaurant of a five-star hotel. And that I would say to them, "Time does not pass for you, teachers. You are just as I knew you, whole and standing tall." They would smile sardonically at the compliment that interpreted my affection for them.

I don't know how long it took me to return to the house I had rented on Mendoza Avenue, with the number four thousand and something or how much time I spent researching the lives of the professors instead of studying medical therapeutics or surgical techniques. What I do know is that it one autumn afternoon when the sycamores were dyed a carotenoid red and dropping leaves on the boulevard sidewalks, I walked with my hands in my coat pockets, savoring the cool breeze. As I strolled along I began to remember every phase of my life. There were so many defeats, and only a few triumphs. My childhood, watching the whistle of a knitting factory to see what time my mother would leave work. My father, resting on a wooden lazy chair while reading the latest American weekly, sold by a certain Miguel Rivero in a kiosk in the city. The small squares of a neighborhood that had to be climbed through narrow streets, where people dressed in percale and cheap wool walked. Then the trip to another city. We had to migrate because my parents had to look for new horizons for a dwindling domestic economy.

The real and invented pranks. My encounters with the port's many inhabitants in search of a joke: making fun of a streetwalker or drinking until you become unconscious. The discovery of psychology and biology books, whose authors were Honorio Delgado, from Cayetano Heredia University, and Claude A. Villee, from McGraw Hill University in Canada. My passion for French and Russian literature thanks to *Les Misérables* by Victor Hugo, *The Count of Monte Cristo* by Dumas, *The Human Comedy* by Honoré de Balzac, *War and Peace* by Leo Tolstoy and *The Brothers Karamazov* by Fyodor Dostoyevsky. All this changed my life.

At that time I discovered the concentric rings in deciduous forest trees and learned about the phloem and xylem as a ring of reproducing cells. The onychophores is a species of a special phylum within the *superphylum Panarthropoda*, a species whose ancestors date back to the Cambrian period, at least five hundred million years old, and possibly in the process of extinction. I discovered methods for understanding neurosis and the questioning of the perception of the routine world.

From a mischievous, half-dollar hooligan, I became a reader on a park bench or in the public library. From a street corner lover, I aspired to apply to a university, believing that this way

I would get answers to my questions about so many novelties that began to disturb me. At first I thought about the School of Biology, until I was presented with the opportunity to work with Professor Quevedo Aragón on a project that consisted of making masks of the faces of elderly Indigenous people who had died in hospitals for the indigent. I had to place brown clay on the face to obtain the mold and then pour the liquid wax over it, once it hardened.

I assumed that these reproductions were destined for a wax museum or perhaps an anthropological museum in order to compare the features of one ethnic group and another, of one race and another, although in reality I did not know the destination. I once heard Quevedo name an Italian scholar, Joseph Imbelloni, a paleoanthropologist specializing in racial characteristics of the natives of the Americas. Imbelloni had studied the linguistic kinship of the different cultures of South America to check for similarities. He then formulated his hypothesis, which stated that the settlement of the Americas was the result of multiple waves of migration from Asia and Oceania.

My friends played practical jokes on me. The little women in the neighborhood made fun of my haircut and the fact that I carried my books in my armpit. Possibly, they were laughing at the effect of the radical change of a trickster boy who had turned into a guy with the appearance of a shyster. I supposed, although they did not tell me directly, that the adults believed that I would give up at the first hurdle and that I was poorly prepared for this life. For them, it was almost impossible for a youth from the interior to compete with the students from the big cities. And they were right. I could prove it when I arrived at the railroad station and took the first cappuccino with sweet bread they called factura, which was nothing more than a sweet baguette. I got a shock when I was selected to apply for a job in a Latin American restaurant. I had had to scramble for any job.

However, there were people who were proud to see that change and, more importantly, my persistence. My father seemed to have gone to Chicago as a frustrated student, when he had to drop out of school and look for a job to survive. He felt like he was suddenly getting revenge because his son was going to get a degree. My mother was hopeful and had already forgotten my drunken returns in the early hours of the morning. I'm sure she and Grandma had disguised my rounds at night so as not to get on my father's bad side. I'm convinced that they died of grief when they saw me hanging out with trashy broads who were trying to extort money from me and the boys. I know they also felt bad when they realized that among my friends there were guys who tattooed themselves on their necks, shoulders and backs, and wore earrings on their tongues, noses, earlobes and navels as was the custom of Malay or Filipino sailors. They were guys of the worst kind who would have swiped the wallet of anyone within their reach, or so-and-so's who cut those who looked at them the wrong way or insulted them and made a comment behind their back. Worse yet, my mother and grandmother felt sorry for me hanging out with crazy women with red, lilac and yellow hair; women who imitated the crazy women who accompanied the punk musicians and metalheads who appeared in the neighborhoods of Liverpool or Manchester.

And then, when they saw that I had risen from the ashes, like a phoenix, my mother and grandmother joined hands to pray to God that this was not a collective dream of theirs or a passing restlessness on my part. They prayed to all the saints that what they were seeing was real.

I could not fail my parents; the expectations they had placed in me, nor could I ignore the memory of my grandmothers.

Even if I had to read back and forth the three thousand pages of Harrison's *Principles of Internal Medicine*, the two thousand pages of Litter's *Pharmacology*, or the fifteen hundred pages of *Physiology* or *Neurology*. I would spend his nights in a room studying. One way or another I had to achieve my goals.

For that and many other reasons, I had to continue my studies until the end, despite the difficulties to retain data; despite the loneliness in a student room, ignoring the internal voices that told me to throw in the towel and go back. I couldn't go back to the port bars to recount a hundred exploits invented by the ravings of alcohol or of a stump of any paste that I had to sniff to forget. To forget that, really, I was a shitter who got all wet after the first exam he failed. I got hives from the mosquito bites that came into the room during the summer because I could never buy a coil of pyrethrin as a repellent to keep the bugs away. In addition, I had to suck up the summer heat without a fan and the winter cold without a heater. My teeth would chatter as I read and reread the same page before falling asleep at my desk. When I woke up I would find the page folded over the chapter on uroporphyrin metabolism, after the release of hemoglobin in red blood cell apoptosis. After the tongue twister, I had to remember the details of the enzymatic cascade and study that this was the way to save iron to reuse it in the formation of new red blood cells.

When it started, it looked like a Mandarin Chinese and then it was a puzzle or a kaleidoscope with hundreds of figures and thousands of alternatives. Each time it showed a different image, even if something remained of the previous model. Every day I repeated a resolution: I had to continue in spite of the difficulties in understanding; in spite of the envy and bad blood of some relatives and acquaintances, who bet on me as a loser.

After the walk along the waterfront, where the drops of water taken from the river by a strong breeze, wet my face, I arrived at my room and lay down on the single bed. I turned many times on the same axis as I tried to disconnect from the events of the day.

The clock struck eleven at night and I couldn't sleep. In a fit of nostalgia, I dressed in a sweater and put on the only raincoat I had in my closet to go out and wander the streets. I walked along Cordoba Street, towards the center of the city. I entered the first coffee shop I found open, on the corner of Mitre with Córdoba. I would have preferred a bar. There were so many bars on the Costanera, near the port. Naughty bars, with their smelly odor from hetairas, liquor and blunts. I wanted to smoke a cigarette; however, it was forbidden to smoke in closed public places.

At that time of night there were no more than six to eight people in the store, possibly insomniacs or distressed people like me. When I saw the sleepy faces of the waiters, I felt ashamed to be in that place. All of them were infected by mockery and boredom. After drinking the cup of coffee, I went out to the street, foreshadowing a persistent insomnia, and walked along a cross street until I reached Santa Fe, where I boarded the first trolleybus I found on my way to the northern neighborhood. The streets were bare, except for some guys who looked like thugs. They were not crooks, but other sleepless night owls. Not a woman in sight, much less a girl of loveable age, except for some old women selling cigarettes on the corners of the commercial streets.

I looked out the window and suddenly I saw a boy. At that time of the night? He was sitting on the edge of the sidewalk, in front of the porch of a chalet in the most fashionable neighborhood along the way. It seemed to me that he was waiting for someone or was lost in the tangled streets of the area. Then I imagined that the boy was me. Not in that fictitious neighborhood, of course, but in one of the suburbs of my childhood. I would stand still, waiting for them to open the entrance door for people, not the garage. Maybe they wouldn't notice that I was alone and sad at the door of a two-bedroom house with five beds in each room. Each bedroom would house several families, as if they were refugees from a war or victims of a great economic depression. I hallucinated that my luck had changed.

In my dream I was a simple guy with a country to return to, and not a stateless person with an important job anywhere in the world. In the end, the image of the boy was lost and there remained an elongated shadow cast by a body and neon light.

The trolleybus continued its trip along an avenue that seemed to be the ring road. Not a soul on the corners; not even the guys who go out to collect material for recycling. I remembered the children of my neighbors from the small streets of San Blas or the Inclán neighborhood. Today they would be bureaucrats for a water company, bank employees or workers in the copper deposits. Perhaps some of them work as stevedores, warehousemen or customs officers at the port.

I was driving along Rondeau Avenue and the ring road. From the window I had seen the front of the Granadero Baigorria pediatric hospital, where the skinny Mirta and Susana, classmates and now interns in neonatology, were on duty. At this hour, they would be drinking coffee to stay awake and without rancor while on-call. The skinny girls were transformed from spectacular girls to haggard and disheveled doctors.

The trolleybus continued through the northern neighborhood. In Fisherton, behind the hedges of pruned bushes, were the luxurious residences. I remembered that Assad's wife waited on us in one of those sumptuous mansions and that I didn't bring any flowers to the invitation. God, what a lack of courtesy! She kindly overlooked this detail.

In my village I had not learned to bring flowers when invited to someone's home. I had the belief that flowers were carried in bouquets to the graves of deceased relatives. They are also carried by the bride or given to a friend on Valentine's Day. In my concept, an Andean cheese or some tamales from the land should be brought, but never a deliciously fragrant flower, much less a crimson rose with plush petals. I had not learned to be fine, or even elegant, until then and perhaps I would never learn. To my mind came a dinner served on fine china with French silverware, Christofle cutlery with an *art nouveau* design. The professor had put on a plaid wool jacket, a silk shawl and vertically striped pants. Maybe it wasn't wool, but cashmere. His wife wore a long dress made by Dior or Versace. I went with my best navy-blue jacket, a white shirt and a maroon tie. It seemed to me that somehow we were all dressed up for a fancy dinner. Maybe at some point I should return the courtesy when I could, at a three-star Michelin award-winning restaurant.

The butler served Pommery champagne and Château Ste. Michelle wine from a vineyard in Washington. The background music seemed to me to be *Capricho árabe*, by Francisco Tárrega, or perhaps it was *Rondó alla turca*, by Mozart. I remembered Cacho Tirao playing *Zorba the Greek* on a Spanish guitar.

The conversation touched on several topics. It started with climate change attributed to global warming. The professor's wife was dismayed that in some parts of the mountain range the snow was disappearing. She mentioned a lake that had left cattails where the edge of the water had been. I told her that condors lived on a mountain with perpetual snow, above the knot that joined the cordilleras. What I didn't know was whether the birds nested in the snow or in the rock.

We agreed that one of the most beautiful spectacles of nature was the detachment of the ice blocks of the Perito Moreno glacier. I imagined the sound of the collapse and the splashing of the water. We did not talk about politics or recession or corrupt governments. We ended by recalling the tragic event of Guimpel's death, which had struck us all. She felt troubled and he seemed to have a poorly disguised anxiety crisis, with trembling fingers and chattering teeth. This was how he manifested his depression. Suddenly Assad said, "Guimpel was as German as Goethe and Wagner. Whoever wanted to invent the plot of the Jew hiding in the sewers was not honoring his memory..." he didn't finish the sentence, but it made me think that his anti-Semitism was hiding behind it.

I didn't mention it that time, but there were other Germans who were descended from Jews: Einstein and Marx. I thought they were not the only ones; in fact, we could mention German Jews, Slavic Jews, Russian Jews, American Jews.

"There is nothing more unjust than intolerance," said the Turk, and his wife nodded in agreement.

I would have liked to add something to the commentary. I do not understand anti-Semitism in people who, on the other hand, admire Charles Chaplin, Marcel Proust and the Marx Brothers. I would have liked to talk about the fact that shortly before I had read *Journey to the End of the Night* by Louis-Ferdinand Céline, a doctor who had revolutionized the literature of his time. A humanist thinker who, at the same time, was a self-confessed anti-Semite. At that moment I thought of the influence of the political situation on collective thought. The phenotype of the fauna during the thaws of the post-glacial era. Louis-Ferdinand Céline was a hero of the First World War; a hero who had been wounded in the trenches, with damage that involved curettage of bones and muscles to remove splinters and prevent bedsores of the devitalized part. This minimized the risk of amputating the entire limb. At the same time that the bone fragments were removed, the tolerance was cut off. Céline hated the *Protocols of the Elders of Zion* but he believed in the economic and political control of Jewish bankers. For my part, I did not want to add my opinion on the matter.

As I traveled at night on a C line trolleybus, I thought about how it had been a long time since that invitation. I thought that time had aged the memory to the point that it seemed as if the dialogue had taken place in the distant past. Perhaps, the dinner and its prolegomena did not happen as I remembered, and it was all part of an imaginative avalanche.

I recalled the Russian Velkovski's face, which seemed to have a stubborn embarrassment; someone in the classroom said that the Russian had disappeared after a raid in his neighborhood. Had it been the hitmen of the Triple A, or a task force linked to the army? We could neither know nor investigate, as it was risky. Velkovski had a girlfriend of special beauty, she had black hair and blue eyes. Every feature seemed to have been composed by a hyperrealist painter. I could not believe, no one could imagine, that Velkovski was linked to a subversive organization or, at least, to a human rights group. Someone commented that it must be a mistake. The Russian played the violin extraordinarily well, and maybe another wind instrument, but we never had any indication that he was linked to a political group. A conversation with a Jewish guy named Rabinovich, a psychotherapist of the new post-Gestalt school, came to mind, "I am interested in primitive peoples," he said, and then gave an explanation of his interest in the subject. I am enthusiastic about the behavior of the people. I would like your help in finding information about some groups living in the Andes, either on artificial islands or in dens in the massifs." At that time there was a fascination for the primitive.

"The Uros live on an artificial island on Lake Titicaca. As construction material they used mud, alpaca dung and totora reeds. I once heard that they may have been the first inhabitants of the lake. As for communities living in open caves in the mountain range, I remember the Catacamaras, who lived in villages of adobe huts with conical roofs. They also lived in hollows carved out of the limestone rock by erosion."

Perhaps they were the closest thing to cavemen and that made the psychotherapist uneasy. Perhaps, at certain times of the year, they used the caves as a dwelling, or also as a refuge after raiding the muleteer caravans that traveled the supply routes. I tried to see if that was the information Rabinovich was looking for. Then I explained to him that the Catacamaran were highwaymen and herders of auquenidos (alpaca like animals) in villages located above four thousand meters above sea level. At the same time, I asked myself: "What could Rabinovich be looking for in this information? Did he want to formulate a hypothesis about the adaptation of a collective to its environment, to affirm the resilience of a tribe that belonged to an ethnic group, or was his interest more predictive, did he want to know something about the adaptive capacity of human groups that survived an atomic conflagration?

I did not want to find out the background of the interest shown by a guy on a subject I knew only little about. I knew that reasoning became complex to the extent that it was nourished by contexts. I had once heard an individual talk about the diaspora as if it were a collective school of learning, in which each person or group participated with its load of experiences. I never came to understand the reasoning of people different from my context. The complexity of reason is hard enough to try to interpret the opinions of others.

I pondered in silence. Then I tried to explain to the psychotherapist the details of the islands and the dens. The huts of these human groups, like the huts of the villages of

Huarochirí, have conical roofs; not like the rest of the ethnic groups, who build gabled roofs. To make myself understood, I drew a conical roof over a cylindrical hut. Then, remembering Professor Quevedo and his colleague Imbelloni, I had to make it clear to him that these differentiated characteristics could insinuate that they were ethnic groups with different origins. Then I kept quiet, because I was not sure that I could remember the migratory currents of America. Perhaps Rabinovich would be able to offer me a more encyclopedic explanation of the movements of groups in other parts of the world.

When Guimpel's suicide occurred, there were those who pointed to Rabinovich as the intellectual author of the professor's questioning. Then I remembered a fellow student with whom I coincided during my oncology internship, Salomon Yelin; a brilliant student whose notebooks were purchased by publishers to produce compendiums on internal medicine. Yelin wanted to return to Israel to practice medicine on a kibbutz in the Negev desert, or perhaps work on the outskirts of Eilat. There is no doubt: there are guys who are lucky or have an uncanny sense of timing that leads them to succeed in their pursuits.

I did not want to speculate on other aspects of emotional intelligence linked to success. Velkovski's bride looked to me like a watercolor by Sorolla; even more, it evoked a painting by Serge Marshennikov. The painter is also Russian, like Velkovski and his bride, perhaps from Odessa or St. Petersburg.

The trip through the deserted streets, the proximity of Assad's house and the memory of Guimpel's death evoked strange associations of ideas in me. I conjectured that Rabinovich was, in addition to being a psychotherapist, one of the commandos of a Mossad cell, or a member of a lodge whose purpose was to capture and torture SS war veterans, as well as those involved in the extermination of Auschwitz, Dachau and other concentration camps. I assumed that this was an unimaginable plot. I imagined that the organization was composed of dissimilar individuals: Velkovski was an agent provocateur, infiltrated within Bolshevism to betray the clandestine members. His disappearance was due to the fact that he had aroused the suspicions of some of the commanders of the most active subversion cells. For this reason, the organization arranged for his return to Israel.

Tamara, Velkovski's beautiful girlfriend, managed to penetrate the organizations of female relatives of the disappeared, as one of those who had also suffered the kidnapping and subsequent disappearance of her partner. Once she learned the names of the women involved in the movement and the support groups, she was kidnapped by the agents of the Task Forces, who received the instruction not to touch her at all. On the contrary, they were to hand her over to the instructors who, in turn, were agents of a foreign power. Within this delirium, Yelin, the brilliant student of the faculty, was, moreover, an informer of student movements and professors who had joined anti-government groups of any flag. Assad blamed the Zionists for the provocation that led to Guimpel's suicide. As I put the threads of the plot together, I realized that I was turning into a creator of thriller novels, as if I were dealing with a plot with intelligence and counter-intelligence implications.

The trolleybus was gliding into the night. I could not tell how much time had passed inside the vehicle, even though my watch read two o'clock in the morning. The last passengers were descending through both doors, which opened with a sound of greased pistons. The squeaking came from outside, possibly from the connection of pulleys and electrical cables. At some point the driver yawned, an unmistakable sign that we were reaching the end of the journey. I don't know if the man used a microphone or imposed his voice, but he blurted out: "Well, gentlemen, the trip is over! This is the final stop. He then parked the bus in an empty space between two vehicles. The remaining passengers inside went down the embankment. I feared I might not be able to find another way back to the city center.

I walked several blocks of streets illuminated by neon streetlamps, until I reached a place that looked like a nightclub. There was an intermittent sound that sounded like villera music, or maybe it was Central American salsa. Nothing identifiable. I guessed that inside the pitiful *boliche* were dancing horny women. A huge guy, standing at the entrance door, a security guard or a pimp, was in charge of hooking up the business. He asked me, "Do you have a reservation?" I replied that I didn't have one, without adding anything about my desire to enter the place or not. There were several vehicles parked at the curb.

I thought I had lived the same story a long time ago. That time the ones having fun were conscript soldiers on their day off. The women were barrack sluts. On that occasion everything ended in a scandalous mess, with several wounded and bruised, after the brawl broke out, first among the women and then generalized to all the attendees. I was rewarded with an internal ulcer in the mug and a tooth that remained loose in its socket for some time. The same scene for having arrived at the wrong place. The same feeling of nausea and retching. I wondered what part of this story was a dream and what part was reality.

I would have liked to analyze my personal life, perhaps motivated by the revelry of that place. Smiling girls at the School of Medicine. Women wearing suggestive dresses, that were sometimes almost transparent. Most of them seemed to combine their beauty with some lightness. They were probably the same kind of girls I would find in front of a night bar in the Quartier Pigalle, in the 9th arrondissement of Paris or outside the doors of the Nouvelle Athènes literary café, which was reminiscent of an

Edgar Degas painting. Maybe it was not Paris, but New York and the neighborhood was Times Square with its diagonal avenue Broadway. Seventh Avenue changed its name to Fashion Avenue, between 36th and 43rd Streets, where the New Yorkers could be seen tearing it up. Suits, dresses, hairstyles, extravagances, everything imaginable. Once one of those girls asked me, "What country are you from?"

Noticing that I was slow to answer convincingly, she stated, "You're not from here."

I had to explain my origin. Small neighborhood streets, some of them with sidewalks or on the road itself, slopes from where you could see the downtown districts and the cathedral, built in the sixteenth century. I could have told her that in my youth I had swum in a small bay in the ocean called Cataratas. The place was at utterly calm with the breakers of the waves at a distance of two hundred strokes offshore.

She looked at me like one looks at a madman. I'm sure she regretted having asked the question. I also confessed that I remembered a professor by the nickname of Osiris, who was trying to explain to us the overlapping of cultures in the development of mankind. Listening to me, the girl must have thought she was in front of a totally crazy guy, a native of some very ancient and somewhat exotic place that she could not locate on a globe, as she did not know if it was on one continent or another.

At the first yawn from her, I finished the explanation. I kept many memories that I did not want to share with anyone. I kept quiet; I wanted to offer her a colorful drink that seemed to me a combination of non-miscible liquids because they overlapped forming layers. After drinking, she walked away down an avenue; I don't remember if it was a boulevard facing the Place de la Republique, in the 10th arrondissement of Paris, or was it Seventh Avenue, in the colorful advertisement area of Times Square, in

Manhattan. After saying goodbye, I walked a few blocks and then hailed a cab.

I went back in memory to my student room, with the dirty cups of granulated coffee and, on the same worktable, several volumes of books piled up. Then I suffered from sighing dyspnea, which explained the melancholy of past times.

Chapter 5
The Colt Gallop

The galloping of wild colts in front of the truck that traveled the trails between muddy fields and dense jungle, seemed to me part of a fantasy. I could see their legs, wet from the sweat of the trot, and their manes waving. At times the road stopped at a speed bump dug by the waters of a stream; then it crossed a pool of dark water. Sleep invaded me as the driver struggled to find his way through the undergrowth and mud.

I had a wealth of recent experiences that left me with a sense of fulfillment. So, I needed to digest the bad times and the good friendships.

I met Zaragoza at the Waldorf Astoria in New York. We were in the Big Apple on business: the great dengue epidemic in Central America, which was why we had come to the United Nations building. He was to explain how the disease had influenced the migratory movement of people. I was to relate the outbreak to the arrival of Asian immigrants. We struck up a friendship in one of the pubs in Greenwich Village, where he went with his wife, a Nicaraguan friend of Bianca Jagger and Rigoberta Menchú. The Nicaraguan woman's name was Estela and, despite her angular features, she boasted an enigmatic beauty, inherited from a Slovenian mother and a Central American Creole father. From the very first moment the lady seemed to me to be on the alert, as if she was afraid of unraveling something recondite. Those were times of double talk and cautious silences; it was better not to take unnecessary risks.

As we listened to a jazz band, Estela justified her residence in New York, where she worked at UN headquarters. "My activities and friendships would have harmed Saul's professional and political career." She was referring to Zaragoza, who had already explained to us in detail the tragedy of some brigadistas who had been kidnapped by psychopathic killers in the north of his country, in an area victim of armed conflict. The captors were drug traffickers and, in turn, hard-core addicts on the run. These guys recruited people from among the ill-fated in the coastal areas of Guatemala, Belize and Honduras; people whose main activity was the transfer of drugs to the southeastern coast of the United States.

After recounting the rampage, Zaragoza asked himself the same question he asked himself at the time: "Who the hell had recruited those sons of bitches?" The answer was in his mind: the Minister of the Interior or the Minister of War. Or maybe a guy who worked in an office in the National Congress Palace itself. And as they recounted the events in detail, we had dinner with Hozier playing *Take Me to Church* in the background. I listened to it, really feeling every detail of the lyrics. It differed from jazz and any other kind of music; it was madness invading the last redoubt of the human.

Zaragoza interrupted the story at times to participate in a toast and then continued. "The subjects were tattooed all over their bodies, they were an orgy of blue and red on the face, back and shoulders. I had to find the brigadistas."

Dr. Zaragoza was head of the Metaxenic Diseases Area of the Guatemalan Ministry of Health. "No one would give me any information. Nobody knew what had happened at the edge of the marshes next to the Caribbean Sea. Comandante Jackal was part of a story of horror and blood, but nobody knew the beginning of the story. Who had the hell recruited that son of a bitch? No one knew the ending anyway. Maybe one of his jackals had attacked him from behind, or maybe the ephebus himself or the androgynous woman had stabbed him in the chest in the middle of a relationship.

"Of the brigadistas, not a shadow. Only a report of a guy who proclaimed himself a witness of the facts in the mangroves, near the Maya constructions. No one could vouch for whether the witness was an individual who had been arrested by the jackals and fled from his captors or one of those recruited by the alienated man with the tattoos.

"I went to visit the family huts of the brigadistas' families. No sign of them or their families; they had surely migrated to avoid the mess. Just a couple of crosses on the side of the road as if it had been a traffic accident. A one-armed man who had lost his mind and was begging for alms in one of the streets of Puerto Barrios, in the department of Izabal. What was not clear to me was whether there were women in the Jackal's group. Maybe there were. I assumed that in the self-defense groups, women were recruited to search the enemies or to prepare the concoction," said Zaragoza.

"In the end, what did you come to know?" interrupted Estela, who had followed the narration in detail.

"Well..." Zaragoza wanted to toast to our recent friendship. "To you and to better times ahead." Then he continued, "We found the witness in a village in the department of Petén. After putting him between a rock and a hard place, he told us the story. The man called himself Comandante Chacal. He had tattoos of dragons, women, mermaids and swastikas all over his body, even on his face. He was as dangerous as hurricanes.

"The brigadistas were his first civilian victims, along with the health personnel of the peripheral posts in the Maya strip. After a mock summary trial, in which they were accused of belonging to guerrilla support groups, which supplied them with medicines and surgical instruments, the shit-eating Jackal condemned them to death. Our informant explained that it was the Jackal himself who interrogated them.

"It was more or less a matter of, 'What are they doing in the zone, don't they know this is a red zone?' Our brigade leader told him that the group had no political ties to any group in conflict, that the only thing they did in the area was to locate ponds in the marshes to spray insecticide, because there had been cases of malaria in the area.

"The subject who informed us of the event pointed out that the brigadista was trembling while the said commander was being fondled by a tomboy. No one knew if it was an androgynous woman or a tranny. Suddenly, one of the madmen swung a machete at a brigadista and cut his arm off." He paused, thinking that the moment was not right for dark comments while we ate veal.

"It is very cruel, but it is better to know what these madmen are made of...

"You know that malaria caused more deaths than the accidents that occurred during the construction of the Panama Canal. The border of Belize and Mexico, through which drugs for the Zetas transit, is in the Gulf itself, a few hundred kilometers away. The issue of dengue fever is recent; we have always had malaria. That was the reason for the sanitary brigades in the National Plan to fight against Metaxenic Diseases. You can imagine the poor man, convulsing in pain while the stooges died laughing."

I don't know why I was presented with the figure of a guy I met many years ago. When I saw him from a distance, I thought the man was black or had skin covered with what looked like a dye, a symptom of Addison's disease, but as I got closer I realized that his face was covered with tattoos, which contrasted with a sclera that I thought was exaggeratedly white. "Hysterical flower," I said to myself as I listened to the story. Perhaps I had gotten the idea that his companion would be a short-haired woman with an androgynous body or perhaps a slender boy with feminine manners. In any case, she was the partner of the tattooed guy, who served as the commander of the extermination group. There was not much to expect from that couple and their henchmen.

The rest of the scene was easy to guess. The guy was shouting like a madman, "I'll leave you cold, you fuckers!" He may have said it in a different tone and with a different accent, but it was just as threatening.

The brigade leader responded, "I would like to contact the Minister of Health by radio. He can explain the reason for our stay in the area. No one would believe it."

Then the tattooed man screamed in his face, "What the fuck do I care about the order of the minister's bagel! I'm the one in charge here, you cunt! Do you understand? Fuck off with the minister's story, you fucking cunt!" The bombastic voice would make the brigadiers tremble. Most likely they would shit their pants, which made a deplorable spectacle that provoked the mockery of the predators.

"The witness described the smell of cattle dung, the stench of marijuana stalks. No one could tell if the witness belonged to a group of paramilitaries who had joined the gang or was a repentant member of the gang itself."

Dessert at this dinner in Greenwich Village consisted of strawberries in port wine. Zaragoza continued to explain how, taking advantage of the cover of the war against subversion, all kinds of revenge and abuses were carried out against the civilian population. The paramilitaries were accused of perpetrating a racist war with the objective of exterminating the Quiché agrarians, the Ixil Indians and the Maya ethnic group in all its local variants. In order to proceed with the xenophobic genocide, they recruited unsuccessful subjects: elements of the local underworld, ex-convicts and agrarian resentments, to create an army of mercenaries with fixed pay and prizes for their deeds. In addition, they were given freedom of action: they could keep the proceeds of looting, blackmail and take over the property of their victims.

The toll was tens of thousands of dead during the internal war between 1962 and 1983. The majority of dead were natives who wore suits with flowered ribbons on the hem of their skirts or embroidered bows on the bottoms of their pants. The women wore multicolored serapes and woven headdresses over their hair. I asked myself: "Weren't these the heirs of the Maya civilization, weren't they the creators of the Maya calendar? At the same time that I was answering my doubts, I realized that the pre-Columbian past of a culture of pyramid builders in the middle of the jungle was no longer of any interest, nor were the papers signed by the encomenderos and viceroys of the kingdoms of Spain. There was no fascination in fighting for the rights of the Indigenous peoples, as enshrined in the United Nations Charter and in the Constitution, the law of laws of the nation. Other issues, such as the discovery of oil reserves in the northeastern zone, in the Ixil strip, were of interest. It was important to preserve the interests of the nickel miners during the time of the highest price of the metal, since it was used in alloys with silver and gold to mint coins. In recent times it was also used in the aeronautical industry and for the manufacture of engines.

Saúl Zaragoza, national director of the Metaxenic Diseases Program, explained that in January 1980 the Spanish embassy in Guatemala City was taken over. Workers, students and peasants took part in the occupation. The episode ended with the death of thirty-seven people who were attacked with white phosphorus bombs. Those who fled through the walls that adjoined the mansion of a landowner were chased from house to house. The troops were ordered to shoot to kill anyone who looked suspicious, whether it was an individual with a strange limp or a guy with half his face bandaged from phosphorus burns. For them, anyone loitering in the vicinity of the embassy was a suspect. Hospitals were also ordered to be searched for people with deformed faces or neck or scalp phlyctenas.

The official version implicated Ambassador Máximo Cajal, who was accused of being an accomplice or, at least, an accessory to the illegal occupants, who had also kidnapped public figures and former public officials, such as former Vice President Eduardo Cáceres Lehnhoff and former Foreign Minister Adolfo Molina Orantes. Both of them were killed during the assault, along with the occupants of the embassy, including Rigoberta Menchú's father. The occupation had no witnesses.

After the episode, Ambassador Cajal had to hide in the residence of some friends, and then take refuge in the headquarters of another embassy, as he was aware that his life was in danger. Later he had to be rescued by an international mission that took him to Spain. By then relations between the two countries were broken.

The news was broadcast by the main television networks and led the newscasts, which denounced the atrocities during the internal war involving different military governments in Guatemala. At the same time, the first voices were heard denouncing the genocide in the Ixil strip. The natives had been executed by the regular army and paramilitary armed groups. The international news picked up the interview of a fifteen-year-old boy who spoke of events that had been suspected but never proved.

"I was twelve years old when they took my parents and my siblings." The young man was a Quiché Indian. "They took them away and we never heard from them again."

"You were twelve years old; do you remember in detail what happened?" asked the reporter accompanying Rigoberta Menchú.

"It is engraved in my memory. You will understand that it was the saddest thing I have ever experienced. I have relived it so many times," he continued, "My father was shot at the door of the bar and thrown into the truck bed. I still cry as if it happened yesterday. It was around 1982. I was twelve years old. I was born in 1970. Sir, my family grew corn. We were all sleeping on a mat when the self-defense groups came and entered the shack, sir. The worst thing is that we never knew if my father had died right there, and they threw him dead in the box."

"And your mother, did you hear anything from her after the kidnapping" continued the BBC London correspondent.

"And... what am I going to know about her and my little brothers? It was President Ríos Montt himself who ordered the extermination of the Mayas and the Catholics. Ríos Montt was an evangelist." This was the fourth interview the survivor had given on the same subject, and he already doubted that it would be of any use.

The boy's statement came before the conversation I had with Zaragoza and his wife in a Manhattan restaurant. What had become of the fate of the Jackal commander? I imagined the son of a bitch with a broad back covered in blue tattoos against a background of dark skin barely visible under the graffiti on his skin. I assumed that his partner had suffered a few bouts of manic-depressive psychosis before taking her own life in an orgy on methamphetamines.

I thought criminals had nine lives, like cats; they were bulletproof in ambushes, stabbed in the back, blown up in minefields. He was almost certain that the son of a bitch was still involved in drug trafficking along the border with Belize. Perhaps he had become the coordinator of a group of hitmen at the service of the northern or Gulf of Mexico cartels. Then I remembered the summary trials in Guatemala during the dictatorships that followed from Peralta Azurdia to Rios Montt, including Romeo Lucas Garcia. Faceless tribunals that left no possibility to file a writ of amparo, *habeas corpus* or any other plea to prove the innocence of the accused. The barbarity was completed with the creation of paramilitary self-defense groups, especially in the department of Quiché, where more than 600,000 members acted with a license to act, carrying out predatory actions. Subjects recruited in the barracks of the city or in the fishermen's coves, who joined the agrarians who resented the lack of laborers for the harvest. All of them were recruited with the promise of a fixed weekly salary and piecework payments for causing damage to the enemies of the regime.

The process got out of hand from the start. The snitches multiplied. Psychopaths reproduced in the bars of the coves and in the villages. And the commanders got permission to kill. Among them, one of the most active, Commander Jackal.

"Saúl, my love, you had news of other deaths of your people: rural doctors, health workers and brigadistas." I heard Estela's Argentinean voice, which reminded me of other powerful voices: Carmen Aristegui and Bianca Jagger. "It is just as they denounce every day in the UN offices. First Southeast Asia, then the war in the Persian Gulf. The fleets of the apocalypse. Steel monsters painted dark blue, with fighter planes and bombers on their decks. The chemical industry manufacturing weapons of mass destruction that are dropped from airplanes and helicopters on territories where there is a population. Napalm bombs and other types of exfoliating explosives used to destroy vegetation and enemy supplies. They use corrosive substances that affect the skin and mucous membranes and cause severe burns.

"To avoid the effects of the bombs, the survivors build thousands of kilometers of subway tunnels, as well as nets stretched in the trees. The men submerge themselves in water to avoid contact with the poison, taking advantage of the lagoons, ponds and even puddles opened by the bombs. They had to keep their bodies under water to prevent the affected skin from detaching from its subcutaneous matrix. They breathed with hollow reeds that soon filled with saliva and toxic substances, so they had to change them regularly.

"Survivors show scars on the neck, armpits, ribs, flanks and pubis. All stigmata. Many have disfigured faces as if covered by plastic masks, with the choanae flush with the face, like two deformed incisions. Those who had aspirated some substance suffered from laryngeal stenosis or high tracheal stenosis. The stridor of their breathing could be heard from a distance as an expiratory whistle.

"It looked like an action movie, with lots of deaths and images reminiscent of the apocalypse. But there was no Cormac McCarthy script behind it, it was fucking life! It was as simple as that. In the Iraq-Iran war, neurotoxic gases with names like sarin, tabun, soman and VX were used on a massive scale. The result was more than twenty thousand dead and toxic effects on another eighty thousand humans in the ranks of the Iranian army. Then, as if on cue, the Iraqis got their turn at the bad end. One for another. The dice were cast on a Persian rug, or maybe it was on a Castilian blanket. The sum of points gave several losers. The fulsome player won, so the die was cast. Iraq would be invaded by warriors from across the sea. Syria was bombed from the air. The oil wells and reservoirs would be set on fire.

"Since then, there has been an all-out war. The cities of ancient Mesopotamia are destroyed. The Sunnis fight against their Shiite brothers. There was death and destruction. And then came the time of the caliphate and the warriors of Daesh, always dressed in black in permanent mourning, with black flags and black turbans. Cities were set on fire and then ended up under the rubble by the action of bombing. No one was spared by the war. Neither the children nor the old. No one was spared the destruction, which came from the air in the form of fighter planes or bomb-laden drones."

"I didn't know you had those reports, my love. I'm sorry. Mine turns out to be a penny a piece," commented Zaragoza, referring to the crude scenario and the drama shown by Estela, his wife.

"The warriors exploded. Collapsed buildings became machine gun nests and bazooka shells fell on every level. There was no blood left to transfuse for those who had lost liters from bone, abdominal or chest wounds. Antibiotics were used on a large scale to prevent anaerobic rot at the edge of wounds and on the stump of amputations.

"The defenders and attackers of the enclave were short of breath. Women and men mourned the death of those close to them by hitting themselves on the head. They even went so far as to mourn the fate of strangers who shared their tragedy.

"In the city, the children lost an arm, a leg, parts of their faces, eyes, and their photographs showed resigned expressions. The attackers had the same face, the same features and the same clothing as the defenders of the territory, as if they had been copied from the others or were the negative of a photograph."

When Estela Zaragoza paused, I felt like applauding the master class we were receiving during dinner. In the meantime, I remembered Jimi Hendrix and Charlie Parker at the Cafe Wha? And... well, excuse me for the length. Excuse me for...

Then I thought of the nomadic caravans of Afghanistan, with the woolly bovids they call yak, the belongings and the children on the animals' backs, behind the fat hump. The men were dressed in winter rags and covered in mud. Snow covered the muleteers' route. The boxes, on the backs of Himalayan oxen, looked like wooden coffins, but they contained smuggled weapons that the Taliban sent to warriors in Iraq and Syria. Someone blurted out, "But if the soldiers of the caliphate are enemies of the Al Qaeda militiamen." No one understood the terms of each group or what the value of the checkerboard was. The Druze remained loyal to the Al Asad regime. The Turks attacked the sites of the Kurdish defenders, and the Russian allies did the same in the cities taken by the fundamentalists. The Islamic brothers were hiding in the barracks. No feeling, not even with themselves or their children, because their fathers were shadows in the gloom; ghosts of memory lost in the mist.

And nothing. In this situation life doesn't matter, not even your own life. I don't know what those men with bristly beards and matted hair would think, nor the young, bearded men who barricaded themselves on the rooftops of the apartment buildings to resist the onslaught until the end. Nor did I know what the women who hid their faces under the burqa or covered their heads with the hijab to comply with the precepts of the Koran - not to show their beauty or their tears - were thinking.

And when everything seemed to presage the end of the sects, the analysts realized that the objective had not been achieved. On the contrary, it was not clear who was winning. Some, the more objective ones, were of the opinion that this war was futile, where no one would achieve victory, not even the initial purposes of establishing a place, activating a generalized sentiment, overthrowing a government or expelling the powers that be.

In the metropolis, discordant voices arose, questioning the war, the futility of the conflict, the expenses, the time wasted, the mountains of dollars lost. The data were published in *Blackwater. The rise of the world's most powerful mercenary army*, by Jeremy Scahill. The transnational security company with more than twenty thousand mercenaries trained in wars of extermination. The promoters had enormously profitable contracts signed by President Bush. Wagner's music covering up the screams of the tortured, the same gimmicks as before. Of course, there was gangrene and an epidemic of pneumonia from opportunistic bacteria. *4321 by* Paul Auster. Just as recondite as the Vietnam War. So much so that the times and objectives were confused.

I had seen the images of women and children before the My Lai massacre. In the sequence, in a second photograph, SP5 Capezza soldiers are seen burning Vietnamese huts. The third photograph shows the corpses of the women and children, almost lined up on a narrow path, which I presume was the entrance to the village. The massacre was attributed to 2nd Lt. William Laws Calley. Commander Nguyên Giáp had anticipated that in an all-out war many combatants would die before the invaders were driven out.

The memory took me back to the images that were leaked on social networks about the torture of Al Qaeda members. In them you could see hooded men with a kind of white tunic covering their faces, hanging with ropes tied to a ceiling beam. The men received electric shocks that made their bodies shake in a swinging motion that simulated a clonic convulsion. Everything seemed to indicate that names and circumstances were simply repeated: Saigon, Baghdad, Aleppo, Huế, Hanoi, Islamabad, the Mesopotamian region, the Mekong Delta, the Persian Gulf, the Indochina peninsula, Laos, Cambodia.

Life was not a drama, but a tragic satire. Then I remembered what my friend Daniel Gutiérrez had told me about his participation in the Gulf War. "Are you sure, that it's not one of your rants to make yourself feel important?" I asked him once again. He went on to talk about the aircraft carriers, with their grappling hooks and steel cables to catch the planes on landing and the thrusters that catapulted them during takeoff. To give seriousness to his explanations, he said it in English: *"Arrivals and departures"*. He thought this made it more convincing.

Maybe it was the war that made him crazy. He was a post-traumatic psycho from the fucking war. Like those who ride the subway trains that run above ground in Harlem and the Bronx. Maybe he played in a band of street musicians inside the station between Seventh Avenue and 42nd Street. Maybe he was part of a city tribe that lived in Jersey City or Paterson, on the other side of the Hudson River. What happened next would be part of a true story, without euphemisms. Daniel walking through the streets of the district. On the sidewalk some men are sitting on wooden benches or on the ground itself. They laugh. They look drunk even though the time of day is not appropriate. I feel sorry for him.

Dinner was over and I returned to the Waldorf Astoria. Zaragoza was leaving the next day for Guatemala City, and I had a pending conversation with Friedman of Philadelphia University. He wanted to lead a team of immunologists to South America and needed to know where he could conduct research on rare tropical diseases. I thought of São Paulo. At the same time, I could have some link with the Hospital Israelita Albert Einstein.

While the couple talked, I thought that the story touched me as a voyeur. I never understood the argument. It seemed to me part of the chapters of Kafka's *The Trial*. But real life reproduced the plot of fiction. Or the fiction had been written in a similar context. There was a putrid smell in the air, of cigarettes and pungent perfumes with an undertone of armpit. The heat of the day irritated all of us, the morning dew bounced off the ground and put us in a shitty mood. People walked along the avenues with the smoke of melted asphalt and the stench of the port. "You have to shut up!" Just like that. Then I started reminiscing about each of the ambushes I had suffered.

Sometimes, not on every trip, a Maltese horse would trot in front of the vehicle, as if trapped by the wooded fence that runs along the roadside. It would pant as it galloped, its nostrils foaming and its back shiny with sweat. Its tail would swing pendulously behind its haunches. The floor of the road, made of gravel and a clay-like mud, seemed to splinter like gravel and crusts of mud flew up against the vehicle.

On one particular occasion I thought the animal was playing with the four-wheel drive truck as part of a reception ceremony typical of the valley; or perhaps it had nothing to do with advertisements or humans. The dark back reflected the last rays of sunlight; the mane moved in the wind as if waving; the haunches moving to the rhythm of an eternal escape. All this made me think of myths with winged horses soaring through the air, the allegory of steeds rising from the seed of Medusa's blood, wounded by Perseus. Suddenly Buraq carried on his back the prophet Mohammed, guided by the archangel Gabriel, in search of the seventh heaven and the face of God.

That horse, which led the way through the forest, was part of the wild herds that remained in the valley that became cloud forest as we climbed the escarpment. I assumed that the horses had belonged to some stable of an old hacienda which, at the same time, must have been a sugar cane mill and a liquor factory. I wanted to believe that were also packs of dogs or cats without owners that, from time to time, would sneak into the settlers' villages to kill chickens and other domestic animals. The next day the foxes would be blamed for the pungent stench of urine they left behind.

The wild horses grazed in the wetlands and ran along the road, taking advantage of the open spaces so as not to get tangled in the trees; perhaps they also climbed along the paths trodden by the goats, and then descended through the clearings until they reached the banks of a sounding stream with sparkling water, where they quenched their thirst.

As the vehicle moved along the road, I kept watching the horse, which trotted, avoiding the thistles of the bank and the branches of the trees that bordered the road. At times it seemed to me that the wet back emitted iridescent reflections, like the reverberation of the flowers of the water lilies or the dewdrops on the wild begonias. It continued to lead the caravan for half an hour, until it disappeared from our sight around one of the bends of the road. What else could a horse with a dark flank, a mix of gray and brown, galloping in front of an English vehicle manufactured in the sixties do? I had to answer whoever wanted to know the answer. A concept similar to reality, like any other idea, not exactly accurate. It vanished from our field of vision as if it had suddenly been swallowed up by the earth or the dense forest growing on the roadside. And that seemed impossible to me, due to the lack of holes for an animal of its size to slip through.

Beyond the pass stretched the low jungle savannah, furrowed by large rivers that meandered through the green surface. From the trail you could hear the mixture of noises that the jungle hides. In the concert I distinguished howler monkeys, colorful parrots, green frogs and insects with chitinous elytra.

I don't know if I fell asleep or was just dozing where I was assaulted by thoughts in which I saw myself on the edge of a trail similar to the one we were traveling with the four-wheel drive vehicle. Suddenly someone stopped the car. Seconds later I was forcibly lowered, with my hands tied behind my back. The leader of the group ordered me to kneel on the edge of the sidewalk. I heard the voice of my captors, although I could not see them because my back was turned to them.

One of the guys listed the crimes for which I was being sentenced to death.: "The son of a bitch wanted to eat up the country," said someone in a nasal voice; perhaps an infamous-looking man with a huge belly and bushy mustaches. Another gave him an answer. From the difference in tone, I sensed that he was possibly lesser than the first.

"These are the worst," he blurted out, and pointed the gun at the back of my head.

I was shaking like a leaf, unable to distinguish between the reality of the trip to the jungle and my execution by those bastards I didn't know. Then I remembered the same images I had experienced in previous nightmares. Then I felt a blow to the back of my head; I didn't know if it was the impact of a bullet or a club. And I felt my body rolling down the slope.

As I fell I thought that, if it had been a bullet, it would have entered through a small hole in the occiput and, after detaching the aponeurosis, it would have exited through a nozzle in the frontal bone. At that instant I thought my body was in a garbage dump, or maybe it was a landing of stinging weeds. My abductors were throwing, from the edge of the slope, dirt and rubble over my body. I wanted to scream that I wasn't dead, that I hadn't committed any of the crimes they listed. I hesitated between begging for mercy or playing dead so they wouldn't finish me off.

When everything seemed to indicate that I would end up in one of the mass graves where other individuals, guilty and innocent, had been buried, I realized that the driver of the van was waking me up by shaking me by the shoulder. It had all been a nightmare.

"Thank you!" I exclaimed.

The man panicked, as if he was having a panic attack. When he was able to speak, he said to me, "You scared the hell out of me. You were screaming like crazy. I thought you had lost your mind."

I don't know if I asked him to forgive me for scaring him or if I kept quiet, as if I had not caused such a scandal. I felt sweaty and with the sensation of having my mouth and nostrils full of dirt and grass. When I reconnected with reality, I looked at the road, illuminated by the light of the vehicle's long-distance reflectors. I could not make out any horses. I tried to fix my eyes on the beam of light, which showed a cloud of insects playing with the glare of the truck's headlights. But I didn't see any horse, so I had no choice but to investigate. "What happened to the horse?" I wanted to know.

The driver of the Land Rover was puzzled, "What horse?"

I assumed I was hallucinating and it was all part of the nightmare. I feared I was raving, experiencing hallucinations and delusions. It had been an exhausting trip. Clammy humidity. Fever of insidious onset, with electrolyte changes and sodium depression from perspiration. These could have been the first symptoms of an illness and any of these alterations could have generated the delirium.

I had the sensation of traveling on a road that had penetrated the cloud forest. Hot air seemed to rise from the ground and from the leaves of the trees. The abandoned shacks brought back distant memories of children in a shelter set up to be a children's home, of old women taking turns caring for the little ones. Perhaps I was confusing Myanmar with another country; the refugee camps on the Thai border and the displaced from the war could have been confused with other children in other homes. I remembered my night duty visits at Centenario Hospital. The general wards with their cots arranged in two rows separated by light tables and screens with metal frames and canvas. I could almost smell the pine floor disinfectant and hear the noise of the urinals and the creaking of the doors of the wards; the whispers of the nurses and relatives crowded in the corridors. I thought I heard a murmur of a river coming down the mountain of rolling stones, the comments of the actors that melted into an unintelligible murmur.

Then I recalled meeting a woman in the isolation ward for patients with infectious diseases. She must have been between forty and forty-five years old. The room could have no more than four beds, where critical patients or those with symptoms of a communicable disease were placed. This time the only occupant of the isolation room was the woman. She looked emaciated from disease; her countenance indicated that she was suffering from periods of fever and consumption; she had sunken eyes and marked cheekbones. So far, I had no definite diagnosis of the disease: hemorrhagic fever due to the Junin virus transmitted by field rats. Or were these the prodromes of another type of illness with intermittent fevers? I prayed to God that it was not a hemorrhagic viral disease with a mortality of over forty percent, like other fevers caused by the arenavirus.

I had examined her carefully and found no ecchymosis at the rubbing sites, no petechial rashes or papules on the lower limbs. Apparently, she had no nosebleeds or petechiae due to platelet consumption. However, I was alert. I also examined the sclerae to distinguish splinter hemorrhages. I observed the palate, uvula, tonsils, gums. Fortunately, I did not find any signs. Then I explained some details that she did not fully understand.

She asked me, alarmed, "Luckily nothing what?"

"No evidence of bleeding," I clarified.

"Is it serious? Am I going to die?" she was panicked.

I didn't know what to answer. She took advantage of those seconds to tell me that she had had to flee the city after the disappearance of her only two living relatives and then had ended up in an abandoned ranch.

"Did you see any rats there?" I asked.

She replied that the area was near containers, next to the river, where there had probably once been a port for loading farm produce for export. More than likely there was a rats' nest somewhere nearby.

"Why? Do rats have something to do with the disease?" she was curious.

I wondered how a beautiful woman lived in such a place. Beneath the earthy pallor, fine features were visible, although her hair was matted, and her face had the ashen color of fever and wasting. I surmised that the woman had been beautiful in her time and still retained some features. It was noticeable in the expression of her lips and the way her forehead was furrowed, as well as in the color of her eyes and the softness of the palms of her hands. Maybe I had run into her on Florida Street in the federal capital. Maybe she was a girl from the Recoleta or San Telmo neighborhoods.

While I was trying to put together a work plan to address her illness, I remembered Professor Assad. I would have liked to have had him around to ask him questions about the woman's discomfort. He would have wanted to know if there were moist rales in the lung bases, or if I had touched the edge of the liver below the ribs, or if the spleen was palpable. I was unclear about the diagnostic pathway. Maybe I would have to go back to the history and question the orientation I was giving to the anamnestic data. The Turk had died some time before and his wife had returned to Europe to live with one of their children somewhere near Paris.

As the days went by, and although the fever persisted, her hydration improved. At times I noticed that she was communicative, as if seeking to clarify my concerns. She wanted to explain the reason for her current situation. "I was living in Villa Constitución, in a farm adjacent to the metal-mechanic factories, when the great workers' strike took place," she said.

I remembered that the event paralyzed the city and industrial steel production for more than two months. That was several years earlier, maybe five or six.

"And?" I urged her to continue the story.

"It was a night of chaos, people were running away trying to avoid being shot," she paused to catch her breath, then continued, "I couldn't see anything because we hid in the farm with the lights off. Suddenly a group of hooded men slipped into the entrance hall after breaking down the door with their guns. They forced my father and my brother to lie face down on the floor. I saw them handcuffed while they pointed their guns at the back of their heads. You don't know what terror. You could only hear screams."

"Fuck," I exclaimed to express my indignation and solidarity.

"And after the raid, they took my older brother and my father. They took them out handcuffed and dragged them to a small pond next to the sidewalk. Then nothing. The next day I went to file a complaint at the police station. There I was arrested for plotting slander, since that was not the method of the glorious Federal Police: kidnapping people.

"According to them, I was part of a smear campaign against the guardian institutions of the nation. Moreover, they suspected that I belonged to a subversive terrorist commando, a group to which, supposedly, my father and brother also belonged. That's what the feds thought," she explained. Then she spoke as if I didn't believe her or doubted the story. "You denounce a crime and the Federales, those sons of bitches, they treat you as if you're lying."

The woman was crying her eyes out as she told me her story, and I was shivering with fear that the same thing could happen to me at any time. At some point one of the residents on duty asked her, "Who were your relatives?"

"My father's name was José Luis Sachetti and my brother Luciano Gustavo Sachetti."

When I heard the name of the kidnap victims, I was reminded of the tragedy of Sacco and Vanzetti, the workers accused of an anarchist conspiracy in Massachusetts to which the prosecutors of the time had added the charge of murder and aggravated robbery. The Italian emigrants, laborers in a textile factory, belonged to a very active cell. Followers of the group led by Luigi Galleani, who, in addition to spreading his ideas in the *Revolutionary Chronicle*, was a supporter of acts of terrorism.

Sacco and Vanzetti were sentenced to death by electric chair. The sentence was carried out in August 1927, despite massive protests in New York, London, Amsterdam, Tokyo and Paris. The drama was made into a film in 1970 under the title *Sacco and Vanzetti*, directed by Giuliano Montaldo and starring Gian Maria Volonté and Riccardo Cucciolla. In the production Montaldo exculpates the workers of the crime and accuses a criminal group known as the Morelli gang, a mafia group specialized in armed robbery of banks and wealthy people.

I had to ask myself if the details of the nightmare were the result of something that happened to me in the past. Perhaps events that had been narrated to me about two guys coming along a trail in a place that looked like a wasteland. The individuals had matted hair and wore filthy rags. The older one told me that he was a doctor by profession and had been accused of curing rebels. The younger one did not tell me his profession, so I deduced that he must be a student. They were fleeing along an abandoned road that had been replaced by a four-lane asphalt road several years ago. The two roads were no more than five hundred meters apart.

The men walked at night and rested during the day so as not to be detected by helicopters or patrols combing the area. In the sunlight they hid among the poplars and weeping willows that dominated the hills. Their beards were half-grown, which told me that they must have escaped fairly recently. The boy confessed that he had become engaged to a Quiché Indian and attributed to that the persecution of the Federales, whom he considered a troop of fascists. The doctor accepted that he had cured some guerrillas for humanitarian reasons, but this did not mean that he was in league with them. At some point the man tried to explain, "If you were to walk through these woods, they would also have accused you of belonging to the rebel gang. To be fair, I thought it was dangerous to walk in the bush when we were immersed in a conflict with irregulars taking up arms against the regular army and the paramilitaries called self-defense groups.

"That time I was in a green pickup truck with silver hood ornaments. The vehicle had the logos of a medical support organization helping refugees emblazoned on the roof and doors of the car. After offering them some protein- and iron-fortified cookies and Coca-Cola, I told them, 'I can take you to a safe place where you can settle down. Do you know of any shelter for politically persecuted people?'

"The older man shook his head as the younger man seemed not to hear the conversation. I didn't know the country, but I assumed that there were hiding places for politically persecuted people or populations at risk of violence.

"After considering it for several minutes, the older man told me,

'Sir, we thank you, but every five hundred meters there are checkpoints for suspicious people and vehicles. We don't want to expose you to the risk of being considered an accessory to thugs or insurgents.' After a sigh, he added: 'We thank you, but we think it is better to continue walking through the bush.'

"I thought it was very considerate of them and very convenient not to risk my person and my mission. After that I saw their silhouettes on the horizon, moving away while I took the opposite direction.

"After half an hour, I found myself in a city of buildings of ten or more stories, with the streets illuminated by neon lights. Shop windows displayed all kinds of products. On the main streets and avenues signs announced art shows and concerts. It seemed that the city lived completely oblivious to the issues of the countryside and the conflict zones. I thought of the two travelers. Both faces had bristly beards. The older man's was gray; the boy's was black. I felt sorry for them. I wasn't clear where they were fleeing to, north, where the border was, or were they looking for a place of refuge? The logos on my van indicated that it was a medical support vehicle of the United Nations High Commissioner for Refugees, UNHCR. So sad. I felt I was living a farce in which I was the dilettante. A lot of slogans for a dubious work; maybe I was afraid of being involved."

My thoughts returned to the story of the woman with the contoured face who was struggling between life and death, I recalled the details of her evolution. It was as if I had to face an exam in a very difficult but important subject in my career. I kept every detail in my memory. I wrote down each finding in a notebook that I used to memorize. The dry mucous membranes. The fauces were congestive and with a membrane detachment in the pharyngeal arches. The sclera with venous dilatations that, at first glance, indicated a subconjunctival hemorrhage.

The fever did not abate despite treatment. I had prescribed three antibiotics, although the main suspicion was that it was a hemorrhagic viral infection. The latest test results showed a decrease in lymphocytes and platelets, which were lower than normal. It was likely that the first petechial bleeds would soon appear, despite the fact that platelet packs had been transfused, and intravenous pulses of polyvalent immunoglobulins had been administered in the last few days. The immunoglobulins were obtained from convalescent patients who had survived the disease. There were no commercial preparations of interferon yet, so we could not use the treatment explained in the updated medical literature. There was also no possibility to resort to specific antivirals or to opt for other drugs that would prevent viral replication. No other treatments came to mind.

I suspected that catastrophe was near, so I reread the latest published articles on arenaviruses. The information was sparse and mostly concerned hantavirus. In that moment of doubt I really missed Assad. "Maybe the professor would have found the answer," I said to myself. Although I was aware that he would have been out of date with the emergence of new diseases that had come out of nowhere, he would certainly have related the viruses of Africa to the microorganisms of the scrublands of the pampas, even though virology was science fiction in his day. I even seemed to hear his laryngeal voice reasoning with me. He would have postulated that a proto arenavirus had generated the current arenaviruses through a succession of mutations originated by RNA sequence breaks or by translocations of genes and codons. Perhaps there had been changes in the host or target organs; nests of T lymphocytes, matured in the thymus, had conditioned C lymphocytes to make proteins that would destroy the viruses. What I would have given for Assad to have come to the scene. He would have liked to help.

The image of the professor evoked memories of him with his wife. I thought about the gauzes and silks of her dresses and their Versaillesque manners together with the professor's intelligence and erudition. I would have preferred not to have witnessed his amnesias, his catatonic depressions, his involuntary movements, which indicated that his dementia was the product of multiple cerebral and cerebellar infarctions, as a consequence of arteriosclerosis in the cerebral ducts. It was probably due to his cigarette smoking. I imagined that arteriosclerotic vessels would have atheromatous plaques in the endothelium composed of foamy cells with a high content of low molecular weight cholesterol, with a proliferation of muscle cells at the periphery of the atheroma core. The changes caused by IL-5 interleukins and tumor necrosis factor (TNF), destabilizing the plaque to the point of ulceration, together with the platelet-derived growth factors that generated their aggregation, had originated the vessel-obliterating thrombi and cerebral infarctions.

If he had quit smoking ten years earlier, everything would have been different. "Why did you miss the opportunity?" I wished I asked.

But Assad would have answered me, "What the fuck are you talking about? It runs in my family, from my father and my father's father. It's fucking genetics."

I couldn't tell if he was referring to the cigarette addiction or the tendency to have multifocal infarcts in the brain. I understood that they too, his father and relatives, ended up in mental health hospitals or nursing homes for the elderly with some degree of dementia. Poor Mrs. Assad, with her paisley dresses and Parisian manners. She had to face the most painful part of her husband's existence.

She had been a student at the Sorbonne in Paris and then worked at the Pasteur Institute, in the 15th arrondissement, on rue de Docteur-Roux. At that time François Jacob and Jacques Monod headed the institute; in 1965 they would receive the Nobel Prize together with André Lwoff for their studies on the genetic control of enzyme and virus synthesis. Possibly, it was here that she met the professor and, after a romance between two lifestyles, the adventurer from Ankara and Beirut and the lady from scientific circles, who met in the 7th district and in the cafés near the Champ de Mars and the esplanade des Invalides, had decided to unite for the rest of their lives. The age difference was at least thirty years.

In the end she knew how to cope with the professor's weaknesses, tolerating his unnecessary courtship with the surrounding ladies, his high-flown phrases, his snoring and the nocturnal dyspnea that made him suddenly get out of bed in order to breathe with wheezing and rapid gasps, almost predecessors of sudden apnea and irreversible respiratory arrest. She respected him even after his death and devotedly kept his notes and articles on communicable diseases of the Rio de la Plata, the professor's main legacy. Within the notes, in pencil or in the margins of the books, was the description of a strange disease, whose etiological agent was unknown. It was attributed a lethality of more than fifty percent. The cases that had been reported occurred in the district of Junín, in the province of Buenos Aires.

I would wait for the professor to come to my aid; this happened every time a diagnosis became a problem. At that moment, he would arrive with the books of clinical pathology and virology and with a page separator in each book; copies that he would place on the table that we used for our discussions. He would then open the books at the places marked by the page dividers and explain to me, "Do you realize, kid, that it was just a matter of rereading the page?"

He would then remain silent.

That night, in the doctors' residence at the hospital, I reread the books to see if I had missed any notes or if it was a matter of waiting for someone to solve the riddles.

The woman, whose full name was Andrea Luciana Sachetti, became ill one afternoon in May. What I don't remember is whether it was before or after May 25th, the Day of the Fatherland. She was transferred to the intensive care unit (ICU) with assisted ventilation and received new platelet transfusions. There was no hope that she would be able to come off the machine, at least in the short term. Those of us who cared for her at the time felt a sense of guilt, as if we had not settled a debt. There was a sense that we had either failed to study or had not retained the necessary knowledge. It occurred to me to consider the shape of the virus in the sieve of an electron microscope. I would see the capsid as a mosaic of iridescent polygons that, in turn, became a sphere wrapped around the nucleic acid core. It replicated using the host's genetic material. I knew that mortality occurred within the first twenty days. Luciana had been struggling for almost a month.

Suddenly I thought of Florida Street and the girls who walked along the pedestrian street wearing semi-transparent dresses during the summer, which they hid under long trench coats and dressed up with boots during the winter. Luciana had little muscle mass; bones traced her contours under the skin. Her languid gaze seemed to say: "I want to live! Help me!". The bad thing is that we were either deaf or too busy to hear her cry.

The next morning I took a bus on the Chevallier line to the capital. I would never see her again, even if she had survived the illness. After four hours, I arrived at the bus station in Retiro square, where hawkers were selling handicrafts. Many of them were migrants from neighboring countries. From the entrance area of the station I could see the Sheraton Hotel tower and the edges of the village, with shantytowns between uneven buildings. I had the same impression as if I were in Villa Constitución or Ciudadela. Before arriving at the station I could make out the port cranes and container warehouses. The place was a berth for black rats and any of those bugs could be infected with the viruses of a field scavenger. Then tragedy would strike, like in those movies where cities are destroyed and the population is affected by a radioactive poison or an unknown pathogenic germ. The survivors would move along deserted avenues or roads without traffic, among collapsed buildings and ghost towns. In this case, catastrophe would follow the exodus of the population trying to avoid the disease.

A video of a city in my country came to my mind. It reproduced images taken in 1950, with narrow streets paved with cobblestones and parallel lines of railroad or streetcar tracks, although I knew we had never had a streetcar. The country people carried bread to market on the backs of llamas that moved with their necks erect and their black eyes peering. The bales hung over their flanks.

The video showed the inhabitants as if they were beings from another century, even another planet. The individuals wore striped ponchos, possibly colorful, and conical hats made of alpaca wool. Their expression of innocence and unconcern, typical of the inhabitants of the Andes, stood out. The women appeared seated on the sidewalk, in front of the wall of an ancient construction of high walls whitewashed with plaster. I presumed it was the wall of the city's central market. They had their produce, potatoes and herbs from the fields, spread out on woolen blankets similar to the ones they used to keep their backs warm.

The video had no audio. I got the idea that the women were talking to each other and to the buyers. Then I decided to investigate what was happening in the rest of the world that year. The reconstruction of Europe and Japan had begun; as had the rehabilitation of buildings on the periphery, destined to house families whose homes had been destroyed in the war. The displacement of entire populations knew no borders. The railroads moved the survivors of the tragedy.

I stopped to think about the personal and family dramas. The refugee barracks were full of orphans. No one knew the fate of their relatives, and no one had any information about the children; for example, their last names, where they came from, their relationship to other groups of displaced people. In this context I asked myself, "How important could each of these children be? How important was Andrea Luciana's individual tragedy? As I said this, I felt a sour taste in my mouth. The children would be taken to cloisters of convents converted into foundling homes. I assumed that Andrea Luciana continued to fight for her life, despite having experienced the pain of the disappearance of her closest relatives, a personal tragedy that impacted deeply on the rest of her life. Then I thought that my job was to rescue whatever was left of the human tragedies: Luciana's health or to bring bread and medicine to the foundling shelter.

The day of my arrival in the capital, at nine in the evening, I met with a couple of friends, López and Ulanovsky, at a restaurant on Pellegrini. It was warm enough to enjoy the outdoor tables lined up next to the road, barely covered by a veranda. At that hour the place was full of streetwalkers offering their company to customers. The two of them, both López and Ulanovsky, had been friends of mine for a long time. I met them when they were backpacking; we met on the bus on which I was going to say goodbye to my relatives before starting my studies. Since then, we cultivated an indelible friendship that recalled in detail the adventures of that trip we made a few years ago. We remembered playing soccer with the fishermen of a lake at an altitude of more than four thousand meters above sea level. In that place we drowned in the rarefied air and our hearts were pounding.

At the end of the meeting, we were invited to a nearby town by the mayor of the town, so we walked for two hours along a muleteer's trail that separated the edge of the lake from the town. We stayed there for two days, got drunk and ate partridge with green rice and chickpeas. We danced with the village girls and listened to the local musicians. Everyone danced through the city like a human chain, hugging each other at the waist. The women wore mid-thigh length skirts and white blouses with embroidered strips and lace on the chest. The men were dressed in raw linen shirts, black pants and narrow-brimmed hat of the same color. Behind the procession were the musicians.

I don't know if my fellow travelers experienced the same thing, but I was immersed in the seduction of the instant. It seemed to me that if I wanted to feel such an emotion again, I would have to travel to this village and meet the same people. I imagine that is why every time I visited Buenos Aires, I tried to meet with them to catch up and tell each other about the latest experiences and achievements; above all, to listen to their recent anecdotes about women and wine. They either forgot the episode or did not give it the importance as I; they never commented on their emotions in the village or at the edge of the lake, where the flamingos soaked their shanks. However, for me, to meet the friends with whom I shared those days was to return to the Andean valleys and the innocence of its inhabitants. At the end, we would end up talking shit and sharing neighborhood gossip or about soccer teams, depending on the passion of the fans.

At the time, López worked as a freelance journalist for various European newspapers. At the beginning of his career, he sent news about political events and artistic novelties in the city; later he became a war correspondent. Not because he wanted to, but because the most important issue in the last ten years turned out to be the internal wars, with violence in the countryside and in the city and the aftermath of kidnappings, disappearances and the trafficking of prisoners' children. Ulanovsky ended up being a psychotherapist and professor at the Faculty of Medicine of the University of Buenos Aires.

"Oscar, did you hear anything about a strike in Villa Constitución?" I asked López, inquiring about the events Luciana had told me about.

"Yes, it was an utter mess. You had to sift what was news from what was gossip. So many things were said, like that every night a leader disappeared, that there were shootings." He didn't tell me exactly when the events took place. "It was at the end of the messy years." I don't know if López was referring to the period of Videla, Viola, Galtieri or Bignone.

I remembered that Galtieri was a dipsomaniac and Bignone a puppet. "The drink left his neurons in misery and his thinking became rocky," I said to myself in relation to Galtieri's unstable behavior. His behavior was erratic. Suddenly he was a nationalist, anti-imperialist when it came to the claim of the Malvinas Islands, and he gave fiery speeches against Great Britain and its allies, who helped undercover groups of the Navy and the Police, who continued with the selective homicides. He promised elections with the participation of the traditional political parties and then ranted about democratic governments, which suffered from a weakness that put at risk the building blocks of the nation. I imagined him haranguing his troops in a heroic drunkenness that he himself did not understand.

"I met a woman who lost her father and brother during the strike and was upset about it," I blurted out. Almost immediately, I regretted it, as if I had insulted or disrespected Andrea Luciana.

"Can you believe we've been collecting data from the war years? It left us with a shitty feeling," Osvaldo Ulanovsky admitted. He was referring to the document that had been entrusted to Sabato and which he published under the title *Nunca más* (Never Again).

"It was a very dark period," I said. "The woman was homeless, rolling from one place to another. Maybe she was hiding from the preacher or she was paranoid and had a persecutory psychosis. She went to live on a farm built next to the decaying deposits. I got the idea of a place with shacks made of cardboard and zinc sheeting. There she contracted a virus that left her in the shit. That crap gets into your body and turns you into dust."

I sighed as if it were something pathetic that would make anyone's heartbreak, as if I were talking about a tango or a Creole tune from a neighboring country. Then I continued, "Don't mind me, maybe I'm talking about someone who has already died. The last time I saw her, she was admitted to the ICU of the hospital where I worked.

"I don't know why, but I imagine that before the disease she was a pretty girl, one of those who walk along Oroño Boulevard, near the courthouse. If we mentally move to the capital, she looked like those who wander along Corrientes Street or along the pedestrian street of Florida. So pretty and with such a face that it was hard to imagine that she lived in a village next to the railway line or a container depot with export garbage" I tried to give them a complete idea of the matter.

"The history of the last fifty years reflects what we Argentines are. It's the same in all parts of the country. You can put the name and surname of any acquaintance and tell whatever you want that will coincide with their own tragedy: the Swedish nuns, the slum priests, the university students, the high school students, the metal workers, the garbage collectors of the capital city, the soccer pool sellers, it doesn't matter who is involved in a story." said López.

"And that's an understatement. An example: I know more than three versions of the attack that killed Rucci." He was referring to José Ignacio Rucci, secretary general of the CGT. "First it was said that it was the Montoneros. Then a sector of investigative journalism thought that it was not them, but the members of the Triple A. There were those who presumed that it was the group of the deceased Vandor and there were those who pointed to a dispute with Lorenzo Miguel, the leader of the 62 Organizations, for the secretariat of the CGT. In the end a cinematographic version was that of a sniper, nicknamed Lino and surnamed Roqué was the author of the execution of General Sanchez in Rosario.

"Witnesses were found among the people who lived near the scene of the murder. They affirmed that the guy was shooting from the window of a car, with half of his body hanging out of the window. The bullets fell on the metal and windshield of the armored vehicle. Most of the ammunition seemed to bounce off; however, the windows of the door of Rucci's car exploded and suddenly they could see that the guy came out limping against the sheet metal, where he was riddled with bullets by Lino. Then he fell on the hood while the men in the other vehicles of the caravan repelled the attack.

"The scene looks like something out of an action movie starring Steve McQueen or Bruce Willis," Lopez emphasized.

The food we had ordered was great and the wine was dry. The streetwalkers were getting bolder and bolder, so much so that one of them offered her fare to Lopez. I don't know what he replied, but I perceived the woman's anger and a hissing sound that I interpreted as an insult. I presumed she had blurted out something along the lines of, "Fucking rude!" Then she walked away before my friend could react.

"If you notice," Ulanovsky interjected, "the violence came from both sides. Do you remember the slaughter of the presidential guards? They were ambushed when they were leaving in a bus near the Plaza de Mayo. It was a real massacre. They attacked them with rocket launchers and then finished them off with heavy shrapnel. And what about the attacks on the Azul and Monte Chingolo barracks."

It occurred to me that his reflection was professional and did not involve a judgment of any of the warring factions. Then he continued, "The worst thing was that, in the end, state terrorism was imposed. It began with the extrajudicial killing of nineteen prisoners who had surrendered at the Trelew airport, after a failed escape from a high security prison in Rawson. Although the escaped and then executed prisoners were not angels, they had surrendered and, therefore, their lives had to be respected. They surrendered to the Navy under those conditions, with the promise that they would be returned to the prison from which they escaped.

"But instead of taking them to Rawson, they took them to the navy barracks and there they riddled them with bullets. The one who directed the murder was a naval commander. I think his name was Luis Sosa. He has been condemned by the Chamber of Criminal Proceedings of Rawson for crimes against humanity. Some time ago we could not even imagine this." I thought he meant that judging actions like this would have been impossible. Then it dawned on me that the slogan chanted by the anti-dictatorship activists, vindicating the martyrs of Trelew, referred to this episode of history.

"What are you saying, Osvaldo? I can't believe you. You can't put state terrorism on the same scale as the terrorist actions of insurgent groups," criticized López.

I remembered reading in the *Encarta* dictionary that *state terrorism* is defined as a 'Systematic use, by the government of a state, of threats and reprisals, often considered illegal even within its own legislation, in order to impose obedience and active collaboration of the population'. I remembered the quote almost by heart. However, I did not want to interfere in the conversation, as I thought it was an internal Argentinean matter and I should not get involved.

"They are diametrically different issues," Lopez continued. The State, with the power given to it by an entire country, and the subversive groups, which use terrorist methods. Of course, I do not agree with the use of this method that terrorizes the population. The insurgents must be punished in accordance with the law, after a due trial and with a just imprisonment.

"Civilians who did not participate in the conflict should not have to endure acts of intimidation and persecution." After a short pause, he continued, "What is your perception of what is happening in the country?" The question was addressed to me. Without waiting for an answer, he continued, "The same thing can happen in Rosario and anywhere else. And here in the capital. A person can be the object of rampant snitching. Any person is accused of an invented crime and the individual ends up executed as if he were a bug. Under such circumstances, the fear of the population grows, as in the worst times of Hitler's or Stalin's regimes.

"There you have Captain Astiz, a son of a bitch who tortured women at the Navy School and boasted of having been the Angel of Death. He brushed off two European nuns and the founders of the Mothers of Plaza de Mayo. The cowardly bastard submitted to the first roar, when he heard the sound of the cannonade of the British artillery. His balls shrunk and he surrendered as the worst whore that had ruled us and also terrorized us."

"As for the woman, what do you say? I suppose you thought she was upset," asked Ulanovsky, evidently changing the turn of the conversation and taking it to his own terrain.

"I don't know what to tell you. Evidently, she had a psychic disorder that could be attributed to her general condition, as she was suffering from a viral disease. Perhaps because she was suffering from small hemorrhages in the encephalic mass or because of the viral toxemia." At that moment I thought that the kidnapping could be the consequence of a hallucinatory delirium or, in reality, it was part of her past, it was her relatives. The truth is that the woman seemed to be out of context in the last place where she lived. Her face was that of an urban girl, with a higher culture than the average country dwellers or garbage recyclers.

I described how she arrived at the emergency room. She was brought by an ambulance from the Provincial Hospital in very bad shape and her appearance was a mess. The nurses had to sanitize her before placing her in the isolation ward for infectious diseases. She barely had the strength to help her admission. She was a specter; nothing like she might have been in the past. I tried to explain that the initial diagnosis was Argentine hemorrhagic fever, whose pathogenic agent was the Junín virus, a type of arenavirus whose vector was the rat that lives in the province of Buenos Aires, near the garbage dumps of the rainy ports or in the soybean fields. The disease was complicated by multi-organ failure and disseminated intravascular coagulation. Then I noticed that my description was boring, so I quickly moved on to talk about my stay in the federal capital.

"What about you? Are you going to settle in the capital? Do you have a place to stay?" Osvaldo asked me.

"I'm staying at a hotel near here, downtown. Do you know the Nogaró Hotel? On Julio Roca Avenue. I will stay there for at least a year while I do an internship in gastric and intestinal diseases related to transmissible infections. I will work as a resident at the Udaondo Hospital" I told them.

At dinner we finished a bottle of wine between the three of us. I had ordered hake fillet in olive cream. I don't remember what they had. It must have been some kind of meat or pasta. I remembered that when I first met them, I invited them for sole and we ate it on the beach itself while the fishermen smoked the flesh of the freshly filleted fish. They were no more than eighteen or twenty years old at the time. They had known each other since high school and from their trips to the *boliches* at Boca and Tigre. At some point it occurred to them to form an experimental theater group and they thought that the next thing would be documentary films or short films. The times were not right for such ventures and, after having met people in the field, such as Pino Solanas and Norma Aleandro, they recognized that their dreams were difficult to achieve.

When I first met them, they seemed to me like a couple of dreamers who were eager to travel to neighboring countries in search of adventures; places they knew about from others, and to conquer a girl or two. As time went by, I got to know more about them. López was a militant for some years in the Partido Revolucionario de los Trabajadores, a Trotskyist group that split off around 1970. The group, led by the Santucho brothers, distanced itself from the founding aggregate of Nahuel Moreno, which persisted in trade union actions. López was not a supporter of either side. For this reason, one stormy night he fled by ferry to Uruguay and then sought refuge in Madrid, where he worked for a while in a publishing company that specialized in self-help books. There he met writers in the field, among them Deepak Chopra. On one occasion he told me that both sides were somewhat delirious. I understood that he had moved away from the party's fevered ideas. Chopra seemed to him to be a guitar playing in the purest gaucho style.

As for Osvaldo Ulanovsky, he had always belonged to those who wanted to interpret society through a snapshot of the prickly pear years, as the time of the scourge or the long knives. It was the period between López Rega and the military dictatorships.

Sometimes I discovered in his voice a feeling of painful nostalgia for friends who had disappeared, for people of his own generation, "people of the homeland", he would tell me. He was divorced and preferred to continue in that state because it allowed him to enjoy transgressions such as listening to jazz in a nightclub in La vuelta de Rocha or ending up in the restaurants near the docks of Puerto Madero, where he met with other crazy people, many of whom were addicted to alcohol and heavy drugs. He confessed that he enjoyed flirting with marijuana, which he said should be decriminalized.

In his professional life he had achieved several notable successes, especially in introducing methods to treat depressed or dependent patients in groups. For five years he had been a professor at the University of Buenos Aires, where he taught at the School of Medicine and was part of the teaching staff of the Neuropsychiatry postgraduate course for medical and clinical psychology graduates. He gave weekly courses on psychotherapy techniques and Gestalt approach in the investigation of neurosis. But he stood out, fundamentally, in his studies on depression in the elderly, which he considered as part of cognitive deterioration.

When we left the restaurant, the tables were almost empty and the street girls had disappeared. Maybe they had already hooked customers or perhaps they had moved on to other places. López had to return to his home in Ciudadela, so a three-hour bus ride or a two-hour subway ride awaited him. Oswaldo invited me to spend some more time in a place that could pass for a disco or a dance club, where we watched a show of Ukrainian dancers.

It seemed to me that we could have a more serious conversation. I wanted to ask, for example, what had happened to his marriage. Surely, he would not give me the answer I expected. Maybe he would say something like, "And... you know that things happen that way". And then he would ask me: "What about you? Then I would answer that I had nothing going on, although I would be lying, because there was nothing more serious than what was happening in my life. Finally, and to evade the answer, I would bring up again the subject of Luciana's illness and her mental imbalance.

And as if he was in a state of narcosis, with irritated eyes and panting breath, I did not notice that he was obsessively looking at the dancers. Suddenly a woman in her forties, blonde and with a beret tilted over her hair, came on stage and began to sing in French *La vie en rose* and then *Candilejas*. I felt absorbed by the atmosphere and reminisced about times gone. I thought that the three of us had passed our thirties. We had been touched by squalls and frigid nights with a shivering dread. Everything had happened and history had turned the tables on us.

It was almost dawn when I returned to my hotel near the José de San Martín Hospital. It took a while to open the door and I was ashamed of having returned late. The evening had been great; however, I thought about the woman at the Centenario Hospital again. I promised myself to call the hospital early to inquire about her fate. It seemed to me that I had more doubts about her recent past. What was she running from? If she had been detained, how did she escape from the holding place? Had she been tortured? Maybe none of that was true. Maybe she hadn't lived in Villa Constitución at the time of the metalworkers' strike. I even doubted the disappearances of her father and brother. Perhaps it was part of the plot of a novel she had created, or the delirium was the result of the fever and the mental deterioration of the illness she was suffering from.

I had seen the delirium of viral encephalitis and cognitive impairment, the shaking from chills and raving. I assumed she was hearing inner voices and having visions. The reddening of the sclerae, which could be mistaken for subconjunctival splinter hemorrhages, and the blank stare, with horizontal nystagmus when fixed on someone or something, indicated to me that the nerve centers had been infiltrated with fluid or fluid bullae, perhaps the blurred boundary between gray and white matter. What would happen if resurrection occurred? Nothing, for the after-effects would turn her into a dumb, almost hebephrenic woman with emotional lability. She might suffer subintrusive convulsions and prolonged absences. Then I thought the die was cast, and on this occasion, with loaded dice on a red cloth.

I didn't want to think about her anymore; it was as painful as if she were a close relative. And I entrusted myself to hope. In the morning, I would call the ICU at the hospital and ask about her. I hoped that on the other end of the line they would tell me, "She's miraculously improved. We hope she gets out of the unit and has few after-effects."

I remembered having read a publication that talked about neuroplasticity and integration of information. The resource of perception to create channels that determine thoughts and memories. Each neuron is capable of receiving between ten thousand and fifteen thousand synapses or connections with other axons or glial cells. Billions of interconnections between the one hundred billion neurons that a human being has, which would explain the plasticity of the brain and its sensory extensions to elaborate thought, since the information perceived by the senses reaches the memory. The hypothesis concluded by affirming the existence of a single higher nervous center: the brain and postulated that each receptor neuron was an extension of the same higher center. The whole system was integrated, like a radiolarian, like the aerial seeds he saw during childhood. The neurons of the retina, the olfactory corpuscles, the organ of Corti and the tactile corpuscles were part of this higher nervous center. It was felt and thought with the fingers when they caressed the skin; with the ears when we listened to music and words. Then I remembered the sound of the saxophone in the *boliche* we visited with Ulanovsky, and I compared it with the sensation produced by the autistic boy in San Telmo.

Chapter 6
Anonymous Beings

We are anonymous beings, masses of insignificant individuals.

In spite of insisting on the search, repeating the same scenarios and watching the same dance group, I never saw again the migrations of yellow butterflies that covered the avenues of that city. The event took place every twenty-five years and lasted one day. In the end I came to the conclusion that nothing I pursued was worthwhile. Rather, I have to admit that nothing turned out as I had dreamed it would. Perhaps it depended on the expectation I placed on the desire.

Those were the days when it occurred to me to lead the brigades fighting against malaria! At that time I had long hair and a rock singer's face, but, above all, I had Gabriela's affection. She still believed in me, despite my cheating with the secretary of the director of a fishing company. When she found out, she wanted to die. I sang so many songs of regret and I told her so many stupid things in order to apologize.

I could not convince her. Her face reflected an expression of sadness, as if she wanted to scream at me "Look what you did, you crazy bastard! Worse, she would have said, "Look what you did to me, you crazy bastard! I'm sure she didn't want to use interjections and that's why she kept quiet, so that it would be her face and my conscience that would speak for her.

It is possible that I went out on a cobblestone street and walked ten blocks, talking like a madman or whistling like a nostalgic. I guessed that the icy wind that hit me that day was coming from the southern lakes. I think I was crying, because my cheeks were wet and I was breathing through my mouth; I even began to have laryngeal stridor. I felt pain, as if something was being ripped out of my chest. At the end of the night, I had to look for a sleazy hotel where I lay on a single bed and smoke a cigarette of disgust. Then I took out of the white plastic bag, or a black backpack, I can't remember, a book and started to leaf through the pages. I don't know if I finished the novel or if I got halfway through it, like so many other times. It was *The Magic Mountain*, by Thomas Mann. The photograph I used to mark the page showed her sitting on a ledge near the ledge that held the bear cage. With her are our three children: the little girl with crossed arms and the same sad expression as her mother and the two boys, who didn't give a damn about anything. They were playing on a tricycle, one as a pilot and the other as a passenger. "Holy shit! How the fuck did I get to this point of misery," I whispered. But it was even worse, for I had no chance of resurrection.

Then I thought she was still alive, even if she was burned by my bragging, so I would impose a tribute on myself: I would bring her every day an ice cream sundae and a red rose. I would tell her, "Tell me to cut off my balls and I'll do it just to have your company again. Do it for your mother or for our children, but don't be angry forever."

She would look at me with eyes wet from crying and answer me,

"It's too late. I can't." And she would have completed the sentence, "Even if I wanted to, crazy man, I swear I can't." Then she would keep quiet or walk away or do both at the same time. And I would feel like banging my head against a concrete wall.

How had I gotten to this state? I debased her, I dirtied her memories, I messed with a girl who was vastly superior to me in every way. And I sent to the garbage can the moments of incomparable tenderness, like the births of our three babies, standing at the altar saying, "I do", Christmas and all the trips we had taken.

I have the feeling of having lived a dream. I remember the factory bell where my mother worked, placing the brand seals on the corner of the blankets. The factory produced alpaca wool fabrics. The whistle could be heard for ten blocks around and had a high-pitched tone that made it shrill on rainy days. When my mother met Gabriela, she told me, "What a girl!" She was referring to her black eyes, which contrasted with her white skin, giving her face an ethereal beauty.

Her eyes were enormous; the delicacy of her face was indisputable, and her slenderness was evident. But, above all, she was the woman who gave me the gift of destiny. She would tie my tie, iron my shirt so that the collar and sleeves were impeccable. She wanted me to look elegant at conferences. She would study with me, even though she didn't give a damn about what I memorized. She listened to me even when I made ridiculous comments about soccer games between teams she didn't care about. Once in a while she would comment something like, "If they already played each other a few months ago, why are they playing another game now? It seems very repetitive to me, week after week."

I explained to her, as if she were a small child, that the tournament had two rounds of all against all and that was called the first and second round. Today I would have asked her something else,

"Woman, why didn't you just tell me to go fuck myself right there? Why did you have to endure every word of every sentence from an asshole who pretended to understand everything?"

She was my only interlocutor in the cafeterias, when it occurred to me to invite her for a coffee and croissants. She was my confidant when things went wrong. When my mother got sick with colon cancer, it was Gabriela who took care of her and gave her chicken egg albumin to prevent edema in her lower limbs. She massaged her back and accompanied her to the hospital for chemotherapy. She was even the one who washed her panties stained with blood from her colon hemorrhages. She cared for my mother until the disease defeated them both.

I would say that the cancer killed my mother and broke Gabriela. My mother's belly bulged as if she were pregnant, and her legs oozed a sticky liquid. Josefina, my mother, died one day in June and I haven't heard the sound of the whistle since. Maybe in Gabriela's life there were similar sounds, but not in mine. Remembering the days of May, with the frost on the cobblestones, I feel the immense loss. I would have liked to have shouted, "Come back, mother, don't die! Come back, Gabriela, don't abandon me! I could not keep them, nor recover them, and even less as they were. I carry my mother with me in a few black and white photographs. Gabriela, in the color photos I took myself.

She, Gabriela, after the mudslinging with which I repaid her immense affection, languished. She lost heart, kept silent and then left for another city. Believe it or not, at that moment I was proud of her for leaving me. I believed, in my conceit, that she would be unable to leave me forever, so sooner rather than later she would return accepting her defeat, even more humiliated. What a load of crap! The greatest loss of my life covered up by vanity.

I kept my pride and tried to replace her with one woman after another. Obviously, I fooled myself into thinking that I could feel anything like the affection to which Gabriela had accustomed me. Soul mates? Not even a little. In the end I had to take refuge at work, running from one place to another to go to the reports of epidemic outbreaks, small or big, and investigate what they were about. I got into a breakneck pace created by my anguish, like those individuals who moved from Manhattan to a village in South America.

I tried to keep busy so as not to feel the loneliness. I studied, watched movies, took up sports, read literature and medical texts. However, the nights were long and the hangover routine. And I had to soften the memories so as not to go crazy. "I have not lost my loved ones," I said to myself, "what I have done is to prioritize my professional duties". Once again, I fooled myself like any dilettante, like a clown mocking his own image.

Suddenly, faced with the loss of my family, and in the midst of nostalgia, it occurred to me that I had to work to forget as if I were an alcoholic who drank to forget. Then, as soon as I received a notification about the sign of a rare disease, I would rush out to look for the patients to learn about their symptoms and signs, to have them tested and, after the tests, to have an idea of what it was all about. I was able to detect hepatitis B in a group of soldiers from a mountain regiment. They had been infected by a prostitute that the conscripts had shared in the Amazon jungle. Similarly, after a while I had the opportunity to visit a small village by a lake, where the school children were suffering from a rare disease that covered their bodies with rashes and caused high fevers accompanied by convulsions. There, I discovered a virosis transmitted by ticks.

In the end, I accepted whatever was proposed: trips to Southeast Asia, the Middle East, Africa. At the drop of a hat, I would grab my backpack and get on the first plane to the proposed destination. Thus, I accepted the assignment to go to an area where they had observed a hemorrhagic disease with a very high lethality.

When I arrived in Kampala, I was met at the airport by two people who identified themselves as Dr. Jalufe, the head of the field hospital in Victoria, and an official from the Ugandan Ministry of Health whose last name I did not catch due to a language issue. After the immigration formalities, I was transported to a hotel downtown. As the limousine drove along the avenues, I contemplated the contrasts between the suburbs and the city center. In the meantime, Jalufe told me about the beauty of Lake Victoria, where the operations center was located, a field hospital with five hundred beds, although there was a project to expand the space to accommodate up to a thousand. The official was silent; possibly he was listening to the conversation to learn about the mission I had been entrusted with.

"Doctor, you must be tired. If you wish, give me a call on this cell phone at your convenience. I'd like to invite you to dinner, so we can chat for a while," offered Jalufe, an English doctor of Lebanese descent.

"Thank you, Dr. Jalufe. Yes, that would be great, would in a couple of hours be okay? I asked him.

"Perfect. I'll be in the lobby at eight o'clock."

At that time Yoweri Museveni was in power. The man had been a guerrilla fighter of the People's Revolutionary Army, with which he came to power by force by overthrowing the corrupt government of the octogenarian Milton Obote. Obote had been accused by his opponents and by the international press of fraud in the elections that gave him the presidency in 1997. As was customary among doctors taking on a mission in an unknown country, we informed ourselves of recent political events to get an idea of the arena we were about to enter.

Uganda was governed, between 1971 and 1979, by the dictator Idi Amin Dada, to whom is attributed the death of about three hundred thousand people and the exodus of a large part of the population to neighboring countries. In 1979 the exiles, supported by the Tanzanian army, overthrew the dictator and organized elections that gave victory to Obote, despite the fact that there was suggestion that the elections had been fraudulent. The old president, Milton Obote, was a puppet of Amin's former army chiefs and the Tanzanian occupation troops. Not surprisingly, in this scenario, the struggles of Museveni's ERP continued.

During the period of the Ebola outbreak there were still pockets of resistance among the displaced and the new guerrillas of the Lord's Resistance Army, with liberated areas in the north of the country. The leader of the faction was the religious fanatic Joseph Kony, who claimed to be a medium, a spiritualist and a healer of diseases.

In terms of health indicators, Uganda had successfully managed to control AIDS with the ABC campaign, which stood for abstinence, being faithful and using condoms. Despite this, the health conditions of the population were deplorable: child malnutrition, multidrug-resistant tuberculosis, diarrheal and respiratory diseases and more plagued Uganda. There were so many problems that wreaked havoc on the population. There were groups of endemic diseases in the vicinity of the great lakes, as well as in the north. I am talking about malaria and other zoonoses transmitted by mosquitoes.

In the evening I met Jalufe at a restaurant in downtown Kampala. The place was reminiscent of any place in a European city. Most of the customers were white and dressed in sporty attire. The predominant language was English. The ambience of the restaurant reminded me of a London pub on The

Thames, as well as an establishment in the bohemian district of Hong Kong.

René Jalufe had previously volunteered for Doctors Without Borders in various missions, particularly in Africa. Tall, rather thin, I would say bony, almost always in shirtsleeves, and balding, he had an extremely friendly manner and an empathy that I found enviable.

"The sight of the mountains," I said, "reminded me of a Hemingway novel, *The Snows of Kilimanjaro.*"

"The character, with a comminuted fracture that gangrenes, remembers every detail of his life in a conversation with his wife while they are in the mountains," he said. "I saw it in a movie starring Gregory Peck. What I don't remember is whether the character was a doctor or a writer?

"As a child I was seduced by the exoticism of this continent. Perhaps it was generated by the safari movies in Tanzania or by the discoveries that took place in the Valley of the Kings, such as the mummified remains of Tutankhamun and his solid gold mask. In my case, I was fascinated by the findings related to early hominids. One of the first books I had on hand was *The Formation of Mankind*, by Richard Leakey, son of Louis and Marie Leakey, who discovered human fossils more than two million years old in the Lake Rudolph Basin in Kenya. The progeny of the *Zinjanthropus olduvaisis* near Lake Olduvai."

Here I wanted to reveal my passion for the subject that made me think about becoming a paleoanthropologist when I was young and flipping through the *National Geographic* magazines that my father collected.

"The truth is that the place is beautiful. It was the first time I was able to see lions in their habitat, wild rhinos, hippos in the rivers, as our vehicle drove across the plains before arriving at the camp," he explained.

"What about Ebola?" I asked to get into the subject.

"Actually, when the first cases were reported, we thought that the outbreak was worse than it is," he said. "When the hospital started operating, we were able to detect it in twenty-five people. Before our arrival, about twenty people had already died with suspicious symptoms, hemorrhages and fevers. We could not prove that it was Ebola because we were not allowed to perform autopsies. The customs and laws of the country prevent autopsies. We did not even get to see the bodies.

"Of those we treated, three died and the rest were treated with general measures, parenteral fluids and, in some cases, a blood or platelet transfusion. Seven people are still in serious condition in the hospital. The others have recovered. In any case, we will keep them under observation for another twenty days to check their stability.

"Collaterally, we attended hundreds of patients with malaria, influenza and other viruses such as dengue, and even cases that seemed to be leishmaniasis. In short, patients with other etiologies," he smiled as if something had amused him. Then he continued, "Mothers brought us girls with amenorrhea and suspected pregnancy; boys with diarrhea because they had heard that some of the symptoms could be liquid stools and general malaise. In those cases, the diarrhea was caused by parasites. In addition, we saw cases of avitaminosis and severe malnutrition, rickets, pellagra, beriberi. Some patients appeared to be suspected of AIDS or tuberculosis." He smiled again.

I interpreted his gesture as expressing the paradoxes that exist in the healthcare system. Nothing is important if it is routine. What is important is the atypical. For them, Ebola was a novelty in their work. It mattered to them as much as AIDS, cholera or any other pathology. Perhaps as much as the emaciated children running through the dirt streets of the shantytowns.

"Thank goodness the outbreak was small. But won't the surveillance extend your stay here?" I asked.

"Well, the work must continue," he acknowledged. "We are also interested in the rest of the diseases, especially those that are common in the area. Maybe that's why they are of little interest to international organizations." He paused for a moment, taking a deep breath as he reviewed in his memory what those diseases were.

I assumed he was thinking of dengue, malaria and tuberculosis. Perhaps in the malnourished children that appear in some photography contests, little ones with dilated bellies, globular, with shiny skin and herniated navel. Children who, in contrast, have thin limbs, no muscle mass, with skin over bone and a skull peeled by alopecia. Perhaps his mind was fixed on the drug addicts of the slums, who lived in alleys or tenements and consumed the vapor of *ice* crystals, which simulated fragments of crystallized plaster, pricked syringes with the oily and translucent liquid or ingested blister packs of methamphetamine, indistinguishable from other over-the-counter drugs.

This conversation took place in 2009 in a restaurant in Kampala. Ebola virus disease was first detected in Uganda, in the province of Gulu. Earlier, in 1976, cases appeared in the Democratic Republic of Congo, near the Ebola River. The first deceased was a primary school teacher, who presented symptoms such as diarrhea, muscular pains, maculo-papular rash. A week later, abdominal and thoracic pains began, with vomiting and liquid evacuations; ten days later, he was in an excited state and then went into coma, with hematemesis, melena, epistaxis. Finally, he died after twenty-five days. Since that first case, more than ten thousand were reported until 2014, when an epidemic outbreak occurred, spreading across sub-Saharan Africa and affecting the Democratic Republic of Congo, Liberia, Ghana, Equatorial Guinea and Uganda.

The Ebola data reminded me of other diseases with which I had had contact in the past: the Junín virus and hantavirus. I had fresh memories of Andrea Luciana, the sick woman in the ICU of the Centenario Hospital, whose final fate I never discovered. Likewise, I recalled a hantavirus epidemic in a village on the border between Peru and Bolivia. There I saw the fallacies that separate the countries. The border line ran along a street and divided the village into two zones. Each of them belonged to a different country. Both had victims of the Junín virus and hantavirus, with similar symptoms, although one of them was less lethal.

The virus was classified as a filovirus with RNA nucleotide and filamentous glycoprotein capsids with projections on its surface. Prior to 1985, subtypes had been discovered that only affected great apes. However, other groups, such as Zaire Yambuku and Zaire Kikwit, as well as the Bundibugyo virus, documented in Uganda in 2007, and the Sudan virus, Gulu, discovered in the same country in 2000, were transmitted to humans.

Human-to-human transmission spread among medical personnel through contact with the blood of the sick, as well as other body fluids. Among the natives, dissemination was caused by the custom of the bereaved to prepare the body of the deceased for burial. They bathed the corpse before dressing it with their best tunic. During the ceremony they had to clean the drool from the mouth and the feces from the sphincter of the anus. Both areas were a breeding ground for the disease.

Another factor that also favored the spread of the disease was related to food. The natives consumed meat from sick animals that had died during the outbreak. The easiest animals to hunt were those that were sick. The mission epidemiologist explained the following to me,

"Sometimes they found the animals in the forest clearings. Then they boiled the bodies and served them in stews or breaded them before putting them on the griddle." The hospital's medical director then justified the consumption of wild animals. "Cattle and domestic fowl are scarce here for human consumption. Eating such food is a privilege enjoyed only by the well-to-do. The humble people and, above all, those who come from the countryside, together with those displaced by the war, feed on what they can hunt: monkeys, pigs, antelopes and also on river fish, such as dorados and tilapia," said Jalufe.

I thought it would be difficult for them to change their eating habits. Besides, hunger outweighs any fear of an enigmatic disease. I also suspected that the virus could be spread by Flügge droplets during sneezing and coughing, although this route had not been proven. Handling body fluids from the sick person was possibly the most frequent way of spread, but not the only way.

Jalufe was a serious guy, with a deep knowledge of medicine in general and tropical diseases in particular. He had had extensive experience not only in Africa, but also on other continents. And his treatment with the mission staff, as well as with the sick and their relatives, was excellent. The doctor had a warm rapport; I would say downright friendly. From the beginning we hit it off. We saw places in the same light. We both abhorred religious wars. It seemed absurd to us that people who shared the same geographical area and belonged to the same racial group should be pitted against each other because of religious beliefs.

Buddhism versus Islam in a conflict with violent actions that resulted in the displacement of Muslim populations. These ended up as refugees of conscience in neighboring countries. So did the people of the Gaza Strip. It reminded us of the intifadas of blood and mourning. We knew that the war in the Middle East was spreading from one country to another. It had broken out in the poppy fields of Afghanistan and then crossed the border into Pakistan. Then the fleeing caravans had taken it to the northern border of Iran, through which the opium shipments transited to the Mediterranean ports once they left Turkey behind.

Taliban and Islamic State soldiers were fighting in the mountains and in the cities of several countries. Syria was a powder keg. Sudan was a supplier of slaves that could be bought in the markets of Libyan cities such as Sabha. Several countries in sub-Saharan Africa were destinations for European women seeking sex tourism. Tuareg rebels were fighting for the independence of Mali and Niger, for which they had organized the National Movement for the Liberation of Azawad (MNLA), whose most important action was the seizure of Timbuktu in 2012.

I imagined the dark-skinned Berbers and the tanned-skinned Tuaregs in wandering caravans in the desert. Few of them had been able to settle in the shanty shacks made of cardboard and zinc that they called *cités*. They stood next to the small towns of southern Morocco and western Algeria, most notably Ifni and Tindouf. In some cases they lived in villages of the same ethnic group, settled in the few places that boasted date palms and pools of clear water. Here they established corrals for their sheep. Most of them continued wandering through the desert, seeking to converge in the oases of alkaline waters, unfit for human consumption.

From those first conversations, on such fascinating topics as ethnicities, their behaviors and geographical distribution, a friendship was born that I consider very heartfelt on both sides. I will remember him in my moments of nostalgia for his long periods of joy, when he was exultant in his comments and in showing affection. Perhaps I compare him to another friend I met in Southeast Asia: the Nordic Olsen. In their own way, they were both intensely human, committed to their time, courageous in the face of danger and certainly not driven by economic interest, but by an inner fire of solidarity.

As he spotted the caravans of nomads, moving along a desert corridor on the border between Algeria, Niger and Mali, with their gear on camels' backs and riding their spirited horses, he commented to me, "I believe they are traders descended from the Phoenicians and other races that settled in the desert."

"Nomads of tradition or pushed by the usurpers of their territory?" I wanted to know.

"I'm not an expert on the subject, but I think it's a matter of encroachment and persecution," he said. "I understood that cities were walled off to prevent their entry. Countries persecuted them with laws created to prevent informal trade and illegal immigration."

Together with a group of doctors and nurses from the non-profit organization Doctors of the World, Jalufe had set up a field hospital in the south of the country, near Lake Victoria. The center was used to isolate the sick during the most severe stages, when splinter hemorrhages were visible in the conjunctivae of the eyes. It was then assumed that a stroke would originate, causing convulsions and the patient would go into a coma. At the equatorial plateau camp they looked like a group of astronauts, with their protective clothing under positive pressure and the curved moon shields in front of their faces to prevent the miasmas from sticking to them along with the droplets that came out with the patients' coughs or sneezes.

The work was both terrifying and addictive because this was, in the end, a drug like any other, like any other vice, such as gambling or kleptomania. It stuck to our bodies like a scab that we could not get rid of. The other thing, that of responsibility and the mystical and heroic burden, could seem like verse, although this idea kept us going.

Sometimes I asked myself, "How much of what I do is due to the overvalued idea of my mission?" Maybe I was deluding myself and what I was looking for was recognition for my work. "From whom?" The answer was not clear to me. It could be from the organization I worked for. Maybe from the country where I had come to solve one of their health problems. Perhaps, more humbly, I wanted the authorities of the region or the province to award me a medal or a diploma. But neither one nor the other. In the end, you would leave the place in silence, just as you had arrived. Maybe you gave a paper at a scientific congress or were invited to publish an article in a specialized journal. This was definitely not my case. It was much less than all that. It was my way of living, my context, my day-to-day life. Something like my skin, which I could not get rid of.

In the camp near the hospital were the tents of the relatives of the hospitalized patients. We did not want those who might be incubating the disease to spread it. The nurses in the group followed a protocol that they completed every day. The questionnaire included questions to be asked of each person arriving at the camp: place of origin, usual food, type of housing, family relationship with the sick person, any flu symptoms in the last four weeks, pain in the joints or in the muscles of the upper or lower limbs, if so, what were the symptoms? In the case of women, bleeding between periods, presence of bruises on the body without apparent cause? The questionnaire was exhaustive and included questions about proximity to areas inhabited by the region's monkeys, both small monkeys and great apes. Questions were also asked about the location of dwellings and the presence of flocks of fruit bats or wild pigs.

The computers, fed with information from areas that were part of the natural habitat of monkeys, bats and wild pigs, provided us with a mapping of the risk in relation to the geographical area. In addition, dietary habits in the area of disease occurrence had to be taken into account. Among the local population, it was common to hunt jungle animals, such as macaques and pigs. Likewise, it was known from previous studies that fruit bats were healthy hosts of the Ebola virus, with which it had coexisted for thousands of years. There was no evidence, but it was possible that fluids from the winged bats' jaws and urine could contaminate fruit for human consumption and, therefore, the possibility that they could spread the disease by this means was not ruled out.

In conversations with Jalufe and other members of the Doctors Without Borders organization, I learned of battles between Tuareg warriors and French soldiers, aided by Sudanese riflemen. In the end the losers would flee to join caravans of children, women and old men carrying their belongings and domestic animals on camels. The children grew up and became adults, and so history repeated itself over and over again.

Jalufe and I bumped heads when we discovered the sub-Saharan slave trade. Until that moment I thought that slavery no longer existed and that it had been replaced by human trafficking. I thought human trafficking was the quota that was charged for the transfer of people who intended to enter a country in Europe or the United States as illegal immigrants. In the past, I had seen forms of slavery in underground variants, such as the exploitation of women on factory ships in the China Sea, where they remained for months, perhaps years, without touching land. The personnel on these ships were fed by the ship's own cooks, who were supplied by the mother ships.

He had also witnessed the exploitation of Eastern migrants, who worked from sunrise to sunset in clandestine ships located on the outskirts of some European cities close to the Mediterranean and in the factories of North African cities. The Senegalese and Syrians fought for jobs in a labor regime of forced confinement, where the doors were closed with chains and padlocks. But I certainly had heard nothing about the sale of slaves, nor of slave traders who engaged in that trade until I overheard a fellow talking about slavery as a business. The man admitted that he himself had checked out slaves in a certain area in southern Libya, almost bordering Niger. The men were gray in color, because of the dust from the dunes on the dark skin, they were chained by the neck with nooses and had shackles on their ankles, which they call herropeas.

I would never have believed it, even if I had been shown photographs. I remember seeing an old image depicting sexual slavery, the major suppliers of which were colonized countries. I don't remember if I saw the painting or a photograph in a magazine of some organization that fought against racism and xenophobia. It showed naked Crimean women showing their attributes to potential buyers, who were wearing clothes used by Arabs.

When I asked Jalufe, he replied that he had seen a raid on a tribe of shepherds south of the Atlas Mountains, involving people wearing tunics and turbans.

"I don't know if they were Berbers or slave traders from Mali or Niger," he explained in response to my doubt. "They carried old long-barreled rifles and fired into the air to frighten the villagers and those in the vicinity. After gathering a group of more than twenty young men, they were taken away tied by the neck in rows of two. The captives were on foot, guarded by their captors, who rode desert horses.

"I don't know if they perceived our presence and didn't give a damn. Maybe they didn't realize we had seen them," he said.

I wanted to know more about the captors or the characteristics of the captives. For example, why had they raided this village of shepherds? Were they Berbers?

Jalufe gave me ambiguous answers, "The attackers acted as if it were a robbery. The victims were very poor people living in isolated villages. They could have been Berbers or traders from any country or ethnic group," he answered hesitantly.

I don't think Jalufe was clear whether they were taking the young men to exploit them in the sugar cane fields, which had run out of braziers, or in order to sell them at the slave trade fairs held in southern Libya. That was what he told me, with a gesture that I interpreted as a mixture of sorrow and indignation.

"I could not identify the ultimate purpose. Perhaps it was to make up for desertions or deaths in the camps on the North African coast. Maybe it was something more repulsive: using the boys for evil practices."

"I find it unbelievable that this aberration continues in the twenty-first century. If I had been told about it before coming to Africa, I would not have believed it," I confessed.

It seemed to me that there were places where people lived according to the codes of the past. Places where today's civilization has not arrived. Villages raided by gangs of slave traders. Deserts through which the nomads, who had been nicknamed free men, Bedouins in the Arabian Peninsula and Berbers in North Africa, roamed. Dunes used as hiding places by warriors to crouch and surprise the enemy.

I should have known that the Arabs of the kingdom of Zanzibar, now Tanzania, were traditionally engaged in the slave trade. That the Berbers bartered sheep's wool, gold, and dates from the desert, even salt from the Mediterranean.

In the end, we returned to a conversation about pathologies and doctors. He then explained to me that the Berbers did not get sick in the great cholera epidemic that affected the coastal towns and fishing coves. This was possibly, because they covered feces with the sand, just like the dead, who did not need to be buried.

We were silent. The coffee in the pots was cold. We had been caught up in the subject. At that moment I thought of the dark gray color of the slaves. Maybe they were oiled to keep the desert sand from cracking their skin. On top of the oil, the powdered sand from the dells would stick to their dark skin and give it a gray color and a prickly, rough texture. I would have to consider it as a method of preserving the merchandise to get the best price at the fair. I don't remember if Jalufe said it or I pondered it on my own, but the women got the worst of it because they ended up in the harems of the sheikhs or in prostitution dens set up in the coastal cities. I thought of Fez and its medina, the historic city of Morocco, where the madrasas were located, and the universities of Ifni. Islam in the lives of the students from an early age.

While he was telling me about the slave trade in Africa, I remembered witnessing the slaughter of a tribe of uncontacted natives in the Amazon at the hands of the rubber extractors. They wanted to expel them from the protected territories. At least, legally that was the condition of the parks protected by the Ministry of Environment and Populations at Risk of Extinction. If I wanted to recount the episode, I have to explain that I saw with pain the murder of an itinerant group, who were then doused with gasoline to burn the bodies and their huts. The killers were psychopaths recruited from the favelas of Rio de Janeiro, or maybe the slums of São Paulo.

Those who hired the services of the vicious killers were even more miserable, even if they were the power of the region or of the State. They hired them to kill the natives who lived in a territory near the Madeira River. They intended to expel them from their territory or to eliminate them like herds of black macaques in order to keep their lands for the denouncements, with the purpose of obtaining gold, illegal wood or exploring oil deposits and then transferring the information to transnational companies or to the national oil company, Petrobras. The was plenty of classified information to sell.

I explained that this region was the habitat of these indigenous tribes, who lived as itinerant groups without harming anyone. They only prowled around with their black bows and arrows with poisoned tips. I told him that this was a method used by the *syringeros* in the golden age of rubber. That way they kept huge areas in the middle of the jungle. When the volume of this business decreased, the invaders continued with the possession of the land. After that, everything was simple: lawyers and notaries registered the property as a *denuncio* and later as legally acquired property with the right to sell.

Nowadays, the business objective has changed. Now it is the miners who strip the protected areas in search of gold veins and precious and semiprecious stones. This is the stage of the informal fortune seekers. The objective is to occupy the territories where there are gold-bearing sands or lands likely to contain quartz, amethyst, emeralds or diamonds.

Jalufe wanted to know if I had reported the massacre to the local authorities. I replied that I had, and not only to the local authorities, but also to the police, even though I was sure that they would not act in defense of the Indigenous population. I explained that the matter was part of the corruption of power and that I even wanted to contact the offices of the Public Prosecutor. I was worried though that they would suspect me; they would even invent stories of how I was affiliated to an extreme left-wing political party or that I belonged to a human rights organization with the reputation of subverting order and screwing the authorities. That's what I told him so he could understand the context.

Jalufe understood my indignation because he knew that murder was a sinister but frequent practice to eliminate enemies of power and those who were an obstacle to the illicit enrichment of mafia groups. Remembering the scene, I felt nauseous again at the smell of roasted flesh, at the musky stench of the excrement released before death. I experienced again that disgust for the bestiality of the strong and the helplessness of the weak. I was disgusted to belong to a rotten race of ambitious people, of individuals who only think of how to line their own pockets. I also felt pity for being part of the infamy, even if I had only witnessed the barbarism.

I could make a psychological profile of these people.

"They are unscrupulous, capable of selling their mothers for money or power. Guys who think they are the kings of the world and can do whatever they want in their arrogance," I told Jalufe.

It was too much to say that the mercenaries' camps were visited by prostitutes hired as part of the pay to keep the assassins happy. Women smelling of liquor, cigarettes and something that smelled of rancid fish. I interpreted these as male secretions. Women with the language of the worst criminal gangs, who seemed to emerge from one of Dante's hells. I described them as beings with greasy bodies and unctuous skin, although deep down I was lying, because I had seen girls who seemed to be out of place because they looked like newcomers to the jungle. Then I understood that these young women had been captured in the nets of juvenile prostitution.

Thus, the mafia turned the area into a paradise for drug trafficking, illegal mining and indiscriminate logging. Then the state-owned oil companies and large hydroelectric plants entered the area, these were expected to respect legality, but the reality was that the abuses continued. The route continued to be plagued by girls and young women who, originally, had been negotiated by their relatives with organizations dedicated to the trafficking of women for sexual exploitation.

Despite that, and many other unsettling realities, both Jalufe and I shared a stubborn hope: "Everything is changing for the better! Everything is changing for the better!" The truth is that I doubted this optimism. Maybe it was not an affirmation, but the way of seeing life of a delirious or a chronic optimist.

Anyone listening to us had a right to think that was the way two idiotic guys talked. But we had to hope, if it was the last thing we did. Maybe vaccines would be created to boost immune systems. Maybe after the war we would live a moment of peace and a new world balance would take place.

Then Jalufe said, "The Ebola outbreak was not as large as expected. It was as if it was self-limiting in time after a boisterous start. We have had no new cases for two weeks now and those who are in hospital are gradually improving."

That was the explanation for our intransigent optimism. The self-limitation in time of the great evils. Equilibrium as a universal constant. Entropy. I did not answer because I shared his criterion.

Suddenly, after a prolonged silence, which he took advantage of to drink the rest of his coffee, he began to narrate episodes related to his life: "We were once told that there was a population of lepers in Mali, near Smara," he said. "It was a new challenge, so we took it on. When we arrived, we saw their faces deformed by the disease, the cavities of the nostrils without cartilage and skin, the gums without lips, the folds of skin over the face, like a bulldog's snout. It was terrible. Instead of fingers, they had stumps. The cause was related to accidental amputations caused by loss of sensation. They had leonine features and ulcers all over the body.

"It was common for them to wear gauze and bandages soiled by the soggy ichor and stuck to the skin ulcers. In the air there was a nauseating smell coming from the putrefaction of the flesh. But what was impressive was not the known stigmata, but the shared poverty. The blankets and clothes. The wooden vessels, with the broth prepared by the women, which went from mouth to mouth after they cleaned the edges with their own hands. For them there was no feeling of disgust. I wanted to tell them that this could spread the disease. Then I thought they were all sick." Again, he was silent. Maybe he wanted to see if I was interested in the conversation.

"What a pity!" I didn't want to say anything else. Then I tried to pay attention to Jalufe's description. His narration brought to my mind the memory of other places where people with common illnesses were grouped together.

"The place was near a small town called Smara," he continued, "where the Tuaregs congregate to practice their prayers. It is a town near Timbuktu, considered a holy city by the Berbers, the Tuaregs and the Mauritanians. Smara does not have the madrasas of Timbuktu; these are sort of universities, built in mud and boulders, where students of the Koran can learn the message of Allah.

"In Smara, the sheikhs, who are the military and religious leaders, gather after having crossed the desert. They arrive in the Holy City after having fought several battles against the soldiers of the Malian army, reinforced by French and Spanish mercenaries. This place is the refuge of the nomads who have arrived from the desert." He took a breath and continued his lecture, "the caravans take weeks to cross the desert. During their journey, it is not the distance that counts, but the nights on roads that only they know. I imagine that, by dint of traveling through this territory, they are guided, like the old navigators, by the position of the stars and correct their route during the day until they see the stars again the following night." His account was intended to provide a coherent interpretation. "They tell how many nights they had to camp in canvas tents. To avoid being buried by sandstorms, they arranged the camels and horses in two concentric circles for protection.

"The sheikhs guide them. When they find an enemy patrol, they are the ones who initiate combat and plot the attack and escape strategies because they use surprise as a weapon." As Jalufe narrated, I thought that the nomads, because of their knowledge of the routes in the desert, could choose where to flee without leaving a trace. Imagine the camels. Each one carries two wicker baskets hanging on either side of his body. In them go the women and children, the elders on the back of the camels. In case of escape, the camels would start the escape with the women. They would be followed by the camels carrying the elders. In the end, the sheikhs would order the withdrawal of the warriors and would leave the slaves carrying the bundles with the provisions as a trophy. They also abandon on the battlefield part of the camels' packs." There was another silence, which I interpreted as a period to remember. Then he continued, "the Berbers are, perhaps, the only people who have the way of life of the gypsies, as if both were condemned to repeat the myth of Sisyphus.

"Picking up their gear every morning and setting out with a goal that was only in the minds of their leaders. I imagine them climbing the slope while pushing a rock and then waiting for it to roll all the way down, and repeating the same action the next day."

It was evident that the figure of the myth of Sisyphus was fortunate for the external perception of the life of the Berbers, the Gypsies and the uncontacted natives of South America. Perhaps there existed in Papua, and in other places I did not know, other ethnic groups that assumed the condemnation of Sisyphus. Perhaps the way of life could be applied to their lucky brothers, the Tuaregs, who lived in the corridors from the Algerian Sahara to the Spanish Sahara.

That is why I asked the English doctor, director of the project, the following question, "Why don't they settle in one place and start another activity?" I said while thinking that I knew very little about that town and its way of life.

"Maybe they have a virtual homeland, without territory or borders. Perhaps it is not territory that unites people, ethnicities, peoples, but the bonds of blood, religion and history. The groups of Montenegro, Macedonia, Serbia, Bosnia and Herzegovina, Croatia lived on the territory of what was the former Yugoslavia, but they had been split by other factors." I realized that I knew little about the migrations of Arabs, North Africans and sub-Saharan Africans and how their displacements had changed the structures of cities like Marseilles, Paris, London, Madrid. Even cities not previously chosen by African diasporas, such as Berlin, Brussels, Zurich, Athens, Rome were impacted.

I remembered the Parisian district of Barbès, where the North Africans lived, whether they were Moroccans, Algerians, Mauritanians or Tunisians. And the Château-Rouge district, where Senegalese, Malians, Kenyans, Nigerians and Angolans lived. Then it came to my mind that in New York, on Eighth Avenue, in Times Square, you would come across people of African origin selling tickets to tourists for the Big Bus. Several generations and hundreds of years have passed since the arrival of their grandparents in these lands. Black New Yorkers were people born in the Bronx and Harlem, neighborhoods in the Big Apple where African descendants predominated. Perhaps they were born or lived in Brooklyn, Queens, New Jersey or elsewhere in the big city or neighboring states, such as Washington, the nation's capital. Who knows, some of them might even be last-minute immigrants, such as Haitians or Jamaicans, Tunisians, Algerians, Libyans, Moroccans, Syrians or Egyptians, who arrived in recent diasporas as a result of political conflicts in their countries of origin.

In Madrid you could find them in the Plaza de Chueca selling to the junkies who approached on their Harley-Davidson motorcycles. Some also control the prostitutes in miniskirts and provocative necklines who show thighs and breasts, despite the unbearable cold on Gran Via, and even more so in the Plaza de Cibeles. In other cities of Europe you could see individuals dressed in white tunics down to their ankles or vertical striped tunics of gray on a white background. At the same time these people wore turbans or hoods that looked like airline stewardesses' headdresses. For them, the clothing represented their dignity in the countries south of the Sahara Desert.

Those who wore white robes had, in turn, very dark faces and very thick lips. I assumed that they came from Senegal. People from the high sphere of the country or members of an animist religion that believed in the spirit of objects, both animate and inanimate. I felt they might have icons in their residences representing ancestors, including the great Changó of the Yoruba Shinto religion. These men, in long robes, walked with an entourage of people: bodyguards or government officials, or part of a delegation of businessmen from their homeland. Or, simply, members of their family.

People with a different appearance were a rarity in the context. Most of the immigrants were poor and lived in apartments and garrets on the boulevards near Montmartre, crammed together in shanty environments, with the elevators out of order and the doors protected by an external trellis. The buildings looked like post-war prisons, where defeated soldiers were locked up. On the rooftops and in the windows hung laundry. I guessed that many of them had to sleep in shifts. Maybe they also had to wait for their turn to use the toilet or use the clothesline. And it was the same in the neighborhoods of the downtown districts, as well as in those built on the urban periphery.

Many of the inhabitants of the Africanized neighborhoods had arrived in waves of migration. Most of them came between 1957 and 1977, when exiles from Algeria, Libya and Morocco arrived. Then followed the sub-Saharans; mostly from Angola and Senegal, who came protected by the International Red Cross to the port of Marseilles or the Baltic ports. After a few months, the immigrants moved to the big cities in search of stable work. The cities of choice were Paris, London, Madrid and Berlin. Later they moved to other European locations: Brussels, Rome, Milan, Barcelona; wherever there was a minimum option of work, even if it was temporary or marginal. The lack of employment turned them, soon after their arrival, into street traders, jugglers, souvenir or trinket sellers, if not thugs of all kinds, from muggers to pimps, drug smugglers and hit men in the service of the mafias. Those who were a little luckier got jobs as drivers of rented vehicles, porters in restaurants and hotels, dockworkers.

In the case of women, they worked as domestic servants, caregivers for the elderly and public cleaning ladies, if not beggars who begged for alms on the curbs in areas near tourist attractions or at the exit of subway tunnels.

In the busiest streets and boulevards you could see the men and women who had had some success in life. Men in black suits and briefcases looked like bureaucrats, businessmen or professionals. Their women wore brand name clothes, Victoria's Secret or Givenchy, in strong and bright colors. Their demeanor and manners clearly distinguished them from the immigrant population as a whole. I imagined that despite being from the same country or sharing the same origin, there were also cultural and economic hierarchies. They all came from sub-Saharan countries, but some were fleeing extreme poverty and lack of opportunity, while others were leaving for political reasons or because the situation threatened their economic stability.

It occurred to me to think of a South African bishop, similar to Desmond Tutu, or a law professor at the Sorbonne, recognized for his professional quality. Perhaps I had to think of other types of success: traffickers of women, clandestine lottery sellers, real estate or stock market brokers, money dealers obtained in the countries of origin by corrupt governments. They might even be the children or relatives of the dictators in power. They would come from places under colonial domination which, after gaining independence, sent their students to European universities or high schools.

Leaving the Château-Rouge district, in the direction of the Place de la République, you would meet white-skinned women with some vice. Women in long overcoats of any color, with a paper bag in which they carried a bottle of red wine or white wine from the Alsace vintages. Women who walked shuffling or dragged by a lapdog who protected them in the raids of vice, because the police did not stop them to avoid the work of transferring the dogs to the kennels that were outside the area of the district. Lonely women who would crane their necks on the sidewalks as if they wanted to cross the street to get to some place where they could sit on the curbs and hide behind the vehicles parked on the avenue. Once settled, they would drink until they were exhausted, waiting for the patrol car to arrive to arrest them and take them to a rehabilitation center or, simply, to a police station with a jail.

The disjointed faces, with a somber expression, evidenced a variant of depression and dementia, or a stage I or II Korsakoff's psychosis. The staggering gait could be explained by Wernicke's neuropathy.

I also saw boys no older than twenty of all races, lining up in rows to get their dose of morphine or naloxone, depending on what phase, withdrawal or treatment, they were in. I noticed that the younger ones looked no more than fifteen years old. I felt sorry to see that there was a painful underworld that was right in front of us and that we did not perceive because of selfishness or because we were distracted by our own issues.

Near the Pigalle and the Moulin Rouge, in the small squares near the Sacré-Cœur, artists offered their portraits for meager sums. This was the Paris of 2000.

Suddenly I recalled the streets of Marseilles along the seafront, steep, with an uneven floor of basalt stone. From up high you could see the steamers used by the emigrants to reach the coast. In the city stood the basilica of Notre-Dame de la Garde, from where you could see the old port and the neighborhood of Le Panier, inhabited mostly by Italians and Armenians, who opened craft stores, pastry shops, and bakeries. At the port, midshipmen and customs and immigration employees checked arrivals on electronic tablets. Images from Charles Chaplin's film *The Golden Chimera* came to mind. The same scene: people huddled together, roped together in groups of all ages. Some in black and white, others in full color. Some appeared to be uniformed in attire that simulated raincoats, yellow coats with lead-colored, phosphorescent ribbons. In reality, they were fishermen's outfits that had been sold to them in the ports and coves of the African Mediterranean. The images were etched on my retina. Although, as a physician, I knew that the retina was part of the cerebral cortex; just an extension of axons and dendrites attached to the receptor neurons, its own modulators, and, among them, its own repressors. Codons and anticodons in the messenger RNAs (mRNA) and in their corresponding triplet transfer RNA (tRNA), which encoded a type of proteins. These became transmitters between synapses. The magic of thinking at the molecular level.

Later, from 2010 onwards, refugees fleeing internal wars in the Middle East and North Africa arrived. They were fleeing bombings, some perpetrated by NATO allies, as well as from battles between Sunni and Shiite.

I don't think anyone can explain how the Russian bombers dropped their shells on the cities taken by the rebels. Then, as if in perfect sequence, the U.S. fighter-bombers would attack the ruins of the city. I wondered how it was possible that the Americans were allied with the Russians; how, in turn, were the countries of the European Union and the rich regions of the Middle East involved in this confusion? There were so many questions that were so very strange.

I assumed they were doing it to support their allies or out of pure humanity, as they were fighting against the forces of evil, so that citizens would not succumb to the onslaught of caliphate fighters or other fundamentalist groups such as Al Qaeda, who could enslave them, especially the women, who were forced to live under a veil without the freedoms of Western women.

Even so, I did not understand it, just as I did not understand the wars against apostates. Maybe the people there knew the verse, but I didn't subscribe to it. Excuse me! It sounded like the lyrics of a tango to me. I imagine that the young men fleeing the conflict did so in order not to be recruited as combatants on either side of the conflict. Among these refugees were those who fled the chaos after the revolution in Libya, which ended with the death of the dictator Gaddafi. The country, after the dictatorship, became a no man's land. Suddenly, one region of the country was ruled by soldiers of the dictator; another by militias paid by transnational companies interested in oil and other natural wealth; another, by the Gulf of Sirte, dominated by the forces of Daesh. Revenge killings and vandalism were the order of the day. I am convinced that, if statistics had been kept, they would be in first place, for cause of death above epidemics and common diseases.

After conversations in the restaurants in Kampala's business district, Jalufe and I had the feeling that we knew each other better. It could be that the bond resembled friendship. At that stage I began to understand his connection to this land of savannahs, deserts and great lakes. And this despite the fact that days before my arrival at the hospital an armed group had kidnapped him; they only released him when they saw how useful he could be to the people of the town. He had described the kidnapping to me after several weeks of work, after the last conversation in the restaurant we frequented.

"The truth," he confessed, "is that I could not identify the kidnappers. Most of them were young boys with guns and uniforms that were too big. I thought it might be a group of bandits who were planning to demand a ransom for me and for the two Catholic nuns who were accompanying me on this mission. Later I understood that it was a commando who wanted to make his presence known in the northern region of the country, on the border with Sudan. Anyway," he said, "I got the scare of my life.

"At that moment you can't know how the adventure will end. You just want to guess the motives and you can think of many: political pressure, revenge for entering their territory and taking away their prominence. Maybe they saw me as an animist sorcerer. I also thought they wanted to ask for a ransom and that a group of hired killers had been ordered to intimidate us into leaving the country. There are so many possibilities," Jalufe explained to me.

"I can't believe it," I declared. "I can imagine your fear in those circumstances. I was also kidnapped on two occasions and felt the fear you experience in those circumstances. In the Rwandan conflict I was surrounded by a group of Hutu boys who had two dead bodies in the back of the four-wheel drive truck. One of them had been shot and the other appeared to have perished from a hemorrhagic disease; perhaps Ebola or something else capable of causing upper gastrointestinal bleeding, because both the clothes and the jaw of the corpse showed traces of bloody vomit.

"That time I felt a paralyzing fear, as well as some resignation for what might happen. I depended only on what our guide and the porters, whose ethnicity I did not know, whether they were Hutu or Tutsi, were explaining. I did not know what they were saying.

"What happened next was that the group leader asked me to feel his belly, just in case he had the same thing as the deceased. After the examination, I reported that the guy was not suffering from anything that would compromise his liver, much less anything that could be the indication of a hemorrhagic disease because he had no ecchymosis on his lower limbs and no subconjunctival hemorrhages or bleeding gums. Then they got into their van and left us to resume our itinerary in the silver-blue vehicle with the United Nations logo." I did not know if my narration would reassure him; however, I continued speaking, "My next kidnapping took place in South America.

"That time I was kidnapped for several days. They were armed people who belonged to a faction of an insurrectional movement. That time I was saved by the conversations I had with a guy who declared himself the leader of the group. He was a fundamentalist who had developed a discourse on the permanent armed struggle, which confused me, because I did not know if it was a group of Maoists or if they were Trotskyists. In either case, I had been taken in one of the raids of that cell, far from their area of action.

"My job was to detect yellow fever and delta hepatitis as a cause of sudden death, as autopsies had noted that some of the deceased had stony livers. Therefore, I had to analyze the organs that the local doctors had kept under refrigeration. I also had to explore the possible sick people who appeared in the area.

"I was kept in a shack that had once been a fruit stand, in the path of illegal loggers who preyed on the jungle. The heat was over forty degrees and I was sweating like crazy, and the damned mosquitoes left my body like a sieve. That time I was left in the middle of the jungle, without guides or health personnel. They abandoned the assistants who accompanied me somewhere in the jungle, with no way of communicating with the outside world. I swear I was so scared that I seriously thought about quitting the job, which, to begin with, seemed like an adventure in dangerous territory.

"Later I found out that from the group that made up the delegation, two individuals had disappeared, although some claimed that they had joined the irregulars. This was after I was rescued by some settlers who were dedicated to the sale of curare in boats going up the river. When I regained consciousness, I was in a post, receiving venous treatment for parenteral hydration.

"Anyway, now I remember it as if they were anecdotes, images that belonged to a dream or experiences that a colleague told me. Nausea and diarrhea screwed up my intestines for at least two or three months. I treated myself with antibiotics, although I was not sure it was an infectious disease, but rather an emotional one."

I remembered the news I had read in some European newspaper; I think it was in *The Guardian* or in *El Mundo*: the article mentioned the massacre of a group of Angolan doctors and nurses in an area dominated by UNITA guerrillas. Nothing guaranteed the behavior of a group of paranoid fanatics who saw enemies in any unknown person.

"That's right, I think I was born again that time," added Jalufe. There was no doubt in my mind: I had been reborn or resurrected.

Despite the incident, I could sense that Jalufe felt attached to the country, even to the continent. His descriptions of the geography and the people who inhabited those places were very detailed. When I listened to him, I had the feeling that I had been there. I think I shared with him the battle of the *Shaykhs* when he told me about the death of his warriors and horses. The individuals fell from the deadly blasts of the enemy riflemen. In a matter of minutes, the military men were eaten by carrion birds, even before the desert sand engulfed them without leaving the slightest trace of their bodies and the din of battle.

I felt sorry for the fate of the nomadic families. To my mind came the figure of a little girl with brown skin and light green eyes. The girl's beauty was evident; the color of her eyes contrasted with the color of her matted hair and wind-tanned skin. Jalufe had told me about the bad winds, which, according to the tradition of the Saharan and Bantu peoples, generated tragedies and brought disease. The bad wind could explain the cholera epidemics on the coast, which left several thousand dead. The sick died after suffering from diarrhea and incoercible vomiting. The bad wind also justified the defeat of the militias of the Popular Front for the Liberation of Azawad. I told him half-jokingly, "In my land we cure bad wind by burning branches of rue, which crackle in the fire. Then we rub the plant on the foreheads of those affected and drive away the ailment."

"What is rue?" he asked.

We both laughed at the comment. Then he told me that Kampala was home to Makerere University, where they taught courses that were in high demand on the continent: law, medicine, mining engineering, economics. Then he told me about the Islamic schools, where the Koran and the Islamic tradition were studied. We talked about the appearance of armed groups of a radical Sunni branch that sought to liberate territories in the Middle East and Africa to create a state they wanted to call the Caliphate; a country that would cover North Africa and the entire Middle East. It was the area that had belonged to the Umayyad Caliphate, between 660 and 750 AD.

"What do you think of everything that is happening on this continent?" I asked.

"It takes time to know what is going to happen in these countries," he replied. With that ambiguous answer, typical of an Englishman, we ended our conversation.

He once told me about the habit of some Zulu youths in Cape Town, South Africa, Rhodesia and Namibia of intoxicating themselves with *ice* (a form of crystal meth). He also tried to explain to me the Yoruba religion, which had spread to other continents as a consequence of the slave trade for the cultivation of sugar cane. And he spoke of the syncretism of the Catholic religion with the polytheistic cult of the Yoruba. I got an idea of the orishás, some of whom were children who protected their followers from the evil of their enemies. And others, like the great Changó, gave them virility in the bid for life, love and survival in the face of the hardships they suffered at the hands of their masters.

On one occasion, probably after an operation for a cystocele accompanying a lymphatic elephantiasis due to filariasis, or after a fasciotomy to avoid compartment syndrome due to viper bites, Jalufe asked me something I did not expect, "What's next after this?"

I did not know what he meant, or perhaps I understood that he was asking me about the next scheduled operation. I replied that after cutting the skin, subcutaneous cellular tissue and fasciae, and exposing the muscles so that the tissues infected by the anaerobes would come into contact with the oxygen in the air, there remained the hyperbaric chambers to increase the oxygen pressure in the areas where the infection had penetrated.

"I'm not talking about the fucking job, but about what I was supposed to do next." Then he added, "For this shitty life I lost my family."

When I heard that, I was cold as an iceberg, even though the temperature was above thirty-five degrees and the humidity was almost one hundred percent. I thought about the programming of hyperbaric chambers to accelerate the treatment of wet gangrene, with its dark phlyctenas in the areas affected by the infection. At the same time I imagined that Jalufe was referring to a very elegant society woman who had refused to come to these wet and wild lands to accompany my surgeon friend. It reminded me of a scene from the movie *The Snows of Kilimanjaro*. In it, the protagonist suffering from gangrene and delirium, a product of the microbial toxin, was accompanied by a woman. I don't remember if it was his wife or his girlfriend. During several minutes of the film the couple talks about unfulfilled dreams and comments on their memories of their now distant stay in London, or maybe it was another city in Europe.

The setting is unique: on the edge of the Kilimanjaro glacier, and what surprises Hemingway's character is that at that height of the mountain they find the skin and bones of a leopard. What could a leopard be doing in that place? One explanation could be that the feline arrived there in pursuit of a gazelle or an antelope. I have no doubt that there are situations that do not occur in the normal context.

Jalufe took advantage of my silence to continue the conversation. The details I remember in a fragmentary way, but the background was quite clear: "My friend, did you know that I was married and have two daughters in London? My wife did not accept that I spent so much time away from home and asked me for a divorce. That left me lonely and without so much as a dog to bark at me."

Perhaps the comment was due to the fact that I had shown no signs of affectionate communication during the period I was working with him. Perhaps he simply wanted us both to come clean. After a pause, which I did not use to answer his question, he continued, "I think, partner, we're both screwed in that respect. Maybe, in that and other aspects." After his comment he let out a loud laugh, which I interpreted as the laughter of a naughty child surprised by an adult who has caught him committing a mischief. Or the smile of a boxer who felt his opponent's punch, which put him in bad conditions, on the verge of knockout.

"I think you're right. At least, that's where I'm doubly fucked too." I told him about my life since the loss of Gabriela and the way I dealt with it, focusing on working to forget. I still perceive it that way. I guess it's a fact of life. But I feel like I've been knocked to the ground. I read recently that there were people who had an orphan's vocation. That must be what happens to me. I didn't comment further, although deep down I felt like shit thinking about all I had lost. I tried to evade questions and cross-examination to avoid useless confessions. So I changed the subject, "Are filarial elephantiasis very common in the region? Is there a prevention program that treats it with triple drugs in the endemic regions?"

I recalled one of the prevention programs that used 400 mg of albendazole twice a year, plus i200 ug/kg body weight of ivermectin and 6 mg/kg body weight of diethylcarbamazine citrate. The result of the triple drug plus vector control, the *Anopheles* mosquito, and the use of insecticide-sprayed bed nets had shown great efficacy in reducing the occurrence of new cases.

However, my mind was trapped in the feeling of orphanhood that at times invaded me. I remembered the months when my mother could not walk because of swollen legs. They were soft edemas that she partially treated with albumin and diuretics. Chemotherapies with the three drugs methotrexate, 5-fluorouracil and cyclophosphamide came to mind. Although I don't remember if the last sessions were with doxorubicin or with cisplatin. That time my mother had explosive vomiting for which she received a dose of six ampoules of metoclopramide before each chemotherapy session. One day she seemed to tolerate the treatment, but the next day she felt as if she was running out of life.

Gabriela accompanied her to each session. She told her countless anecdotes about her family, who had emigrated to Buenos Aires from an Italian city, Bologna, in the Emilia-Romagna region. I'm sure she explained to her that the city's tourist attractions were the palace of the Notaries, the mill canal, the Neptune fountain and the two medieval towers. Her mother, according to her, was an expert in seafood, in addition to preparing typical dishes of the region. She made *tagliatelle* and lasagna Bolognese particularly well. Her father had been a sales agent in South America for the Lamborghini.

My mother's attention was focused on her as if it were a chaptered novel in which the characters had conflicts of interest. I understand that Gabriela was trying to distract my mother so that she would not feel the symptoms of the therapy and she would listen to her attentively, trying to forget her own drama and the undesirable effects of the medication. Years before, my mother would bake us a baked corn cake that I thought was delicious. I never got to eat the cake again. I was never again served cocoa and cheeses on wheat bread.

I also remembered that as a teenager I was an asshole who was nicknamed *Pata de Cabra* (Goat's Leg). I was a scoundrel and I was a friend of all the bad guys and pimps who all led me astray. In the end I gave up my vices and my friends. I left the girls, who called themselves the *Tóxicas*. I gave up the slums and the wanderings. In the end I came up with another madness: to be a good son. Maybe it was too late and the mitotic chaos had already taken hold in my mother's descending colon. Maybe she needed to see that I had gone the other way to feel relieved. I'm sure she was happy when I returned to the homeland with my medical degree. She saw my first performance in a hospital. Then she swore that she was not in any pain; on the contrary, she felt so satisfied, even though I knew that she felt intense pain in her lumbar spine, which at times prevented her from walking or bending down to lift an object from the floor or simply tying her shoelaces. She even confessed to me that her own mother, who was no longer in this world, would have been very happy to know that I had graduated, even though she was already entering the delirium that preceded her death.

Suddenly, when the conversation seemed to be over, Jalufe said,

"We stay in the area." He was referring to the people in his organization: doctors, nurses, assistants, laboratory technicians, sanitary technologists and coordinators. "We will remain in the hospital. We want to be seen as an outpost in places where there are no other health services. We want the population to perceive that this is a right that should be demanded not only from their authorities, but also from the rest of the world.

"Also, for me, it is exciting to investigate the customs of the inhabitants of this continent. He paused to sigh. Although that part is just a lot of hot air. The truth is that this is my world now. At least, that's how I see it."

I kept thinking about the nomadic Berbers, so different from the sedentary Berbers in Marseille. Not in racial traits, but in the way of life. Something like the eagles that live in a zoo and those that inhabit the peaks of the Alps. I also pondered about the photograph Jalufe had on his desk, showing a very elegant woman with two young people at her side. The woman looked very haughty, and the children were clearly proud of something. I instantly imagined that they were Jalufe's ex-wife and their two offspring. Because of their age I guessed that they were in high school or the first years of college.

The young woman resembled her mother, and the boy resembled his father. I don't know in what detail of the photograph I noticed that the woman must belong to an evangelical church, whose pastor could be her own father. Maybe it was just my imagination, or maybe she reminded me of another woman who belonged to the Methodist Pentecostal church in the Chilean province of Concepción. The one who didn't fit in the picture was my friend, the doctor at the Ugandan field hospital. With the canvas scout hat and sleeveless vest over a polyester twill shirt. I could imagine him in the desert region of Mali talking with the sheikhs, or visiting a lazaretto somewhere near Timbuktu or Smara. There, where the sick lived in shacks made of twigs and mud from the alkaline water lagoon, he ate dates and eggs from laying hens he had himself brought from a nursery on the upper Nile to be raised in the village.

I am sure that he had air-conditioned barracks built in each room to create a sort of field hospital, which ended up being a permanent facility for leprosy patients and their relatives. There he recruited, among the relatives of the sick, young girls to train them in the work of nursing assistants. In this way, he created the first school for nursing assistants in the region. In the leprosarium hospital, he checked the open wounds on the stumps, took photographs of the patients before and after treatment, and checked for stigmata and bumps on the skin, especially on the face.

Maybe it wasn't all work; at some point the professor would have met an Arab girl or a European volunteer with whom he fell in love. I guessed at this. I even believed that he might have the courage to break all barriers to conquer a princess with very tanned skin and green eyes that he would have met in a caravan of nomads in the Spanish Sahara.

"There is so much to do on this continent," I sighed, thinking of the leprosy treatments with dapsone and rifampicin and in some cases clofazimine. "I would like to stay longer to help them. Besides, as you say, that way I could learn something more about the Islamic religion and the religious syncretism of those who profess Santeria. Maybe I would learn something about the customs of the people." I paused. "Professor, I swear to you that knowing other peoples is not just a joke. I have so many questions to ask. I would like to understand them better."

I was thinking about how the Berbers keep their horses beautiful, how those lustrous animals withstand the heat and sand of the desert. Camels and dromedaries have reserves of water and food in the hump, but the horses ridden by the sheikhs, who look so spirited, needed water and fodder to subsist. Perhaps the water bottles carried by the dromedaries supplied both humans and the animals of the caravan, including the goats and the occasional bird that seemed to be used in falconry to ward off the crows and vultures that approached the retinue.

I kept thinking about the slave traders and their slaves. I imagined them traveling through the jungles, following the course of the rivers and then crossing the savannah and the desert until they reached the fairs, on the southern border of Libya. The buyers, who were not the final masters, but the intermediaries, would come to that place. These, in turn, would sell them to the captains of the Libyan ships, who would take them out of the continent to turn them into slaves. In the end I realized that I knew very little about the subject.

Normally, I would think of nothing and only complain about the unbearable weather in the afternoons, even with the ceiling fans and air conditioning in the hospital wards. I also complained about the mosquito bites when I went near the mud flats and the taste of the water, that had a chlorine aftertaste that made it undrinkable for me.

"It would have been fortunate to be able to count on your support for longer, but I understand that, in our profession, we are beholden to commitments already agreed upon beforehand," he said, looking down at the floor, which made me assume that he had miscalculated the help I could give him.

"The bad news," I said, "is that my return trip to Europe is scheduled for next week. Taking advantage of my stay in the region, I would like to visit Marrakech, Fez, Casablanca, Algiers, Cairo and the pyramids."

I kept thinking about the quarantine period I would have to undergo after my visit to a place facing an infectious disease outbreak. Possibly, I would have to remain in isolation in a hospital in Rome until I completed the clinical tests that would indicate that I was neither sick nor a carrier of any tropical disease. Once I was discharged, I would visit the Vatican Museums and the Trevi Fountain and stroll through Piazza Navona to see the Fountain of the Four Rivers with the Obelisk of Domitian. I also planned to visit the church of St. Agnes in Agony, with its white facade and dome.

Then I would like to travel to New York to walk around Manhattan. I would also like to visit Tisch Hospital and Bellevue Hospital Center on First Avenue, where I will be able to see some friends I have not spoken to for several months. At the same time, it could serve as a way to relive the past. In the early years of the eighteenth century, cholera, malaria and yellow fever were treated in its wards.

Similarly, I will visit the United Nations headquarters to reminisce about meetings with the directors of the World Health Organization and the overseers of the new global commitment to end to tuberculosis. They organized the first international conference of health ministers, with seventy-five countries, in Moscow in November 2017. The conference declaration aimed to achieve "a world without TB" by 2030. I thought then of the numbers affected by tuberculosis in the world, which exceeded ten million. I also thought of those suffering from AIDS and those multidrug-resistant to first-line drugs.

Possibly, after walking around places related to my work, I could invite a couple of Brazilian doctor friends who work directly with Dr. Tedros Adhanom, the director of the World Health Organization. My friends were Drs. Airton and Monica da Silva. Perhaps we could go to dinner at Carmine's restaurant in Times Square, where we could enjoy our favorite Italian dishes. There we would reminisce about our previous meeting at the Waldorf Astoria many years ago. On that occasion I would be staying at the Hilton Times Square on 42nd Street between Seventh and Eighth Avenues.

The Waldorf Astoria was the hotel of the gangsters of New York, on 300 Park Avenue. When you walk through its corridors, you get the feeling that at any moment you are going to run into Marilyn Monroe and other glamorous New York celebrities. However, those of us who attended the conferences of the International Convention of Infectious Diseases also stayed there. Kofi Annan, then president of the United Nations, stayed at the same hotel and occupied the luxurious presidential suite. I didn't know whether to enter through the Ladies lobby or to walk along the Pavos promenade. Nor did I know what outfit to wear in the large dining rooms or when walking through the corridors of that luxurious hotel.

Years before working in Uganda, I had worked in the field hospital of the world's largest refugee camp, Mae La, in Thailand's Tak province. That time my job was to rule out an outbreak of yellow fever among the Mekong villagers. We went after some suspected cases of the disease had been reported following the mass death of monkeys in the jungle. The place was not a hospital, but a refugee camp for those persecuted by the Myanmar government, the Rohingya Muslims, a minority living mostly in the state of Rakhine. The barracks inhabited by the refugees were similar to the wards of the Doctors of the World hospital near Lake Victoria, several kilometers from Kampala. The refugees were fleeing the conflicts that took place between 2000 and 2008; conflicts that became really violent in the last months of 2007 and the first months of 2008, although ethnic hatred had been present in the area for many years before, perhaps half a century.

Undoubtedly, the situations were not the same. However, the circumstances and the scenes seemed to me like *déjà vu*, something I had already experienced, an anticipation. The commander, with a military background, was nothing like the doctor Jalufe, but I have a similar memory of them both, a time-proof friendship. It's a kind of empathy that I can't help but compare. Perhaps they reminded me of peripheral people I also met on my visits to those places. For example, an Irish woman who worked as a mission coordinator for Doctors of the World. She seemed very committed to her task; I even got the feeling that she was keen on Jalufe. I would have liked to warn my friend about it. Maybe he already knew and maybe he was already involved with that slender woman. I remember her with a white face and some freckles, very blue eyes and reddish hair.

I don't know if it was out of emulation or healthy envy, but I also had a name in mind: Nadia. She could fill the gaps in my life. At least, that illusion generated in me an intense desire to see her again at the Cappuccino Café or in a seafood restaurant next to the Pacific Ocean, or perhaps in one of the cities of southern Chile. I would look for her and tell her, without any shyness, what I was keeping inside: "I just fell in love with you." I imagined that she was watching me with smiling eyes, as if she was waiting for a declaration.

Other images also stayed with me. For example, the Burmese woman carrying children and elderly people through the jungle to the Thai border. She looked like a soul in pain, an ethereal vision, with her white robe over an almost flat chest. Or the image of a girl no more than ten years old, Berber or Tuareg, with a dark face and black hair, and with light green eyes that made her a child of exotic beauty. She was part of a caravan traveling through Western Sahara. The group, after several months of enduring the dry heat, which destroys the skin and mucous membranes, as well as the dusty winds, which sneak through the respiratory tract to the alveoli, and those cold nights as hostile as the noontime without shade, would stop in Smara to stock up on water and food.

She traveled on baskets attached to the hips of a dromedary that swung its load from one side to the other. The girl was between eight and ten years old, but her features already showed a face that would seduce the warriors of other caravans, or the Arab traders who came across her on their journey through the bazaars of Mogadishu or Algiers. She might become the last wife of a Saudi prince, or perhaps bad luck would cause her to fall ill with tuberculosis or pneumoconiosis from breathing desert sand and dust. Perhaps she would have to emigrate to Europe with other women seeking to escape persecution after the defeat of her tribe's warriors. Maybe there was no longer a place for her in the caravan because she had grown up or because those who made up the retinue had separated. In those circumstances, it was likely that I would cross paths with her in some European port such as Marseilles or Algeciras, without our recognizing each other.

But the images that stuck with me the most were not those, but those of other women. In this case, they were cadaverous-looking women who, in turn, were nursing stunted children. They wore green and yellow tunics. Also, those others who accompanied a group of armed men who fought to recover street by street a city in the hands of their enemies. They were in charge of carrying the baskets with ammunition for the machine guns in wicker baskets or on their shoulders. In the same way, they carried, in linen bundles, omelets prepared with eggs from free-range chickens.

Chapter 7
Walking the Path

Today, walking along the machete-opened trail, guided by a native expert and with several porters who came from the creek to the river strait, I think of the conversations with Jalufe and our experience in Uganda as I contemplate the turbulence of the waters. It seems to me that I should have stayed longer on that mission. At least until those with symptoms similar to hemorrhagic viruses were discharged, or until people stopped looking at me with pleading eyes.

Nothing compelled me to leave like I was in my evil hour, running from something I couldn't figure out. Maybe it was the typecasting, the single task, which was in the service standards manuals. Maybe it was an imprint on my life: leaving one place to find another where I could find my lost steps. I kept reminiscing about the women who fled from the armed forces. Emaciated women who carried their children clinging to the breast that had stopped suckling them. Perhaps there was something I should return for: the mountains near Lake Victoria or the bones of the first hominids that obsessed me in my youth. Who knows if I wanted to discover the last village attacked by Arab slave traders or sail the Nile in a ten-meter boat to reach some sacred place, Luxor or the Valley of the Kings, and thus find the ghost of Howard Carter.

The narrow pass was a gorge known as the Pongo de Aguirre. The two mountain ranges, which bordered the gorge, were separated by a distance of no more than two kilometers. At the bottom of the canyon the river became narrower and more sonorous, with rapids that meandered between rocky outcrops and bevel-cut edges. No one would think of braving the turbulence down there. Somewhere the rafters lay on shore and lifted the canoe to carry it on their backs along a path barely visible to experts and invisible to guys like me.

We had to walk along the paths that bordered an abyss cut at an oblique angle, with a depth of at least five hundred meters. At that moment I relived the time when I traveled along such dangerous roads as the road to the Yungas in Bolivia or the Bhutanese gorge that ran along the border with Tibet. The vertigo was unbearable for much of the journey, and then left a feeling of persistent nausea. From that goat path we could observe the water of the pongo, which was turning brown with swirling foam due to the turbulence.

At the end of the strait, in the pass, it was possible to continue downstream by canoe. They had attached a small motor that propelled the canoe to the area of the logging colonists who depredated the jungle with excessive logging, leaving bare spaces, without vegetation. From there they looked like mycosis ringworm on children's heads. We continued in the small boat until we reached a cove with a wooden dock on stilt houses that sank into the mud of the riverbank. It was the last point of river navigation. From that place we had to continue on foot along a path opened by the settlers with machetes.

I continued to walk, limping due to the wounds on the soles of my feet that reminded me of chilblains or wet ulcers from palmar and plantar dyshidrosis. In addition, my body was weakened by fatigue, which forced me to stop every fifty meters to catch my breath. Thus, we arrived at a town whose name was not defined by its inhabitants, who sometimes called it Platería and sometimes

Pueblo Madero. I assumed that the names somehow interpreted the main activity of the inhabitants. When I inquired, they told me that there were open pit mines in the mountain from which they had extracted argentite, until the seams were exhausted a few years before. Sometime later, perhaps a hundred years later, the settlers began to cut fine timber trees and built a sawmill. The change of occupation gave rise to the name of Pueblo Madero (Wood Town).

The settlement, which I would define as a small village in the low jungle, had huts separated by spaces of bushes and reeds. Before reaching it, we passed by the remains of two market spots where fruit and refreshments had been sold in the past. The only street that the town had was of earth and it extended from south to north. The population, made up of some two to three thousand inhabitants, was sustained by the harvesting of coffee, cultivated in its wild form on the hillsides surrounding the town.

When we arrived at the village we were greeted by a bustle of children and the smiles of the women sitting on the platforms at the entrance to their huts. I got the feeling that the chatter was due to their curiosity about my high-waisted boots and khaki uniform. Perhaps they were impressed by my canvas hat and beard. Suddenly, as if waiting for us, a group of men in colorful shirts appeared across the street and came to greet us. Most of them had skinny faces furrowed by wrinkles, toothless smiles and caked and unctuous hair, which contrasted with the brightly colored shirts.

"We've been waiting for you, doctor," they said, and I was left wondering if they were waiting for me or if there was a mix-up with some ministry official who would be arriving shortly.

I was then taken to a camp where the women served a plate of meat, which I presume was picuro or some other edible rodent, accompanied by boiled yuccas dipped in chicken eggs.

"Thank you, it was delicious," I thanked them. The food reminded me of my childhood, when an aunt or my own mother would prepare one of the guests' favorite dishes. That was so long ago, long before I became a lone wolf; long before I left the land and the homeland.

As I was tasting the food, I was observing each of the people present. "How is it that they came to this place and then stayed to live forever and ever?" The answer was not known to any of the attendees at the meeting because the arrival of the pioneers had taken place a long time ago, perhaps several generations before. "We stayed because this is where we were born," I imagined the most astute of the group would reply. Of course, I would understand the message, just as I understood why other human groups lived in similar regions, such as the Inuit peoples of the Arctic tundra or the Lapps of Scandinavia.

Days before, we had separated from the other members of the mission: Antonio Gonçalvez, a Brazilian microbiologist and biochemist expert in virology and detection of atypical bacteria, and the sanitarian Joao de Fonseca, who would be in charge of the treatments and of obtaining the samples for the studies. They had stayed in a rural hospital in a city near the place I intended to reach. There they would have the necessary comfort to embed the tissues I would send in kerosene. There they could also process the blood samples and run the lab tests. That way, the etiology of the disease could be found.

Both Antonio and Joao belonged to the research group at the University of Arizona led by Professor Michael Worobey, a prestigious scientist and pioneer in AIDS research. He and Professor Oliver Pybus of Oxford University had discovered the origin of the human immunodeficiency syndrome in the capital of the Democratic Republic of Congo, Kinshasa.

I presumed that the city was in the maelstrom of the riots that anticipated the independence of the Congo in 1960, with the joyfulness mixed with the problems of migration and overcrowding of rural people who had fled from the battle fronts. Shacks and cardboard sheets surrounded the city in an impressive disorder. The sidewalks were public urinals, and the dirty weeds of the mud flats were used as natural toilet paper, mosquitoes infested the suburbs and people bought their water from tanker trucks.

Armed gangs and merchant robbers were hiding on the outskirts of the city and remained very active. It was in that city that a disease previously considered a disease of apes, chimpanzees and gorillas, produced by the SIV virus (simian immunodeficiency virus), which depleted the primate population in the clouded mountains, began to be studied. I did not know the symptoms in primates, but I imagined that it caused a madness similar to rabies, the adynamia of sleeping sickness and diarrhea like those of cholera; until the great apes were consumed like rags and ended up on the floor like dead cats, dry and without fat or muscle.

The history of the country was a horror story since the allocation of the territories by Leopold II of Belgium, consecrated by the Berlin Conference in 1885, which formalized the scramble for Africa, a division of the continent among the colonizing countries. Leopold II kept the territory that today is the DRC.

This king ruled his colony in a personal way, hiring the English explorer Henry Morton Stanley, who was famous for having found Dr. David Livingstone. The territory, a colony dedicated to timber, rubber, ivory and slaves, reminded me of Joseph Conrad's novel *Heart of Darkness* and of the punishment to which children who stole precious stones or were late in the collection of rubber latex were subjected: amputation at the wrist. Those who were lazy for the sugar harvest also suffered from this evil. When King

Leopold II transferred his private colony to Belgium, thousands of people had stumps instead of hands.

I presumed that Michael Worobey had encountered the old men with amputated hands upon arriving in the capital; even the imprint of the iron nooses with which slaves were transported at the turn of the century. I'm sure he was appalled and, above all, pondered whether it was worth punctuating Europe as the continent of civilization. I am convinced that he had the same doubts as Jalufe when he witnessed the slaughter of the Berbers by Senegalese riflemen, who were armed by French mercenaries.

To follow up on AIDS, Worobey would search the dirty slums of Kinshasa. There he would find that the disease had spread like wildfire. He could have seen the earthy pallor, the visible lymph nodes on the neck, the skin lesions, the dirty sarcoma ulcers, the encephalopathies and the atypical pneumonias. The first cases looked like a rampage: continuous diarrhea, encephalopathies, emaciation and languor. He tried to discover in the kerosene cubes the origin of the disease sown by rare but very active prostitutes. Thus, at first it was interpreted as a disease linked to promiscuity, which predisposed those who were vulnerable to other infections and malignant processes that depended on immunity. Diseases that, as usual, have some degree of self-limitation. For example, herpes simplex, anthrax, sarcomas. In turn, it made tuberculosis resistant to first-line treatments.

In this context, he was presented with a search of medical records and laboratory samples from 1905 to 1908. The plan was to find rare pathologies: liver tumors, splenomegaly with seeding of accessions, caverns in the lungs and lacunar degeneration in the brain. He found little, almost nothing, until he suddenly came across a hatching in 1960. He attributed it to factional warfare, displacement of people, extreme poverty, promiscuous habits, contact with apes in the mountains where coffee plants were grown.

I felt like I was in that scenario, although I did not know Kinshasa or Congo; however, I imagined the city to have busy streets, tricycles and motorcycle cabs avoiding passers-by and those on bicycles, as well as long-horned, high-muzzled oxen. It would resemble Kampala or Kigali. Worobey resembled Jalufe in an older version; perhaps also the Leakeys researching early hominid fossils at Olduvai. Meanwhile, it was unclear to me whether I was describing AIDS research or chronicling my trip to Uganda.

I had the feeling that the Congo and Nile rivers had forests with palm trees along their banks. Nearby, trees with umbels and evergreens denoted the humidity of the mangroves, which shaded an undergrowth of ferns and mosses. Likewise, in the lagoons one could observe enormous lilies with their huge leaves and white flowers.

On this side of the world, close to the tributaries of the other longest river on earth, the Amazon, my brigade continued walking for three ten-hour days, until we reached a religious mission run by a foreign priest and a nun. She seemed to have arrived from the lands of the sugar cane plantations built near the sea and the priest was a white guy with pink cheeks due to chloasma or rosacea. The nun's name was Elisa, and the parish priest was a Pole named Román. The last name was difficult to pronounce: Brzezinski. When I met them, I had the feeling that these figures were out of place, surrounded as they were by poor farmers, who stayed in the area after the fine timber forests were depredated, even after the coca crops were moved to more accessible places.

Beyond the village, the Yagua natives lived in the surrounding forest. Years before, the place may have been more attractive to adventurers in search of auriferous sands in the canyons. But once the vein they exploited for decades was exhausted, they were convinced that there was nothing more to do. Those who could, went upriver in search of new beaches rich in minerals. Others, the most deluded, got the idea that they had to exploit the emerald deposits. Only the oldest, or the poorest, remained.

The elderly missionary, who had replaced an even older missionary who was said to play the ocarina, explained to me that the parish had once been a mission in Yagua territory. Then he took me to a shack with a veranda of transparent fabric that resembled tulle or plastic. For me, who was sweating profusely from the tropical heat of the place, it was a cool haven,

"It was Sister Isabel and I, who asked for your help." He looked me in the eyes and continued, "The reason is very simple: suddenly, in a way that no one is able to explain, many people became ill. Some died after an agony that lasted several days. The illness began with fever and then passed into a state of madness from which no one ever emerged. The bellies of the sick swelled to the point that the skin shone, and the veins became translucent. All this was accompanied by dark diarrhea and, later, relaxation of the sphincters." This reminded me of the wounded with blowguns poisoned with curare.

That too had been a trip through the jungle with the same purpose: to try to find a human group at risk; in this case, a disease characterized by fevers, jaundice and digestive hemorrhages. First, a trail that penetrated the jungle, surrounded on the sides by the forest. Then a woman, with a Greek or Andean face and a Hellenic profile, tried to cajole me with a dance of tarantulas on her chest. This was followed by an invitation to her five-courtyard residence, with a disproportionate number of rooms overlooking courtyards and stone steps. Finally, there was the walk along a route plagued by mosquitoes, puddles, colorful butterflies and poisonous vermin. I had to walk entangled in the rhizomes of the lianas, pissing me off with the low branches of the tree ferns and cedars. In this new scenario I thought that the priest of more than eighty years was the valid interlocutor to find the thread of the emergency. The euphoric children, the cheerful women and the men in colorful shirts were the chosen troupe of the religious for the reception.

The territory was in the middle of the jungle, surrounded by forests and clearings, mudflats and streams that flowed into the great river that meandered between islets of lush vegetation. In the mountains next to the savannah, the settlers had coffee and coca plantations. In these muddy lands and the surroundings of the great rivers, the natives lived grouped in small itinerant communities. I thought they might be families with endogamous ties or survivors of systematic extermination. The men painted their faces with achiote, and the women wore ornaments that seemed to be shadows around their eyes and blushes on their cheekbones. They lived by fishing and hunting small mammals.

The religious men took me to a village on the riverbank that was actually wooden huts lined up on each side of a single street. The last was larger and I considered that it must be the communal house, which was also a school and a food store where they kept coffee seeds and berries similar to a tomato.

I was told that several natives had succumbed to fever and black vomiting. Others showed sequelae, such as extreme thinness and skin color, between green and black, with a yellow sheen over the sclerae and wrinkles at the corners of the mouth. I had the intuition that it was a disease that affected the liver to the point of acute hepatic failure, as the most severe variant, with massive hemorrhage and death of the affected person. I had to study the fluids of the patients, from blood to urine. I even analyzed the waters of the ponds and the river. I looked for dead or sick rats, in case of leptospirosis, and monkeys to decide in favor of yellow fever.

The settlers, mostly old people, women and children, also fell ill, although less seriously than the natives. I had to meet with the shamans of the Yagua ethnic groups, who cured diseases with stones heated by fire, which produced hyperthermia and burns. I remembered the history of the treatment of syphilis in its different phases, with hyperthermia generated by physical means or fevers related to other diseases. I remembered that Wagner-Jauregg proposed to cure the disease, in its secondary phase, with blood from malaria patients transfused into the luetics and having infected mosquitoes bite the sick. I thought it was a crazy idea: to treat a disease with another disease just as serious as the one it was intended to cure. Likewise, the Yagua shamans tried to eliminate any evil by heating the environment with charcoal embers or hot stones. They also boiled a macerate of jungle fruits and fleshy leaves and gave it to the sick person to drink until the last drop of the container was consumed.

When I made the first inventory of the sick and dead, I realized that the prevalence was twice as high in displaced natives. I had to consider several hypotheses to explain this trend. The first took into account the history of contagion of susceptible populations, without previous immunity to protect them against viruses carried by wandering populations that had arrived in occasional migrations. The second hypothesis was more sophisticated. The prevalence was explained by the location of the huts in the forest or near the pools infested with mosquito vectors of metaxenic diseases. Or perhaps because of their feeding habits, as they depended on fish caught in backwaters contaminated by excreta, including those of the sick. The shores were the place where animals, of any species, drank and urinated, which increased the spread.

The nun told me about the sexual customs of the natives, where polygyny was frequent. She told me about Jacob and his wives; among them, Leah, Reuben's mother. The priest observed that the issue of polygyny was pure realism in a population where for every male there were seven females.

While they were explaining to me about the customs of the natives and the settlers of the place, a blue fly of half a centimeter was hitting the glass of the room.

"Is it a horsefly?" I wanted to know.

"No, these are called flesh flies or *Calliphoridae*, they feed on decaying flesh. They do not bite like horseflies." He didn't tell me that these bugs announced death, because they appeared when there were epidemics. I don't think it's superstition, but you run into them when someone is going to die.

I reasoned that the bug could pick up effluvia. Maybe the same insect was the one that left its eggs on the corpses. Something similar to what happened in the Chamo desert, when the vultures would fly over an old animal that had fallen behind the herd. They could sense the vibrations of the sick and the carrion from thousands of miles away and they could spot carcasses from the nimbus of the mountain ranges.

"Was the white dress because she was a nun or because she was sanitary?" I wondered. The priest was wearing ratty jeans and a fleece shirt that, I thought, might have been Canadian. From the clothes, he looked like he was in Alaska and not in the jungle suffering from intense heat. The gray beard hinted at a square jaw and a scant jowl. She was thick and he was rather scrawny.

I remembered, by association, the first novels I had read in my life: *Crime and Punishment* and *The Brothers Karamazov*. It seemed distant to me the time of my childhood, when I read and got fully involved in the plot and identified myself with the characters in a setting entirely different from that of the pointed domes of St. Petersburg or Moscow. Perhaps it was the isbahs of the lower Urals or the gulags in the Siberian steppes. Perhaps it was nothing like the taiga with its coniferous forests. This time my scenery was reduced to puddles with the smell of wood rot, to swamp sloughs inhabited by vermin.

Of course, in the area there were no colossal constructions decorated with lapis lazuli and gold leaf. Just shacks built of planks cut with hatchets and sheds of balsa wood branches, weightless, covered with banana leaves. However, it seemed to me that the priest could evoke any of the Dostoevskian characters, with the red beard, black hair, bright eyes, dark eyebrows and aquiline nose. I saw a broken personality, with periods of transition between melancholy and anger, for no apparent reason.

He could have asked suspicious questions: "What do you do around these parts, macho man?" As if he were a judge to whom you had to account for every step of your life. Then another question, "Why did you choose this job?" He wanted to know what kind of work I had to do, even though he was the one who requested my presence. Naturally, he said nothing of the sort, but his penetrating gaze told me of unhealthy suspicions. Suddenly he seemed to be unraveling the riddles of my life to scrutinize his own. If he had to raise any doubts it was to his own person: "Why on earth had such a priest come to the Amazon jungle?"

As far as I knew, people were driven by interests, one of which was money. Another was pleasure. There are also more heroic motivations: love, science, religion or politics. The exemplary choices seemed to me pure ideological lucubration. I did not recognize in him or in me a complex or altruistic reason. Maybe I was in this profession unconsciously, as a result of running away from my own weaknesses, my own limitations. Maybe I started with this and never knew how to stop. Everything was cajoling me until I became an exegete who could not leave the stage.

I remembered what happened a few years ago, in another place but with similar actors, while I was fighting one of the diseases that had ravaged the place. At the end, when I thought I had accomplished my mission, like those lunatics who, after a theater presentation, go out to receive the applause, they looked at me with melancholy, that which arises when you say goodbye to loved ones. Then I, with a sly look and a hoarse voice, told them, "I don't need to be paid; I did everything for free."

I finished tying the laces of my boot, hiding a tear that had long since stopped rolling down my cheeks, and carried the backpack. Then I handed over to the porters the medicines, microscopes, reagents, forceps and everything I had brought to accomplish the mission, stored in the containers with cold chain. I took a deep breath and went out into the open field to retrace the path by which I arrived. Same thing every time there was a health emergency. The same at any time. The same anywhere in the world.

"Why are those memories that I thought were buried coming back?" Maybe it is due to the temperature, because it was over forty degrees and the humidity was almost one hundred percent, as if I had a fever and uncontrollable delirium. That day, walking through the swamp, with my shoes sunk in the mud of the mangroves, I remember the climb up the escarpment of some dark mountains crowned by snow. That time the soles of my boots slipped on the straw that the natives called ichu or icho, as they pleased. I skidded and fell on my face, on my back, on my buttocks, on my knees, and my companions laughed at me. That time it was a path next to a stream that collected water from the thawing of the dark mountains. Today it is a path opened with a machete.

At that moment I realized that mine was a matter of childhood frustrations and racial complexes. I had grown up in an environment where the average size of women was five foot six, with little voluptuous, petite girls, with candid faces and simple clothes. Every return to places where beings similar to those of my childhood lived was a return to the past, to the cobblestone streets, to the neighborhoods of tailors with thimbles and needle stitches, to the wood carvers and mystical goldsmiths. I felt at ease, I longed to return to my paternal home, with a sunny courtyard presided over by peach and cherry trees. In my memory, bougainvillea climbed up the carved stone columns to the balconies and corridors of the second level. The red-tiled roof of the house had sprouted clumps of moss hair and lichen, resembling birds' nests. I figured I must have missed something to end up in these backwoods in search of high-risk diseases. Maybe I had to give the same credit to the priest. The man must have been totally nuts to take up residence in the middle of the Colombian Amazon.

I was not sure if I had guessed the characteristics of the Pole's personality. My mind was drawing a mixture of thoughts that blended two of Dostoyevsky's characters: the monk Zosimo with Dmitri's second son, Ivan Karamazov. The priest combined the mania of wanting to be a mystical miracle worker with spaces of silence in which one could guess his feelings of guilt for something that had happened in the past. I presumed that he was experiencing intense grief, like the death of a parent. Somehow, the son always claimed to have wished for that death.

Or maybe it wasn't a father-son thing, but something just as dirty and cruel. I immediately imagined different scenarios. The cities he had lived in - I did not yet know at the time that he was Polish - were ravaged by a protracted war. Maybe it was a racial thing; maybe he was a Polish Jew descended from Holocaust victims, or a shipyard worker from Gdańsk.

There was something about him that had transformed him into a suspicious and intriguing individual. He was betrayed by his cadaverous appearance and his elusive yet inquisitive gaze. His long silences observing the jungle, as if he was waiting for a dragon or a madman with a machete to emerge from it to hurt him, were evidence of his misgivings.

For her part, the nun had a clear personality. She fit into a convent in a South American city nestled on the Atlantic or Caribbean coast. The woman was of an astonishing simplicity, which was a paradox to the stoicism of the priest's disposition.

One morning, after breakfast prepared by the priest himself, with eggs and bacon, he invited me to walk along a path with an earthy floor illuminated by what looked like exotic begonias. The sun was scorching, and a damp mist rose from the floor. He explained, "The relationship between cultures settled in geographically distant places seems to interpret the same story told in several languages. It is a concept that starts from the universalization of historical contingencies, such as the universal flood, described in the Judeo-Christian texts, even in the apocryphal version of Enoch. In other words, the flood was sent by Yahweh Eloah as a punishment, not only to men, but also to the angels called watchers and their giant children, the nephilim, who had allowed the disorder on earth."

Román compared them to Mesopotamian texts that narrated a similar disaster with the Chaldean Utnapishtim, appointed to save the species. "Likewise, the pre-Columbian Maya and Chibcha cultures admitted a divine punishment with water and fire to conclude with the forgiveness of the gods and the release of the waters through the Tequendama waterfall in Colombia."

We walked along a path that penetrated the thick forest. Román explained to me that this trail connected the mission with a road built by the loggers that was used to transport the logs to the riverbank. These solid stems were transported in rafts, or simply placed in the middle of the stream so that the river would carry them away. Suddenly, changing the subject of his long monologue, he told me, "I was almost seven years old when the Warsaw uprising took place in 1944. Since then, nothing has been heard of my father. I deduced that he was one of the thousands of victims of Nazi repression. "As a result of the war, the historic center of the city was destroyed, including the royal palace and the Warsaw synagogue. The walls of the buildings bore the marks of bullets and shells, and the windows were turned into anchovies. I stole bread from the markets, even though there was almost nothing for anyone. Famine became widespread in the city." He shooed away the mosquitoes, which stuck to his face, and continued, "People looked like specters, with dark overcoats that were too big for them. The food was brought in on the carriages of those who had been large landowners before the conflict."

With this information, I was able to estimate his age. The priest was between seventy and eighty years old. He did not look it. I would have guessed between sixty and seventy years old.

Román filled me in on the terror. First, he told me about the uprising of the Jewish ghetto against General Jürgen Stroop, which ended in April 1943, and then the repression of Warsaw the following year. The number of corpses was so great that it was impossible to remove them from the sidewalks and from the vestibules of the collapsed buildings on Nalewki and Przyrynek Streets. According to him, the bodies were deposited in carts pulled by young men to the wall that divided the ghetto from the rest of the city; a wall erected by General Fischer or by the *Generalgouverneur* of Poland, General Frank.

Before the Battle of Warsaw took place between the Polish army and the Red Army of the newly formed Soviet Union, he was taken to one of the concentration camps together with a group of boys, mostly black-market food and clothing traffickers. That is why he did not witness the explosions and sniper fire or the house-to-house action. After leaving his country, the streets along the Vistula, the fields near Lublin; the fighting that culminated in the demolition of the Orthodox Alexander Nevsky Cathedral were fixed in his memory. He could even imagine wild boar hunting in the forests near Krakow and peacocks in the gardens of the zoo. What he could not be entirely sure of was his participation in the skirmishes that left the country dismembered and under the political domination of the Soviets, who occupied the cities and the countryside. It was as if he had erased those memories. He was not sure what happened to his mother and sister, who were rescued from the concentration camps and then taken to a town near the Russian border.

I sized it up. I would have liked to be friends with him; also with the Caribbean woman, who, by accent, I assumed to be Dominican. Possibly, they are still in that part of the jungle, considered a conflict zone between the army and one of the Colombian guerrillas. Maybe they were waiting for the army sappers to prepare the final assault on the positions occupied by the subversives. When that moment arrives, the boys of the irregular troops, acting as porters, will guide their enemies through the pongo ravine and make them leave the area by the bridge that crosses the river, at the point where its course reaches three or four hundred meters between banks, with two small islands in the middle of the course. In that place the tropical flora is exuberant, and hundreds of birds of different colors and shapes can be seen. Cranes over a meter tall, birds of paradise with huge tails, cock-of-the-rocks with orange crest and plumage. Even, if you are lucky, yellow finches and black toucans with yellow-edged colored beaks.

For some time, there will be no more war in the bush. The settlers will remember the epidemic as a past condemnation and some will try to avoid mosquito infested puddles or rodent urine. The natives will avoid the dense forest so as not to get sick from the plague which, according to them, came from the monkeys, although they were not clear whether it was the nuthatches or the howlers that caused it. I will regret not having been able to determine the diagnosis and cause of the outbreak. I imagine it could have been a germ affecting liver cells.

The objective is not always achieved; sometimes a substitute is enough. That time Román had explained to me something about conflicts and human relationships. "It seems that men feel the need to do something heroic."

Was he referring to the illegal boys hiding in the region, or was he talking about the ones who rose up in Warsaw?

"Do you think it is a psychological need?" I asked him, not understanding why these men wanted to give meaning to their lives. Then I told him, "I believe that it is more a matter of objective conditions, such as the poverty of the settlers. And what to say about the natives." Then I kept silent.

"These woods remind me of wild boar hunting in my homeland," he confessed.

At that moment I imagined packs of dogs running after the prey. The dogs must have been Irish setters. In the Amazon jungle, peccaries gather in herds of hundreds of specimens. The madness of hunger transforms them into ferocious animals that attack any living being, of any size. Jaguars, big apes, boas and yacaré succumb in their wake. Sometimes they invade villages and attack humans, dogs and other domestic animals as if they were a plague of the kind that ravaged the land of the Pharaohs, according to the Bible. On a settler's stand I could see a jaguar chained to an unfinished cement column, peccaries in a hole in the floor and a tapir in a hole. It was the village zoo.

In the same village of scattered shacks, I spotted a boy wearing a threadbare brown shirt. He was dull and emaciated. Then I thought he could be suffering from multidrug-resistant tuberculosis. The boy looked at me with the coldness of those who seem to accept their hopeless condition. It was a look of glistening corneas, no eye movements, no hint of sentiment. Perhaps he was judging my indifference. I even thought it was a reflection of my own gaze, which watched me with the same indolence.

Suddenly, the boy disappeared into the jungle grove. He disappeared from my sight. He would continue to watch me while I tried to discover his brown shirt somewhere in the vegetation. I imagined him leading the soldiers to the bridge that would take them out of the area. That way he would prevent the military from being able to find the subversives' shelters and, therefore, locate the native reservations. Possibly, it would be the last heroic act of his life, because his body could not take any more. He could not even return from that place.

Once his mission was accomplished, he would stay at the edge of the pongo, near the low jungle. There he would spit blood until he breathed his last breath. After a few days, someone would find what was left of his body, after the scavengers had torn it to pieces. They would only see the carcass of an emaciated body.

It was clear to Román who the skeletal boy was. He could place him among hundreds of seminarians or other young men who lived near the mission. Therefore, when he learned that he had died on one of the cliffs, he cried as when he talked about the wagons full of corpses in Warsaw. As when he went to visit the shrine of the Black Madonna of Częstochowa, the patron saint of Poland. Just with the painting, depicting the Madonna with the infant Jesus in her arms, he had been moved. Darkened by a fire, the female face showed two scars on the right cheek caused by the sword of a Hussite warrior who had fallen fulminated, before causing other wounds, the result of subintrant convulsions of epilepsy. There was no Polish Catholic who was not moved by the historical image of a people that had been invaded several times in the last hundred years and, nevertheless, maintained its identity and faith in its destiny.

Román admitted to having cried that time, infected by the fervor of the pilgrims and the memory of the hardships of the war. The icon painted on the miraculous wood reminded him of the black-market speculators, of the women who had prostituted themselves or begged in the streets of Warsaw, of the children who had died of starvation and had been discovered in the attics, of the little ones killed by the bullets of the Gestapo soldiers, who had been shot at point blank range as they tried to break through the ghetto wall through the holes that had been dug by the reservation men, and of the German soldiers taunting Polish prisoners when they replaced Jewish prisoners in the concentration camps.

Most of these prisoners were vandals who gathered in groups to raid markets and food suppliers along the roads leading to the cities. Finally, the Black Madonna reminded him of the arrival of Russian troops entering ruined cities and turning to rubble what was still standing of commercial buildings or houses.

He would remember the cloud of dust that rose with the fall of the buildings, which left the atmosphere unbreathable and plunged the city into a gloomy darkness of bad omen. It was evident that hatred can cause a feeling similar to grief for losses and Román continued to feel grief and hatred, which conditioned any further reasoning. Time had not healed his pain even though redemptive amnesia had fragmented his memory. Thanks to this, he had managed to forget the darkest, most painful parts.

Thinking of the cachectic boy, who had diverted the route of the official troop, he knew that the militia scouts were pursuing the patrol until they verified that it reached the opposite bank of the river and went back into the jungle, where it ran into another patrol that had also been diverted, this time by a group of native women with children who were the children of the irregulars.

I didn't believe any of that and still thought the wars were unnecessary, especially the one they had waged. In the end the army troops will return, despite the attempts to get them out of the area. They will return with the objective of exterminating the rebels.

Román continued to narrate his memories of the war, including how young Poles were burying hundreds of corpses a day but how this was not enough to put an end to the putrid smell that permeated the neighborhoods. He told me that the hollows of the buildings, a product of the fire of the Luftwaffe, harbored thousands of crows that during the night tore the carrion to pieces. I thought that it would have been better, for the sanitation of the city, if instead of crows they had been vultures from the Carpathians or Lower Silesia. These birds, after flying over the city for hours, would come down to the streets to feed on the corpses.

To this day I firmly believe that wars are useless because there are no winners. The Poles, the Hungarians, the Romanians, the Czechs, the Germans, the Japanese; even the Americans, the British and the Russians. They all lost the war. They would end up traveling in wagons on their way to exile or wandering from one city to another, from one train station to another. The convoy cars would be pulled by a coal locomotive, with its stoker and its shrill whistle.

Roads were another way for deportees who did not have access to trains to get around. The men marched on foot along the edge of the roadways. At times they would be forced to pull off the road to allow trucks carrying troops, American Sherman tanks and Russian T-34 tanks to pass. Walking deforms the bones at the epiphyses and the articular facet and destroys the surface cartilage, which affects the synovial sacs, which then fill with a mixture of synovium and pus. This is followed by aseptic necrosis, which shortens the lower limbs by at least ten centimeters after remodeling of the bones and joints. At the end of the exodus, those who fled appeared as if they were old and dwarfed in shabby clothes several sizes too big for them.

As an exercise in resilience, his mind imagined meetings with the girls he played hopscotch with to initiate a romance. Román ran errands for the housewives in exchange for plates of black lentils. He could not remember if he was buying legumes or selling scrap metal. On one occasion he ran into men who appeared to be Gypsies or Slavs. They had been accused of being smugglers and profiteers. They were darker skinned and had black mustaches. Also, their language was rough. Or maybe he didn't see them; he could only imagine them as guys with bloated faces and globular bellies. He didn't know where they were taking their merchandise, maybe to the Middle East or to Venice, as in the days of the silk trade. They would say that they belonged to the nobility that had been stripped of their power and patrimony by the revolution and the wars. Their elegance was measured by the satin palettes they wore, the trench coats and borsalino hats.

Those were times when I was being cured of something. Could it have been the excesses? Had I had any vices? I didn't think so, but maybe I had. It could be a covert workaholism. Who knows, maybe an affair. A romance came to mind that seemed to have manifested itself only in my imagination, or maybe I had seen the woman in *Vogue* magazine, with a little star tattooed on her cheekbone that gave her face an artistic expression. A lock of long hair seemed to move in time with her body as she walked. In addition, the eyes, which reflected an enigmatic expression, somewhere between sadness and exultation, stayed with me.

It could be that I had made it up because I was going through a period of compulsive need for affection. I thought it wasn't just me; everyone has a compelling need to seek admiration or affection, perhaps both feelings together. That lack of affection is what drives politicians, professors, preachers, scientists, everyone, and makes them addicts and romantics. The craving for affection is a Freudian interpretation. I thought I had read something about that in Otto Gross's books, which tried to interpret the relationship between anarchism and Freud's libido. Perhaps I should have been informed about how Jung approached the social imprinting to give rise to the formation of the archetype and the collective unconscious. Or I should have imbibed Alfred Adler's theories. That way, I could interpret the neurotic outbursts as part of my inferiority complex. Perhaps if I reread the classics of psychoanalysis, I would find the explanation for my mystical and heroic affections and romantic dalliances. Was eroticism one of many vices inherited from my ancestors or the imprint of my nationality?

Suddenly I found myself in a group of people walking through the jungle. They were clearing a path for us with machetes. The path ascended along the edge of an escarpment or a gorge. I don't know why the battle of Thermopylae between the Greeks and Persians came to my mind. It seemed to me that the rhizomes and roots of the great trees held the path that otherwise would have ended at the bottom, a hundred meters deep.

I was sweating from the heat and the humidity remained on my shirt, which stuck to my back. The faces of the boys who led me along that path seemed to me to be the same or similar to those of the porters, perhaps because they were their sons or brothers. Among them were tonsured young men who could have been descended from the natives. Some wore glasses and others showed marks of youthful acne. Their hair was always greasy and almost all of them were skinny.

I thought I'd seen them on Sunday at the village fair, receiving the quota of eggs and chickens delivered by some women. The supply was supposed to feed everyone for a whole week. Perhaps I was mistaken and had not seen them, since they were not carrying any weapons, but were a group of catechists attending mass. Likewise, they were wearing worn out clothes and high rubber boots to avoid being bitten by vipers and other crawling vermin that hid in the branches of vines. When I looked at their faces, I didn't seem to be seeing the faces of killers. None of them had tattoos on their faces or neck or the salamander face of the hired killers I had seen in the marshes of Honduras; however, I thought about their AKMs and realized that the boys could be as fierce as any homicidal madman. They were capable of killing the miners who screwed the village girls, the loggers who destroyed their jungle hideouts, the black-shirted soldiers who covered their faces with shoe polish to make themselves look fiercer.

I imagined them marching down the trail in single file, looking to either side so as not to fall victim to the booby traps the soldiers had planted. I could catch their crooked and slippery looks, the same expression they used to intimidate the farmers who refused to hand over the quota demanded of them. Then I realized that I had been kidnapped and those who had plotted the abduction or, at least, had allowed it were Román and the nun Isabel. When I realized how precarious my situation was, I began to shiver like a malaria patient. The heat turned into a cold that rose from my body. I could lose my life, because they didn't give a damn about my work, nor did they understand anything about bacteria and viruses; not even about infected monkeys or bush rats and mosquito vectors. They were more practical. They wanted me to heal the sick, especially if they were their fighters or their collaborators. I would heal them, or I would be listed as a suspect, because I would be considered an asshole. Therefore, I felt vulnerable to their popular judgments and to the accusations of the relatives of the dead.

I understood the message, so I would have to make a point of using the entire arsenal of medicines that the porters had brought and those that the Polish priest might have in his commissary, which were the product of donations from some non-governmental organization. I would make a mix of three antibiotics, an antifungal and a test antiviral. Needless to say, the treatment would have some effect: some would reduce their fever, others would come out of their stupor and stop breathing in a stertorous manner; in other cases, their urine would clear and their stools would return to normal. The number of new cases noted by the Polish priest in his little notebook would also decrease. Of course, things could be truncated and, by bad luck, the symptoms of the sick would continue beyond the period they judged tolerable. If that happened, I would find myself in imminent danger. "No way," I said to myself, and put my fate in the balance.

When I thought the wind was blowing in my favor, I talked to the commanders. They looked like university students, graduates or rural professors. I found them gathered in one of the huts without walls and they were willing to listen to me, although I could sense their doubts about me; doubts that centered on knowing details of a matter that worried them: who was the one who hired me? Why was I in that place?

I had to explain it to them. I told them that the matter was not only about curing them; it was necessary to know what had caused the disease in order to stop contagion and, with it, the appearance of new cases. They almost died laughing. Then they looked at me with contempt. They were judging me.

"Look, sir, for us it's the same as curing them with cattle poop or bee stings," said one of them with a hint of bitter sarcasm. I assumed that the man had lost a loved one to the disease, maybe his brother or a dear friend. He could have confessed his anger and fear before threatening me. By the time he realized he was sick, he was already spurting blood from his mouth. "Maybe they gave me ground glass or bamboo canes," he sputtered.

The guy had the face of an elementary school dropout. His hair was cropped short and his shirt was open at chest level. He wore dark glasses, perhaps to look cool or to avoid corneal burns, or to avoid being recognized by the army sappers or the infiltrators hiding among the local farmers. All the time he thought it was the fifth columnists who gave him ground glass or pieces of sugar cane in a contaminated drink when they invited him to one of the cabins before arriving at the pongo.

The hut was where travelers, irregulars and, sometimes, soldiers snacked. I thought that the man with the appearance of an Antioquian would have taken revenge on the owners of the boarding house. Surely, he hung them by the balls and cut off one of their hands, although he even spared their lives before the wife's pleas and the husband's tears.

When he questioned me, I responded with another question,

"How did he realize that it had been a poisoning and not a disease?"

He answered me that, before taking them down, he had trained the cooks to give him some indication. They sang that it was no poison, unless the whole river was toxic. They claimed that it was a disease that was killing many in the mission and was most deadly with the natives, who perished as if they had been given chicken distemper. He then told me of other pathologies that he himself had discovered, such as skin streak, which I assumed could be bejel or uta ulcers, or perhaps leprosy itself. He also told me how some boys who had hidden in some caves to escape from the troops that were chasing them had died. There they had been bitten by blood-sucking vampires. After a few days, they developed a sickness that made them go crazy, they even foamed at the mouth and convulsed, until finally, one after the other, they died. In this case I imagined that it was rabies, transmitted by the bite of contaminated vampires or bats.

When, somehow, it seemed that the tough guy had become my friend or, at least, would tolerate having a conversation with me, it occurred to me to tell him, "I do not think that this was the correct way to bring me to your camp., I would have come if you had asked me to, maybe through Román or one of the farmers. It was disrespectful that they kidnapped me."

"What kidnapping are you talking about?" he asked me, which made me hesitate. It was true; they did not blindfold me or use force, much less point a gun at me. I followed them, I understood the message they were sending me in a coded form as if I were a collaborator or I had no choice but to accept the conditions.

"I'm sorry!" I said, looking for a convincing explanation; maybe I should apologize for the protest, although I didn't know if it was the most appropriate thing to do on this occasion.

We were next to the bank of a river. I thought it could be the same riverbed that penetrates the strait of the pongo. Perhaps the yellow color was due to the brown clay. In that place there were some huts that were supported on thick reeds or thin sticks. Maybe they were the aerial roots of the ficus trees that grew in the mangroves. Suddenly I noticed a group of men in uniform resting in the clearing, among the trees that cast huge shadows; they were different from the other irregulars, even the ones who had led me to the camp. The uniform consisted of gray pants and an earth or grass-colored polo shirt with camouflage spots. On their shoulder they wore a pennant with the national colors. I thought that this must be a badge of their faction.

The men were armed with rifles and long-range machine guns; they also carried grenades, which hung on the sides of their chests. They kept their distance from the new arrivals and covered half of their faces with black scarves. In addition, most of them wore iridescent glasses. I imagined that this was a minimum precaution in case the irregulars were captured and tortured in search of information about the identity of the leadership.

Among them was a guy with scars on his face that, I presumed, were caused by injuries during the campaign, from scratching himself with the adventitious ivy or with the thorny catingas, although I did not rule out that they were the imprint of juvenile acne conglobata that had left indelible marks on his face. When I arrived at the place, someone introduced me to him, "This is the doctor who is curing the disease in the ravine." I didn't know if he was referring to the village or to the mission of the priest Román.

In spite of the introduction, the guy wanted to hear it as a confession, "Have you been asking the natives about things that involve us?"

I had no choice but to tell him the truth, "Yes but I had no intention of knowing any strategic secrets." I wanted to tell him that I didn't want to know anything about their location or their numbers, much less their firepower.

I only intended to find out what had caused the disease. I tried to explain, "My intention was to try to find the origin of the epidemic." I thought about explaining to him that in other conflict zones that had caused displacement of people, changes in environmental conditions and overcrowding had led to an explosion of disease, a phenomenon we sanitarians call acmé or climax epidemics. I would have warned him that his thing, i.e., small and medium intensity wars, was not unknown to me. Nevertheless, every time I came into contact with these groups, my nerves were on edge. I am not used to violence, even though I have been in countries where it was a daily occurrence. I was referring to the Middle East, the Indochina peninsula and equatorial Africa. Perhaps I should also mention the Central American countries, the south of the continent and the Amazon jungle of Brazil; even Colombia itself.

"Don't tell me," he answered me in a rough tone, by way of a challenge.

According to my perception, the guy thought he was the bravest guy on the planet, or else he was crazy. As crazy as the hierarchs of the gangs of hired assassins in Central America or Mexico. Maybe he thought he was a Cambodian Khmer Rouge warrior, or a jihadist in an area conquered by the Caliphate, between Iraq and Syria, with a machine gun mounted on a four-wheel drive truck.

Suddenly, while talking to this crazy guy, I realized that the disease could be leptospirosis. It was as simple as that. Instead of thinking about the danger to my life posed by an individual like that superb eraser, it occurred to me to shuffle through the diagnoses. Somehow, I was just as nuts as the guy. Not as much as those around me, but just as scattered, albeit with quick thinking, with quick mental flashes.

I mentioned that the disease could be leptospirosis. It is possible that I said it in a low voice, because he didn't hear my words and asked, "What did you say, sir?"

"The way doctors reason is heuristic, which means that previous experiences, geographic location, statistics and a calculation of probabilities must be applied to try to find the explanation to the enigmatic. In this case, the diagnosis of the disease and its causes," I stated as a challenge. I wanted to say, "I can't imagine you'd understand though, asshole."

Realizing that I was trying to confuse him, the man blurted out in a high-pitched voice, "You're risking your life here, you bastard!"

"No, sir. All I am doing is putting forward a hypothesis that can save your people and the whole gorge," I replied. I used the name they had given to the area.

The symptoms were clear: jaundice, renal dysfunction, hemorrhagic diastasis. The clear triad of Weil's disease: hemorrhage, jaundice and renal failure accompanied by hemolytic uremic syndrome, thrombotic thrombocytopenic purpura and even coma and melena or hematemesis before death. Death is rapid after delirium and the smell of drains that indicated that something was rotting inside the body.

I still had to detect the tiny helicoidal microorganism, which would be visible under the microscope with a Chinese ink stain as it moved on the cells of the biopsy tissue. I would send the kerosene blocks, in which the tissue damaged by the disease was included, to the laboratory improvised by Gonçalvez and Fonseca in the city of Mitú, in the department of Vaupés. I could send a fragment of hemorrhagic lung extracted from the corpse of a boy, still a child, who accompanied those of the central command, or from the liver of another deceased already examined. I presumed that the boy would have died after enduring respiratory failure. He was walking up the mountain panting, feeling the chills before the fever peaks, spitting out fragments of lung tissue with frothy blood.

It was my second autopsy. The first one I performed on a guy who presented lividity in the back and cadaveric pallor, which spoke of massive hemorrhages before death. In the boy I found the lung turned into a gelatinous mass of lax tissues and bubbling blood; it had the appearance of a bloody mucus, of a rotten viscera. Despite the mask, I could smell the stench of anaerobes on the dead tissue. And despite my gloved hands, I felt the softness of the crackling, friable viscera as I was overcome by an insidious dizziness and nausea. As I was about to perform the third autopsy, the individual with the cratered face, the one with the acne scars, spoke,

"I don't think it is necessary in this case. He died from the damage to his spine."

I understood that the man suffered paraplegia due to a vertebro-medullary injury caused by trauma after falling off a cliff or perhaps being wounded by an enemy bullet. In that case, he would surely have been transported on a litter or stretcher. At that moment I thought that the injured subject must have been an important commando or an ideologue of the movement; otherwise, they would not have taken the trouble to carry him on their backs through the jungle trails.

In the backpacks that the porters had loaded, I carried a small laboratory: microscope with immersion objective, kerosene oven, alcohols of different grades for the dehydration process of the tissue sample, several reagents and staining substances. Antonio Gonçalvez and sanitarist Joao Fonseca were waiting for my samples in order to unravel the epidemic. Once they reached their hands they would immediately process them to obtain the serotype result. That way we could know if it was a mutation of *Leptospira interrogans,* which had been detected in some places in the Amazon rainforest, or a *Leptospira Copenhagen,* a strain carried by field rats in some countries in Central America and the Caribbean. The guys would be elated to receive the samples and it reminded me of their experience in AIDS research in the laboratories at the University of Arizona, where they shared experiences with Professor Michael Worobey.

Of course I made up my mind that I was a Worobey in my own style. I associated his name with expeditions in the Congo, as he toured the cities overcrowded due to migration from rural areas to the suburbs to escape poverty and war. I wasn't clear if I had seen his portrait in a magazine spreading the story of HIV findings in the shady neighborhoods of the city. Perhaps I was confusing his features with another scientist: Friedman, from the University of San Diego.

Extreme poverty, promiscuity, violence, overcrowding, vice, shantytowns. One of the most dangerous diseases of the century was incubating in that place. I still needed to get closer to the mountains where gorillas, chimpanzees and baboons lived. Worobey would have tried to find the source of the disease in the apes. It was in those damp-smelling, humus-rotting jungle places that the virosis that would later terrorize mankind had begun.

Surely, he would have found that many of the tuberculoses and pneumonias were associated with skin cancer and encephalopathy caused by microbes that attack only a group of people without defenses. Perhaps there he discovered that the viruses infected CD4+ T lymphocytes, which were destroyed by natural *killer* (NK) cytolytic lymphocytes that injected their lytic proteins into the diseased cells. I envisioned Worobey as an explorer in the slums and villages of the Congo, somewhat like Jalufe in the hospital in Uganda. Both seemed like safari adventurers in pursuit of the big game, even if the big game was the virus or pathogen.

At that moment it occurred to me to think of the first cases I had diagnosed with AIDS as a young man working in a field hospital. The building had the architecture of French post-war and post-German occupation hospitals. It had been built in the middle of the century and was located on the outskirts of Buenos

Aires. The corridors connecting the wards were in the open air, and in the extensive gardens one could see cats of various colors, almost all of them obese. They were probably there to deal with the rats.

The pavilions looked like barracks. Inside were two rows of cots with a passageway between them and bed-to-bed spacing of no more than five feet. The first patient diagnosed with AIDS was an African-American man. He had a carbuncle that ulcerated his face and was almost cachectic. In the brief conversation we had, he told us that he had arrived some time ago in the Rio de la Plata. I deduced from that confession that the guy had enjoyed a short stay in Uruguay with a job that he did not want to explain to us. It seemed to me that he might have been a hotel manager in a shabby hotel or, simply, had been a small-time pimp. Most likely, he was infected in this way.

During his hospital stay, the man collapsed despite treatment. By the time the Elisa and Western blot tests came back, confirming the disease, he was in agony. I learned that the man might be Panamanian or a native of one of the Guianas and that he had migrated south because of problems with the police in some Central American country.

On the second occasion, I treated a patient admitted to the medical service who had lived with a guy who had abandoned her to join the pleasure circuit of the Côte d'Azur. The man had probably contracted HIV in Marbella or Ibiza. When he became ill and destitute, the cheeky man returned with his wife, whom he then infected. The girl was in her twenties and had a baby, who was at this point, no more than three years old. She turned out to be the darling of the service, despite the fact that we isolated her with a kind of reverse asepsis to avoid intra-hospital infections that would complicate her immunosuppression. When she passed away, we railed against her husband, against bad luck, against science, which had not advanced AZT and other antiretrovirals or, if it had, they were unaffordable for poor patients. Finally, we complained against the system and against the context; maybe against ourselves, who could not do anything to rescue her.

Returning to reality, and my being kidnapped by an armed group, I noticed that the camp seemed calm. The women had stopped whispering; the fireflies seemed like lanterns illuminating the gloom and the cicadas scraped their transparent wings against their chitinous abdomen, drawing notes of a monotonous and redundant rhythm.

I spoke by radiofrequency with Román to inform him that I already had enough material to send to the central laboratory and that the time had come to return to the city. My decision did not fit his idea. He wanted me to stay at the mission forever and perform the duties of a post doctor. If the Polish priest had been present, he would have looked at me with anguish and pity; he would even have given me a desperate scolding. It was as if he had suddenly left behind the good old days and the contact with his European past, as if he no longer had a friend who understood his nightly disturbances, when he had dreams that he could not remember the next day, as if he had suddenly jumped from Europe to that place they called the ravine. He ended up understanding that, with my departure, his legitimate personal aspirations had collapsed and he only had to get fully involved in solving the problems of the rest of the people, even if those problems were hard and demanding.

If I had had him in front of me, I would have noticed him more nervous, giving high-flown answers to the nun Isabel, spilling the coffee from the cup due to the trembling of his hand, turning the fan on and off, carrying his pipe everywhere so as never have to stop smoking, telling those who asked him for a mass on Friday to go to hell. Finally, after so much grumbling, he would come around to the idea and help me carry the bundles on the backs of two large mules and on the backs of four porters, two of whom were resuscitated from illness. They would be the ones to carry the material to the small town where my four-by-four was located. In their eyes I could make out the glint of something like a tear, concealed to prevent a guy, whom I had only met weeks before, from witnessing their grief.

All this I had to imagine because neither the Polish priest was on the scene nor had I returned to the mission. On the contrary, I found myself surrounded by individuals armed to the teeth, with surprisingly little feeling towards me, even though I had discovered that the disease that decimated his entourage was leptospirosis and I had cured twenty of those interned in their field hospital, which was nothing more than a canvas tent camouflaged with palm branches to which they had taken me, blindfolding me and tying my hands to two people who dragged me or restrained me as needed.

When we arrived at the place, they removed my blindfold and released my wrists. That way I could see the sick lying on the floor on their sleeping mats. They were jaundiced and pneumonic; encephalopathic and prostrate. Some were in a state of agitation and others with symptoms of narcosis. All were wiry and with tremors that I attributed to chills and beriberi due to vitamin deficiency after not eating for several days. While I was busy verifying the diagnosis, one of the girls accompanying the group approached me and told me that she was a doctor or almost a doctor.

"Great!" I exclaimed, and explained that we had to prepare IVs with polyelectrolytes and saline to hydrate them while they received antibiotic treatment. I did not share my hypothesis about the causes, nor did I inform her of the complete treatment, because I thought that my knowledge guaranteed my survival.

When I noticed her sweaty and engaged, I asked her, "How long have you been with them?"

"A long of time," she answered. That didn't mean anything to me, because it could be several months or several years. I left it at that and asked no more questions to avoid the distrust of the group.

On the third day, the jaundice continued but the urine was somewhat clearer, which I attributed to the dilution of the saline sera, or because there was an improvement of the hepatic function. The fever decreased due to the lysis; they only suffered tremors in the afternoons and there was no more blood in the stool. When I saw the evolution, I almost jumped for joy.

"What do you think?" I said to the man who was looking at me with some anger, as if I was winning a poker game or wishing that somehow the treatment would fail.

Barely moving a muscle, the guy answered, "They are still weak and yellow."

I would have liked to shout, "Give it more than two seconds, you asshole!" but I didn't. Instead I kept quiet, thinking that this madman had a trauma that he could only fight with the blood of the executed.

His gaze seemed cloudy and stubborn; his eyebrows were furrowed, his was face hidden by his handkerchief and his cheeks were concave. I recognized in him the pallor of the mentally insane, the perspiration of the feverish when the action of the sympathetic nerve predominates. I had no choice but to continue doing what I was doing and gamble with my life. I relived the nightmare in which they tied my wrists behind my body and shot a bullet in the back of my head, and then buried me, still alive, in the first ravine with a slope that existed in the vicinity. I, in anguish, felt my nostrils fill with dirt and grass from the landslide that my executioners made fall over the edge. I wanted to scream and tell them that I had not died while thinking that it was not the most appropriate thing to do because they would come to finish me off. That same dream repeated itself every time I feared for my life, as if it were a premonition or if I had witnessed an execution in the past.

If I had to report to someone or if I had to narrate a plot set in that place, it would be difficult for me to describe the beauty of the landscapes, full of tree trunks of fine wood covered by lianas and fungi; green tree ferns mottled with blue; giant, bell-shaped, orange flowers with vermilion stamens. I witnessed paradisiacal exteriors and unimaginably beautiful animals; little spiders that look like pearls and hang from webs. Probably, no one would take me seriously if I tried to describe this beauty.

At times the scenery became a gloomy place, with swamps full of lizards with menacing jaws and snakes on the banks showing their venomous fangs, while from the greenish swamp emerged clouds of mosquitoes transmitting various zoonoses. The same, green and orange lights filtering through the thicket; young men with high boots; songbirds raising their din among the branches and tops of the giant trees; insects that seem to have been created in the Cambrian period without having changed one iota since then. All in a range of psychedelic colors, like luminescent scotomas in the prodrome of a subintrusive migraine attack or an epilepsy with tonic-clonic seizures. I thought that it was the announcement of a cerebral arrhythmia, represented, in an electroencephalogram, by sequences of acuminate figures resembling the edges of a saw.

At a certain point, I don't know if it was because they put a drug in my infusion or shot me in the ear with a blowgun, I had visions caused by some hallucinogenic ivy; the same visions that a someone would experience on meth or acid.

In my hallucinations I was in a place that I identified as the port overlooking the Pacific where I spent my adolescence. I thought I was in the Pakistani merchants' neighborhood of Inclán, near the wooden dock next to the train station.

The planks were weathered by time and use. I could see through the cracks the foam of the high tide waves. There I felt the chill of an autumn afternoon, after the beach season had come to an end. However, I did not see my buddy Daniel or the boys from the neighborhood. Much less could I recognize the girls of that time; among them, the girl to whom the neighborhood gave the nickname of Lolita.

The scene gave me an attack of jealousy. Then I became aware that envy had dominated much of my emotional life. I had harbored that feeling when the girls in the cove were flirtatious with my friends and left me aside. Maybe I felt jealous because they would only fool around with me when they were drunk. I would experience jealousy or envy when they turned me down at parties. That emotion was lost in my childhood; maybe it wasn't envy, but frustration for not achieving what I had set out to achieve, for having lost what I once had.

I started to think about where the kids I was envious of were. Of some of them I had no news; of others, the grades had not turned out as good as I had imagined. Some of them were alcoholics who frequented the bars of the port; others got married young to the girls on the boardwalk and, after a while, had left them because they became fat, neurotic and vulgar. I was told that one of them left the country, maybe to Europe or North America. Daniel was a whoremonger and drug addict in the Big Apple, with a luck that I wouldn't wish even for a desolate night with winter cold that came with a persistent wind. I asked myself why I was jealous of them.

I had the feeling that my thinking was becoming more and more scattered, trying to interpret life in its real dimension. At times I thought I was alone and stripped of the armor I had been wearing since the moment of my birth or my early childhood. I felt my body naked, without any defense, exposed to any aggression. However, it was true that I had felt the same thing before in many other places and in other circumstances, so it should not be strange for me to feel the same anguish again. I had already experienced it on a road in Rwanda and in the Amazon, when armed gangs opposed my arrival at the epicenter of a health disaster. That time it was one of the psychopaths who shot me in the chest or in the temple; as in my nightmares, when after the shot, I fell into an abyss. I might have been infected by the filth I around me and suffered from pneumonia or typhus through lice bites. Or through the poisonous bite of vermin.

In that moment of loneliness I remembered Román, who always tried to be supportive of me. He was smoking a pipe and I was drinking a cappuccino he had served me. He talked to me about so many subjects that I felt he had not talked to anyone in the last months, maybe years. With me he broke the dam of his silence and began to talk about all the topics he wanted to get off his chest. Then he told me that the wolves of the tundra only attacked men when they were hungry or rabid. He told me that the Lapps came out on moonlit nights in June to paint the backs of sheep and caribou with their dogs dragging the troikas. Just like the agrarians of my land, in the same month of June, on the eve of St. John's Day, during the solstice, when they painted the backs of llamas, alpacas and vicunas green and scarlet red. I thought that at the same time they would count them, but someone told me no, "We only paint their backs and necks so that they don't catch the plague". With that clarification I was happy.

Then Román referred to the coincidences between the phases of the moon and the madness of the insane; he sought to coincide the greatest follies of war with the appearance of a pack of steppe wolves howling in the distance, in the Nordic tundra where the Lapps lived. He told me that discipline was important for survival. That's why, during the evacuation of the cities at the end of the Russian invasion, when the troops of men with purplish-red faces burned by the arctic sun disappeared, the mothers tied their children around their waists with tattered sheets. In this way, they did not allow any of them to get lost in the long column of civilians moving into the refugee camp to stay in prefabricated barracks. In the meantime, Russian troops were clearing out the strongholds of resistance, those Nazi snipers who had not yet learned of the surrender or simply did not want to end up in the Russian gulag camps, where they would be exterminated just like the Jews in Auschwitz or Dachau. This time the concentration and extermination camps were in the Urals and Siberia and had other names, but they served the same purpose: to eliminate the enemy.

Suddenly, landing in the time of my visit, he explained to me the current situation in the area. He informed me of the areas occupied by the troops and by the irregulars, for which he used a map he had drawn himself. In the geographical representation he had drawn the course of the river with its meanders and rapids to the north, where the riverbed narrows in the pongo. He also demarcated the territories of the natives and sketched the huts and the hunting areas that, in some way, were respected by the troops in combat.

Then he said to me, as if emerging from a dream, "You don't have to be afraid of being hurt."

I didn't know what he meant by that phrase; nor did I want to inquire what implications it might have for my own safety. I wanted to believe that he had cured a few of the kids involved in the movement struggle. One of the boys, the one who looked like a catechist, a witness to the healings, had returned to the mission with the task of informing Román, "The companions are grateful." This brought a smile of satisfaction to the priest's face.

I had no choice but to trust what the Pole was telling me, sensing that many young university students, the kind who organize street marches and lead student protests that involve the hijacking of vehicles, had been placed at the head of the militia.

On the other hand, there were the army commanders; positions held by cadets who graduated from military schools. These elements, with some degree of culture, could understand my work or, at least, accept what I was doing. Moreover, it was possible that the males had consulted with the members of the Central Committee, who had received the reports of the epidemic with concern. Surely the old men of the Committee had told them that they had no choice but to trust me, no matter what. Maybe the army generals had ordered the troops not to harm me, as they needed to have an ally in the fight for positions they did not want to abandon. Otherwise, they would have to evacuate the soldiers to hospitals and leave the advance camps in the hands of the enemy. They would have been happy to see the helicopter gunships with their load of soldiers leaving the place for the duration of the illness. They would take it as a triumph for their troops.

In the same period, the results of the analyses processed by Antonio Gonçalvez and Joao Fonseca arrived. I thought that the serotype brought surprises and that the mutation was due to the new environmental conditions. Perhaps the rats in the field were infected by some microbe that multiplied the litters. This could be due to several options: the animals' own endocrine system and the activation of serotonin receptors in the brain and hypothalamus, which had led to a hormonal cascade with the maturation of several eggs in each period. The result could be measured by the litters of mice found in the tunnels dug under the roots of the undergrowth or by dissecting the uterus of pregnant rats to assess the number of offspring they could have.

Overpopulation of rodents would invade city centers, villages and camps. This situation would make contact with sick animals more frequent and the possibility of contagion greater.

"I want to talk to you," the pissed-off man said. "I don't know how you feel about our battle. I can understand that it is not important to you. We are pragmatic people. You will understand that those of us who have embraced this life also accept death as a tragic option," he sighed, perhaps reflecting on the ups and downs of his adventure, the deaths, deserters, betrayals, recruitments of volunteers or by obligatory quotas demanded. "I don't want to tire you, but you have our eternal gratitude," he said as he glanced sideways at the group, seeking their approval.

"Thank you for your words. Believe me, I needed to hear them," I said. My heart went out to him as I listened to him.

At the end of the dialogue, he got up from a folding bench, which he had used in the barracks to threaten me and then to thank me for my work. Then he shouted, "At your orders, comrades! Attention! Platoon, march!"

Then I saw their backs crossed by their military webbing, their camouflage gear, and berets. I watched them walk away along the path, until they were lost in the thick forest. The irregulars, with Crato in command, stayed with me. I don't know at what moment I felt my legs weaken to the point of not being able to take a step and my hearing became so distorted that I could barely hear their voices. The light seemed to reverberate and I felt dizzy. I had the sensation that they had dissolved a dose of benzodiazepines or zopiclone in my soda; a mixture that they gave me to drink while I was speaking the command of the hosts.

I woke up in the mission. The mulatto nun was giving me an infusion of a sweet herb and Román was telling me about Warsaw and the Vistula.

Chapter 8
The Roads of Paris

I give several examples. A woman could be absolutely transcendent and then become almost nothing after a few years: consider, for example Zoya and her ego. She had arrived on an international flight of a European airline. We met in the baggage reclaim halls of Charles de Gaulle Airport. Or rather, her eyes met mine after we found our suitcases. Maybe I helped her with her heavier bags.

A few days earlier I had been given a description of the lady: six foot tall, slim, slender, with light brown hair. She would be wearing a white two-piece suit and an Irish miner's cap. The image I had of her before I met her was similar to that of other slender women. I imagined her as that woman I noticed at the Melbourne Zoo, in front of the gorilla area. Impressed by the largest anthropomorph on earth, I almost didn't notice her arrive next to me. I saw her enter the area, where there was an open cave in the mound covered by dwarf palmettos and a spring through which water flowed. I was stunned by the slenderness of the woman and her poise as she slipped into the ape enclosure. To my surprise, one of the silver-backed gorillas approached her and stroked her face. I couldn't believe the ape was able to do that with the back of a huge paw. The woman looked fragile and received the touch with a tender expression.

Airport woman was just as slender, tall and stylish, with rather blonde and curly hair. She wore boot-cut pants and a waist-length jacket. Perhaps the woman who cared for the mountain gorillas had been very beautiful when she finished her degree in biology or when she did her internship at a zoo in Europe. However, the Australian woman had nothing to do with the French woman; she didn't wear boot-cut pants. Perhaps, in my fantasy, Zoya looked like a Russian spy or a runway model from the fashion world.

To ensure I could recognize her, her sister gave me signs that were easily recognizable: she would be wearing a white outfit and an Irish hat. Seeing her looking so stunning and dressed in that style, I thought she looked like a couture mannequin, a doll sent by the Russian mafia for methamphetamine smuggling. I couldn't imagine anything more enigmatic, despite the intricacies of the last few days.

Days earlier I had been at the Humboldt University in Berlin with Zoya's sister Irina, who was almost as glamorous and beautiful as the woman I met at the airport. Both had the surname Polyakov. Irina looked a few years older than Zoya. I met her at the break after a lecture on viral genetic engineering that seemed like a runic version of the Old Testament, which I didn't understand at all. The woman seemed out of context at a scientific meeting. She gave the impression that she was one of the university hostesses, or those who accompanied the old scientists. I also felt out of place despite the Armani suit I had bought for the occasion.

I had been invited to talk about a hantavirus epidemic in a South American country, although there was really not much to talk about. Maybe I could have given them a description of the high plateau with hurricane winds and morning frosts; suddenly they were interested in knowing something about the customs of the people who lived in that forgotten village with huts made of mud adobe and straw. I could also have told them that the children seemed to have erythrocytosis as an early adaptation to living four thousand meters above sea level. I would have to explain to them that it was not I who identified the disease, but a group of scientists from the UCLA laboratory after analyzing the blood and other fluid samples that I had sent them.

What else? I would also have to tell them that it could not be diagnosed with certainty, since it was an inhospitable place, which seemed to belong to a community of deportees or very poor people who had arrived there as a result of the exodus of Auken herders or due to a drought in the plains. They had been there for so many years that they had become accustomed to that kind of life. At the end of the lecture series, the hostesses introduced us to the participants. This is how I officially met Irina, an epidemiologist from the Karolinska Institute. I knew that the chance of getting to the Swedish institute was very small for biologists in Europe, one in ten thousand. Undoubtedly, Irina must have been an excellent scientist, which explained her research there.

After the presentation in English, Irina conversed with me in Spanish with a Madrid accent. She told me that she had learned the language during her internship at the Complutense University of Madrid. I deduced that she had been in Madrid for an inter-institute talent exchange scheme, or to share experiences as part of the globalization of research in academic centers in Europe. Our talk began by addressing findings that had not yet made the news, such as the issue of the detection of a polio outbreak in a village in East Timor. Perhaps not that topic, but something more historical, such as the evolution of typhus during the Russian Revolution. We even mentioned the death of some characters from that disease. I don't remember if we talked about John Reed or other war correspondents who had also covered the uprising.

Later the dialogue turned to less professional topics, such as the blizzard on the Spree, and finally to the beauty of some South American cities. She remembered Rio de Janeiro, Buenos Aires and Cusco. She had been impressed by the South American jungle and the design of Rio, which seemed to blend the urban with the mountainous environment of the Tijuca jungle. Buenos Aires reminded her of some parts of Prague or Paris; she even felt the same when she saw slim young men playing a tango in the street to the beat of a bandoneon. It seemed to her a picture of her childhood in Odessa, or maybe it was part of a dream.

Cusco seemed to her the result of a delirium, as if the city did not really exist. She had a vision of its past, even though she had never experienced it. Its streets, with sloping walls, and musky smell evoked in her what she had felt in Samarkand and Jerusalem many years before. She remembered the names of some streets, some tango lyrics and Brazilian sambas. I don't think I heard the name of any of the Peruvian Andean songs, or maybe I did. Maybe she was told that *El cóndor pasa,* sung Simon and Garfunkel, was an adaptation of an Andean song.

After a while of pleasant conversation, Irina returned to the subject of hantavirus as if she was very interested in my work or had no other business to discuss with me. "In the Bolivian outbreak in which you intervened," she said, "what was the distribution of cases of HFRS and HPSV? I am referring to patients presenting hemorrhagic fever with renal syndrome and those showing symptoms of hantavirus pulmonary syndrome."

"The cases were of the hemorrhagic type, with jaundice and anuria. They suffered petechial flare-ups and ecchymosis before presenting with hematemesis and hemoptysis. Cases with pneumonia seemed to me to be rare." This last one I assumed, as I could only check the melena and ecchymosis; not the respiratory pictures. I would have to clarify that the cases were more complex than could be explored in the scientific literature.

Her question had left me blank. The issue of the classification of syndromes seemed to me similar to the process of manufacturing vaccines by genetic engineering, using brewer's yeast or *Escherichia coli*. In other words, it was a tangle that at the time interested me to no end. To be honest, I should have replied, "The disease was an enigma until I was informed from headquarters that it was hantavirus. If I had not been given that information, today I would still think that it was a hemorrhagic or pneumonic disease of any etiology. Thus, I took it as a disease whose origin was still to be determined, with high lethality and high transmission." That was my limit and that is what I gave her to understand.

"I can only tell you that the first place it was detected was a rural school. The teacher reported the outbreak, alarmed by the number of deaths that occurred for no apparent reason. The disease was characterized by intense fever and stupor with psychomotor agitation that eventually led to coma," I explained. I was relying on the references the teacher gave me: fever and insanity. What she had described was not very precise.

"She also informed me that the students and their sick or deceased relatives had varied symptoms. Some had fever and showed signs of encephalopathy. Others appeared to be suffering from severe pneumonia, similar to miliary tuberculosis which causes respiratory distress. I could not determine how many had kidney failure or how many had pneumonia because at no time did I have the laboratory tests or X-rays to make a diagnosis."

I thought to myself that this explanation sounded as I was making excuses. I should have been more observant at the time, so that I could have observed changes in diuresis and hemoptotic sputum with respiratory distress.

"I really congratulate you," she said, "for your ability to make the diagnosis despite the lack of technology at your disposal." It seemed to me that she was patronizing me, perhaps due to her Madrid accent.

"The hard part was facing people's mistrust. The same as always, everyone believed they were predestined to survive. Nobody thought they could be next on the list. We had to convince them of the danger they were in. Despite that difficulty, it was less exceptional than you imagine." I wanted to tell her many details, such as the fear I felt about the possibility of catching the disease when I arrived in the village. I wanted to tell her about the precautions I took in feeding myself and washing my hands, the panic I experienced when removing the schoolbooks and books of the schoolchildren that gave off a musty and dusty smell, the itching and sneezing despite the mask I wore. Finally, I said, "The crumbled hero is just an ordinary man, one among many." Or maybe I whispered it almost to myself.

She did not understand or did not want to understand me. She watched me with an expression in her eyes that I interpreted as one of tenderness and admiration, as if she were in front of a guy with enough guts to get into one of those unimaginable villages hidden between the mountain ranges and the plains of the plateau, where the thatch and the rhizome weeds grew.

"How I admire you!" she exclaimed. And without waiting for a response, she continued: "I imagine you in that isolated village, walking the access roads free of vehicles, attending to people and sharing their anguish."

I should have replied that I was the one who admired her knowledge and scientific work. I should have told her about my participation, a long time ago, in a study on organ transplants in newborn chicks that had been removed from the bursa of Fabricius and given immunosuppressants in minimal doses. And that I had met two scientists who had received Nobel Prizes. She would have made an admiring face, despite the fact that her university was home to more than fifty Nobel laureates.

At that moment I understood that this extraordinarily beautiful woman was trying to show her admiration for a South American who had moved into a village of scattered huts on the plateau, where he had lived with the schoolteacher in a building that had no glass in the windows or any protection against the icy wind from the mountain range. I didn't mention it, but I felt ashamed to have thought that the teacher, a woman in her forties with an Andean face, had intended to seduce me and take me to her one-room hut with walls covered in peeling plaster. I wanted to hit myself in the chest with a rock as I compared the beauty of the Russian woman with the humility of the elementary school teacher. "What a moron," I said to myself. "It's like comparing a frontier village with the city of Berlin."

Zoya, her sister, was dazzling. She knew it; of course she knew how much she could unsettle the passers-by waiting for their relatives or acquaintances. Seeing her gave me the feeling that I already knew her. Maybe I had run into her at a ballet show, or maybe on an English mystery film set in Hong Kong. I was waiting for her with a little sign on which I had written her name. I imagine I looked like a moron in a crisis. She must have classified me as an old-fashioned nerd.

Nevertheless, she smiled at me as she wiggled her neck and shook her hair out. She added a smile. Everything about her seemed fit for a Parisian boutique fashion show, for a musical performance accompanied by a Moscow-born violinist with pink cheeks. And in my mind I rambled on about the presentation, which would take place at the Lido or some other venue in the Pigalle district. It could be at the Moulin Rouge itself or the Folies Pigalle. In my hallucination, the man with pink cheeks had the style of the musicians who played in the nightclubs, plethoric and roaring. I assumed he would have been part of the Bolshoi ballet orchestra.

She made me think of the fragility of the women in Tolstoy's novels, Anna Karenina or Natasha in *War and Peace*. At the same time, I thought about the fact that, behind the beauty, intrigues and contradictions were hidden. Perhaps I should think about the slender body of Maria Sharapova or the graceful movements of Svetlana Zakharova, the prima ballerina of the Bolshoi Theater.

"Your sister gave me a description of you," I said. "However, she fell short when she said nothing about your beauty." Irina had informed me that her sister was somewhat taller, younger and more stylish than she was.

As I took the seat in the van that was taking us to her hotel in Republic Square, I kept quiet thinking about the magnificent woman next to me.

"Do I disappoint you?" she replied, making a studied gesture of sadness.

"No! On the contrary, you are the most beautiful woman I have ever seen in my life," I said, blushing up to my ears. Then I remembered that I had seen a woman just as beautiful in the Berlin subway. Maybe another equally beautiful one at the Turner Hotel in Rome. That time the woman looked Italian. The girl was in the lobby of the Roman hotel and looked like a young version of Angelina Jolie. She was also about four inches taller than me. Sensing my daze, she said to me, *"Buona sera!"* she greeted me with a splendid smile that I matched with a rictus grin of fear.

The good thing was that, in my case, any compliment to a beautiful woman was only a kindness with no hope of return. Zoya would have taken me for a Cro-Magnon living in a hollow somewhere in the Alps, thus interpreting my astonishment. I did not want to pay attention to her features, and even less to the exultant expression on her face; nor did I want to notice the beauty of a body that I could only imagine as perfect. It was obvious: her size and slenderness and fine features reminded me of the last trip on the Berlin subway. Not only because of Irina, her sister, whom I had met at the Von Humboldt University, but because of an anecdote with a young woman I could only see that time in one of the *unterBahn* cars. The girl looked to be the same age as Zoya. She possessed identical whiteness and was equally beautiful. I guessed her to be Russian or Lithuanian.

Of course I could not explain that interpretation of where it came from, even though listening to it I found the language to be different from German, with a Russian-like hiss. It was one of the last days of my stay in Berlin. The scientific congress had ended a day earlier. While at the hotel, it occurred to me to visit some museums before leaving for Paris. My tour included the Pergamon Museum, where I was impressed by the Pergamon altar, the market of Miletus and the Ishtar gate; the latter, with the glazed bricks depicting lions on the blue porcelain background. The now-restored altar came from the acropolis of the Greek city of Pergamon. Later I could check the classical features of Nefertiti in the Neues Museum, and conclude with a visit to the Altes Museum, of classical architecture, with an equestrian monument at the entrance that seemed to be Greek or Latin.

When I left I found myself in the park of the Berlin Cathedral, with its central bronze dome, which had regained its original green color from copper sulfate or some oxide such as malachite, and its side towers crowned by smaller domes. The night of that late autumn was frigid and the first snow of the season was falling. The Spree received the snow on its surface, where the white flakes melted with the dark tint of its waters. The wind brought drops of icy water that wet the faces of those of us who dared to walk through the streets. I had to walk several blocks to find the entrance to the Berlin subway train, through the Hackescher Markt station, in the direction of Wall Street Plaza. I had not finished settling in when suddenly three people got on the carriage, one of whom was a stunningly beautiful woman. She was accompanied by a young man with an unkempt beard in a wheelchair, and another young man who was pushing the chair. He was maneuvering it in front of the car seats.

All three spoke a language that I guessed to be Russian or Polish. I assumed they were soldiers from some country at war. The man in the wheelchair had a splintered femur. His disability attracted attention, but could not compete with the beauty of the woman, who stunned the occupants of the wagon.

Every detail reminded me of a night in another city, on another subway train, perhaps with another woman traveling next to me. On that occasion, I was the one who got into the car. The girl in that other city was alone, I even felt her to be melancholic, as if she was thinking of something sad or remembering a great loss. The city was Buenos Aires and I was taking the subway line D, between Tribunales and Palermo. I found the girl's desolation seductive or, at least, enigmatic. She had very white skin, although she might have been pale with grief. I thought then that the young woman was coming from a grief over the loss of a very precious one. Her boyfriend? Maybe the grief was over her job. Or maybe it was both. Many years later, in Berlin, I was once again contemplating the beauty of this young woman with a very white complexion, who was accompanied by two young men.

I would have liked to understand what they were talking about, or at least get lost in their exotic faces. She was talking in a language I couldn't understand and I couldn't fix my eyes on her to avoid the reaction of her companions, who did not look friendly. I had to dissimulate by looking in another direction, like someone who watches the other people who also travel in the subway. Me and my delusions. I spent the day elaborating arguments for every situation. Maybe I was obsessed with inventing a script for each person. That time it occurred to me to fantasize that the girl was accompanying a war wounded man suffering from a gunshot wound, and not from a traffic accident or a simple fall. Quite a novel.

The young men could have been of any other nationality, not necessarily Russian or even Lithuanian, as I was unable to identify the language. What was certain was that the girl possessed a sensational beauty. The boy pushing the wheelchair pretended to be a nurse. At that moment it occurred to me to think of every woman I had ever known in my life. It hurt that among them was Gabriela, my ex-wife. It hurt because I should have been with her and my children, who were by now old enough to go to college. Maybe they worked in an office somewhere.

The train hesitated on the curves. From the window of the car we could see the walls of the tunnel, illuminated by light bulbs placed on the top of the reinforced concrete. The light was dim and the tunnel dark. Every now and then you could hear the screeching of the brakes and the route was illuminated by the reflectors on the embankments of each station. There were the access platforms and the transit corridors with their illuminated signs. Slowly the cars emptied of passengers, perhaps because of the blizzard or because of the night schedule. My mind immediately imagined lonely passengers on an old train in some city in Europe or South America. Some of them would be dreaming of furtive encounters or some surprise for which they were not prepared. Maybe they were humming a song that in one of its verses said, "The house without you is as empty as the cars of a train in the last hours of the night." That made me think of an old, narrow street with many nooks and crannies. On the street there was a little sign advertising the sale of artistic masks from the Venice carnival. The street was called Di Fiore and years before flowers were sold there.

The train arrived at the next station. There a group of tipsy boys got in the carriage and reminded me of some young men who were putting on an allegorical performance at the end of the Unter den Linden avenue in front of the Brandenburg Gate. The boys in the street theater were dressed in the uniforms of Russian, American, British and East German soldiers. I imagined that they were acting out the moment when the troops of each country found themselves in the city divided by a concrete wall. The boys were playing at reenacting what happened while making fun of passersby. Some were carrying flags. I spotted the one with red stripes and white stars on a blue background, the red flag with the hammer and sickle at one of its corners and the red, yellow and black striped flag of Germany. And, of course, the red, white and blue vertical striped flag of France.

The tipsy boys were trying to perform a stage act that I couldn't identify. Some had gothic faces and others looked like they had been recruited at a punk party. Their hair was gelled, painted in outlandish colors: purple, blue, green, violet, crimson. Maybe they wanted to imitate the plumage of exotic birds.

The girls' clothes mixed different styles; the boys, on the other hand, looked as if they had come from a costume party or a fashion show. I thought they wanted to represent citizen tribes or the variety of European youth fashion. Or maybe they intended to make a show of dementia that they boasted about as if by doing so they looked different. Lately I had noticed the same self-denigrating or self-destructive tendency in kids from the big cities. The scene reminded me of young men from New York's Seventh Avenue, Chelsea, New Orleans Mardi Gras; very thin boys and scrawny women on the busy streets, with wiry faces adorned with noses eyebrows and tongues pierced and tattoos everywhere.

The reaction they produced in the travelers was diverse: the older ones looked at them with fear while muttering between their teeth; the younger ones shared the joy of the group and joined in the dialogues. As I watched the Russians I realized that they were strangers to the show. Then the girl turned to me; she had noticed my gaze on her during the trip. Her eyes were a deep sky blue and she was smiling at some joke her companions had told, or maybe she was amused that an older guy couldn't take his eyes off her. Our gazes met for a few seconds, enough time for the color and shape of those eyes to remain engraved in my memory as one of the many pleasant memories of my life. Perhaps I could compare it to the sight of a very beautiful woman dancing the tango on Florida Street. The tango woman was very thin, almost spiritual, and as she danced, her dark brown eyes stopped to linger on mine as she smiled at my enthusiasm.

When I had to get off the train, the station platform seemed silent and I felt the damp cold penetrating through the entrance to the station, as if the icy Arctic wind was blowing. The chill entered my bones and froze the tips of my nostrils and my ears. As I glanced at the cars of the train, like someone looking at a doll for the last time, I saw the graffiti with drawings and vulgar phrases.

The custom of painting graffiti on street corners was a globalized phenomenon. The same message was repeated on the subway trains of any city: Moscow, London, Paris, Berlin, Mexico, Buenos Aires, New York. I imagined that the authors were young people who belonged to some underground tribe, indignant youths who invaded the big cities of Europe protesting the economic crisis. What they were writing was part of a story they considered interesting, but I didn't understand the plot. I don't know if they were trying to express crazy ideas or a deep regret for some unresolved issue. Perhaps it was the expression of a generation in the hands of an artist seeking to create symbols.

When I met Zoya, I relived the moment when I saw the girl in the Berlin subway. The two looked alike. "Maybe in the color of their complexion or in their manners," I said to myself. Although the similarity was also in the perfume and the color of the lipstick they used to paint their lips. Or was it the carefree look with which they observed what was going on around them?

The vehicle that transported us from the airport to the Place de la République, where the Crowne Plaza hotel was located, crossed the Boulevard Peripherique and left behind Gentilly and Ivry-sur-Seine, neighborhoods with immigrant populations. We then continued along the Rué Bobillot. Between the Place de la Bastille and the Place de la République we spotted the drug addicts and alcoholics, who zigzagged as if suddenly the passersby in the central streets felt a generalized vertigo, an earthquake perceptible only to the addicted.

Then Zoya broke the silence with a question, "Do you know Paris?" she said in French-accented Spanish.

I replied that this was the second time I had visited the city. The previous one had been a working visit. I explained that then I had the opportunity to visit the Pasteur and Sanofi laboratories in Montparnasse. Zoya smiled at me as if I were a child who had yet to learn more about life. I would have liked to tell her that I knew other cities, such as New York, Chicago and Sydney. Chinatown in Los Angeles and Manhattan with the crazies in Central Park and Greenwich Village came to mind. I should have told her that I had traversed dangerous areas of São Paulo and shantytowns near the marshes in Honduras. And that I had also visited historic sites in Europe and other parts of the world to let her know that I was well traveled and that I knew such cosmopolitan cities as Paris.

However, I kept quiet thinking that maybe she was offering to serve as my guide for the next few days. Although, to tell the truth, there was no point in getting my hopes up, since there was nothing to indicate that she wanted to thank me for having met her at the airport or to bring her sister's package to her. I thought the package might contain an Indian shawl or a Spanish scarf. "Something small but meaningful," I thought to myself. My commitment to her sister, Irina, could be considered fulfilled.

I must have retired that same afternoon, after leaving her in the lobby of the Crowne Hotel, when I accompanied her like a mute to her service, listening without understanding what she said to the receptionists. The bellboys took care of the luggage and escorted her to her room. I remained in the lobby for a few minutes at her request. She had said something like, "Stay, I'll be right out," or, "Wait for me so we can schedule something." It was all the result of my fully-fledged innocence.

When she returned to the lobby, we arranged to have breakfast the next day at a restaurant on Boulevard Saint-Martin. After breakfast we explored. It felt like a dream, like a delirium. We ascended by funicular to the esplanade of the Sacré-Cœur basilica, from where we contemplated the Montmartre district, with its narrow streets and nooks and crannies, like the rue Saint-Rustique or the rue Norvins and the Place du Tertre, where painters exhibited watercolors and oils while sketchers traced a face in charcoal in ten minutes. We passed through the immigrant neighborhoods, le Barbès, where North Africans used to live, and Château-Rouge, a stronghold of sub-Saharan Africa. We walked along the Avenue de Clichy, passing in front of the Moulin Rouge, the Opera Garnier, the Louvre Museum and the Place de la Concorde. Then we walked along the Champs Elysees until we reached the Arc de Triomphe. We took a cab to go to the Trocadero, cross the Champ de Mars and reach the Eiffel Tower. There we ascended to its apex on a freezing cold afternoon to see the Seine, the Chaillot Palace, the Invalides and the Bourbon Palace.

At that moment, I thought that the Sacré-Cœur, without Zoya's company, would not have the warmth that the funicular had given me. It would have been an experience like the one I would have had climbing Christ the Redeemer or Corcovado, in Rio de Janeiro, with a bunch of Cariocas singing sambas. It would be interesting, but without any added excitement. Accompanied by Zoya, the Sacré-Coeur seemed to me a place of enormous beauty, with its magnificent domes. During the ascent to the atrium of the basilica, I don't know why I remembered a picture of Indigenous people with their wool or toquilla straw hats yellow with age. It occurred to me that they could be Ecuadorians.

As an association of ideas, I remembered having been near the salt flats of Uyuni observing the locals with their black suits. I noticed black eyes, with incomplete epicanthus, looking at me from the banks of the Madeira River in Brazil. As if I found myself in the southern lakes with the Mapuche Indians on the outskirts of Buenos Aires. Maybe I should have hummed a tango:

> Under the mocking gaze of the stars that today see me return [...]. Back, with withered forehead, the snows of time silvered my temple [...].

Then, finding Zoya by my side and realizing that she was not a chimera, I was reminded of Édith Piaf singing *La vie en rose*. Zoya changed my world, she sweetened it in the old streets of Paris, on the bridges over the Seine River, at every turn of Montmartre, in the gardens of the Champs Elysées. I was convinced that her slenderness contrasted with my vulgarity; her style was another note in my life. I thought she could fit in with the Montparnasse of pre-World War II American writers: Hemingway, Ezra Pound, T.S. Eliot, Henry Miller. I imagined her rivaling Vanessa Redgrave when she played Isadora Duncan, as beautiful as she was, though much younger and more divine. I even thought that Zoya could be found among the members of a Caucasian ballet group performing a classical dance piece.

Next to her I felt tiny. When I studied that face of perfect features and her body of soft lines, it seemed to me that I was looking at a model of an haute couture designer. Especially when I lost myself in her enigmatic eyes, which I considered to be the heritage of the Crimean Tatars. I was reminded of Warhol's paintings, which showed the most beautiful eyes on earth. I perceived a tearing of the outer corner that gave her an air of mischief, noticeable from the first moment.

In the end, when we went to dinner in the Latin Quarter, I was already head over heels in love. Just like that! Like a teenager coming out of high school. I was studying her to figure out if her eyes were dark green or reflected a range of very dark blues. Maybe it wasn't her eyes I was contemplating, but her magnificent diva-like gestures.

She ordered *foie gras;* I ordered swordfish in pea cream and sautéed mussels. As we waited for our plates to be brought to us, she started a conversation that sounded like a police interrogation to me: "How do you know my sister?" she asked me, as if it was difficult for a South American to receive orders from a European woman who was a researcher in a Swedish scientific institute.

"I met her at the Von Humboldt University in Berlin." I didn't want to tell her that both Irina and I had participated in an international congress on infectious diseases because it seemed pretentious on my part. I did not want to break the charm of a cloudy afternoon in a city that looked just stunning in autumn.

"Did she tell you about me?"

"Well, when she found out I was coming to Paris, she asked me to deliver a package to you Besides, she guessed that it would be a pleasure for me to meet you."

I don't know if I made that part of the conversation up. Maybe Irina told me between the lines while talking about the twenty-nine Nobel Prize winners of the Humboldt. I will not exonerate Irina from having been able to say that her sister was breathtakingly beautiful, and also had an extraordinary warmth.

"Irina is a wonderful sister. She is very much like our mother, who was a professor of biology at Lomonosov University." She paused and let out a sigh, recalling some moment from childhood. "A good woman." Possibly she was referring to her mother, or maybe it was Irina, or both. "It is curious that my mother and Irina are engaged in the same business, as if the vocation was inherited. "I remember that my mother, instead of telling fairy tales, would talk to us about the cellular processes to generate responses from the defense of the organism to the accumulation of memory. She did it with such enthusiasm that she seemed to be narrating chapters of Tolstoy's *War and Peace.*" Again, another sigh. Then she continued, "Suddenly, I became an obsession for both of them. They thought I would take a wrong turn in life and become a dancer at the Moscow ballet or a circus performer on a tour of the most important cities in Europe if I didn't end up as something worse, perhaps an adventurer with a tendency to addictions.

"They had fixed ideas about my future. I can even say that today they are still almost maniacally obsessed with me. For them I am a permanent concern. It is as if they always want to rescue me from something they consider bad life and bad decisions."

"I can't believe it."

I got it into my head that her looks were the problem. Being very beautiful could attract all kinds of people, including scumbags and rascals. I saw it in Pigalle, when I saw beautiful girls perverted by the traffickers who seemed to have robotized them. Beautiful women on a cliff of the senses.

"For them, the world continues to be a confrontation between good and evil, in the purest Cartesian style. For me it is *carpe diem.* Living each day without thinking about what will happen tomorrow. Nothing is regulated by the rules of the moralists." Then, talking about them, she said, "You should know that natural laws contemplate aberrant mutations, bizarre individuals, altered processes.

"I remember my mother used to explain the chaotic reproduction of cells in neoplasms. Maybe she thinks I'm an atypical daughter, like my father, an alcoholic musician, or her own brother, a crazy anarchist," she concluded.

At that moment I began to review Hellenic mythology, the heretical one, and not the classical one. I thought of Saturn devouring his children, as ordered by Titan, his older brother. The explanation was intended to demonstrate the destruction of the children by the parents. Then I turned to Achilles' revenge for the death of Patroclus. Aeschylus explored in his play *The Myrmidons,* the affection between the warriors hinting at the possibility that more than friends they were lovers. Achilles the *Erastian* and Patroclus the *Eromancer,* or the other way around. The truth was that I did not know then what it could mean to be an erastess and an eromaniac. Later I learned, from a psychologist who had a fondness for classical history, that the affair alluded to pederastic relationships between an older man and an adolescent.

If I had guessed her addiction to alcohol that evening, I would not have ordered the glasses of port. Maybe that would have prevented her from going on a multi-day binge until she was exhausted. I admit that when she asked for more port that night, even though we were both tipsy, I was assaulted by lubricious obsessions with the desire to have her beautiful body, slender and softly contoured, and to caress that wonderful face with its languid gaze and sensual lips. It was as if I had suddenly gone mad. I felt unbridled lust and did not know how to take the next step. She noticed that my eyes showed a pressing sexual desire, so she took the initiative and told me that she knew a hotel in Montparnasse that was run by a Lithuanian woman.

When we arrived, I noticed that the place was discreet and apparently hygienic. The designer had tried to reproduce the image of one of the famous hotels in Saint-Tropez or Nice, on the Côte d'Azur, to set it in the bohemian quarter of Paris. The courtyard was adorned with red bougainvillea and the interior walls were lined with climbing plants. They had arranged the tables and chairs of the cafeteria under a veranda made of wooden slats, over which a green canopy of vines had been woven. The walls of the rooms had been covered with colorful patterned paper reminiscent of the early twentieth century, which contrasted with the classic rococo furniture.

By undressing her in a place like that I relived one of the hallucinations that assaulted me from time to time, the result of the ravings of a brain with islands of neurofibrils and amyloid substances. I even thought I was suffering from kuru because of one of my trips to Africa. A prion disease of the cerebral cortex whose initial symptom was scattered thinking, then ending in soporous dementia. At the same time, I began to suspect that port was loaded with a soluble aphrodisiac and the effect was that numbness replete with sexual fantasies. Then I realized that I didn't need any stimulation. The beautiful body I admired on those sheets of impeccable whiteness was more than enough.

The rest was a delirium, an utter fantasy. It was as if I had come out of seclusion after many months, perhaps years. She responded to my caresses discreetly, without the need for fuss.

I am certain that she felt as admired as all the paintings in the Louvre, as the most sought-after supermodels. She sensed my admiration, greater than the admiration I had for the geniuses who had used the restaurants to converse and create their masterpieces, such as Joan Miró, Amedeo Modigliani, Pablo Picasso, Marc Chagall, Juan Gris, Jean Cocteau, Max Ernest, Diego Rivera, Vicente Huidobro, Salvador Dalí, Henry Miller, André Breton. For me she was much more than all of them. She was an authentic composition of Russian classics. She was the Nastasia Filipovna of Dostoyevsky's *The Idiot*, or Tolstoy's Anna Karénina, or both in one person. Beauty combined with fragility in a single woman.

I don't know where I got the conclusion that Zoya felt the pain that the privileged experience when they look at the mass of anodynes and envy their luck. Paradoxical indeed. The pain of having burned her life in the candle of beauty or in the embers of success. I had perceived it in other people and in other scenarios. Like the cardiovascular surgeon Favaloro, who committed suicide at the height of his professional success, when the scientific world admired him for his contributions to coronary surgery and mammary artery bypass grafts. Just as it had happened to modern music legends such as Sid Vicious, Kurt Cobain, Amy Winehouse: self-destruction as part of fatalistic thinking, as if the overload of feeling different was too much weight for the backs of those human beings.

When she could no longer conceal her anxiety, she cried as if her suite at a luxury hotel, the Bellagio in Las Vegas, had been taken away from her; as if she was remembering the loss of a very dear one, her last boyfriend, a Russian with curly hair and classic features.

I took the opportunity to ask, "What happened? Maybe it wasn't a good idea to go to this place."

"It's not you." She paused. "It's a matter of bipolarity. I try to forget, but I can't. Everything comes back like a vertigo. The sleepless nights trying to listen to my heartbeat to know if I'm still alive. The day, which is slow to come with each sleepless night. I don't know what to think. Maybe I should return to my land, although I don't know if I should go back to work either." I remained silent to see if she could continue her narration. Seeing that I was all ears, even though her story was enigmatic, she continued with her explanation: "I would like to find someone to take me with him. In the end, it breaks my soul to realize that I am on the opposite side of the street, and I cannot cross to hold his hand."

It started after the first toast, or maybe the first shot, or maybe with the first love. Then she could not stop in time and ended up in free fall. It was the self-destructive fury in the exceptional, spoiled by luck. People who have extraordinary beauty, like Zoya; people with outstanding intelligence, like Barnard or Favaloro; famous artists, like Kurt Cobain; stars and movie stars, like Marlon Brando or Lindsay Lohan. Each of the characters has their suicidal tendencies and their bipolarity, their addictions to alcohol and drugs. Then I remembered my friend Daniel Gutierrez, in a rut I didn't understand, looking for someone to fuck on Manhattan's Seventh Avenue. I also thought of Gabriela's niece when she relapsed into addiction. Both would end up lacerated on a table of stone sacrifices, in a temple that had hollows in which the transgressors of a universal order were imprisoned, which spoke of punishment for those who could not stop at the edge of the cliff.

Certainly, the addiction presented by some people linked to hereditary depressive dysphoria, genetic alterations of intolerance and dependence to drugs could not be minimized. Its locus in areas close to the limbic lobe, where the pleasure centers were located.

Dependence is as serious as any other chronic brain disease. In some cases the addictions even overlap with brain diseases such as Alzheimer's or Parkinson's disease. I had witnessed the encephalic destruction of the elderly who abused drugs and alcohol. I had seen them totally wasted, muddy in their own feces, urinating on their mattresses. I had also seen children or young pubescent boys on the sidewalks, shaking as if they were attacked by a disease that affected their balance and caused vertigo. I had seen very young girls throwing empty beer cans or whiskey bottles into garbage cans. I came across them in the vicinity of gambling houses and brothels, as if they wanted to enter to play the slot machines or be part of the pleasure offer.

Zoya had it all: beauty, culture, elegance. Why had she ended up in that pit? I got no answer. Then I remembered a woman who had a television program for children. Actually, there were two women who hosted the program: one of them was very tall, the other not so tall. They were both very beautiful. One early morning news leaked out: the body of the smaller had been found in a luxury hotel. The details were not known, except for some speculations, one of which referred to the use of anxiolytics in lethal doses to achieve suicide.

It seemed to me that Zoya suffered from a similar picture of depression and anxiety. For her, every moment of happiness was interpreted as the beginning of desolation. It was something akin to the chronic illness that haunts some women in countries like Sweden and Japan. I had heard of mass suicides in Tokyo subway tunnels and seasonal suicides during cold or rainy periods in

Stockholm. I attributed the incidence to funereal landscapes, overcast skies, demanding, competitive environments that led to frustrated young people, graffitied streets, drug proliferation, erratic feelings and, above all, the recycling of depressions in people of the same community. I imagined the forests of Aokigahara, located in Shizuoka Prefecture, near Mount Fuji, Japan. It is reported to be the place with the most suicides per year, more than thirty thousand.

On several occasions I observed the eyes of those who had tried to take their own lives. They were those of a dead man. Their gaze was lost in space, or rather, they seemed to convey the pathetic sensation of an old suffering. They remained motionless in their sockets. There was no corneal luster and no sclera.

Then I noticed Zoya's eyes and I understood the expression of pleading, of help not to go down the slope of self-destructive immolation. I imagined that she was looking for a plank of salvation, even if that plank was a third worlder without lineage who did not even know Paris, much less had been associated with the world of celebrities and luxuries that she frequented. She had no choice. If it wasn't me, it would be anyone else with Samaritan tendencies. I had arrived at the right time; I was in the right place. How not to believe it. So much so that I would avoid recounting my affair lest it be thought that my travels had done irreparable damage to my brain. The damage consisted in the inability to delimit reality and fantasy.

As I realized that time was running out in paradise, I felt a kind of despair. I would have to leave and continue my routine of working in an office with computers and a lot of paperwork. I would return to my excursions through almost deserted mountains or hot jungles to keep an eye on those places where I thought the unwelcome might be found. In my new travels I would meet again the tarantula woman and a dwarf in the mountains. I would meet a Polish priest and the children of the settlers and the children of the Indigenous. I would interrogated by a multisectoral commission that was inquiring about the facts that led to the massacre of uncontacted natives on the banks of the Madeira. On a muddy road, a dwarf horse with sweaty legs would gallop in front of the jeep. Thus ended the reverie to give way to the harsh reality, although at every moment I dreamed of returning to the little hotel in Montparnasse.

For Zoya that had been a very nice moment, very tender, but it could not last because of the absurdity. At some point I would ask to be free, even if my eyes were flooded with tears, even if my feelings were ambivalent and even if I struggled to have it all. I knew she didn't fit into the geography of the third world, and conversely, I had no place in her rarified atmosphere either. She needed pedestrian streets that would simulate civic walkways; places where people would admire her as she passed by, even if only out of the corner of their eyes. She required an entourage of people interested in beauty and fashion, whether in Brussels, Rome, Paris or Berlin. She would pose nude in front of a homosexual photographer in a session contracted by a magazine specializing in beauty or haute couture. She would walk down the Champs Elysées with ease, appearing nonchalant, even if deep down she reminded me of a half-exotic and very affectionate individual.

I had no illusions about prolonging the happiness of that moment either. The idea that I could take her away from her world of enchantment, so different from mine, full of inhospitable places with small people without aspirations, did not fit the reality.

"We could live in a very big city, maybe as big as Paris. With streets and customs similar to those of European cities," I suggested, thinking of Buenos Aires or São Paulo.

"I don't like to think about tomorrow," she replied, faithful to the *carpe diem* that governed her life. "Let's dream that today is our only day. Tomorrow does not exist. Let's take advantage of these moments of surrender." And she tucked the sheets under her body.

At that moment I was reminded of the supermodel Natalia Vodianova, tall, slim, not anorexic, with an angel's face and full lips. I thought she already knew in advance at what point the affair would end. She had it figured out. I was the unwitting one.

I pondered the difference in the two worlds, in their qualities and in my own limitations. She saw me as a scientist who moved around in helicopters and four-wheel-drive cars. She could in no way imagine my travels in ancient vehicles or long treks down slopes to reach villages with inhabitants so humble that they seemed to belong neither to these times nor to this world. Nor could she imagine my lodging in small hotels with huge rooms, where I had to accommodate my body among those who were already resting, on a mattress that was a simple sheepskin or foam as thin as a sheet. No way, she could not know my daze before her beauty.

What happened? Every moment I asked myself the same question to explain our strange relationship. Maybe she was looking for her childhood in me.

"I would like to return to Red Square, to contemplate St. Basil's Cathedral, to belong to the ballet cast of the Bolshoi Theater, to throw flowers into the river from the Andreyevsky Bridge when spring comes. To have the opportunity to talk with my father or to meet an Argentine friend with whom I fell in love because of his jazz and Latin music interpretations on a piano in a downtown hotel, close to the hyperboloid towers of Shukhov, on the banks of the Moscow River."

"Tell me more." I didn't specify whether I wanted to know more about her family or about her youth.

"I don't know what else to say. My partner died a year ago from a heroin overdose. It was the biggest loss of my life," she sighed. "I gave up drugs after that. I'll give up alcohol any day now." She didn't mention what her former partner was like at all, she didn't even name him. Rather, she spoke of overcoming her own flaws and vices.

It seemed unlikely that I could evoke her childhood, being a South American with an accent she didn't know, with a skin color that could be described as bleached white and the body of a man in his fifties, with tufts of gray hair at his temples. Perhaps I reminded her of her father or maybe a Latin American friend.

Something like that happened to me. Zoya felt a zest for life, as if she suddenly found herself in a lyceum with young people dancing around a bonfire. She was in the middle, dancing to music that came from a balalaika or a *matrioshki*. She wished she could go back to her younger years, when she wore a kilt and combed her hair in braids. She thought it might be the only chance she had to return to tenderness, to the teddy bear with glass eyes. She thought that, with my support, she could leave behind all the excesses, alcohol and bad company. Saying goodbye to heroin must have been a real tragedy. I can imagine her despair at being locked up in a nursing home, without the right to have visitors, receiving her naloxone or any other morphine agonist, or doped with benzodiazepines; all with the aim of leaving the hell of consumption. She needed to be admitted to that rehab clinic to isolate herself from her environment and thus overcome the dependency. I suppose she had to endure the anxiety and tremors typical of periods of abstinence, perhaps also moments of catatonia reminiscent of a quadriplegia of unknown origin.

I would mistake her mood swings for depression over the mourning of her one-time companion: a young, curly-haired Russian with the look of a Renaissance angel. I suppose she had loved him as her soul mate, as someone who suffered the same falls into identical pits. She had loved him for his snobbish elegance, for his hysterical breakdowns and his permanent and incomprehensible paranoia. If I had asked her how one could love a man with so many problems, she would have replied that special people have an unusual seduction. I speculated that the man had been the first figure of the Bolshoi ballet, undergoing demanding tours of various cities in Europe and the United States. Perhaps he did not belong to classical dance but was a journalist who had covered the war between Serbia and Croatia. He had then become a freelancer for several large-circulation newspapers. I assumed that he fell into addiction to get around the stress of work and extreme passion.

When the man died, Zoya would have felt like her life was ending. Worse. She sensed that the rest of her life would be lived on a cliff-edge. How much did she suffer while overcoming her addictions? I'm guessing the hyperkinesia of withdrawal crisis and depression. I'm sure she was given intravenous, fast-acting benzodiazepine to sedate her during times of psychomotor agitation. She might even have received electric shocks during periods of major depression, when she suffered from absolute immobility or suicidal compulsions.

After the hospitalization, which had lasted several months, Zoya underwent occupational treatment that involved her participation in group therapy. She tried to get out of the crisis of melancholy by traveling from one city to another, looking for someone or something that would give her back her illusion or, at least, make her enthusiastic in some way. Maybe I was part of those attempts. Maybe when Irina sent me with the parcel she intended to motivate her sister, presuming that that primitive and sentimental something she saw in me would be able to break her sister's nihilism. She was referring to that boundless disenchantment, which she interpreted as the first phase of a major depression. She thought that Zoya needed a dose of tenderness, someone who did not come from the hedonistic world in which she lived. Perhaps the hunter of emerging diseases could have the affection that her close relatives and former romantic partners had not given her. Irina thought she had let the moment pass because she was too busy and because of the damned habit of judging her before loving her as she was.

"It seems that I inherited from my father a chip that leads me to dependence. My mother knew it. Addiction has to do with an issue of neural receptors that have a predilection for chemical mediators activated by substances coming through the bloodstream. She knew that.

"Many years before, she dreamed of the possibility that my father could be treated with a lobotomy to stop his compulsive alcoholism and, in that way, save their relationship. He relied on all kinds of treatments: receptor blockers, acupuncture, group therapies, plus anything else that might make sense. She waited for him every night, until he arrived with a dull face, drool at the corners of his mouth and a foul-smelling stench that could be perceived from several meters away.

"I grew up believing that this was the relationship between the addict and his family environment. Maybe that's what they call codependency. My mother even thought about ending the conflictive relationship; however, she backed out with the argument of the children and other elucidations, such as not being able to abandon a sick person when he needed her the most. She would not admit submission as a disease. She did not accept that she had tried to get away from her husband several times without being able to free herself definitively.

"Tatiana, my mother, had to admit the hatred she felt for her husband, an emotion she shared with fear of his angry outbursts. Perhaps she was afraid that the man would be mugged on the dangerous streets or beaten by the gangs of juvenile delinquents who roamed the city on their motorcycles."

"What do you want me to tell you," I replied. "It's true: the whole environment accompanies the sinking or the resurrection."

I also wondered if there was a relationship between depression and climate. I thought of the Lapps of the Murmansk Oblast, in Russia, and of those of Norway, Finland and Sweden, raising reindeer or fishing in the ice of the northern seas, between the Norwegian fjords, the Barents Sea and the Arctic Ocean. I had seen portraits of families in front of their reindeer-hide huts. I was aware that when people spoke of this people it could be assumed to be pejorative. Besides, the Lapps liked to be called Sami people. I found out that during the Beiwe Festival, at the winter solstice, they danced in homage to the goddess of fertility who favored the procreation of reindeer and plants. In this way the sustenance of the people and the transport in sledges pulled by the deer was guaranteed. Beiwe was the same divinity that remedied the mental illnesses of the inhabitants of the northern regions of the globe. It reminded me of the great Changó of African and Afro-American animist religions. Both deities could cure depressions and addictions.

I left a few days later and she returned to her world of nihilism. I imagined her walking down the Champs Elysees in a state of inebriation, swaying on the sidewalks from where she observed the Chanel, Dior, Hugo Boss windows. In my nightmare she was wearing an exclusive Louis Vuitton ensemble and trying to avoid her own vomit so as not to ruin her dress. She had a haggard face and dark circles under her eyes that enhanced the beauty of her eyes. Seeing her this vulnerable, any guy would try to seduce her by inviting her to a restaurant with indirect lighting or a half exotic place with the air of a kiosk dedicated to the sale of handicrafts.

I would never hear from her again and the memory of her would make me sick. I felt again that it had all been a huge deception, a tremendous fraud involving her, me, Irina, the Lithuanian friend at the hotel in Montparnasse, the bellboys and receptionists at the Crowne Hotel and the waiters at some restaurant in the Latin Quarter. Possibly, she remembered in detail the last conversation I had with her. I raised the possibility of her getting serious treatment to quit alcohol. To do so, she needed to check herself into a sanatorium for addicts or be recruited by a therapeutic group such as Alcoholics Anonymous or join a rehabilitation institute based in Switzerland or Romania.

"I swear I want to get off the fucking booze and the fucking drugs," she insisted. And she added in an ironic tone, "The thing is that the whole world drinks. Even in your case, I've seen that you like martinis and port. Am I wrong?" The statement seemed unfair to me. I didn't want to contradict her to avoid self-congratulation. Nor did I want to humiliate her. Then she continued: "Maybe you think it's easy. You can't imagine how much climbing you have to do. It's quite a trauma." She meant that she didn't think she could handle the discomfort of a long treatment like the one she'd had with the opiates.

The day was approaching when I would have to leave for Madrid, my last stop on my European journey before the return trip to South America. There was no alternative. Zoya was part of the city that had enraptured me for a few days. I took a watercolor of her. The portrait showed a small tattoo, like a dragon of less than half a centimeter, on one of the cheekbones. The painter captured the beauty of the face. I would place it in a special place in my studio on Tiradentes Avenue in São Paulo. I recounted that trip: Irina, in an amphitheater, chatting with several internationally renowned professors; among them, Michael Worobey of the University of Arizona and AIDS researcher. Zoya, in Montparnasse. The Lithuanian streetwalker in her little hotel with retro decor.

I was returning to my continent to dress in the mist with my newsprint windowpane and the pants with the open fly, for lack of buttons, from my childhood in the working-class neighborhood. I remembered my plaid percale shirt that I used to wear when I was a teenager. I remembered the taste of the frog or swallow-head broth that my mother used to prepare in the market restaurants. She feared that I would transform from a dreamy child into a lonely adult, on the verge of isolation due to a mental weakness caused by a lack of phosphorus or enkephalins or phospholipids.

The route from school to home was through narrow back streets with many nooks and crannies. Sometimes I would stop at one of the corners of the square to watch a little girl with green eyes and brown hair combed in multiple braids pass by. Four centuries before, a stone church had been built in the square, with friars in brown cassocks and chasubles coming out of its portico. My father taught English at the university's School of Economics. I took advantage of his subscriptions to *National Geographic Magazine* to discover other races living in different regions of the world. I was also interested in learning about the riches of other regions. My mother felt sad when she understood that I sought solitude to draw tanks on zigzagging roadways in my notebook. Perhaps those colorful lines I drew were interpreted as a delay in mental development. For me they were part of a fantasy without borders.

That happened to me with the memory of Zoya. My mother was no longer there to give me broth. Then I lay down on the sheets to play with the two possibilities I faced: that it was all true or that it was just a dream. By then the neighborhood weasels saw me as an adult who, right off the bat, ran away from the neighborhood to get lost in the backwoods in his denim jumpsuit with straps crossed behind his back. I would look at them sideways, like someone who doesn't see them, and between my teeth I would grumble: "Old busy-bodies!"

I felt immense sorrow for having left Zoya, for not having convinced her to come with me to fill all the spaces I had left empty. Before returning, I filmed her kissing me on one of the bridges of the Seine, the one closest to Notre Dame. Of course, I didn't show anyone the pictures or the footage either. After all, no one was happy about it.

There are so many inexplicable situations. Like, for example, my not knowing English when my father a teacher of that language. However, it was he who induced me to be a wanderer in places all over the world. On those trips I met different people, some of them fascinating. On this trip I had met Zoya and Irina. Earlier I had met a dwarf on the Andean slopes, in a thicket with cactus with red flowers and cottony seeds. They all had something indelible about them. Perhaps there was a mixture of the seductive and the deplorable. Beauty has some stigma.

I'm sure I could find the arthritic finger of El Greco's characters; see a pitched battle between the street tribes of the Goutte d'Or in the Barbès district, a few blocks from the Louvre Museum and the Sorbonne university. The gang members would carry all kinds of weapons: guns, daggers, chains, construction iron. The sirens of the police cars and ambulances would silence the screams of the wounded and the shrieks of the women who, by their appearance, looked like streetwalkers looking for ten euros.

Zoya had the euphoric mood of drunken Cossacks and the melancholy of old Nordic men as they sit waiting for extinction in front of a fogged window, like elephants in a cemetery in Abyssinia, or like reindeer lying in the snow in Finland. However, this is how I loved her. That's how she crept into my soul. That's how I remember her as the best thing I have ever known, with her cyclical contradictions: quarter hours of happiness and silent sadness.

I was intensely sorry for every moment we shared and didn't share, when she didn't speak and I had to guess. It would have been better if she had been the one to tell me that her previous boyfriend had belonged to the Russian mafia, the Bratvá. I guessed by interpreting her face tattoo as part of a message. Maybe she had nothing to do with it and the affair was nothing more than a fad for girls her age, or maybe she had to flee the country using her contacts among mobsters who trafficked women and drugs.

I remembered hearing that St. Basil's Cathedral, with its brightly colored towers and pointed forms, was built on the orders of a paranoid genius, Ivan the Terrible, after he conquered the Kazan Khanate. He erected it to honor the Virgin of the Mountain. Ivan hallucinated like a madman suffering from syphilis, so much so that he had his own son murdered and, according to some sources, he gouged out the eyes of the architect Barma Yakovlev so that he could never again build anything equal to St. Basil's Cathedral.

The first tsar of all Russia reminded me of other genius crackpots, among them Nietzsche, Toulouse-Lautrec, Van Gogh, Gauguin. All of them were sick with suicidal compulsions or paranoid crises in which they mistook friends for assassins trying to take their lives. They were like people tormented by neurological diseases or by infections that caused syphilitic gum in the brain. In the end, it could not be known if the genius was due to the mass of the tumor located in the brain or to an electrical disorder, product of ectopic stimuli generated in the lesions of the cortex.

I wondered, in Zoya's case, if the opiates and alcohol turned her into a ragdoll with cyclical periods that oscillated between euphoria and melancholy. I accepted that the girl was fascinating, both for her physical beauty and for her emotional ups and downs, which created a sense of continuous expectation. I could find her in her hysterical phase as during the crisis of absence, when she suddenly seemed to remember something very sad or a problem she could not solve. Maybe she was an anorexic supermodel who understood that behind her there were other young women waiting their turn to replace her.

When I realized how complex she was, I felt the impulse to leave her, claiming I needed to go to the supermarket and leave the little hotel in Montparnasse and never return. The situation was complicated: Paris was a beautiful city; the girl was a mirage. I had dreamed it all. I had to face the reality that was on another continent and with other companies.

At Charles de Gaulle Airport, where I saw her for the first time, immigration control was receiving the forms filled out by visitors while the loudspeakers announced departures and arrivals. My flight had no delays, it would depart at the time indicated on the electronic board. When I took my seat on the plane, observing the rest of the passengers who did not even turn to look at me, I realized that it had all been a beautiful dream, with no possibility of repeating it on another occasion. Maybe there was a little sign in red lights under "No smoking" that said: "No turning back".

Chapter 9
The Trial

In the villages we found the natives with their naked bodies and their faces painted with achiote. Most were of indefinite age; the youngest were barely out of childhood. The older ones had tonsured crowns and missing teeth. They all studied us with distrust, even fear. I tried to explain about lymph nodes in the neck and why they had difficulty breathing as products of scrofula and pulmonary tuberculosis. I thought I would find the paralytics and the handicapped in the group. I did not find them, possibly because they had been abandoned in a wasteland that served as a cemetery. Only fragments of skeletons covered by the mosses and rhizomes of the ground could be found there.

That was all they were: an ethnic group ambushed on the banks of the Madeira River waiting for someone to remember their existence in order to protect them. Or maybe they wanted to be forgotten so that they would not be subdued, infected, enslaved or hunted as if they were wild animals, in order to exhibit them as trophies in the colonists' camps. I imagined the miniaturized heads hanging on the columns of the barracks, tied by the hair one to the other as if they were a bunch of garlic or onions fastened to the post of a greengrocer's shop. I remembered the shrunken heads on the waists of the Jíbaro and Huitoto people.

Looking closely at the shrunken heads, without touching them out of disgust or fear of anaerobic bacteria that could be stuck to the parchment-like skin, I realized that they retained the dominant features and expression of the individuals of the ethnic group, to which was added a gesture of astonishment or terror, which was hardly surprising given they found death at the hands of their enemies.

I discovered the same thing in the settlers' camp: shrunken heads of the natives, with long, dull hair. Moreover, one could perceive the same expression of astonishment at the time of their death. Surely they searched for them along the machete-opened trails and in the thick jungle, full of trees with reddish bark, of stems parasitized by climbing moss, by lead-colored lichens adhering like scabs, by the fungi that looked like small ledges. They chased them near the riverbank and in the cloudy mountains. They searched for them without exhausting themselves, with persistence and patience. When they found them, they riddled them with bullets that had blunt and excavated tips, which produced air voids and explosions with lead fragmentation. What I am not sure of is the method they used to reduce the size of the heads, whether it was the same as that used by the tribal people.

I surmised that they might have used some Jíbaros from the upper Amazon so that they would have done the work for money or in exchange for local sugarcane moonshine. In keeping with their methods, they would have brought the Jíbaros tied by the neck on a long chain like a rosary that, instead of beads, had knotted attachments. Once they had tamed the natives, they used them for their dexterity in reducing the heads. I could not believe that delirium and barbarism had no limits. The reducers were accustomed to masato (an alcoholic drink) and hallucinogens that passed through the external auditory canal; however, they were seduced by the sugarcane liquor. The warriors became submissive to the point of licking the wooden floor on which the liquor had fallen.

Once enslaved, they were forced to reduce the heads of the natives who had died in the hunts. They boiled them over and over again, introduced fleshy leaves in the jaws and in the nostrils a green mass that was the product of grinding the leaves of creeping herbs. They sewed the mouths with a xerophytic fiber, which gave them the expression they wanted to achieve, as if they were masks. Some of the faces seemed to show panic, others seemed to mock their killers. Some showed both expressions at the same time. Then the predators placed the reduced heads in visible places in the camp, at the entrance of the main barracks, in the container used as a dining room, on the stilts of the first huts. Some of the assassins carried their heads around their waists.

Definitely, cruelty had no limits. It was cruel to the natives. Trophies became fashionable, as did tattoos, earlobe piercings, tongue piercings, nipple piercings, and lower nasal septum piercings. Possessing reduced heads had a connotation of fierceness, cruelty. Therefore, the trophy qualified the best in the pack.

In the camp, the sicarios organized nightly sprees with prostitutes. Among these, the best had been recruited by the bosses and others had come to learn of the prosperity of the business from their companions. The boys in the camp were intoxicated by narcotics and drinks with high alcohol content. In the throes of ecstasy, they danced, naked, to a rhythm somewhere between rap and capoeira while the prostitutes danced with each other. Suddenly, Northeastern rhythms from the states of Bahia, Ceará, Pernambuco or Paraíba were improvised.

For the companies, the invaders of the indigenous territory, there were two ways to choose: the first one consisted in driving away the natives with airplanes, hunting dogs, bombs and other unholy methods; the second one was simpler and supposed to exterminate those who lived in the regions that the colonists intended, for which they created troops of assassins with the people of the cities. Then these were in charge of hunting the natives as prey of the bush. They left the corpses in the middle of the jungle, in the open, generating the miasmas of putrefaction. In this way, they were devoured by scavengers, lizards and another ophidian somewhere between the anaconda and the python. At the end came the insects, which created worm nests in the rotting flesh; later, the vegetables sucked up what was left of the organic waste. Carnivorous plants with fleshy leaves, the Venus flytrap and the sundew finished the process without leaving traces of annihilation. No corpse, no skeleton. Then someone will say, addressing the officials of the Secretariat for the Protection of Minority Populations of the Ministry of Justice: "Nothing happened here."

The result was predictable: the territory of the Akuntsus and Korubos ethnic groups was limited to the edges of the canyons, far from the main channel of the Madeira. They took refuge in the cloud forests and in the impenetrable zone of the bush to avoid contact with the explorers of the oil companies, with the hired killers of the chestnut growers and with the prospectors of gold and precious stones. In addition, they avoided the loggers who razed the jungle. They avoided even missionaries, sociologists from non-governmental organizations, government officials and all strangers who poked their noses into the forest.

Few had seen the palisades of their huts, their jars dug out of palo balsa, where they kneaded cassava starch with the spittle of toothless old women to prepare masato. The natives believed that any contact with foreigners brought dire consequences, as if a hurricane wind would tear giant trees from their roots and they would fall on their huts with them inside. Perhaps they feared being attacked and consumed by a disease that would first cause diarrhea, accompanied by weakness that would plunge them into lethargy. After two weeks, paralysis of the lower limbs would set in and they would have to be carried in portable hammocks by the young people of an erratic community, accustomed to changing shelters from one place to another. I assumed that the disease they were referring to was paralysis due to HTLV-1, a sexually transmitted virus, which could be a reactivated endemic or a new disease brought by promiscuous settlers.

Perhaps the paralysis was the consequence of heavy metal poisoning from the tailings and the contamination of the rivers with the mercury used to burn the gold. No idea; it could have been any infectious disease or neurological damage from heavy metals.

FUNAI, the National Indian Foundation, was also outraged. Anthropologist Mario da Cunha told me about his own experience, "The same shit with a different scenario," he told me. "That time it was at the triple border, between Colombia, Peru and Brazil. The victims were a group of Jíbaro Indians. On that occasion, the sugar was poisoned with arsenic."

"Fucking hell!" I exploded.

Da Cunha gave details of the symptoms found on the corpses, "Skin desquamation, accelerated cadaveric processes, sphacelation in parts, with giant liquid phlyctenas."

"I imagine so," I replied, although I had never actually seen the result of arsenic poisoning.

Those who were still alive suffered from diarrhea as liquid as rice-washing water and a whistling respiration, with laryngeal stridor. I thought the noises indicated a laryngeal or upper tracheal spasm, or perhaps they were due to plugging of the bronchi by purulent mucus.

Da Cunha said that the natives who survived the poisoning went underground. To do so, they hid in the jungle upriver.

Those who could not flee because they were immobilized by the poison died because of their inability to ingest liquids, since they could no longer even swallow. They perished from thirst even though they themselves were bags of water. There was water in their abdomens, water in their subcutaneous tissue, water in their sclerae, water in their lungs. This was the paradox of their agony: they were thirsty hydropics.

"I denounced the massive poisoning to the Iquitos Public Prosecutor's Office," Da Cunha explained, "for which I brought as proof of the crime a sample of three kilograms of contaminated sugar taken from two bags that the natives had stolen. The sample had been previously analyzed by the bromatological laboratory of the water service of the city of Leticia. They crapped on the news. It's as simple as that."

FUNAI's anthropologist told me that they had performed the autopsy on one of the deceased, despite the hostility shown by the indigenous survivors. After a few days they had the results of the investigation of the gastric mucous membranes, analyzed by the Institute of Legal Medicine of Colombia. Here they examined the changes in the tissues and the residue adhered to the folds. The investigators evidenced cellular alterations on the mitochondria with lysis, collapse and disappearance of the organelles. In addition, a lot of fluid was found in the tissues and bleeding, perhaps due to hemolysis of the blood.

Da Cunha told me that they had also sent fragments of sphacelated skin, clumps of hair and fingernails from other corpses to the Institute of Legal Medicine in Manaus, but they did not receive a response on the pretext that the samples had been sent without a presumptive diagnosis. After several months, the Iquitos Prosecutor's Office closed the case because the facts occurred in Brazilian or Colombian territory and not under its jurisdiction.

"They didn't want to be responsible for the investigation of the facts either," Da Cunha reasoned. "For our part, we suspected food poisoning."

"How many deaths did the poisoning cause?" I asked.

"The number of deaths could not be verified because of the Jíbaros› distrust of any intrusion by outsiders. They preferred to throw the corpses into the piranha-filled rivers or simply leave them in the termite-infested part of the jungle. Someone informed us that there had been a piranha poisoning. The backwaters of the river and the banks were stained silver by the fishes' bellies. The piranhas also ingested the poison.

"Those who survived hid in the jungle to avoid any contact with the killers of their relatives. The rubber tappers and other settlers did not want to talk to the FUNAI investigation group for fear of reprisals from the killers. During the investigation, one of the settlers made a comment, 'And... it seems that the perpetrators are the thugs of a businessman named Jáuregui.' Later he regretted the comment and did not want to continue the conversation.

"The Organization for the Protection of Uncontacted Native Peoples found out that this Jáuregui was a trader of supplies for the miners and food for the settlers in the area. The man had a network of warehouses along the villages near the Amazon River. For the security of his businesses he hired dozens of thugs with the same physical characteristics as the assassins employed by the Madeira rubber tappers. Subjects of bad living who didn't give a damn about taking anyone who opposed to their purposes. The guys would set up huge bacchanals, with alcohol and drugs such as *ice*, crystal methamphetamines, while copulating with the women who lived with them or with those who came as visitors for the weekends."

"Little angels." I commented.

"Yes, sons of bitches of the worst kind," said Da Cunha. "They killed each other for money or drugs."

I imagined their faces. Young men with scarred or tattooed bodies, bare chests, faces with furtive or openly aggressive looks. Some of them were wiry, while others were athletic. Images of women they were having fun with came to mind. Brazilian or Colombian, and perhaps some Peruvian women from the ports of the upper Amazon. All of them looked exactly like each other, slim, with wide hips and proportionate breasts. Some were older, obese and with flabby skin. They all used obscene language, and all reeked of liquor. The atmosphere of drinks, music and cantinas permeated the camps.

When I thought of the type of mitochondrial degeneration of cells resulting from arsenic poisoning, I imagined the inner ridge organelles inside a double-layered membrane, collapsed into their original structure. I reviewed the concept: mitochondria come only from the mother, unlike all cell organelles, which come from the combination of genetic material from the parents. They are different from the cells of higher organisms. Their genome is smaller than that of their cellular host, similar to that of bacteria. Therefore, once affected by the intracellular toxicant, they disappear without any possibility for the cells to reproduce.

These organelles, with a folded inner membrane, with corpuscles attached to the crests, which are nothing more than ATP molecules, are the ones that provide the energy necessary for cell metabolism. Without them, metabolism would stop, the membranes would cease to be selective and there would be no transfer of ions. Lysis by extracellular fluid would occur. There would be no response to changes in the internal environment. The sodium-potassium pump would not regulate ionic exchanges. The cells would swell and then burst like hydrous balloons. First, hemolysis of red blood cells would occur, resulting in jaundice, with an increase in indirect bilirubin. Then other toxins would follow, such as ammonia, a product of liver cell degeneration, and finally the individual would fall into a coma due to cerebral edema and lysis of the supporting cells of the neurons. Death comes in accelerated stages, perhaps minutes, hours or a few days, depending on the dose of the poison.

Similarly, someone commented that the archiving of the case and the general distrust were due to the fact that the state apparatus had an obtuse and partial vision, which hindered anything that could be a police or judicial process against the power groups or against the soldiers of the border garrisons, strategic allies in illegal businesses such as the transfer of gold, drugs and timber. Protection had a cost that was paid by corruption.

Da Cunha was convinced that the death of the natives was not accidental. They did not ingest any poisonous berries or mistake them for their edible counterparts. It was not they who poisoned the river in which the dead piranhas floated. They had not been ambushed or shot; nor had their village been destroyed, but they had been poisoned. The result was the same as in the massacre in the Madeira basin: dozens of unpunished murders. The police authorities knew it and even the natives who had fled knew it. It was enough to look at the fingernails or hair to find the poison in lethal doses and thus prove the thesis of Da Cunha's group.

"When I tried to provide evidence," Da Cunha continued, "they told me at the Leticia Prosecutor's Office that I should not be the one to file the complaint, but rather I needed a duly accredited attorney; the complaint had to be made in writing. Then, in a week or more, they would give me an answer as to whether the statement was admitted or not. That time I did not understand why an accusation of crimes against humanity or genocide perpetrated against an itinerant group of natives should not be admitted."

"The same nightmare," I said, thinking of the uncertain path involved in denouncing a crime against minorities.

I imagined the police station, with the agents in charge of administrative tasks taking notes on their computers. The usual questions: "Why do you think the sugar was poisoned? Or "Why do you think the village was burned?" Perhaps they believed that the sugar was accidentally contaminated with rat poison or an organophosphate preparation to kill insects. Maybe they thought that the fire was set by the natives themselves while cooking their food. Also that the lead fragments were part of my imagination and that the bags of sugar that Da Cunha seized and then had analyzed did not link anyone to the perpetrators, least of all the poor little armed angels in the camps, who were doing their job of protecting private property against theft and intrusion by settlers, miners, loggers and indigenous people.

"In short, they could not define the relationship between the toxic substance and the perpetrators of the poisoning. It was as simple as that. It made you want to send the administrative staff to hell. You wanted to leave the facility snorting with rage, swallowing foam. But it was not pertinent, because if we withdrew the complaint, we abandoned the victims."

"What, you don't think the link between the poisoning and the sugar with the traces of poison that the natives stole is enough?" he asked me with a certain degree of resentment.

I explained to him that we detected arsenic in the bags of sugar that were rescued before they were consumed. In addition, we had histological and cellular studies of the damage caused by the poison.

"I'm on your side, Mario," I reassured him. "It is more than that. I went through the same dance when I denounced the massacre of a group of the Akuntsu ethnic group. The same ordeal: deaf policemen, disinterested prosecutors."

The bags of sugar that remained in the camp barracks were uncontaminated. The smoke from the burned village had vanished and the charred remains had been swallowed by the humus and undergrowth. The thugs of the Putumayo pit, like the henchmen of the Madeira River, got drunk on weekends. One of them drank until he lost control and went out with his gun after one of the women, whom he was threatening out of pathological jealousy. The others laughed loudly. Then someone from inside the barracks fired his gun and blew a hole in the ceiling. The revelry continued until dawn when the cantina fell silent. The women had a hangover and the men had stopped shouting.

Returning to the subject of the isolated natives of the Amazon, I imagined myself watching the lifeless bodies sailing on the surface of that great river, whose delta was the size of a Central American country, a surface of silt and red clay. The skin of the bodies had a bluish tinge. A smell of rancid fish hung in the air. The corpses showed eyelids inflated by the accumulation of liquid or colloid; the testicles looked like black balloons. An apocalyptic figure. Chilling. That picture was not in the files of the bureaucrats in Brasilia or in the offices of the NGOs, which were struggling to write hundreds of contradictory reports, some of them delirious.

"Who could possibly care about the fate of ethnic minorities in a country that claims to be among the ten most powerful countries in the world? Who could possibly care about the fate of minorities in a country that elected Jair Bolsonaro as president of the republic?"

Today I evoke the mudflats and the exotic-colored butterflies, the lianas tangling on the ground and climbing the branches of the big trees in the middle of an impenetrable forest that you have to break into with a machete to keep walking with the tip of your boots facing the same point. In this way, the rhizomes and holes in the ground were avoided.

Suddenly, at one point along the way, I came across a clearing that resembled the field of a soccer stadium, this was where the villages were located. In that area I found the huts covered with araucaria branches and huge lanceolate leaves. Inside, sheltered hundreds of women with flabby breasts and about thirty men with swollen bellies. The men showed me and my companions their genitals and arrowheads made of xerophyte leaves that they had soaked in a mixture of curare and other poisons. They looked menacing.

To get closer, we raised our hands to show that we were on a mission of peace. The leader looked at us suspiciously, squinting, and said something in his dialect. I didn't know if he was addressing us or his clan. We explained that we were there to save them, as if we were Franciscan missionaries. What clowns we are! No one believed us, not even the most innocent of the group, not even the oldest of the bunch, who looked like toothless old women, even though they were no more than forty years old. "God, where had I sinned that I couldn't help them?" An ambiguous answer comes to mind, "It's a matter of time and deceit. Besides, it's a matter of mischief and double-speak."

I think of Nietzsche and the morality of slaves as a contribution of Christianity. I feel like a Coptic Christian or a primitive catechumen. Then I ponder, "Are there variants of ethics?" The answer must be yes to differentiate the morality of the powerful, wise, strong, from the morality of the oppressed, ignorant and weak. "In which group would you classify the little Akuntsus, among the superlatively weak, despite the myths that defined them as cannibals and dangerous savages?" Everything turned out to be a chimera created by the colonists who usurped their territory as well as by the missionaries who wanted to convert them to their creed after teaching them their language. *The war against heresy:* how many crimes were committed under that banner? It would be necessary to review the history of western civilization to really consider this question.

Suddenly we found what was left of an itinerant village, with the palisade smoking, with the branches of the roof still burning. Among the trunks, reduced to ashes, we found charred bodies. I don't remember if I felt faint, if I experienced tingling, dizziness and loss of strength in my lower limbs. Maybe a very rude interjection escaped me, or did I lose my voice, as if I had no air in my lungs?

I remember the smell given off by the burnt human bodies, a stench that extended for several kilometers around. We could smell it two hours before we arrived at the clearing where the village was located. We knew of similar massacres, we had even been informed of exterminations using helicopters, but I had never been able to observe the perversity before. Everything was as horrific as the vomit produced by the stench of the environment.

The bodies looked like burned tree trunks after a forest fire, like black logs with white ash stains. A gray smoke rose from the ground and faded into the thicket. Among the remains of roasted meat there was the dull sheen of bullet fragments. I deduced that first they had shot them and then sprayed their remains with fuel, gasoline or oil to set them on fire.

"What sons of bitches!" I exclaimed, thinking that the only thing they had missed was to cut off their scalps to collect from the bosses for each death, or to cut off their right hand as proof of their deed. "Fucking psychopaths!" I blurted out to myself, imagining a gang of criminals taken from the underworld of the coastal cities.

When I looked up, my eyes full of tears, I realized that, from the grove of trees that had escaped the fire, a group of indigenous people who had survived the massacre were watching us. I felt like running to embrace them and ask their forgiveness for the deed perpetrated by the hired killers. I didn't; they would mistake me, even mistake our group, for the assassins.

I could make out the crumpled bodies, the primitive nakedness, the sad eyes, even the faces of dread. Seeing them so helpless, so vulnerable, made me want to scream, howl, snort and keep crying. I cried, drowning in my tears; I sobbed for what I had left behind, for the bad times, for the emotional losses, for the frustrations, for the people.

They, who at first glance looked like children to me, continued to watch me with distrust, understandable because of the atrocities they had suffered some time before at the hands of some sons of bitches recruited in God knows what brothels. How could they not confuse the hit men with us, who arrived later? After all, we had the same skin and hair color, even the same face. When I felt the gaze of those beings, no more than one meter fifty, relatives of the annihilated or members of another itinerant tribe that had heard the shots and had looked out to see what was going on, I felt muddy with shit, dirty and stinking, ashamed as a child who has pooped in kindergarten. And I said to myself, "Surely the survivors are shaking. In their logic, in their primal instinct, they should be shaking." There was no doubt. At the same time I wondered how we could be any different. Well, nothing. The same appearance, identical clothing, from the khaki shirt to the high-waisted boots.

At that moment I remembered some guys whose corpses were hanging in the four winds of a pedestrian bridge in Mexico. They had the same appearance as the hired killers who had murdered the natives. The same matted hair, the guayabera shirt, the sadistic face; tattoos decorating their backs from the nape of their necks to the coccyx and identical attire to the executioners of the natives of the Amazon jungle. I even had the feeling of having recognized the one with a paunch one or the skinny guy with the mustache. The same thugs who were dedicated to harming others, with that expression of arrogance and the stupidity of the thugs.

The indigenous thugs turned out to be hired killers of the rubber tappers who had invaded the reserve to find a vein of gold that, they said, had surfaced after a mudslide uncovered a vein hundreds of meters long and several centimeters thick. The find was reported by an informal miner in his seventies who was later identified as being delirious.

What I was sure of was that I was never the same after witnessing such a tragedy. In my fantasies, I dreamed of annihilating predators with a gun. Against a blue background with greenish tints, a winged man with a flaming sword appeared, destroying the bad guys and saving the good guys. In my version, the good guys were the little natives with achiote-covered skin; of course, the bad guys were their killers. I invented avenging characters that descended from the heights in chariots pulled by winged steeds. These characters would gather the criminals in an open field and burn them alive to repeat the scene in which they set the weak on fire. "With the rod you measure by you shall be measured!" I predicted.

I relived those images in my nightmares. I felt scarred for life, with a destroyed soul and a constant desire for revenge. I was not to blame for the crime. However, I felt like shit for seeing the scene and having witnessed the barbarity. I felt sorry for not being part of the avengers. I never knew which feeling was more intense: pity for the underdogs or hatred for their aggressors.

I had been told that in the days prior to the massacre, Hummer H3 4X4 pickup trucks had been seen on the trails in the region. The people behind the wheel were guys with unkempt beards, like the supporting cast of a western movie starring Clint

Eastwood. I didn't know if the bums in the Hummers were the killers. What I imagined was that the psychopaths wanted to be more and more cool and were buying trendy toys. Deep down I knew the whole crime thing was a genocide that would splatter the foreheads of those involved, even the officials of the Secretariat that catered to national minorities. Perhaps the executioners thought that the victims were part of a mass of nobodies who had not received Christian baptism; therefore, they were in limbo, which is a place where Moors and atheists of any stripe go. I don't know what they meant by limbo. To me it seemed to be an idea that hid the unbridled ambition and absolute disregard for the lives of the natives.

I thought I had experienced similar scenes in another place and time. Some time ago I was shown some photographs while being told the facts captured by the witness. In the first image, an armed column could be seen entering a hamlet. The group was made up of people of different sizes and different clothing, which made me think that they were irregulars. The second photograph showed two young men with their hands tied, one of whom was a boy of no more than thirteen years of age. The third photograph showed the same boy hanging by his neck suspended from a tree branch. On close inspection one could see that his neck had been broken by the rope; it looked like the disjointed neck of a chicken. His eyes were wide open and his expression was one of pure fear.

The individual who showed me the photos told me that he had bought them from an army graduate who, in turn, had explained the facts to him. The invaders were subversives retreating after having suffered several casualties in a confrontation with army troops. The boys in the second image were survivors of the subversive column and had been taken prisoner. The boy was hanged by the villagers. The man boasted of his possession, so much so that he displayed them as a war trophy.

I didn't know who was crazier: the villagers who had taken the law into their own hands, the rebellious child at such a young age, the individual who took the photos, or the guy who bragged about them like a moron displaying a shrunken head or the scalp of a deceased person. I thought about the attitudes of the insane of all stripes, from those cracked out from snorting crystallized methamphetamines to those who had burned themselves out as a result of their evil deeds. I heard the battle cries as I pondered the causes of the victims' submissive attitude. I assumed that the boy had pleaded for his life with arguments ignored by the mob.

I did not need to think too hard to imagine would have happened if the victim had been a rubber tapper killed by the poisoned arrows of the natives. I am sure that the police and the army border command would have organized a punitive action against those responsible for the murder. Conversely, with the natives as victims and the rubber tappers as executioners, no one would have thought of the same disciplinary action. In weeks the facts would be forgotten. Moreover, the progress of the denunciations would be impeded and the witnesses of the barbarity would suffer threats.

As soon as the intimidation happened, I denounced it loudly. A surly fellow came up to me and said in my ear: 'We have been told that you are spreading lies about a matter involving some miners in the camp.'

"What miners, asshole?" I answered him. This was a murder with advantage and malice aforethought.

I then explained the story to my interlocutor, who was a journalist from an international newspaper and television network. "The worst thing is that I tried to report it to the police, so I went with a small group of people to the police station in that village, near the site of the massacre. They sent us away. I then sent a report to the organization's directors, a document that turned out to be a report between the lines to the FUNAI's Secretariat for the Protection of the Environment and National Minorities."

"What did FUNAI do about it? Did they investigate the facts? Did they take the complaint to the Ministry or to Congress?" the reporter of the international network wanted to know.

"Nothing. As far as I know, no authority ever thought of starting an investigation. It was better to hush up the matter to avoid any kind of political scandal that would touch the government and its allies." To reaffirm my statement, I added, "*A posteriori*, and so that there would be no doubt, a woman in her fifties, ragged and haggard, gave me a threatening message, almost an ultimatum, 'You do very well not to get involved in trouble. No one wants your harm, much less your death. The boys don't want to hurt you. Do you understand me, doctor? Besides, there is no evidence, do you understand me, sir?'" I paused. "The woman was referring to the fact that the jungle erases all traces. The ficus trees absorb the charcoal, the callampas digest the organic remains and the bones of the incinerated.

"In addition, we all knew that there is no official registry of Indigenous populations. No census was ever taken. No one knows exactly the number of members of a clan, not even if there is a classification by ethnicity, overlapping groups and families in the outdated records of bureaucrats. The uncontacted natives were not inscribed in the civil registries. Legally, they did not exist. Those who said that their souls would be transported to limbo are partly right. I don't think they need to die to be in limbo." I paused again, "An old FUNAI man, by way of reflection, told me, 'Comrade, don't get tired. This is coming from behind. The surviving natives will go into the bush to flee from the bandits.'" Here I remained silent so that the journalist could show some emotion. "They will move farther and farther away. They will walk along the river so as not to leave a trace and so that their smell is lost in the water. They will avoid the settlers, the priests, the sociologists, the whites and anyone who comes near their environment."

"What do you plan to do?" asked the interviewer.

"I don't know yet. I am sure of one thing, and that is that I will not give in. I will stand up to threats and intimidation.

"I take this opportunity to give you film footage and photographs that a woman from the group with whom I found the burned village took the precaution of recording. You will find images of the burned village, the victims and the survivors. This material has not been handed over to FUNAI, much less to the Prosecutor's Office," I informed him, even though I felt it was irresponsible.

"Can I use the material for the report?" asked the man.

"Of course," I should have told him. I was aware of the threat of the Rubber Tappers. The Prosecutor's Office will use this evidence as an indication of its thesis of cover-up and will add another accusation: that of concealment and obstruction of justice, if not against public faith. He knew that the warning of the 'administrators of justice', in quotation marks, weighed heavily. Besides, he knew that the psychopaths would not pause before eliminating whoever stood against them, as they had done before in the jungle or in any slum of any town in the interior; even in Paulista Avenue itself if they needed to do so. What I could never have suggested, in any way, was that I was involved in a genocide.

My heart fell when I saw the summons to the Public Prosecutor's Office, which was investigating the facts that had been reported by the Ministry of Environment and Native Populations. The headline of the accusation: actual cover-up.

On the day of the first summons testifying at the Criminal Prosecutor's Office, I waited two hours with the lawyer for my turn. After that time we were called by a guy with a gallows attitude. It was a miserable office with a desk and a computer in front of shelves overflowing with files and papers filed haphazardly. After arranging a pile of documents, which turned out to be the file of my accusation on a wooden table, the guy who was acting as prosecutor asked me for my personal accreditation and the lawyer's documents. He then reviewed the documents and asked for my general information, which meant that I had to give him my affiliation with data on my age, my nationality, my marital status, my profession.

Then he asked me, "What institution do you work for? How long have you been working with that institution?" He wanted to get an idea of the person he was dealing with. As I answered, he transferred my answers to the computer screen. A typewriter with the letters on the keys erased would have been more in keeping with the environment; an Olivetti brand.

"Were you at the scene?"

"Yes, I was there." I didn't want to go into details, waiting for the next interpellations of that character, who had the face of the bureaucrats in the state offices of any city in South America.

The man was wearing a dark-colored three-piece suit, which included a vest, a white shirt and a red tie. I thought I spotted a sheen on the collar of the jacket that I attributed to the grease in his hair.

He continued, "Try to describe the scene of the events as explicitly as possible." He wanted to know my impression of the burned huts and the charred bodies.

"The Madeira and Marmelos Rivers, are about three hundred kilometers from Porto Velho, in the territory of the Parantintin," I said. When I mentioned the name of the tribe, I was sure that the exterminated natives belonged to that group, or perhaps they were nomads of another ethnic group in extinction with few survivors.

"Give a description of the place" I understood by this that he wanted me to describe the environment, whether it was wooded or an open field, perhaps a swamp or wetlands with a lot of steam, where colorful butterflies that seemed to drink water settled.

"The place was a few meters from the bank," I explained, "in a clearing surrounded by low jungle. I mean twigs, ferns, bushes and vines, with no large trees. It is the kind of place where the natives might have a roving camp, with huts surrounding a larger building."

I tried to detail the scenery as accurately as possible, although I had to admit that I could be mixing up images from other places, even inventing details I didn't remember.

"What did you see?" he continued. I thought the question should have been more specific, something like whether I had witnessed a massacre of human beings or whether the huts were set on fire with the villagers inside.

"We arrived after the events had taken place," I said, so that he would know that I had not made the discovery alone. "The first thing we noticed was that the huts had been set on fire and that the smell of burning flesh was impossible to bear."

Maybe the guy looked at me with a stupid expression and a hiss that I was supposed to interpret as "Did I ask you that, asshole?" At that moment I remembered that how everyone looked as if they had been roasted in a big oven. After observing the bodies, I had saw the dull sheen of melted lead. I presumed the bullets had melted in the fire. First they shot them and then set fire to the village. Taking advantage of his lack of reaction, I added that they were burned in agony or already lifeless inside the huts built with branches and the mud of the swamps, and dung of wild animals. I would have liked to tell him that the purpose of my visit was to find the origin of an outbreak of yaws, a disease caused by treponemas in its ganglion variant, with gums that destroy the bones and cartilage of the face. Those affected end up looking like turkeys because of the alteration of the facial structure. It occurred to me that the man, who was acting as a prosecutor, had not understood one iota of my explanation.

"I found a burning village," I said, trying to describe it in ordinary words. "Ashes, burnt sticks and embers, huts still standing and charred bodies..."

"What kind of bodies? Could they be animal carcasses?" he asked. It was a leading question that confronted me with a concise answer.

"Incinerated corpses of human beings," I answered without the slightest hint of doubt. How could I confuse the skulls of human beings, orthognathic, with the enormous encephalic box; the long tibia and fibula, almost as long as the femur; the classic spine of the erect position. All are characteristics of human beings. They could not be confused with animal bones, not even with bones of large African monkeys.

Finally, I could also tell him that there were clothes and hair stuck to the bones. Long fingers joined by tendons and parchment-like skin on the hands. They were definitely corpses of uncontacted natives who, in addition, had lead fragments lodged in their muscles and bullet shrapnel. I told him all this in all truthfulness. I was convinced that this was an episode of immense cruelty.

"Why didn't you, knowing that it was a crime, file the corresponding report?" That was the key question in a context that he considered criminal.

"What do you mean, 'didn't'?" I answered. "Of course I denounced the massacre." Maybe I shouldn't have described the action as such, but as a confusing event.

The hired killers had a special look, their eyes were charged with hatred, they had eyebrows reminiscent of Mephistopheles, and their arms and forearms were tattooed with characters and phrases of understandable content in the context of their perverse codes. Behind the auricular pavilions, animals and trifoliated leaves had been engraved with ink. They reminded me of characters from a movie filmed in the suburbs of Hong Kong or in the streets of the Bronx, with stoned people emerging from a basement.

"Explain to me, to whom did you report the incident?"

"To the government agency that oversees the defense of national minorities: FUNAI." I thought the section was the Secretariat for the Conservation of Nature and National Minorities. I could have made it clear to him that, in my opinion, that was the best way to make a full-fledged denunciation, avoiding entrapment of the process in some corrupt instance. What I was not sure about was whether the report I had submitted in writing could be called a complaint. In my opinion, it was. It had nothing to do with the report of an epidemic, even if the same number of people had died.

"We have carried out an investigation of the proceedings during that period and I can assure you that there is no complaint in any of the offices of the Public Prosecutor's Office. Sir, do you realize that this constitutes a cover-up of a multiple homicide?" He accused me in a direct way, with the figure framed as a real cover-up. In other words, I had remained silent in all languages.

"Just a moment," I replied, prepared for that part of the investigation. "First of all, we found the burned huts and the remains of the charred corpses. Those of us who were part of the group cooperating with the natives, in which I participated as a doctor, were not witnesses to the action." I should have specified the massacre. Therefore, we did not know who the perpetrators were.

"Secondly, I emphasize that we went to all public agencies without finding any positive response. First we went to the Police, then to the Prosecutor's Office itself."

I assumed that the crime would go unpunished due to the antecedents of other genocides in the country and the history of extermination of the native ethnic groups of the Amazon basin. I was aware that the documents would be hidden, the evidence would disappear and the minutes would suffer mutilations of the pages where the evidential manifestations were found. I even had the intuition that there was a notebook of classified records in the police premises, which they tried to keep secretly in an archive inside a dark room, like the one used for the development of photographs.

"You should have reported the facts immediately to a Public Prosecutor's Office or, at least, to the nearest police station," he reproached me in a hesitant tone, as if he himself was not sure that this channel was the right one to proceed with the complaint.

"Sir," I replied, emboldened, "I went to the police and demanded that a police report be drawn up. I even asked for a delegation of agents to accompany us. They told me that they were not authorized to accompany anyone, unless the events were taking place at the time, which could not be confused with a finding already made, as was the case," I explained simply and, at the same time, in detail. "Sir, we demanded an investigation of the events and the identification of the perpetrators. The police officers told us that only a report could be made." When I heard about the report, I figured that this document would record what we, the complainants, had seen.

At that moment I assumed that among the cover-ups were some government authorities. It occurred to me that the affair was an intrigue in which I was the victim. I even thought that there was no police record because it was never drawn up at the Porto Velho police station. Maybe the FUNAI bureaucrats never even sent the report to their superiors. Maybe the superiors did receive the report, but since they had had similar complaints in the past, they thought they had already read it before, without specifying when the incident took place. I imagined that some high-level official would say: "About the killing of natives, where was it?" And one of the secretaries would try to explain that the village was located in the state of Rondônia or perhaps in the state of Amazonas. Maybe there was someone who wanted the matter to go unpunished and that is why they filed the complaint under seven keys in a metal cabinet in one of the agency's offices.

At that instant I felt the enemy's hand getting heavy and that I would have to look for allies to face this. "Who could be my allies?", I pondered. At the same time, I was discarding some of them, because they had died or because they had emigrated to distant lands like Alejandro and Professor Guimarães.

It was a kaleidoscope, a mental labyrinth with shouts from the subconscious: "You did not make any denunciation to the Prosecutor's Office! Who are you to denounce facts in which the body of the crime does not exist? You are crazy!" This after so many unpunished crimes, after a colonization with blood and fire, after the extermination of the indigenous peoples in several states, especially in Mato Grosso do Sul; tribes to which the "Figueiredo Correia Report" alludes. Of the mass murders of the Guarani-Kaiowá community during the settlement of soybean farmers, or when the rubber company Arruda, Junqueira & Co. wiped out the long ribbon ethnic group by bombing them from the air. With hundreds of denunciations in the forums of the

United Nations and human rights commissioners for aboriginal peoples, including Survival Intercare. No! I could not believe that the genocides of uncontacted natives were denied. Nor that the gang of criminals would become a choir of angels.

I could not believe that there was a sordid threat against the most primitive and defenseless beings on earth. They were on the list of those doomed to extinction. They were slaughtered in the clearings of the low jungle or in the cloudy mountains. They were hunted like a herd of animals. They also received the scourges of the invaders. In some of the FUNAI reports, the collateral damage suffered by the native populations was pointed out. The most important was that caused by the construction of the Itaipu dam and other similar dams in the south of the country. The works were carried out without taking into account that the reservations assigned to the indigenous tribes were being plundered.

This led to the migration of entire populations to inaccessible and inhospitable areas. They had to move their camps to areas plagued by mosquito vectors of microbes and nests of poisonous vermin. Their diet changed from one based on fish and birds, to one composed of berries and other fruits, as they had to move away from non-forested clearings and rivers, where it was easy to hunt and fish for carp and bream.

The peccaries fled from the explosions and the noise of the engines of the heavy machinery. The jungle itself changed as a result of deforestation caused by the felling of fine timber trees and the construction of roads and camps. It was not only the bullets and poison in the sugar; it was also the unsanitary conditions and damage to the environment. Vampire bats spread rabies, transmitted it to other animals and eventually to humans as well; monkeys became ill with yellow fever and parrots with psittacosis.

Nor could I understand my situation in a process in which I was included with the legal figure of actual concealment. "Actual cover-up of what?" Maybe I had missed the killing or maybe I was not tenacious enough in reporting the facts. I felt like a monkey found stealing a packet of peanuts in the Corcovado Christ Forest in Rio de Janeiro. I could not believe that this shit had turned against me and I was being investigated for a matter of criminal violence against the human beings I tried to defend. I asked myself over and over again who cared about the facts. "Fuck. Nobody gives a damn!" I answered myself. Least of all the State.

Maybe I should be happy because it somehow meant that crimes against minority groups would not go unpunished. The absurdity was that I was one of those charged in the investigation. Perhaps the first one to be charged as part of a cover-up without there being, in sight, the perpetrator of the crime.

Today it was my turn to pay the land as the old Andean Indians did, spilling *chicha*, a traditional fermented corn drink, on the grass and burying fetishes in a hole ten centimeters deep. It was August, the time of the ceremonies to fulfill the payments to the land and water. Today I was cleaning my shit-covered shoes on the creeping grasses, not realizing that the filth was soaking into my skin.

"Prosecutor, may I make a comment in relation to the complaint I filed together with a colleague from the foundation, Mario da Cunha, about a massive poisoning that took place in the triple border between Brazil, Colombia and Peru" I asked with little expectation, hoping that he would not take me seriously, like the time I filed the complaint and they looked at me like I was crazy.

"Does it have anything to do with the murder we are investigating?" he asked.

"Of course. In both cases we are talking about massacres of non-integrated natives. In the case of the Madeira River, firearms were used and the village was set on fire to make the evidence disappear. On the triple frontier it was different. There, the natives were poisoned with toxic substances. An equally inhumane action, although in that case they had not resorted to firearms." I felt it was time to state my position on the issue of the extermination of national minorities. "I have to tell you that I am an activist for human rights and native communities. Therefore, my intervention has always been to defend minorities." I would have documented my statement with a registration card or a membership card of a group working for human rights.

"Sir," he said, "we have an ongoing investigation of an act reported to this Prosecutor's Office. It seems to me irrelevant to admit your political or religious affiliation. Here we are studying the components of an illegal action in which the direct actors, their accomplices and the real accessories are involved. We are not at all interested in the religious or philosophical confession that you may profess."

"Excuse me, can I ask you something?" And without giving him time to refuse, I continued, "Who are the direct actors in the crime you are investigating?" I was convinced that the man was going to answer that I was the one being investigated, which meant that the questions were for me and not for the special prosecutor investigating a crime. You had to ask what crime.

"I am not authorized to give you that information," he replied. He had become nervous because he did not think that I could ask him that question that sought to resolve the issue of the authorship of the genocide and then that the identity of those directly responsible would be revealed, the accomplices and those who had covered up the action would be located. In general terms, if there were no defendants accused of a crime, how could there be cover-ups. It was an obvious tautological logic.

Among the accomplices were the authorities who had allowed the barbarity to go unpunished in the time between the event and the accusation against me. They had used their influence with judges and officials of the Public Prosecutor's Office to cool the situation. The police officers and, directly, the agents and commissioners of the jurisdiction, who received the denunciation of the massacre and did not lift a finger to investigate the facts, should also be judged. It was evident that they refused to verify the event and did not inquire about the suspects.

I would have liked to add to my statement that I was not the only one who filed the police report. On the contrary: we went to the State Police station, the doctor of the health center, two ladies who worked in an NGO dedicated to the protection of the environment, a young missionary and a Parantintin leader who was, at the same time, a delegate of the ethnic group to the Andean Parliament. With these people, I went to the Public Prosecutor's Office on duty, where we were given the run around. We were sent to the police station for the ex officio investigation. That time I was able to perceive that the skein was tangled up for the purpose. I would have liked to say that I was not alone during the discovery. I was part of a group ready to testify at the right time, during the process or after it was over. They could provide the missing data to put together the puzzle in which they intended to involve me.

"The same old bullshit! The whole system against the fool who operated against its interests," I said to myself. Then I kept quiet so as not to involve other people in what seemed to be a conspiracy against me. The matter was clear: it was about judging the first fool they found. In this way, neither the material perpetrators nor those who ordered the killing were accused. Nor those who had the obligation to investigate the genocide and did not lift a finger. Nor, of course, the politicians involved in these crimes against humanity that were committed throughout the national territory.

I remembered the trucks where the army troops traveled and the 4X4 Hummer trucks of the rubber tappers. The panorama was similar: armed elements, perhaps border soldiers who were relieved every two months, and hit men hired by the rubber companies traveled the trails opened by the bulldozers mounted on caterpillar tracks and front loaders on rubber tires. It was a swampy terrain of ochre soil. It seemed that the transfer was organized in such a way that no one was ever missing.

I had doubts about the killers. They could be the hired thugs of the companies, but I also suspected a column of soldiers. Maybe it was neither one nor the other. Who knows, maybe the sons of the rubber tappers were out partying for the weekend and, like someone committing a prank, went out to hunt indigenous people from the reserve. I was reminded of a news item related to a group of boys, sons of wealthy people from the northern Mexican states, who embarked on cartel like activities including the illegal trafficking of prohibited substances, smuggling and entry of illegals into the United States and the trafficking of young girls for a prostitution ring. The ranchers' sons became known as the Prepa Juniors. At the end of a career of economic success, luxury, escorts, licentious living, drugs and pleasures of all kinds, there remained only a few of the hundreds who started the adventure. Most of the kids had been mowed down by cartel hit men; others died of narcotic overdoses or simply went underground.

To be honest, the culprit of the slaughter of the natives on the banks of the Madeira and Marmelos Rivers could have been anyone, even a group of boys under sixteen years old, hardened by ecstasy or *crack*, or by a maceration of hallucinogenic ivy alcohol.

Then I remembered a Dantesque episode in Africa. On a gravel road we came across a four-wheel drive truck whose bed was full of boys. They were all children and adolescents under the age of fifteen. The weapons hanging from their shoulders and the cannons on their shoulder straps were disproportionate to their bodies. The boys had the hardness drawn on their faces, the same grimace as the genocidaires. I got it into my head that I had seen those expressions in some inhospitable place in the clouded Chaco, or maybe it was in the vicinity of a swamp with millions of black lizards measuring less than a quarter of a hand and with prominent eyes on both sides of their skulls. What I couldn't be sure of was whether the setting was Darien or the Ucayali basin. What I do remember is that the boys carried heavy machine guns on their shoulders.

In that context of killings and psychopaths I imagine the murderers of the natives as a group of guys who used hard drugs. That put them in tune, like all the addicts I knew. I guess they were whoremongers who fucked women dedicated to the trade, who recruited pimps of all levels.

At some point during the cross-examination the prosecutor asked me, "What were you doing at the scene?"

"I was in the area to investigate an outbreak of yaws among a group of settlers who had developed buboes on their arms and face. The patients went to the health center, where they mistook the scabs for secondary syphilis, with dermal lesions in high relief or atypical condylomas. The same was true of the laboratory tests, where the VDRL serological tests were positive. However, it was not entirely clear to them whether the outbreak had started as a result of accidental contact with other nomads who were sick with bejel, a variant of endemic syphilis that deforms the nose and presents symptoms similar to lepromatous syphilis, with a leonine-looking face and a turkey-nose."

The yaws had affected the settlers who washed gold in the Marmelos canyons; it had also crept into the camps of the workers dedicated to the construction of the dams and the hydroelectric power plants. Faces disfigured by subcutaneous infiltration; they looked like masks with grotesque features. Then I remembered a dance I had seen a few years ago. The masks of the dancers represented Indians with their plumes of feathers and settlers with black capes and top hats. But what was surprising was that they manifested the same deformities as the real-life markings. It was evident that the manufacturers of the masks tried to imitate the alterations produced by this disease in the face of the Creoles.

The dance depicted an episode of colonization, a battle between the invaders and the natives. The costumes of the dancers reproduced the customs of the time: the lawyers with law books, frock coat and top hat; the feathered natives; the soldiers in uniform.

I once visited a colony of sick people who had been misdiagnosed as lepers, which is why they were isolated. Most of them were descendants of sub-Saharan Africans, which made me think about the greater susceptibility of that racial group, or that they were the ones who had imported the disease when they arrived as slaves for the sugar mills. That time there were three of us physicians who detected a type of spirochete similar to the one that causes syphilis. We could see treponemes among the foamy cells, surrounded by nests of lymphocytes and fibrous tissue protecting the nodule. The spiral-shaped bacteria appeared in the tissues of the buboes that we analyzed in the biopsy. We were also able to verify that the scabs disappeared after a single dose of benzathine penicillin. In the end, only the keloids remained.

The cure for children affected by yaws was total; not so in the case of adults, who suffered for years with symptoms in the skin, bones and arteries, since the alteration produced an aortic aneurysm similar to that of syphilis in its tertiary or quaternary period. The wall of the artery had the granuloma under the endothelium, which weakened its structure and made it prone to dilatations that deformed its course. Yaws had similarities with other treponeme diseases, but also some differences. For example, no alterations of the nervous system were observed, perhaps because the patient did not reach the most advanced stage of the disease. Therefore, we could not study the tabetic gait in the patients, nor the insanity due to gummas (swollen tissue) in the brain, which were not described, nor the involutional dementia, similar to other vascular diseases or due to infiltration of amyloid substance. But the most important difference was that its contagion was not necessarily venereal, but by contact with the fluids of the patients.

It occurred to me to think of syphilis as a variant of yaws. Paleopathologists postulated that the syphilis epidemic of 1493, which ravaged Europe, was imported from the New World by Columbus' sailors. This generated a more aggressive mutant that spread throughout the Old Continent. Later, xenophobia attributed the disease to the enemy. French soldiers believed that the contagion came from Naples; the Russians attributed it to the Poles and the English to the Celts.

I had observed the chain of contagion of an epidemic that started with bejel (endemic syphilis) and, after being transmitted to several individuals, mutated into a pathogen that produced yaws. As a second variant, in the same community, dyschromic spots of the carateas could be seen. This served to develop a research thesis on the evolution and mutations of the bacterium: treponema *pallidum*. Mutating into subspecies: *pallidum, endemicum, pertenue* and *carateum*. There was even the possibility that the disease, in its *carateum* variant, had initially been an epizootic of macaques that was somehow transmitted to humans, which generated a zoonosis, possibly due to the handling of viscera or liquids of sick animals.

It occurred to me to imagine the caravans of northerners with a number of sick individuals, with their faces covered with veils or tocuyo cloths to avoid being looked at with repugnance. Perhaps among the gray-haired were those who conserved the stigmata of the yaws and the caratea, which gave them the appearance of masked people with white spots that were lost under the hair and the beard and invaded the neck and the chest.

There were also thousands of slaves, brought for the harvest and sugar mills, with lumps and circular spots all over their bodies. It was most likely that the disease was confused with others of identical characteristics that produced alterations in the face, with loss of structure, deformations and mutilations; similar to the effects of leishmaniasis and leprosy, which had the same geographical scope. Many of the patients died before the disease was diagnosed. There were no tropical disease research units in the area. The care of the sick colonists and the contacted natives, who were part of the workforce, was provided in health centers, which had only a few beds.

I had so many issues to explain to the prosecutor, even if he turned a deaf ear to my arguments. I wanted to tell him that groups of uncontacted aborigines moved through the gorges along the tributaries of the great river. They were small groups of no more than a hundred people. They had been filmed from the air. Most frolicked on the riverbank, but others shot poison-tipped arrows at the scout plane. All were naked or nearly naked, with loincloths covering their genitals and exposing most of their bodies. There were cases where the natives had approached some miners' camps to avoid bad winds and spells that would turn them into tatters, without strength and without soul. In their experience, nothing good could come from approaching reservation invaders.

From all this, it seemed likely that the disease had been started by the excessive sexual practices of the settlers coming from the big cities and not, as they presumed, by the miasmas of the natives. I did not check to see if the migrant huts were located on the reserve itself or outside the protected areas because that seemed unimportant to me. I had to explain that my job was to investigate alerts about unpredictable disease alerts; alerts that came from anywhere in the health network or from the affected population itself. That was my job and that is why I was there when the events occurred.

I had to explain to the prosecutor who was interrogating me that it was not possible to compare the cover-up with a guy to whom one could attribute some degree of idealistic insanity. I could be accused of being an imbecile who was involved in all sorts of entanglements, such as trying to find sick people with a type of malaria that had carried off more than a hundred miners who were washing gold in some yellow mud flats. I could even be blamed for being a fanatic who had climbed the snowy mountains to discover typhus, with its exanthematous spots, in a population that lived in the same place where the rats died, emitting a pungent odor that permeated the whole atmosphere. The truth was that I could be accused of any stupidity, but not of being an accomplice to the crimes.

I could explain to those who would listen to me, including the judge who was to judge me after the stage of the prosecutorial investigation, that I had discovered a type of malignant malaria, with a higher mortality than all other known variants. That this type of malaria was characterized by a tremendous headache and was accompanied by vomiting of a liquid that looked like lumpy coffee. From one day to the next, the sick would develop an encephalitis from which they never woke up.

I could also have told him that the little men of the frozen mountains had spots on their chests. On closer inspection, I realized that they were not spots, but pinpoint hemorrhages that together looked like exanthema. By the time I reached the village, more than twenty people had died of the disease, which I diagnosed as exanthematous typhus in an unusual outbreak.

Suddenly, I remembered the discovery of a cemetery where we came across hundreds of burial mounds covered with medium-sized stones. The bones were those of miners who had returned from the lowland jungles suffering from a disease that caused fever and headaches. It occurred to me that it could be malaria or a type of encephalitis caused by the bite of an insect vector. And I asked myself, "Why had they been waiting for death in that place?" I then assumed that they were not allowed to enter the nearby villages for fear of contagion.

I would explain to the judge that during my stay in Acre and Mato Grosso I had investigated a disease known as yaws that very similar to leprosy. In many of the cases the patients presented a variant known as caratea, apparently more benign, because it did not produce the grotesque deformations of the face; rather some gray spots with a distribution similar to vitiligo, although the macules of the latter were white. The chroniclers of Christopher Columbus' time had attributed to the promiscuous habits of sailors and soldiers the spread of the disease to Europe, where it spread explosively and gave rise to an epidemic.

With these explanations I was trying to show that I could never be a cover-up for alienated people. Then I affirmed again and again,

"You can be sure of that, Mr. Prosecutor, I would never cover up a crime, much less the murder of defenseless human beings." I don't know if he cared about my statement.

I also wanted to tell him about the great swindle suffered by the native communities living in the Ucayali basin, where the oil companies extracted gas and gave the State royalties of more than one billion dollars a year. During the negotiation, the State had promised that the money from the royalties would be used, for the most part, to improve the living conditions of the natives and poor settlers in the area. The tribes had not received a fucking dollar nor did they benefit from the road or sanitary infrastructures, as stated in the mining and oil concession law, although this communication generated doubts in me, as I did not know the benefit it could bring to the uncontacted people. On the contrary, I thought that the roads would be a way of entry for diseases and ambitious people who wanted to take away their lands.

The same roads would be used for the Creoles to fuck their wives and make a fair with their children, who would be exported to Europe as children supposedly abandoned by their parents. There they would be adopted by childless couples. I had to mention to the prosecutor that the children were taken by a religious sect that was very active in the area, which profited from the export, since it obtained a few thousand dollars in donations for each child sent to the first world. What are we talking about, Mr. Prosecutor, in a mess like this? Who is the good guy and who is the bad guy? I'm sure the official would have given me an evasive answer, "Sir, we are not judging the world; focus on the issue and answer my questions."

I would speak as if he were the supreme judge in a court of pygmies awaiting the death penalty for a crime they did not know about. I had to give him a forceful answer that I had not yet prepared. I was to remind the fellow that the world turned many ways, but that in any one of them he was upside down, like a cat falling off the roof. And I would add, "With the yardstick you measure you will be measured and even the last hair on your head will be counted. The devil has many children and the river runs through many villages without stopping its march."

In addition to firearms and poisoning with arsenic or other poisons, genocides also occurred by poisoning the water as a result of heavy metals used in illegal extraction. It was part of an apocalyptic thinking that had seeped into the reports of the bureaucracy's salubricians, although it was said that new legislation was being drafted to penalize ecological and environmental damage.

The reports of the *ad hoc* commissions were discussed on the floor of Congress. Hundreds of complaints of environmental contamination, including river water, were received. Inorganic waste from gold panning was suspected. The presence of heavy metals, including mercury, nickel, copper, lead and chromium, could cause serious nerve, respiratory, liver and kidney damage. I pictured children with pink face and hands, characteristic of hyperkinesia, due to blockage of catecholamine grain depletion in intersynaptic spaces, which is caused by inactivation of the enzyme S-adenosyl methionine. The noradrenaline vesicles, recaptured at nerve cell axon endings, produced excessive sweating, subintrusive panic attacks, hair loss, furfuraceous and lamellar desquamation of the skin of the hands.

The question to the system, not to the prosecutor or the judge, but to the system itself in its governing bodies, legislative and executive, was the following, "What part of the nation cares about the damage to the health and life of the Indigenous people, contacted and uncontacted, who fed mainly on fish contaminated by the detritus of illegal mining?" The answer was simple: no one. Images of the confrontations against the dictatorship between 1964 and 1974 came to my mind, with young people in the streets believing they were drinking blood.

I had heard that the bodies of those poisoned had macerated skin and bloated bellies due to the gas produced by the decomposition of the food ingested before death. Mario da Cunha had told me in detail about the sequence of setbacks he had gone through after finding the corpses of natives of the Uitotos ethnic group in the triple frontier region. At the end he told me, "I did not see maggots in the flesh. I figured they would be under the skin, like fly larvae in cutaneous forunculous myiasis, which could nest in the scalp or in the deltoid muscles of the shoulder."

Then he explained to me his sleepless nights, when he replayed every moment of the discovery, when the faces and blackened skin of the corpses appeared to him. He told me that in his nightmare he would try to bury the bodies of the dead on the hillside, taking advantage of the earth that had been moved, to avoid the rhizomes and thus end the hell of those people, similar to the hell described by Dante in *The Divine Comedy*.

"When I returned to the site, it was empty," he continued. "There were no bodies, no ivy, no worms. However, the ponds still smelled of shit. I realized that the victims were part of an ethnic group of head shrinkers who believed that the dead were still alive in another dimension, but in the same place. The natives of the Shuar ethnic group, following their belief, reduced the heads of their enemies, which they called *tzantza*. They kept them as war trophies and as talismans that protected them from the revenge of the deceased."

After listening to Mario, I dreamt so many times about the scene that it became an obsession; a hallucination generated by my brain as a result of intoxication with some substance I had inhaled in the jungle thicket. Nobody wanted to pay attention to me. I did not find anyone involved in this bullshit. I was even given to understand that they didn't give a damn about the matter and that I should forget the tragedy because there would be no intervention from the authorities against the thugs or the merchant who had hired them.

The forensic medicine report had the same value as the result of the analysis of a pregnant woman with urinary infection; nothing or almost nothing. What judge would take into account the study of a pathologist from Manaus who spoke of the disappearance of mitochondria in the cells of the poisoned? At that moment they would not give it validity, as if it were a tall tale narrated by a doctor over sixty years old with hypermetropia and little experience in this type of analysis, who was studying cellular alterations due to toxic substances.

The prosecutor consulted with the medical examiner, "What are these myths...?"

To which the medical examiner replied, "Mitochondria are cellular corpuscles that exist in red blood cells."

When I heard this, I thought that the doctor had studied the book backwards, that he had no concept of it. I wanted to rebuke their ignorance. I said, "Prosecutor, get the advice of an expert who knows more about the case." And I reproached the medical examiner for his lack of knowledge, "Sir, the cells that have no corpuscles or nucleus are red blood cells; therefore, they have no mitochondria."

The man blushed when he saw himself exposed while the prosecutor, furious, shushed me claiming that any impertinent answer could be considered contempt.

The process was archived for lack of evidence. On the contrary, a process could be opened against those who were involved in an autopsy without legal authorization; that is, against us: Mario da Cunha, the doctor at the nearest post office, the doctor at the hospital in Leticia and, of course, against me, who got into the mess as if I had been involved in the matter. It was a disaster.

Then I thought I was carrying a backpack full of other people's guilt. Mario had to submit a report to FUNAI and accompany it with the results of the analysis of the sugar and gastric contents found in the stomach, according to the autopsy of one of the presumed dead by poisoning. In addition, I had to send the results of the histological examination of the stomach that had been studied by the pathologist from Manaus. In the same vein, I was to submit another report detailing the finding of the burned huts and the incinerated bodies. The results did not matter much, because the mere act of reporting was like washing the body with soap and rinsing it with lots of water.

We never knew what happened with the complaint or with the actual crime of cover-up. Those who opposed any investigation were in league with the prosecutors and judges, as well as with the political authorities of the State. They were all linked to the owners of the syringe companies, bribed by the money of the rubber tappers and illegal miners who poisoned the water of the rivers and caused the Minamata disease, which caused severe and irreversible neurological damage due to mercury poisoning, including blindness, ataxia, peripheral paralysis and paralysis of the respiratory muscles; a disease that ended up being fatal.

It occurred to me that the denunciation could reach the Ministry of the Presidency or, failing that, the Ministry of the Environment. Perhaps the matter would be discussed in the Council of Ministers and thus reach the ears of the Executive. Perhaps it had an echo in international organizations dedicated to the defense of human rights and vulnerable populations. I spoke several times with João Carlos de Queiroz to make noise about the trial and the prosecution's accusation. Ideally, the stone would have hit those who should have been hit, that is, the murderers and the assholes who hired them for this and other similar actions. Ideally, public opinion would have been sensitized and would have stood up against crimes against humanity and against xenophobia as an inducer of homicide.

When I heard it, it seemed to me that my expectation was as delirious as believing that someone with power, a kind of angel of the apocalypse with a flaming sword and the desire to punish the cruel and the psychopathic, would arrive with plagues like those of Egypt or with any kind of condemnation. Perhaps a superior being would send them Kawasaki's disease, which destroys the walls of the arteries and produces aneurysms or stenosis of the coronary and cerebral arteries. In the long run, it produces myocardial infarction or leads to a neurodegenerative vascular alteration due to multiple cerebral infarctions. Perhaps the angel of the apocalypse brought with it an epidemic of Epstein-Barr virus, affecting only the thugs and their prostitutes, with fever and asthenia due to infectious mononucleosis. But it did not stop there, but continued after years with Burkitt's lymphoma, caused by the oncogenic virus. It could not only be the Epstein-Barr virus, but others such as CTLV-1, capable of causing Hodgkin's lymphoma.

That could be the first punishment for the degenerates who had ordered the massacre. More obvious methods could also be used, such as an accident-causing damage to the cervical spine, with spinal cord section and disabling quadriplegia.

I thought I was delusional. However, I liked the fantasy as an alternative to my limitations no matter how stupid it seemed. Then I remembered the syphilis epidemic in Europe in 1493, just after the discovery of America. Maybe some variants of oncogenic viruses ended up in the Old World. Many of them were known to develop into cancer after several years of evolution. The viruses, incorporated into the cytoplasm of the human cell, induced proto-oncogenes, such as c-myc or c-fos, to activate the kinase, which initiated the anarchic and unruly cell division that leads to neoplasia. This is a process that eventually mutates from one disease to another. I remembered that after a major malaria epidemic in sub-Saharan Africa, the oncogenic potential of some viruses was discovered.

And conversely, I wanted to imagine that the higher power would heal the lesions of yaws patients, bejel deformities, tubercular caverns and other diseases, without having to use penicillin injections or a four-drug scheme. In the case of children with Minamata disease, the angel of the flaming sword would heal them with chelating agents, which sequestered heavy metal ions, with which it competed to bind receptors in target tissues. It could be chlorophyll, vitamin C and flavonoids from the long leaves, and not precisely D-penicillamine or calcium edetate disodium (EDTA) and dimercaprol (BAL).

These were the chelating agents created by the pharmaceutical industry laboratories. These chemicals have a higher affinity for heavy metals than the ligands in the metabolic system, thus preventing them from having a deleterious effect on the organism. By binding with metals, chelates are formed, as a non-toxic chemical form and, in some cases, susceptible to elimination by some metabolic pathway.

I imagine that the miraculous cures would be similar to those produced in people resistant to disease, as in the case of that obese woman who worked as a nurse in the tuberculosis ward of an old hospital. The woman was the only one who could enter without a mask or rubber gloves. In the ward she looked like a spectral figure in her white smock over a beef vendor's face at the local market. This woman never contracted the disease. Her body had non-specific resistance mechanisms, inherited from a family with a special genetic load, or maybe they were the product of the mutation of a certain gene. This was a mechanism similar to that of some individuals who are resistant to AIDS due to a variant that causes their HLA-B57 type genes not to produce the receptor proteins on the surface of T lymphocytes that allow viral proteins, epitopes such as gp120, to adhere to them. This means that the viruses cannot enter the cytoplasm of the lymphocytes and, therefore, do not destroy the cells.

It was hard for me to recognize that the nurse worked in the ward where patients with primary stage tuberculosis and multidrug-resistant tuberculosis were admitted, along with other patients with pulmonary mycosis, fibrosis, and lung cancer. In that mess I could confuse patients with respiratory diseases with those suffering from degenerative or allergic diseases. The pulmonology ward was an environment infested by mycobacteria, *Coccidioides*, *Aspergillus* and histoplasma. This was a breeding ground of pathogens that could wipe out a eutrophic giant in less than a week. However, the obese woman would age, retire and live a number of years longer without contracting the disease. I speculated on what the outlier cases represented before refocusing on accusations and blame.

At that moment I understood the effect of the black potion, a substance that the natives gave to the poisoned; even to those who had suffered the bite of a viper or any other poisonous bug: spiders and scorpions. It was given in a very high percentage, even between seventy and eighty percent, and it meant the cure or attenuation of the symptoms, once a period of stupor had passed. The potion, prepared with red and black berries, was an example of natural chelators used by native healers for all kinds of poisons, including arsenic. Then I thought maybe it would also work for mercury and other heavy metal poisoning.

"God does not forget his youngest children!" I said to myself although I had some doubt of that statement after what I had seen by the work of hired killers and other predators such as miners and loggers.

On Saturday, after an intense week full of worries, I ended up alone in a coffee shop in Leblon. The coffee was bitter, as I like it, and the memories fresh. I felt cold and lonely, even though the temperature in Rio de Janeiro was over thirty-five degrees and the humidity was almost one hundred percent. I noticed that my strength was renewed again and again; indeed, it was renewed in uncertain moments. Later I called Nadia to talk to her and tell her in detail about my interrogation by the prosecutor and my subsequent delusions.

Chapter 10
The Wooden Hut

I had stayed in a wooden hut with a tin roof. The temperature was over forty degrees. The heat was complemented by a cloud of blood sucking mosquitoes, among which could be the vectors of dengue and malaria, or yellow fever. However, the barracks seemed to be the appropriate place for those of us who had witnessed the massacre of natives on the banks of the Madeira to gather.

The shed was the last thing left standing of a miners' camp next to a pipe that brought dirty water. We had chosen this unobtrusive place, just in case we were being watched by the rubber guys' snitches. Of course none of us wanted to be in that pigsty of rarefied air, with the little light that filtered through the cracks. The doctor would have preferred to be exhausted and overworked at home or in the medical residence, and not in this place. The priest would rather be giving a three-hour sermon on Good Friday than shitting his pants and sweating in this dump of a shed. I could feel the people in the group yawning from the temperature and humidity. We were all sweating and exhaling an apple-scented mist that I interpreted as the product of a cascade of chemical mediators that had been initiated by the adrenaline secreted during the panic.

I heard the buzzing of horseflies landing on the reed walls and ceilings. As I felt the fear, I remembered the stench of the incinerated dead. Inside the barracks I thought I smelled the same odor I had smelled in the camp where we found the burned bodies. No, it was not the same smell, but a pungent stench of pork rinds watered with skunk urine. I thought it was a false perception, a product of the brain's receptors, which could create the same sensation even though I was no longer in the place or at the time. It was unbelievable that I noticed the same smell just by the presence of the witnesses of the slaughter.

The stench and the darkness masked by the light from outside gave me a shudder similar to the panic I felt that time in the jungle clearing. I experienced the same fear as if I were in a Rio favela, where drugs were being trafficked in full view of hitmen armed with Uzi submachine guns. It was the same feeling of having entered a neighborhood of raggedy Chinese people eating on the floor and dealing narcotics in the outskirts of a city in the Philippines; in the same neighborhood where the dens with skinny, smelly Thai people were located. In the scene the Chinese men were smoking opium while the women attended to them with erotic massages. Suddenly, in my fantasy, blond sailors appeared, possibly Swedish or Norwegian, all in an aggressive curtsey and matching the women's shrieks, insulting each other. I couldn't tell which I feared more, the Nordic thugs or the intemperate shrieks of the prostitutes.

As if it were a group therapy session, we all unpacked our panic.

"I'm afraid that murderers will sneak into my house and grab my son by the neck and rape my wife," the doctor confessed.

"I have received telephone threats and messages on my Facebook page," said the priest.

"It seems to me that the trial is a sham," explained João Carlos. He was convinced that there would be no trial and everything would remain in the accusation phase. According to his hypothesis, there was collusion between the prosecutors and other authorities to cover up the crime by putting one of the witnesses on trial.

After this cathartic session, we went to the heart of the matter for which we had been summoned. We knew that the prosecutor's investigation began with me, but it could have a greater connotation and involve all the people who witnessed the crime. The priest and the doctor thought that I should not mention them, because they were weaker, because their jobs were in that area while I could get away with it if things got dangerous. I would have liked to send them to hell and tell them that, for the moment, I was the only one who was fucked. I didn't say anything because I realized that it was fear that put the words in their mouths. So I changed the conversation to talk about inconsequential topics and in that context I asked the priest, "What do the sons of God mean in the book of Enoch?" When they heard me, they must have thought I was panicked and delirious. I wanted to hear something about the Nephilim. It was a mystery to me that the book of Enoch spoke of the presence of gigantic beings, different from normal men, different even from the dolichocephals of the city of Ur and the Semites who tended the sheep in the valleys of Mesopotamia.

"They are titans, fruit of the mating between the female descendants of Cain and the angels expelled from the celestial choir along with Luzbel," explained the priest, expanding on concepts such as pride and rebellion, in this case, of angels who ended up as demons. Their children would be the Nephilim. Half human and half angels expelled from paradise.

In my mind's eye I pictured them with huge backs and hands with fingers that resembled blood sausages. The Nephilim would be physically different; however, most discordant were the convolutions of the frontal lobe and those of the cingulate gyrus bordering the corpus callosum. In those cerebral areas would

430

reside their genocidal madness, their base instincts. Under that hypothesis, the different brain configuration, with the prominent uncus and a laminar limbic system, could explain his unrepentant amorality. That structure and the connections with the cerebral cortex made them hallucinate. Therefore, they believed they were judges with the capacity to choose their victims according to their criteria. I had the concept that these types of monsters ended up being murderers and their relatives, undercover: the prosecutors, judges and the policemen who protected them.

The old man from the Parantintin ethnic group came to me days after the prosecutor's investigation began. The old man wanted to explain what had been happening, "That's nothing! Last year the bush pigs reproduced like red-ass ants and attacked the villages."

The herds would appear after natural disasters, such as floods or seasonal droughts; perhaps after man-made disasters, such as predation and the invasion of settlers. Perhaps the old man could explain to me the overpopulation of pigs as a periodic phenomenon that recurred from time to time. Sometimes it's the peccaries, sometimes it's the parrots, giant ants or green locusts.

I recalled having cleared a harbor of rats. To check for success, we captured a pregnant female and sacrificed her to determine if the number of offspring per litter was above the normal average. When adverse environmental conditions or aggression from hostile neighbors occurred, the number of fetuses and births per time period increased. This was a way of adapting to extreme situations, thus avoiding extinction.

The older man told me that the hematophagous vampires bats reproduced in the dens near the roads and mining camps. He also pointed out that in recent years snakes and other vermin would sneak into settlers' homes when excavators destroyed their nests. I could add to the empirical knowledge the confirmation of outbreaks of diseases that had not existed until then, such as wild rabies in vampire bats and monkeys, as well as a variant of lethargic encephalitis in some migrants who, by chance, had taken refuge in some caves in the cloud mountain. I didn't know if those shelters were infested with bugs that could transmit any disease.

I once heard that the lanugo of vampire bats intoxicated the animals that sought refuge in the caves. I also heard that the jaws of colored lizards had a poison that affected mammals. I thought that rather than a poison, it would be anaerobic bacteria that infected the wounds. Then I remembered seeing twenty or thirty natives with their faces painted dark, as if they were part of a postcard of Māori from New Zealand in the early nineteenth century. The men carried bows of chonta, a black wood with a fibrous texture and, they had long arrows with tips of xerophytes, similar to bone, smeared with curare to produce the death of the victim by blocking the nervous system. The women had drawn stripes of achiote on their cheeks and some carried their children on their hips, fastened in a kind of hammock tied around their necks. Their only clothing was a loincloth of linen fiber.

The whole group seemed fragile to me despite the weapons. The old man told me that I was one of the few individuals who could approach the Parantintin village. He explained the matter to me as an effluvium that could be picked up by the natives and that I had impregnated in my skin. According to the little man, it was the same friendly smell of the healers or witchdoctors who could heal eye ailments. Then I remembered that one of the natives gave me a necklace made of peas, similar to fava beans, because he thought that his son with a globular belly had been miraculously cured by the medicines I had given him. I had to keep quiet in all languages so as not to break his illusion, even though I knew that the matter did not go beyond a deworming with albendazole. The old man mentioned something about the invasion of opossums that stole the canned food cans that then appeared in their nests as if they were carcasses without contents.

The old man could make a list of diverse situations that had ended with calamities for the natives inserted in society, who were dedicated to commerce and tourism with canoes or rafts with outboard motors. He spoke of plagues of snakes that entered the shacks and bit the humans, whether they were Christians or pagans. Apparently, this had resulted in more deaths than any of the wars they had been involved in in the past. He also told me a story that I could not place in its proper context. It told of the death of the greatest native killer of all time. The guy had several names including Pitaña and João Matamoros. The man, a giant who could break the backbone of any human with his brute strength, had killed more than a thousand natives. Then he bathed in the water of the yellow river near the village of Taumaturgo where the inhabitants witnessed the disappearance of the giant in the whirlpools of the river, as big as a mountain hollow. Neither his body nor his remains could ever be found, so they presumed that he had been swallowed by the river itself to collect the deaths of the innocent. Or perhaps an anaconda that first wrapped him up and then swallowed him. They affirmed that the anacondas there could measure more than twenty yards long and up to half a yard high.

He also told me about the black fate of the uncontacted. They lived in the jungle and avoided the farmers, the miners, the water prospectors and the natives themselves who had been included in the civility. He could have drawn up a list of evils that included inter-ethnic wars, massacres, plagues of vermin or bush animals. He would not take into account that the greatest mortality occurred as a consequence of unknown diseases, which they described as chest ailments or witchcraft, which dried their bodies and caused them madness before the evil sleep from which they could not wake up. Then they told of their own delusions, such as the arrival of prodigious beings from the sky, with some human trait; beings that protected them from catastrophes.

I did not know if the old man was telling me these details to prevent me from falling into a depression, because I had failed in an ethical commitment to God's youngest children. The life expectancy of those men was below forty years at best. Many did not live past twenty, if they did not die of natural causes, they would be killed by the assassins. Later, the assassins would take the trouble to set fire to the huts to make all evidence of the massacre disappear, as if this were necessary, when they had in their favor the commissioners, the officials and the prosecutors, who would never do anything against the assassins.

In the opposite case, if a patrol of thugs invaded a native camp in a suspicious attitude, with malicious intentions, they had every right to shoot in self-defense or to safeguard the property of the bosses, whether they were traders of supplies, rubber, loggers or miners.

According to the chief, I should not feel any guilt if I was exonerated from the trial. I was even supposed to feel joy if the trial broke down due to lack of evidence or procedural flaws that neither he nor I understood. Perhaps he was trying to explain how the tribes avoided contact with civilized people at all times, even in their most benign models such as missionaries who wanted to preach the word of God.

Today I found myself in a long-abandoned shack with leaky tin walls and roof. The shack had been plundered after it was abandoned. The fans, light fixtures and furniture had been taken. I found myself in that place surrounded by these shitty friends who claimed to be defenders of human rights. I would have liked to send them home with the peace of mind that I would not mention any names. I wanted to promise them that I would not involve any of those present there so that they would avoid any kind of later problem; even though we knew that their participation in the discovery was known by the murderers. In the semi-darkness I could not see their eyes, but I suspected they would have pinpoint pupils due to the low light, or mydriatic from overt fear.

Seeing my fellow adventurers in the throes of panic, it occurred to me to compare their attitude in life with that of other people I had come to know at some point. Alejandro Erquinigo Ascuez, the Black Janus, had had a similar experience when he was accused of supporting secessionist groups in South Yemen. It was a time of running through zigzagging streets that continued up steep stairways. Government troops searched door to door for subversives, allies of the secessionist troops. Snitches and informers were the order of the day. Every night there was a raid in the suburbs. At that time Jano's wife still accompanied him. When he was caught in one of the many police raids, she had already left for Madrid.

I imagine him in the dungeons with the rebels, as black as the darkest Shiite Berbers, with a bristly beard and gray hair, using English to communicate with the policemen interrogating him. He would claim to be South American and the policemen trying him would think they understood him to say he was South African. Possibly from that statement they got that Jano belonged to a group of militants of the African National Congress (ANC), a group led by Nelson Mandela, who was, at that time in prison. Perhaps they did not confuse the nationality but tried to demonstrate to the international press the foreign interference in the Yemeni civil war between separatists and unionists. What no one could have foreseen was the emergence, twenty or thirty years later, of groups linked to Al Qaeda with a more belligerent fundamentalist practice. Moreover, no one could have guessed that these groups would recruit soldiers of all nationalities, including some of South American origin.

We had assumed that Jano had been mutilated or left brainless, depending on the type of interrogation and torture used by the henchmen. Once, one of the few times he touched on the subject, he told me his fingers gave him a terrible pain that went up his arms and reached his neck. He also confessed to having felt the proximity of death while his body was submerged, hanging upside down, in tubs of dirty water. The torturers held his head so that he could not take it out and inhale air. He went through extreme of pain and experienced a seizure-like sensation during sessions with electric prods, which were applied to his nipples, scrotum and penis. Later, rubber rods and wooden sticks were inserted into his anus, tortures that were almost always complicated by perianal abscesses and lesions that caused tenesmus and intense pain.

However, for Janus, the interruption of sleep every time he closed his eyes caused him to lose his sanity. Moreover, the repetitive interrogations, seeking contradiction in every sentence and then in every word, had been designed to destroy his phrenic defenses until he became a human wreck. Under these conditions there was no room for tenacity or political conviction, let alone fundamentalist faith. The fortress was crumbling and all kinds of weaknesses were appearing. Then he begged for the torture to end. He asked to be killed. The executioners confessed to having turned more than one into a collaborator, an informer of his comrades.

Jano did not have much to give away, except for his ties to the NGOs supporting refugees. He repeated over and over again that he entered the country on behalf of the UNDP, the United Nations Development Program, and the UNHCR, the United Nations High Commissioner for Refugees. During the interrogations, when he gave his professional affiliation, the agents demanded that he sing one of Caruso's songs before they turned him into a living dead. They forced him to point out, at least, two names of associates in the underground or two names of people linked to the people's aid. I suppose that the interrogations ended when they could not get anything new out of him.

The detainees were then transferred to political prison camps, consisting of insane people surrounded by barbed wire and round-the-clock armed surveillance. The guards were ordered to shoot at those who attempted any kind of escape. Many prisoners had suffered injuries that prevented them from fending for themselves and needed other inmates to help them move around. The inmates were subjected to a diet of bread and water, or a frugal diet equivalent to a starvation ration, with greasy, tasteless polenta at noon.

Inmate deaths were a frequent occurrence. Some caught pneumonia due to overcrowding, unhealthy conditions or temperature changes, which were amplified by the zinc sheets under which they lived. Others were driven to madness and committed suicide by ingesting desert sand that destroyed their intestines as if it were ground glass. Those who survived envied those who had gone ahead.

In that context, the hope that the vesanic version of an informant, who had muddied the South American black man, would be questioned was, in practice, null. In this prison camp Jano recalled his childhood in the sugar plantation near the Pacific coast, in the huts next to the sugar mill. He evoked the breakfasts eating bread with chancaca made from the molasses of the sugarcane dregs.

When he had lost all hope of regaining his freedom, a chancellery official appeared, as if from heaven, with an order for his immediate release. The seized documents were returned to him and he boarded the first plane to England. He later learned that his release had been arranged with the Russian embassy by the European Union's refugee finance office.

Remembering the Janus tragedy in South Yemen, under the current circumstances of the prosecutorial investigation for a slanderous accusation of actual cover-up, I wondered: "Could something similar happen to me? I might not be tortured, but I could be unjustly imprisoned or have my neat work vilified. Slander was still the method of choice to tarnish the prestige of the accused. The same story in a different context, as if its narration was transferred to reality. Those were the years of opprobrium, by one name or another: the chumo or the five-year period of Operation Condor. The tortilla was still upside down.

In the case of Jano, the aim was to demonstrate foreign interference. In my case, the mess of a formal investigation of the real murderers was released, involving a scapegoat who after a while would be left in peace and with that the affair could be swept under the rug. It would be as if nothing had happened in that clearing in the jungle near the right bank of the Madeira River. You didn't have to be a fortune teller to know where the prosecutors' program was headed.

At that moment I remembered the faces of the crazy people. It was as if I was watching a short film on YouTube showing the wildest groups in the world. I recalled the ones jumping over the turnstiles in the Paris subway. They looked like herds of agile and bellicose beings who wanted to demonstrate the existence of a strange world, not obedient to the rules. I relived the face of the Rocinha gang members. All of them had a twisted look, the convergent squint, the fury in the form of foam at the corner of their lips. They were just like the psychotic madmen admitted to a hospital where mental emergencies were treated. To compare one group with another, I thought of the natives. They always looked at the floor, as if they wanted to avoid meeting the eyes of their interlocutors. "Perhaps they had become accustomed to behaving this way to avoid tripping over moss-covered roots and creeping plants."

I couldn't see their eyes, but I could see their faces: dull, expressionless, almost pleading. I felt immense pity for them, as if I were looking at a group of children cornered by serial killers. Their dwarf bodies and small stature gave me the impression that this was a group of dwarfs due to hypopituitarism. Some had bristly beards, prominent cheekbones and matted hair.

They were totally different from their killers.

When I arrived at the burned village, I had the feeling that we were being watched from the dense part of the jungle and from the high branches of the trees. I imagined the Indians fleeing, hiding to watch, horrified, what was happening in the village. I was convinced that they had observed our arrival and the shock we felt at the annihilation of the group. At no time had they approached us because they presumed that we were part of the gang. For them there was no difference in the color of our hair and skin, nor in the shape of our dress, not even in the smell of tallow soap.

Without a doubt, the psychopaths could destroy them in a few minutes. It was possible that they had been shot with bullets with a truncated, dug-in tip, which fragmented the projectile into splinters that would stick in different parts of the body. "Dum-dum bullets or hand grenades," I thought to myself. When they saw the bodies of the little men jumping through the air, expelled by the force of the discharges, they burst out laughing, as if they were bowling or attending a carnival. After the first attack, they threw incendiary cocktails on the branches of the trees and the trunks of the huts, so that the fire would spread and consume everything, even the bodies of the dead or the wounded that were left on the ground. I could not say for sure, but it was possible that they had burned the wounded without finishing them off so as not to waste more bullets. It was also possible that they were hunted in the middle of the flight, while the natives wanted to reach the wooded area to blend in with the vegetation. Once the killing was over, they moved the corpses and the agonizing wounded to the village to burn the bodies and the huts in a single bonfire, avoiding leaving traces of what had happened. That part I didn't understand, "Who did they want to make nice with?" I assumed it was a conditioned reflex situation, like a child's regret after breaking a piece of pottery or grandmother's vase.

When I remember the event, I associate it with another passage of my life. That time the scene was not the jungle, but an American city. A guy with shabby clothes and a bristly blond beard paralyzed the traffic on a busy avenue. He seemed drugged or immersed in a severe psychotic crisis. His aggressiveness was out of the ordinary: he hit anyone who crossed his path and he threw rocks at vehicles. It took ten police patrols to bring him down.

During the time that the rampage lasted, there were scenes of collective panic, as if a shooting had broken out or as if a wild animal had been unleashed from the zoo. It seemed to me that the massacre in the jungle was just as frightening. The men who had unleashed their fury against the natives were psychos from the favelas or slums of the big cities. I presumed them to look just like the madman. I imagined the face stigmatized by drugs: the sunken cheeks and the lost look.

In my nightmares I saw myself walking next to a very thin and tall woman while smelling the smell of ashes, of charred bodies. At one point the woman, who remained silent, showed me the bodies lying on the floor. They had empty eye sockets. Then she explained,

"With fire, the eyes explode like eggs in an oven or microwave."

Then she fell silent and the image receded as if it were a spectral vision.

I saw Jano again, evicted by his own wife on the pretext that she could not live with a guy with so much trauma, unless she exposed herself to madness. After the defection, Jano could be seen walking along the colored cobblestone streets of Ipanema, or sitting at a table in a coffee shop in Leblon. Always solitary, sometimes disguising his loneliness like someone who reads a book and does not turn the pages, or turns them so fast that it is evident that he is not reading. I never saw him cry. I presumed that his tears had dried up or his pain was so great that he passed into catatonic melancholy without undergoing the cathartic mourning. My furtive gaze here was the same as when I saw that beautiful young woman on the Berlin subway train. I don't know why the ideas were so linked for me: a melancholic man and a woman of unquestionable beauty.

Jano died of an aneurysm of the aorta artery, which originated below the intima of the endothelium with a growing hematoma that was separating the layers of the artery wall, sequestering blood and leading to heart failure with arrest in systole. The cause of the weakness of the wall was due to tertiary syphilis; a disease contracted on one of his trips to the Near East, or maybe he caught it in the red-light district of some European city.

I imagine that the pain caused by his wife's betrayal was greater than the torture he was subjected to. Before the abandonment we used to go out in the evenings for coffee at one of the fast-food restaurants that dotted the beaches of Rio de Janeiro. Jano would arrive with his dark glasses on as if he were having a busy day, or as if he wanted to hide his swollen eyes. I never dared to ask about his state of mind to avoid any intrusion into his life. Neither did I ask about his ex-wife nor his children.

On those breezy nights we would sit facing each other, in silence, watching the people passing by. There were the blondes from Ipanema and Leblon, the fine brunettes from São Gotardo, the brunettes from the favelas built on the hills near the Sheraton Hotel. That time I would have told him, if he would allow me to be frank, that any of those girls was better than his ex-wife. Perhaps he would have approved of my assessment and then talked about the women of Abyssinia and the beauty of the lines of Nilotic females. The model Naomi Campbell and Dominican Arlenis Sosa were of South Nile, Maasai ancestry. I imagined very tall women, with slender silhouettes and graceful gait.

When I heard of his death, in the emergency room of the Albert Einstein Hospital, in downtown São Paulo, my heart broke and I ached. People like him reminded me of other places where I could contemplate the best of mystical attitudes. I reviewed the lives of people shaking the leaves of an old tree that stood on the main street of my city. The tree had red leaves and reddish flowers; maybe it was a variant of chlorophyll, or it was the absorption of soils with a large amount of iron oxide.

I began to think of Müller, the scientist who had sketched out the unitary concept of cancer as a spontaneous or induced mutation in the genetic material of cells, when there was no evidence, not even in my wildest dreams, of the existence of proto-oncogenes and cancer suppressor genes. At one point, the man tried to take his own life, after a period of stubborn isolation, because he felt misunderstood by his thinking. Ten years later, in 1946, Müller received the Nobel Prize in Physiology and Medicine.

His theory of mutations of genetic material had been supported by virologists, immunologists and radiologists. New hypotheses were created in which the damaged or altered genes received the noxa that changed their structure. It was a genetic mutation. These noxae, whose name derived from a Greek root meaning harmful, were the ones that produced cancer. They could be viruses that were included in the genetic material to replicate and ended up damaging the DNA, or chemical substances such as cigarette tars, soot from chimneys, benzenes from paints. Radiation could also alter the sequence or structure of DNA itself, and gamma rays from the atomic bombs dropped on Hiroshima and Nagasaki, as well as nuclear power plants, such as Chernobyl.

It was the mutation chain in the Ras/MEK/ERB pathway, which gave rise to the mitotic changes in cancer. These generated the enzymes necessary for DNA strand duplication, a pathway for activating cyclin kinases that opened the cycle of massive mitosis. It could be that the strands of normal genetic material themselves underwent gene translocations, sequence fractionation and strand repair. All the chaos set ablaze by proto-oncogenes.

Undoubtedly, Müller's contribution to human knowledge was extraordinary. However, his history of isolation and depression was common in successful characters with different qualities. That story could be repeated in any human being: neurosis or severe paranoia that led them to behaviors that were difficult to explain. Some committed suicide, others entered a world of obstinate silence. Some madmen sought the sewers of a city to isolate themselves from the world. Many of them spent their last days in an old people's home or in a fifth-rate hotel on the outskirts of any city. Names of famous musicians came to mind, such as Kurt Cobain and Amy Winehouse; heart surgeons, such as Christiaan Barnard and René Favaloro; notable mathematicians, such as Alan Turing. All of them became suicidal, suffering from insurmountable depression or loneliness that they could not overcome.

Contradictions in people's lives occurred quite often. People would go from success to failure or vice versa, so that the last part of the movie would stick in our memory. We would not come to any rounded conclusion. For some of his enemies, Janus was a covert anarchist and for others a salesman who used that disguise to live off the funds that financed that ideology. To a few, including myself, he was a master of geopolitical knowledge. Meanwhile, the man was crying out for a little affection.

He spoke more than seven languages and had graduated in three disciplines, Social Anthropology, Sociology and Politics. In the end, he was an old man tired of the hustle and bustle, firm and recalcitrant in his thinking. We erased the final impression to keep the most successful idea, possibly ten years before his death, when his conversation was erudite, but still accessible. I remember meeting him on one of my visits to New York. He was wearing a black suit with blue vertical stripes and had just given a lecture at the United Nations on the subject of fourth world geopolitics. At the end of the lecture, we left with the desire to find a restaurant in Greenwich Village where we could listen to classical jazz from a sixty-year-old guitarist.

Returning to the meeting of those involved in the slaughter of the Madeira River, the hut was empty. The gloom, typical of the late afternoon, seeped into the thicket of the grove. We walked along a sidewalk not suitable for vehicles, with crisscrossing roots and creeping plants, until we reached the beginning of another trail where a four-wheel drive truck with three rows of seats was waiting for us. Despite the warm weather, some of my companions were shivering as if they had a fever. I guessed that it was the result of their fear of being discovered by a gendarme patrol or by a commando of henchmen in the service of the rubber guys. They were even afraid of the snipers that dotted the route we had to travel.

I was sure that at that moment they thought they should not have attended the meeting, even though they wanted to extort a promise from me that I would not involve them in my statements. Perhaps their fate depended on my answers to the prosecutor to exclude them from any responsibility. Of course, no one knew whether events would end with their exclusion. No one could claim that they were off the hook and that was why they had not been cited in the first proceedings. Not even João was convinced that he knew in depth the argument that would free the whole of the legal process. He claimed to know how the law worked in cases like this one; what he could not explain was where he got that information, giving us to understand his reasoning based on past experiences.

"The Public Prosecutor's Office is rotten inside," he said. "Networks of bribes paid to judges and prosecutors by those involved in criminal networks have been discovered. When the hydroelectric plants in the south were built, with the Jirau and San Antonio dams, there were killings of natives without any of the companies or suppliers being accused. Everything came to nothing, despite the fact that more than a thousand people were reported dead. This time, everything is rigged to free the criminals, which would end with the exclusion of all of us."

His explanation was an antithesis that exempted us from any verdict with legal penalty. According to João, the perpetrators of the massacre would not be tried because there was no evidence of the crime. He believed that no one had been interested in locating the place, much less tried to find any evidence of the crime.

Therefore, in the absence of evidence, there were no culprits or accomplices, much less accessories to the crime. The minutes of the denunciations had been mutilated from their folders and erased from the computer files. As far as he was concerned, I could not be held responsible for anything if the guilty parties had not been tried first.

His thought outraged me. Why had we filed the report with the police? Why had we written the report for FUNAI if in the end it all came to nothing?

"No, that doesn't work for me!" I told them, and they all felt cold again. Even João turned his gaze to the trees that bordered the gravel road.

It was clear to me, today more than ever, that the investigation sought to intimidate me in order to obtain my premature surrender. The prosecutor realized that my narrative was coherent in time and space. He sought to entangle the plot so that I would feel his harassment and that would modify my behavior. "No, asshole! That doesn't work for me," I thought silently with conviction, "You're not going to intimidate me."

I remembered my walk through the citadel of mud and stone in the jungle, in an area close to the wildest region. In that place the savannah reached up to the clay columns, which seemed to have been formed by a subsidence or a tectonic outcrop of the cliff. This was hidden under a carpet of blue and red colors. In reality, it was not a phenomenon of changes in the flora, not even of the vegetation clinging to the escarpments, but was due to thousands of parrots clinging to the ochre wall to ingest iron and other minerals.

I thought of the children who ate dirt, a custom we knew as pica and which was a consequence of a dietary deficiency in iron and minerals that led to the ingestion of unfamiliar substances; among them, chalk, gum, dirt, stones, soaps. Perhaps I was also part of the group of children who felt the sweet and salty taste of wet earth. To my mind came the image of the children fishing for silversides and hunting ducks in the nearby lagoon to take to the teacher as part of their homework. The teacher was a mature, lethargic woman who, as fate would have it, had no husband or children.

Attached to the escarpment were the ruins of a citadel of mud and stone abandoned long ago by its inhabitants. The walls rose above the undergrowth and showed the passage of time in its cracks. Thousands of bugs peeked out of those cracks; they looked like white termites or a type of yellow ant. Perhaps they were neither one nor the other, but milky arthropods, similar to woodlice, which belonged to the subphylum of the crustaceans, of the order of the isopods. In the foundation was the entrance to the galleries of the arachnids, hairy like the Mygale tarantulas, or hairless like the black apasancas, which were more than ten centimeters in size. The place was inhabited by urodeles such as spotted salamanders and gold-colored newts. Giant dragonflies seemed to be part of a Jurassic landscape, along with cicadas, the machaco parrot and a green poisonous snake.

In my opinion, the village had been a refuge for the Tupi-Guarani, who had migrated there to escape the rubber tappers, who were increasingly penetrating their territory. The Tupi Indians had become extinct or had gone into hiding in the jungles of Paraguay and the Bolivian Chaco. In Brazil, some individuals remained isolated or included among the settlers and workers; however, their influence could be perceived among the present-day Indians of the states of Acre, Rondonia and Mato Grosso, especially in some idiomatic roots common to the natives of that area.

A Catholic missionary in the Acre region had explained to us that, among the ethnic groups that were most affected by the gold and cocaine traffickers, were the Korubos of the Javari valley. This ethnic group was distributed in groups of no more than fifty people; in some cases they were even small communities of no more than ten individuals. Their ancestors had been persecuted and killed during the golden age of rubber exploitation, when the city of Manaus, with its marble buildings and gold railings, flourished. I once traveled through the logging colonies and toured the stands of the northeastern settlers. In my adventures I sought to rule out bejel and yaws as historical predecessors of syphilis. My notebooks contained notes of places and names of people whose faces were invaded by granulomas and subcutaneous nodules.

On one of those trips I learned that the natives who inhabited the mud citadel attached to the bluff had abandoned their dwellings to enter the impenetrable jungle zone, where they had joined the Awá tribes and acquired their isolationist customs. The Tupi-Guarani brought their skills in land cultivation and the domestication of paujiles, a type of naked-necked hen. The Awás, for their part, taught them to prepare poisons to smear on the tips of their arrows.

I remained silent, just like the prosecutor. A sad silence that reminded me of Janus' depression on the verge of catatonia. In silence I recalled moments of loneliness. I needed all the encouragement I could get to go ahead with the complaint. I wanted the guttural cry of the natives not to be silenced when they communicated from branch to branch while hiding from their enemies; a cry that was confused with the howls of thousands of monkeys jumping among the araucarias and the giant ficus trees. Somehow, I had to make their groans heard at the sight of the bodies of those close to them lying on the undergrowth floor. I had to transmit, not to the prosecutor of the trap, but to the people who had preserved their hearing and sensibility, the silent cry of the survivors. I would tell them that from the edge of the clearing and the forest we were being watched by people with the same number of chromosomes as any neighbor's son, demystifying the story that they had two more pairs of chromosomes, like the giant apes of the African cloud mountains.

And at some point in the trial I would scream, "Sir, that was a crime full of treachery and malice!"

More than one would listen to me and maybe reflect on it.

Chapter 11
The Colony

I had to travel approximately ten kilometers cross-country along a goat path that crossed a narrow pass between two mountains until I reached a spot that the geographer Javier Pulgar Vidal had called the Suni. The place was about three thousand five hundred or four thousand meters above sea level. The climate could be described as mild to cool during September; the rainy season had not yet arrived, although in the sky one could see leaden clouds that announced the presence of a rainy season yet to come. Before arriving at the strait, I had traveled along a spit of land that divided the blue lagoons in two. At times it seemed that it was a single body of water with unclear contours.

The lagoons had white edges; at first glance, it seemed to be the foam of the water, which wet the resinous stems of the cattails that grew on the shore. The puna, with its rocky surface and coarse sand, was a wild place covered with thatch mats or *ichu* and the dwarf cacti, wrapped in their own fluff, sprouted succulent, red flowers. Birds with dark plumage and citrine-yellow beaks nested in the thatch. When they flew up, you could see their tails were as yellow as their beaks. On the escarpment of rocks and caves frolicked vizcachas with gray fur and bushy tails.

As we reached the lower part of the esplanade, the flora became varied, from radially shaped amaryllis and bulbous roots to bilaterally symmetrical orchids, tuberous roots and rhizome or corm stems. The plants were not tall, as in the cloud forest or high jungle; however, they created the appearance of a fertile landscape.

In that place there was a village that was reached via a shortcut through stone fences. The ground was covered by weeds and thorns, with spaces in which feldspar was noticeable. The two-story houses were lined along a single street. At the edges were corrals. A herd of sheep could be seen on the horizon. Maybe they were not sheep, but goats or perhaps alpacas that looked like goats at such a distance. On the platforms surrounding the huts one could see the plucked-necked mountain chickens. Guinea pigs peeked out of the cracks that opened under the mud stoves. In some corrals there were cows with bony haunches and sunken flanks, with flaccid udders that perhaps gave some milk. The dogs were boisterous in the evenings. I suspected that the hollows on the neighboring mountains were inhabited by pumas that fed on the deer and mountain goats. I could also smell the musky odor of the mountain foxes that ate the viscachas, field mice and marbled quail; sometimes they would come down to the village, where they would feast on the tartar-born young and the bare-necked chickens.

At that moment I thought of the circle of time, as if I had suddenly awakened from a very confusing dream in the immense pit of the past. I recalled anecdotes that evoked parts of a movie with actors whose names I do not remember. Then I realized that I was no longer the same person. I had been hit by a camber on an anvil after having passed through the forge; I had waded through a meltwater stream to reach the site. The riverbed was fairly deep and made me dream of my childhood and the porters carrying travelers from bank to bank. I found, in another place of the riverbed, a tectonic fault cut to bevel; among the strata of different colors I could find dark and white stones, with reliefs of fern leaves and fossilized ficus roots.

When I arrived at the village I immediately saw the faces deformed by the disease. I saw cavernous nostrils and perforated bony palates. Some people showed ulcers on the skin, dark chloasmas on the forehead and cheekbones. At the edge of the street, seated on flagstones, the sick, covered only with ponchos and blankets, they were waiting in the cold.

When I saw them, I assumed all the leprosy patients were together, and the tuberculous patients with those with malaria. At first glance one could distinguish the stains of pellagra and the weakness caused by beriberi. It seemed to be the same village, attached to a mudflat of phreatic waters and bubbling geysers, where a tribe of malaria-infected individuals lived, only that one was in another country and a thousand kilometers away. Perhaps they had the same fevers and the same headaches that left them hunched over with stiffness and tremors.

Before reaching the village I could see a cemetery with white painted crosses. It was on a bend in the road, not too far away and yet not so close, either. Many years before there had been an indigenous cemetery there with its own graves. That time I came upon a crowd of disheveled men weeping. I passed among them as if I were a ghost; a chill wind that is felt but not seen. I breathed in the melancholy that came from the hollows of the mountains, turned into a flute and a guitar to emerge as a drum. I would have liked to sit at the back, on the wall to see the faces of the mourners and reflect my own feelings in their gestures.

It gave me the feeling that I was in the Good Friday procession in Calca, with the recumbent Christ inside a glass urn placed on top of a platform carried by the mestizos. The image was taken to meet the Sorrowful Virgin on the main street, which itself was carried on another platform of wood and trunks carved by the women of the city. The faces were drawn with the exaggerated seriousness of devotion. To me it looked like an impostured compunction. As in the Andean cemetery, the same expression was reproduced, making me feel the pain on the surface of my skin.

I could not stay in the place. I could not be part of the scene or part of the sadness. So I withdrew from walking among them. On the way out I passed under a stone arch with a Latin inscription carved on it. I don't know what it meant: "*Dominum humanum*". Perhaps it indicated that this was the place to which one finally entered, the end of a temporal life. I resurrected the scene of the women serving a plate of corn and turnip while the men moved as if they were dancing to the rhythm of the flutes that only they heard. Suddenly, I felt an immense heaviness, something that seeped into my bones like an icy air crawling under my suit and skin.

The cold made me imagine a priest in a brown habit sitting on a mound of stones. The monk was concentrating on an idea or a nostalgic memory. I don't know if he was rambling on about the ephemerality of human existence or recalling a story played out between alleys in a Mediterranean city. The man was very old, he wore it on his eyelids and in the cataracts of his eyes. I imagined the monk climbing the nooks and crannies and the slopes. Along the way he would meet women with their faces covered by a tulle mantilla. Then he wandered into the past, when he was in the monastery of Kikkos, in Nicosia. And she was moved by the image of the Virgin and the child in her arms. The face of the Virgin, hidden behind a tulle, and the face of the child, of the Cypriot brown color.

This time I was in a village similar to other villages in the area. The houses had one or two floors, and the walls were covered by a layer of plaster. However, it was a village converted into a therapeutic colony for the sick with spundia. That had been the intention of the priest, Guardamino: to convert an open field with boulders and bushes of flexuous branches into a population of sick people, following the European model of Thomas Mann's *The Magic Mountain*. He had previously organized an association of spundia sufferers. He then managed to obtain financing for the purchase of a hacienda, which was reached by crossing speed bumps, along a muleteer's path with uneven ground and rocks that camouflaged snake and lizard nests. The hacienda eventually became a village with an autonomous utopian model: with its own currency, a cooperative system for agricultural production and a mutuality with the vulnerable, that is, with the sick, the elderly and orphans.

The founder's idea was gradually adapted to reality: they started growing quinoa and achiote for export; they began to breed alpacas in the high plateau and highland cows in the yunga zone. The idea was to have the sick close by so that they could receive treatment and control their relapses or complications. In addition, a self-management model could be achieved to export fine wool and products from the cultivation of quinoa, pumpkin, highland potato and a type of small-grain corn. In the area near the river, achiote, oil palm and dwarf pineapples were planted. And there was a grove of orange trees that were sold at a good price to fruit merchants.

The population of the village grew with the arrival of other sick people and their families. Never in his wildest dreams would Guardamino have believed that the village would become a small town of more than five thousand inhabitants. However, the old part of the village continued to be home to the sick with spundia, malaria, leprosy and bejel. On the lower part of the hillside, almost next to the river, a small dispensary had been built and was run by another Salesian, Ernesto Corrales. When I arrived at the place, the service continued to treat people who came to cure everyday ailments: diarrhea, respiratory ailments, bone pain, trauma from accidents and children with parasites. Most of all, he was in charge of treating lesions, lepers and tuberculosis patients. Sometimes, primary malaria patients and others who had a flare-up of the disease also arrived.

The dispensary evoked nostalgia for my stay at the Doctors of the World hospital in Uganda. I felt like going back to the cafeteria in Kampala for my last conversation with Jalufe over a bitter-tasting Senegalese coffee. I was reminded of the images of health workers of different nationalities, the patients' rooms, the surgeons in their green operating room uniforms, the nurses with their trolleys.

That was not all. As I turned the page, I remembered the Centenario Hospital in downtown Rosario. The figures of Turkish Assad and his wife, indelible in my mind. I relived the dinner at his residence and the huge library with a multitude of works, from philosophy classics to history tomes, treatises on probabilistic mathematics and medical books, with yearbooks in different specialties. The rose that the lady placed in a long-necked vase resting in the center of the dining room table remains in my mind. I recalled Professor Fracassi's advice when he placed me in one of the stalls at the sanatorium for the elderly with dementia. I landed on Professor Guimpel's story, disrupted by the slander of his enemies, who accused him of philonazi behavior. He was able to do research on the different stages of congenital toxoplasmosis in pregnant women in the hospital. I was shocked when I felt the measured, more than that, perfidious accusations that induced the professor to commit suicide with a Luger pistol.

The Centenario Hospital was a huge block attached to the School of Medicine. On the second floor of the faculty, at the entrance to the anatomical museum room, one could find glass jars with organs deformed by disease. I assumed that the collection had been accumulated over generations of pathologists or anatomists. Inside one could guess brains with tumors, gummas or gliomas; cavernous lungs; livers with bullous surfaces and nutmeg texture, typical of cirrhosis. In short, each jar could correspond to a pathology. But what most caught my attention that time was a glass urn, placed on the front wall, containing the mummified body of an obese woman with oriental features. Upon inquiring about her, I was told that she was the wife of a Chinese or Korean merchant, who had embalmed the corpse because he loved her passionately. The story seemed to me like an Edgar Allan Poe novel, with a large dose of madness and compulsive obsession, and even schizophrenia on the part of the husband.

The naked body showed abdominal obesity and deformities of the breasts, with axillary extensions. It did not seem to me that there was anything artistic about the work; on the contrary, it was a grotesque monument. However, it was not out of context.

I was reminded of my walks along the waterfront, without fearing the drunks who made a racket in the gambling dens near the port. At that time, I loved to walk through the naked city, enjoying the caresses of the breeze of the river and the coolness of the night. I loved to drink coffee in any of the *boliches* at the pedestrian street and then return to my student room to sleep if I was tired or to continue reading the page of my microbiology book if I was not. Sometimes insomnia allowed me to advance in the study of Harrison's *Principles of Internal Medicine* while I smoked Marlboro cigarettes accompanied by cheap coffee dissolved in boiled water and sweetened with sugar. Other times those sleepless nights made me re-evaluate the tenderness of distant or lost loves. Those sleepless nights I felt the most prolonged and anguishing defeats.

No! The hospital in the village, which had become a health colony, was definitely nothing like the Centenario Hospital, or any other hospital in any other city I had ever passed through. Likewise, the village of the therapeutic colony was nothing like the old part of the city where I spent my childhood, nor the port of the Pacific, scene of my youthful antics. Much less did it remind me of the city where I pursued my professional studies.

It was useless to make sense of the past. Perhaps in a sick mind or in a misplaced dreamer. What I really wanted was to rediscover the worn-out human being, the idealist who was nostalgic for yesterday. In that colony of sick people, I recovered my passion and understanding of the value of my work, which had collapsed under the weight of the investigation. I felt as if I was getting younger, despite the stiffness of the spine due to the appearance of bony bridges between the vertebral bodies and the dehydration of the intervertebral discs. I returned to my youth, despite wheezing when walking, a consequence of an incipient pulmonary fibrosis. I would recover the enthusiasm of the first adventures to leave behind my depression due to so many losses.

I was foolish and let myself be fooled into thinking of love at first sight. Today I realize that what is repeatable is not happiness. Edmund Hillary explained it after having climbed Everest, "After reaching the top of the mountain, everything else is descent. You are never the same again." It's as simple as that. What is replicable is to return to places with millions of mosquitoes and thousands of butterflies, with snow-capped mountains on the shores of the dark blue sea, with clouds on the horizon, where the fishermen's ships swayed to the rhythm of the tides. Unrepeatable were the sensations I experienced with a woman of extraordinary beauty in a place that seemed not to exist in real life. That ebb and flow was possible; the other, romantic cities and women with a passionate I don't know what, was akin to finding a mountain higher than Everest and climbing it.

Today I had to land on that esplanade that sprouted from the scree and weeds. I was in a village that had been built on a field by sick people suffering from a madness characterized by passion and delirium. The place reminded me of the trip through the Palestinian settlements in the Gaza Strip. That time the children were training their arms to throw stones in the intifada. The battle had begun with the firing of Qassam rockets at Israeli settlements.

For years there had been a debate as to whether jihad was the sixth pillar of Islam, as the Sunnis claimed, or a religious decree, as the Shiites advocated. I imagined that among the barracks were war cripples, their limbs amputated at the root. Some would have wounds over their faces; old scars that crisscrossed the face from ear to jaw and from chin to neck. In other cases, part of the skull had been replaced with a slab of acrylic, with prickly hair around it. Suddenly a child appeared with a stiffened hand. It was larger than the other, the result of ulnar nerve palsy or a muscular dystrophy of which I was unaware. The nails, thickened by the accumulation of calcium on the keratin gave him the appearance of a feline paw.

When I saw the child's hand, I thought of the Andean dancers who represented black bears and covered themselves with the skin of the animal, of which they kept the claws. The children were skinny, those who did not have war wounds as well as those who trained with slingshots woven with colored wool. The men boasted bulging bellies and the women a flabby and deformed body due to the fat, in the form of an apron, that accumulated under the belly and reached the pubis, which prevented them from seeing their intimate parts. In addition, they had fatty panniculus on the scapulae, on the wall of the axillary hollow and on the back of the arms. They were adorned with many embroideries that decorated the chest, the sleeves, the shawls and the headdress typical of Palestinians. They cared for crippled children with a religious neatness. It occurred to me to think of the zinc-roofed barracks, too hot at noon, too cold at night.

The elderly had vesicles caused by scabies mites and scratching lesions that itched intensely at night. The machine gun nests of the mujahideen would become cesspools from the accumulation of sewage.

There, in the trenches and air-raid shelters, the warriors were exposed to sexually transmitted diseases and respiratory ailments. The overcrowding in which they lived for weeks at a time, hiding during the day and coming out at night, made them more vulnerable to neurosis and many manifested paranoias. Infantile diarrhea became more frequent during periods when the temperature increased, while more water transported in cisterns and desalinated water from the Mediterranean was consumed. The daily water use per inhabitant was seventy liters, far below the World Health Organization's recommendation.

Given the unhygienic conditions, an outbreak of cholera or salmonella poisoning was foreseen. I remembered that typhus was the disease that caused the most deaths during the First World War; it affected more than a million people, between military and civilians, in the countries in conflict and in the regions of influence of those countries. Perhaps the emerging disease was a zoonosis carried by rats arriving on cargo ships from Gaza.

The city had the minarets and mosque domes at the same height as the highest buildings, and the activity resembled that of any Mediterranean coastal city. During the summer the heat seemed to be concentrated in the dwellings, whose windows were wide open, which was the reason for the entry of many mosquitoes. The stench that came from the food markets or from the sea itself also seeped in, as if the detritus of the other cities along the coast were flowing onto that shore. The surface of the streets seemed to reverberate as the sun beat down on the city. The suburbs were filled with people walking with jugs of water that they carried to their homes, since the public water pipes did not work.

After a long time, having left youth and sacrifice for assholes, I evoked the face of that child. Perhaps I would have preferred the scene in which I felt the gaze of a black-eyed girl. She suspected that an individual had arrived, in the condition of a fireman, to mire himself on the shore of the Mediterranean for the sole purpose of being a mystic. The girl was Palestinian, although she was born in Ankara. Of course, I was not what she thought I was. Not even a look-alike.

She didn't understand why I was in a colony of starving refugees stuck with a shitty disease. I couldn't tell her that my brain had been burned out by some philosopher's mumbo jumbo that had put a hype of redemptive culture into my head. As if I had been intoxicated by a shot or smoked a joint, I had believed the whole verse. Of course, she wouldn't understand why she was in her own trench and involved in the intifada either. Maybe she suspected that I had come for love, following a girl who was killed in a mop-up operation led by elite Israeli troops to wipe out jihadist strongholds. Perhaps she believed that I hated the Zionists or that someone had paid me to join them, in her mind maybe I had received as much money as the soccer coaches hired by the sheiks of Saudi Arabia. But neither of these was correct. I was in that place for the fucking reason that I was a passionate and adventurous individual; a bastard who got it into his brain to be around those in need. He was, no more and no less, a nutcase with a redeemer's floppy disk, even if neither she nor anyone else believed it.

Just as I remembered the shantytowns of the Gaza Strip with their frosted walls, in that village of the sick I found the adobe walls sagging outwards. Perhaps that impression was because the base had been eroded by the rainwater running down the streets. The plaster had grown a green fuzz that seemed to me to be moss from the silt. The trail leading to the village had been tamped down by the traffic of people and cattle.

I had to admit that poverty was similar in any latitude. The Andean village and the towns of the Gaza Strip resembled each other in the smell of old rags and dampness. I could see the poor living in abandoned warehouses at train stations, crammed into barracks; beggars dressed in a light blue sari and a white headdress in some Parisian rue or the Senegalese destitute in the streets of Madrid. The women would carry children in their arms and others clinging to their skirts, sitting on the ground while they begged. I had seen Gypsies, Bulgarians, Romanians and Turks in the streets of Europe with the same expression on their faces and the same percale dress as the slum dwellers in the outskirts of Buenos Aires and the beggars in their ripped clothes in the slums of Santiago de Chile. Exactly the same image as in the hills of the favelas of São Paulo and Rio de Janeiro too.

It was worse in the countryside. The rural poor looked as if they were taken from a black and white postcard portraying a family from the first five years of the last century, with traditional hats, knee-high boots and knickers. The same photograph was reproduced, in sepia, of the colony of the sick, where the rural people were sitting on a stone fence.

The sky was still overcast and in the distance I could see the mountains with their peaks covered by clouds that were illuminated by lightning. I thought I recognized the blackness of the hollows of the yungas mountains, where the nests of vampire bats infected with the rabies virus are found near the ranches of the lumber settlers.

Dawn saw the steam rising from the mudflats covered by aquatic plants with mossy leaves. The steam came from the lagoons, whose surface was covered by water lilies with huge leaves and white, fleshy flowers. The women covered their bodies with poplin robes and the children, with disproportionately large heads, sucked milk from exhausted breasts.

I remembered visiting the Yungas villages during a very hot summer. I made my way through the thicket of lianas and palmettos, clearing the thicket of the wild jungle with a machete. I arrived after two days of trekking, subjected to the attack of a bloodthirsty mosquito strain, which simulated a cloud that accompanied us the whole trip. I protected myself with a tulle netting that came down from the brim of my white felt hat. The porters, in turn, had smeared their faces with a foul-smelling repellent.

I had been tasked with checking a health alert, a possible outbreak of rabies in humans caused by bats biting the toes of the inhabitants of the shantytowns. To reach them, I had to pass through a village shrouded in mist rising from the lowland jungle. The wooden huts had been erected on the wooded hillside and the walls were painted in bright colors: green, terracotta yellow and orange. It was as if some Christian had thought of harmonizing the village with the forest and begonia leaves.

Perhaps the pioneers were the ones who created the first ranch, which grew little by little, until it reached the main road and became the town of more than a hundred huts and more than two thousand inhabitants that they called Marcapata, perhaps because it was the last place that could be reached by a muleteer's trail. From the road you could see the clothes hanging on the rusty wires; the orchards with the ground covered in sheep dung and parrot shit from the birds that lived in the branches of the peach trees. For hours the village seemed empty, as if everyone had left at the same time to run some errand, or as if the people had agreed to take a siesta at that hour. In the dirt and stone streets, one could see the occasional dog dozing near the doors of the huts, as well as green parrots perched on sticks in the stucco wall.

At the village health center I met a young doctor, who panicked when he learned that I had come from inland. The boy was trembling with fear, for it was unthinkable for him to travel to the places where the sick came from. Misadventure did not go with him. Nor did he dare to perform autopsies on the deceased.

When I arrived at the post, after crossing the mountain pass in a four-by-four van, I could not avoid the subject. I had to check the drool coming out of the corners of the lips, the reddened conjunctivae and the inexpressive fury of the sick to establish an analogy with what I understood to be the terminal phase of human rage. I was late and could not check the most obvious signs. Thus, I was content to observe the agonizing groans of the sick and the drowsiness that preceded the convulsions. I also found corpses hidden in rooms that had a musky odor from the emanations of the deceased.

I had to confirm my suspicions before initiating any action, before fumigating the caves and huts with cyanide gas and slaughtering any dogs that showed out of context aggression or languor. Then, once the inhabitants had vacated the dwellings and moved their belongings and pets, we would also disinfect the huts. Likewise, I would autopsy the recently dead and remove their brain mass. I would have to send the boys of the village to hunt bats in the hollows of the mountains, even if they ran the risk of contracting rabies. I would send the bats in wooden boxes, just like the ones they used to send oranges to the markets. The brains would be carried in wide-mouthed glass jars, to be analyzed in the laboratory of the Institute of Tropical Diseases.

There the pathologists would try to discover Negri's inclusions in the pyramidal cells of the hippocampus of the brain. I had seen them once under an optical microscope; they were small eosin-stained images located in the cytoplasm of nerve cells. I had not had the opportunity to study these bodies in any electron microscope that would help me to verify that the spots in the cytoplasm were the nucleotides and capsids of the rhabdoviruses that cause rabies.

Perhaps if I had been able to discuss the subject with Irina, I would have told her that I had treated a woman with rabies. She had to be tied with sheets on an iron cot without a mattress. I would have told her that the woman was conscious at times and crying, perhaps her crying was because she knew she was dying. Irina could tell me if she had seen photographs and consulted documents about peasants in the Siberian taiga who had died of rabies; people who had been bitten by Arctic wolves that preyed, in packs, on poachers. The bizarre part of the Siberian report was that these organs had been donated to patients in need of a kidney transplant. The result was catastrophic: the organ recipients died of human rabies. That's day-to-day life, *carpe diem,* she would tell me, and I could deduce that stupid things happen anywhere in the world.

The poverty of the people in this area was visible underneath the cotton polo shirts proclaiming political campaign propaganda. One afternoon I attended the funeral of an old man. The people improvised a coffin from milk cartons. They used ropes to tie the cartons and the body of the dead man as a strut or rigid pillar. The pathetic thing was that they used this material for the coffin when it was a town full of sawmills that scrapped the trunks of illegally cut trees.

Upon returning to the city I wrote my report about this human rabies outbreak. I needed to be more thorough on the context part. Then I asked myself, "What is context?" It might have been the time lived. I could have described the working conditions of the rural people, or perhaps I should have detailed the geographic location, without dwelling on the presence of heavy machinery in the vicinity. There they worked tirelessly around the clock, in three shifts, digging the slopes of the gold-bearing canyons and opening craters in the clay soil, plundering the jungle with the front loaders that uprooted the trees.

I was not to mention, at all, a Chinese emigrant with a lot of money, who was the boss of an illegal mining company that explored the vicinity. The man had bought the machinery and hired the laborers who lived in the camp's barracks. He allude to other Asians who seemed to be his entourage of thugs and bodyguards; they walked with dark glasses to avoid the sunlight and prevent their identification. Of course, he refused to acknowledge that they were murderous psychopaths who were reputed to have carried off more than two dozen people among natives and Creoles. Once, one of them was interrogated by the police for illegal possession of weapons and suspicion of homicide and the henchman argued that he had mistaken the deceased for a tapir and, therefore, had shot him with a burst of ten bullets with a gun that looked like a double-barreled repeating rifle and dum-dum bullets.

In this illegal business were involved criminals of many nationalities. Possibly, the subjects belonged to black-market gold and gemstone trafficking mafias and had boats stranded some twelve miles away awaiting shipments that would arrive at any time, when their inland cronies would have the opportunity to approach the boats in rubber dinghies with outboard motors.

The village continued in the same place, between the hillside and the riverbank. Upon entering, we found black pigs in the open fields, taking advantage of the waste from the dumps. On the slopes of the Andes, the entrances to the caves were covered by araucaria trunks and tree ferns. Climbing plants clung to the escarpment. Flocks of green parrots preyed on fruit trees, mimicking the vegetation, while red and blue parrots burrowed in the clay of the slopes eroded by the floods.

The disease will have its moment and then disappear like so many other phenomena of life. The explanation could be simple: the infested animals died before transmitting the disease. This seemed improbable to me, since one of the characteristics of the disease is the aggressiveness of the vermin in the terminal phase, when the virus affects the brain and provokes fits of rage. Perhaps the decline in reported cases was related to changes in ecological conditions that caused the outbreak to occur. These could be changes in climate or human predation of animal habitats.

Among the measures we improvised to protect people were prophylactic treatments. We administered parenteral vaccines to domestic animals and prepared baits mixed with oral vaccines to immunize wild animals. We also fumigated the caves where the vampire bats lived with cyanide, trying to eliminate those animals that were sick. Likewise, suspicious dogs were euthanized and those that could be considered free of any premature signs were vaccinated. Most importantly, we treated people who had been bitten by wild or domestic animals with post-exposure prophylaxis vaccines placed in the adipose panniculus of the abdomen or in the shoulder.

Today, more than ten years after the outbreak of rabies, time seems to have stopped in the area. The villages are still hidden in the bush; the women wear the same clothes; the children wear only underwear; and the old people continue to sit on the boards of the paths built on wooden stilts to prevent floodwater from entering the rooms of the houses. However, much has changed. Asphalt has reached almost every village in the basin. The excavators grow ever larger and the beaches of the camps have become inhospitable mud flats, with stone cairns on the clay surface dotted with pools of yellowish water contaminated with mercury.

Heavy metals reached the large rivers in the basin and poisoned sensitive species while destroying the ecosystem. The Chinese were still in the area. They used state-of-the-art technology for vein detection, satellite maps and ultrasound equipment. Gone will be the guy with that bush mouse face. But there will be others. Behind them will come the informal miners, like the remoras behind the sharks, with shanty camps, built in wood with zinc roofs, full of filth.

In the future in Boca Colorado and Laberinto there will still be traders with their rigged scales to buy the weekly production of gold sands. In the same village the deafening noise of the loudspeakers will still bring tropical music from other latitudes, from salsa to Colombian cumbias. Inside the cantinas, the alcoholic whores and the queer cooks will still wait for the night to come to manage the business. The hidden villages will be the same and there will be no change. Or maybe not. Maybe it was two rickety kids ten years ago. Or two jaundiced women. Life really is the closest thing to a dream. It is a colorful fantasy, with the blue river, the red leaves, the orange trunks and the smell of lead in the air. In the case of the children who played in the ponds, the dream will be like a scalloped feather or a balloon with holes in it. One of them will pull from the mud a silver-colored fish with frozen eyes. You will never know if the animal died of poisoning or because of a natural phenomenon that repeats itself every five years. Then I will feel sorrow, an immense pity, both for me and for the child with the fish. And I will imagine that the world is a punctured balloon with inhabitants that look like caricatures by a poor cartoonist.

My report had been brief and very scientific, focusing on the important details of the disease. The study on the reservoir mentioned chiropterans as the primary affected. Possibly, it was the bats with frugivorous habits, and not the hematophagous ones, as we suspected at the beginning. The first victims of zoonosis were a woman with five small children and a man who had a store of mining tools. The bats, once attacked by the hydrophobic rage, came out of the damp hollows and went cross-country for miles to attack livestock and humans.

Why had the outbreak occurred? I pointed out more than one hypothesis to explain the matter: the sick bats left the dens frightened by the noise of the backhoe excavators and traveled long distances before reaching the places where they attacked their victims. I also pointed out as another option the possibility that the bats migrated from their natural habitats due to deforestation.

The report described the symptoms of hydrophobia presented by the patients: trismus, stertorous breathing, muscular contractures in the neck, the nape of the neck and even the face. Then came the opisthotonos, similar to those of tetanus, which curved the spine until the body was pinned to the nape of the neck. This resulted in the fracture of the vertebrae. I also mentioned the evolution of the patients, the states of agitation and psychomotor excitement and the irreducible impulse to bite. The patients seemed to be wild beasts dominated by the anxiety to sink their teeth into healthy people, even if these were their loved ones. My report ended with a description of the coma and respiratory paralysis that resulted in death.

Those days were for me the revelation of so many unknowns that I had not been able to solve. First of all, who was I? The second question was even more pathetic: What was I looking for? After more than half of my existence, I still had no answers to these questions. Maybe because I had let time go by without any explanation, or maybe there was none at all. I was like the junkies after having overdosed, totally dazed, burned, seeking to cover my genitals with my right hand to avoid damage from aggressors. I had seen that kind of madness on Thirteenth Street in Los Angeles and on Tenth Avenue in New York; also on the Reeperbahn in Hamburg, in every fucker who lived for the sake of living without even figuring out how the mess went.

Then this person I imagined would become sick, like all the victims of emerging diseases, including that of immunity deficiency. Perhaps he was like those suicidal children to whom Rafael Correa, the former president of Ecuador, referred when he spoke of the great economic crisis in South America and the emigration of the economically active population. In the successive swings of inflation, recession and depression, hundreds of thousands of young people emigrated to developed countries and left their children in the care of grandparents and other relatives. The children, abandoned by their parents, committed suicide in the most poignant picture of chronic economic bankruptcy. I immediately imagined the burials, small white coffins on the shoulders of the elderly.

I also wanted to commit suicide or immolate myself in my own way, like those children in the Ecuadorian village of Chunchi, where there had been so many child suicides. I would do it by exposing myself to danger, entering places that could be risky for my life, unhealthy or conflicting places, escarpments where it was possible to fall into the abyss or jungles with swamps and quicksand. It was as if my subconscious had evaluated my situation as an outcast, without giving a damn about anyone, or as if I considered myself a chronically depressed person, with a compulsion that forced me to continue following a routine.

I did not realize the advantage of being a dreamer over the rest of the population who live the routine of reality. Those were clear about what was true and what was fantasy. I, on the other hand, confused the terms. That was my way of looking at events, perhaps with some advantages over the pragmatists. At that time I compared myself with them. I saw them as successful businessmen, as higher-level civil servants, as professionals in the highest academic category. All of them sweated the shirt off their backs like nobody else and in the end what was left for them? Nothing! It was as simple as that. They were sinking into old age with presbyopia and presbycusis, unable to read the small print of the newspapers or hear high-pitched sounds; barely understanding what was said to them for one reason or another: deafness or dementia.

In the meantime, I continued with the delirium, like a discomforted person who does not understand what is happening to him or simply does not want to understand it. I thought I resembled the elective uncontacted natives, who do not want any links with the specimens of the other civilization. In the end, it all came down to profiles. There was nothing unconnected. The villages and bat-borne rabies connected with the colony of sick people in the mountains. There was no difference between malaria in the swamps of Central America and epidemics of classic dengue fever in another part of the world. Poverty, overcrowding and predation could occur in any environment.

On that trip I met other deluded people who talked about beaches, mountains, jungles and hospitals as if they were the same thing. They told you about their exploits. With them, I began to get an idea of what it meant to be on the lookout for notifications from the epidemiological offices. As soon as I was given the order, I would go out like a dog after a rabbit, running to the place in question.

The report of human rabies made me reflect on the ambiguity of my relationship with humans who may or may not be sick. On the one hand, I considered myself a useful man to others; on the other hand, I thought that was what I believed because of my pride. This ambiguity could be summed up in a portrait of the memory. In the photograph I appeared mounted on a dwarf woolly horse at the top of a hill that appeared to be the highest in the world, because in the snapshot I could see the blue sky and white clouds in the background. But, in reality, it was a small hill, so perspective played a role in taking the picture, with the photographer on his knees and me stretched out on the saddle. Maybe that was the compendium of my past. Me stretched out on a dwarf roan and someone taking the picture from a deceptive perspective.

Suddenly, I landed in a village refuge for stigmatized patients. I had been invited by its founder, Antonio Guardamino. I had met the priest some time before, when we both attended an assembly of leishmaniasis patients. The purpose of the convention was to share experiences between the afflicted and the stigmatized. The delegates were of various nationalities: Colombians from the departments of Amazonas, Vichada, Vaupés, Guaviare, Guainía; Peruvians from the departments of Loreto, Pucallpa, Madre de Dios, San Martín, Amazonas; Brazilians from the states of Acre, Rondonia, Amazonas, Mato Grosso, Mato Grosso del Sur, Pará. The delegates from Bolivia, the host country, came from the departments of Beni, Pando and Santa Cruz.

The assembly took place in a parish school near the city of Cobija. I assumed that this place had been chosen because of the sometimes unpresentable marks of some of the attendees. Fear of contagion was an insurmountable barrier to trying to gather them in other cities. Of course, I reasoned, not all the sequelae were visible. Many had had hepatic, pulmonary and cardiac variants. Some could be recognized by their hoarse voice due to damage to the larynx and vocal cords. Others had wheezing due to lesions in the cartilage of the trachea. Among the Brazilian attendees were those with the visceral variant of kala-azar.

Many years ago, when the headquarters of my work was in São Paulo, I was able to attend to the children of a colony of informal loggers. When I examined them and found many with swollen abdomens, physical asthenia and general wasting, several alternatives came to mind: could it be ascites due to liver failure? Maybe a virus or bacteria such as *Leptospira*? Maybe a trematode worm, such as liver fluke? Of course, I kept other options in the deck: delta hepatitis or visceral leishmaniasis, similar to African kala-azar. That disease was rare in the Peruvian jungle yet somehow frequent in the Brazilian jungle. I reviewed from memory the articles published in medical bulletins on endemic diseases in South America. I remembered reading a report on the arrival of leishmaniasis in America. It had been brought by emigrants from the Mediterranean or by the African population that arrived in Brazil during the years of slavery.

The viscera of the children examined in the logging camp were larger and palpable below the costal ridge. It involved painful growth due to the sudden increase in volume, which stretches the membranes of the hepatic capsule, rich in pain receptor nerve corpuscles. The disease began with afternoon fever, ecchymosis in napa and massive hematemesis, until reaching, in some cases, coma and death.

In real life I had no choice but to continue writing on my logbook and then insert the data of the samples of exsanguinated viscera, mark the test tubes with the content of centrifuged blood and the glass slides on which I made the spread of leukocytes and the imprint of the marrow obtained by a puncture in the iliac crest. Everything would be labeled with small stamps with the patient's data. The material would be sent to the agency's laboratories for research. The biochemists would then report the findings to the central processing center to generate regional alerts. After the whole process, some of the agency's scientists would go on the media to report the finding and the temporary limitation of the disease. When I heard about the interview, I thought that dilettantes rule the world and mendacity is profitable.

Tracking the disease seemed like a crazy thing to do. First I found out that the cases occurred more or less simultaneously, with just a few days difference between them. The relatives caring for the children did not get sick, so I concluded that it was not transmitted by droplets from the sneezing of the sick. The affected children had been scratched by the cats. They had eaten carrion from a mule that had died after a jaguar attack. I could not believe it, but it occurred to me that I was dealing with a zoonosis that could well be glanders, with accumulations of dark brown pus in the liver, putrid and foul-smelling. A few days earlier I had checked for pyogenic abscesses by cutting into the nodular liver of a little girl. She had died the same day of my arrival. It was the only autopsy I had ever performed.

The cuts were made with a scalpel on a pale yellow viscera with brown spots protruding from the surface of the organ. Suspecting zoonosis or pyogenic superinfection with staphylococcus or gram-negative bacteria, I requested that nurses from nearby health centers be sent to me and that they bring ampoules of antibiotics, including imipenem; hundreds of cephalosporin capsules, tablets and dissolvable powder to prepare suspensions of doxycycline and clarithromycin.

I sent samples of the abscess fluid and some viscera fragments obtained during the autopsy to the headquarters laboratories. Perhaps the disease was not glanders and had nothing to do with eating the putrid flesh of a mule, but a variant of visceral leishmaniasis or kala-azar due to a mutation of *Leishmania donovani*. In this case, the vector could be a phlebotomine sandfly and the predominant sign, hepatosplenomegaly.

Similarly, I could consider another option: mutation of a pathogen that was already present in the village, in the skin lesions of spundia or in granulomas in the jaws of utosos. At some point, *Leishmania* mutated into a variant that nested in the liver and other organs.

I don't want to imagine the parents' reaction if they had been present when I opened the tummy to find the percuded liver and then aspirated, through a cannula, the contents of the blisters or bullae that had formed inside the parenchyma. The mask barely attenuated the pungent odor of the milky white, I would say shitty, liquid that had accumulated. I felt nauseous at the sight of the contents; worse, I could not contain my gagging when I perceived the stench. At first, I held it in so as not to dirty the mask; then I could not resist any longer and a single, explosive vomit ensued, while I felt as if I were dizzy from a long trip along the serpentine of a highway.

That was my fucking job. At the same time I felt that there was something great in the mixture of ennui, putridity, disgust and perspiration to save human lives. I was certain that I had fulfilled my destiny after listening to the speeches of the infectology professor, Turk Assad; of having read my father's *National Geographic Magazines* in my childhood. Maybe it was a genetic thing, with a wandering father who had lived in Chicago and felt the cold wind coming off Newfoundland and kicking up waves on the surface of Lake Michigan. I was left wondering about the motivations for my behavior, whether it was due to emulation of my teachers or a matter of isolation and emotional loss.

For several days the children received venous solutions through catheters placed in the arm, in the inguinal flexure and in the shaved skull. The loggers watched me like an alien who had come to resuscitate the dying and bury the dead. The children received antibiotics by vein and orally, just in case it was glanders. Maybe they could receive amphotericin B in case it was visceral leishmaniasis. "God knows with what results?", I said to myself, and then kept silent, praying for a miracle.

Suspicious, we tried to follow up on cats, dogs, sheep, cows and horses. We examined the men with spundia to see if any of them had a painful liver on palpation or a giant spleen. We were looking for the origin of the misfortune so as not to repeat it.

Suddenly, the children were better, the fevers subsided, the smiles reappeared. The fathers and men of the village seemed to have been resurrected along with them. This massive resurrection included me. Days passed. In the end I considered that the goal had been achieved. No new cases appeared. The sick were cured or improved. Even I could not believe it. At the same time, the foul smell cleared up and the children's skin became clearer.

As I listened to the delegates of the assembly of leishmaniasis patients, I imagined I was in a very old city with buildings with peeling walls. From every window a woman seemed to emerge, looking like an actress in a horror movie. One of them screamed that I should flee the place before I got scabies or worms crawled into my brain. Then I realized that I had lived in infected communities without even knowing that the women had dark brown spots on their skin that looked to me like Kaposi's sarcoma herpes lesions. The spots were bluish ecchymoses from extravasations, then they became hemosiderin brown from the destruction of red blood cells and ended up as maculopapules that grew due to infiltration of lymphocytes and malignant cells. They eventually became hard, woody masses.

However, I thought the most at-risk women were the androgynous women of New York's Tenth Avenue and those on 13th Street in Los Angeles. I thought of them as morphine-addicted sluts who required injections to keep from slipping into madness. I recreated them as carriers of sexually transmitted diseases.

The assembly peaked after the second day. The first day had been for registration and credentialing. From the second day on, I was able to listen to the testimonies of the sick, "We worked from sunrise to sunset, from dawn until the moment when shadow replaced light. Half our bodies sunk in the mud and half our bodies hidden by the stains of blood-sucking mosquitoes. When they recruited us for weekly payments and gold quotas for participations," said a delegate from the department of Guainía, "we made up our minds that we could subsist on that. They did not fulfill anything.

"The bosses were heartless. I prayed to the Virgin of Montserrat for my life. I didn't know if I would come out of the laundries alive or dead. The little money we earned was taken from us by the canteens and women. In the end, as a reward, we manifested deep wounds in our legs. At first we thought they were the result of the shit in the pools, due to the infection of the flesh. The wounds never healed and jumped from one side to the other, from the leg to the other leg, from the other leg to the face or to the mouth.

"When I saw the Cumas with their mouths or noses as red as shrimp, I was convinced that they would heal when we got out of the plague of the ponds and marshes. Maybe with pills or injections. Not a bit. No treatment would work for the rash on the skin or for the wounds in the nose, nostrils and mouth.

"One night, tired of so much abuse, we met to plan our escape. We would have to do it as a group and we would not stop even if they shot us in the back. We had to escape; otherwise our flesh would rot as part of a punishment.

"I was born in the forests of Bahia. My mother was very poor when my father abandoned her, God knows where he was going. I found out about the man's fate later. He had gone astray, robbing with other bandits the *fazendas* of the northeast, where he received the mortal wound from a blade or with a shot from the capangas or other rustlers. My mother, left alone, had to go out every day to the forest to hunt some vizcacha or catch some free-range chicken. In that way she fed the six children. She didn't care if snakes were hiding in the bushes.

"One afternoon, as the sun was setting, we saw her coming from the beaten earth, kicking up dust as she walked. When she reached the hut, my brothers and I knew she would die that very night. She had been bitten by the coral viper.

"At night she was delirious and in the early morning she was gasping for breath in agony. After her death, each one of us knew that we had to find a life anywhere to survive. It was my turn to go into logging in Mato Grosso do Sul. At that time, logging was illegal, now I don't know. We never saw the owners of the denouncements; they only sent people to recruit us and pay us a miserable salary. We became experts with the chainsaws to cut the trunks and remove the branches.

"I had been working for more than two rainy seasons. I don't know at what point I started to feel like shit. Then came the fevers and the tremors. I got weaker and weaker until I couldn't stand for an hour at a time, much less use the chainsaw. When they became aware of my illness, the foremen beat me with the rubber rods and snakeskin whips. Later, when they realized that the other peons were getting angry, they put me on a canoe and deposited me in a leprosarium next to the swamp.

"The doctors and health workers thought it was tertiana, until they discovered that it was *Leishmania*. The missionaries in Paraná treated me with amphotericin.

"I think I am cured now, because I don't feel the same. Before, I couldn't walk and I was in a bad place, even if I was eating. Now I feel better; I can work in soybean harvesting and land breaking.

"I have come to tell my experience to show the fate of young people like me, exposed to the plagues of mosquitoes, the bites of snakes, the evil diseases."

Each of the delegates, registered as speakers, gave their testimony. I did not have time to record everything on my cell phone. During one of the breaks, I was introduced to Antonio Guardamino, the Salesian priest who founded the therapeutic colony in a place close to the cloud forests of my homeland.

I also heard this testimony that mentioned him: "I am from Peru. My land, where I was born, is a small town of thirty huts called Colca. I want to give my testimony. First, I am going to tell you how I was hooked. In the small square Limaqpampa there was a grocery store where there was a recruitment agency for boys and girls. The manager was a woman who was known as Marga; I don't know if that was her name or her nickname. She not only looked for the peons, but also for the little women, known as the *pasñachas*, the poor girls. Their luck was worse than ours. They were all-terrain, that's what they called the *pasñachas*. They had them as washerwomen, cooks, barmaids and whores in the camps. Most of them were no older than fifteen.

"The work was on the beaches; that's what they called the puddles left by the pipes that came down from the highlands and flowed into the Rio Grande. In the spillways that were in the bush they put the troughs of the washing places. We laborers had to carry the mud up to the top of the spillways with the buckets and buckets and then roll the mud over the wooden trays so that it would pass through the screens. Then we had to wash the mud to look for sparks and burn the sand with mercury. The gold stuck to the quicksilver.

"When someone got bored with the working conditions, the foremen would accuse him of theft, and if he ran away, they would go after him. I never saw a runaway again. I think they didn't want to capture them to bring them to the camp, but they would tie them up them in the bush.

"One day a prosecutor arrived with a National Police garrison. We peons complained, as did the *pasñachas*. The prosecutor released us, that is, he freed us and offered us protection all the way to the highway. I don't know anything about the bosses and their foremen. Some say that they pay and, at a touch, they let them go free, as if nothing had happened.

"When we returned to the mountains, we were all infected with *Leishmania*. Some of us had ulcers on our legs; others had worse luck and the disease spread to our faces and reached our mouths. It ate my septum and palate, so when I ate, part of the food came out through my nose. And it was worse when I vomited, because it came out through my mouth and nose.

"In the mountains we looked for any little job, but people were disgusted. They thought we were sick with leprosy or yaws and were afraid of catching it. There I met Father Antonio Guardamino in the parish. He ran a leishmaniasis medicine dispensary on a piece of land next to the church, where we were injected with amphotericin.

"The dispensary became more and more crowded and looked like a market. Every day different sick people registered: the unhealthy, the lepers, the tuberculosis patients, people with malarial. They queued up in the street. Sometimes the police or the municipal police would intervene. Many times the townspeople stoned us so that we would not walk on the street or near the school. They were very afraid of catching the disease, so they forbade us to bathe in the hot springs and to go near the church. One day, one of those men of ill will had the idea of bringing together the market's stall owners with the police and women of the town, known for their craziness, and they organized a beating against the sick people. I don't know why. Someone had brought an iron bar, known as a diablo, and with it he beat the sick people who were waiting to receive their treatments.

"When the nuns, Teresa and Carlota, intervened, among them they were almost beaten too. Four dead, two men with skull fractures were referred to hospitals in the capital of the department, and others suffered various fractures and bruises. When Antonio returned from his pastoral trip to the province of Sandía, he was told that the sick members of the association had been expelled from the town and the dispensary destroyed by vandals. He then became ill with a nervous breakdown.

"First he went to look for the bully who had organized the beating. When he found him, he punched him twice in the face and left him unconscious on the floor of the atrium of the church itself. The unruly man's wife filed a complaint against Father Antonio, which was in the hands of the District Prosecutor's Office. In the end, with the intervention of the nuns and the bishop himself, the accusation was dropped and the agitator was found to be in the right. The priest was ordered to pay civil reparations for the physical damages and to close the dispensary.

"The father, regretting resorting to violence, pleaded the defense of the constitutional right of citizens to have decent health services. The agencies turned a deaf ear, so he came up with the idea of creating a larger dispensary. He bought a ranch between the grasslands and the valley: from where the height of Tres Cruces de Oro begins and ends in an abandoned village called Patria. There, a village was built around the hacienda. Now it is a colony for the sick and their families.

"I have to recognize the work of Father Antonio for his kindness..." he was interrupted by sobs and applause from the audience.

I felt intense, inexplicable cold. Maybe it was the climate of the altitude, the winds coming from the mountain range, or it was the air coming from inside the body, similar to the dryness of some organ that has not finished repairing itself. As I felt the chills, all kinds of bad omens came to me. I thought I was suffering from some kind of undulant fever, with chills preceding the rise in temperature. However, I suspected that it was not an illness produced by external organisms, but something simpler: it looked like fatigue, with its accompanying loss of body temperature, muscular asthenia and lethargy. It was as if the cold of the winds of the South Seas in Melbourne or Comodoro Rivadavia, had gotten into my bones. It was an icy sensation that hurt in the bones.

I reflected on how often cultures isolated their sick. We were familiar with the loneliness of the leper communities in Asia Minor and those on the island of Molokai. There were Chinese immigrants suffering from leprosy. When they arrived in the Hawaiian Islands, they were immediately segregated by order of King Kamehameha IV to prevent the spread of the disease. The same could be said of the syphilis of Tahiti and Hawaii: the isolation was due to the population's fear of contracting a disfiguring or mutilating disease. History repeated itself and the sick were intercepted by the guards of King Kamehameha with the order to shoot at anyone trying to escape.

I had been invited by Antonio Guardamino to visit his therapeutic colony. For the trip I took with me Thomas Mann's *The Magic Mountain.* I don't know whether I identified myself with Hans Castorp or Dr. Behrens. Perhaps I was meeting a cousin, Joachim Ziemssen at the colony.

I drove the four-wheel-drive, rural-trail pickup truck. The sweaty horse did not show up, nor did I find any woman with tarantulas on her chest. On the contrary, I noticed that the route was followed by spotters who watched us from the mountain. They shouted the alarm to each other. After crossing the bend where I found the cemetery, I left the vehicle parked in the open field, accompanied by the noise of dozens of children who made fun of the height of the wheels. Perhaps they were also laughing at my boots and my leather jacket. Suddenly I heard a bugle sounding an alert, or maybe it was a sound reception.

I was just entering the narrow street with a central drain, through which crystal-clear water flowed from the mountain springs, when I heard the sound of flutes and seashells, which are called pututos. The ensemble was followed by a group of young women who danced and sang in high-pitched tones. I almost started to cry. I hoped they would not mistake me for someone valuable to them. I doubted if in that place they were paying debts of some beneficiary from another time and another space.

When I returned from my trip to fantasy, I found that the townspeople looked me in the eye waiting for an answer that was slow in coming. At that moment, they thought I was crazy, because I remained silent like schizophrenics in their catatonic phase. They discovered in my eyes the sly, dark, and confused look of the insane, and that made them fearful. I was sure that they had scrutinized my silence, understanding that there had been a gap of consciousness.

The patch of sick and poor villagers reminded me of my early childhood, when I met a child affected by polio. Then came back memories of that child in a wooden crate, which had been fitted with wheels and ball bearings. The healthy children pushed and pulled the makeshift cart. The child's expression was painful and his lower limbs were thin and wasted. That time I was terrified of contagion. I was so nervous when I was near the invalid. I felt sorry for myself when I saw the solidarity of the children who pulled the stroller while I pouted in disgust and tried not to touch the wood of the stroller. Life made me pay for my blunder.

During the afternoons, as the wind blew the ice from the mountains, I was reminded of the boardwalks of the coastal cities. Along the sidewalks solitary individuals walked with beige raincoats, hands in pockets, silk scarves around their necks to prevent the cold from penetrating their chests. You could feel the chill from the shivering during the march. Someone whistled a tune that seemed to be a jazz verse or a tango of yesteryear. The place looked to me like part of a Manet watercolor, a photograph entered in an international competition except for two differences: one was the marine avenue of an Atlantic port city and the other a village in the lower part of the grassland, four thousand meters above sea level. In both places I could feel the sensation of loneliness that had been weighing me down lately. There was no difference between them.

I identified myself with the guy who walked along the boardwalk next to the bluff that cut the waves; at the same time, I was the same guy who walked along a path between stone walls joined without mortar. Yes, he was the same globetrotter with a face splashed with drops of water escaping from the foam of the waves that burst ten meters out to sea and, later, the madman who traveled the roads from one place to another to find the same solitude, the same cold, in a mountain village.

At that time my desire for isolation was stronger than the fear of being assaulted by gang members who are experts in robbing drunks and melancholic loners. Today I repeated the same experience with the wind in a village of stigmatized people. This time there were no gang members and no one would think of mugging me; however, there was the disease, which could be unmanageable, with a lethality superior to any armed gang.

I pondered about the pending issues in my logbook, issues that hurt me and for that reason I put off dealing with them. I was getting old, the hikes exhausted me, the steep slopes made me gasp and my legs cramped; my moods blackened, to the point of believing that I would end up being an outcast without an home. The cold and the landscape of the puna made me gloomy; the jungles made me sweat until I was exhausted, languid, without strength. Then I thought I should look back to what I had lost: the company of a woman, the warmth of a home, books on the shelves, a barbecue with wine and soda, a chat with friends. I had time left, I had desire left. The time had come to accept the invitation of a couple of elderly friends I hadn't visited in a couple of years.

The woman would prepare me a *carapulcra*, a traditional Andean dish with pork and lamb. In return, I would cook a grilled hake fillet, or maybe I would spread it with egg batter for the breading. I would take my her to a music session and she would feel as young as my children.

Then it occurred to me to justify my way of living with a parable of Cicero. In it, some old men were planting an orchard with fruit trees. As they passed by, a young man asked them, "Why do you plant trees that will bear fruit when you cannot enjoy them?"

One of the old men answers him, "We do it to pay for the fruits we have already eaten and so that those who come after us may eat new fruits. In that way we will continue the cycle of God and of life."

On second thoughts, the narrative could be in the *Catilinaries* or not belong to any book of Cicero. Perhaps it was a confusion of the one who long ago thought he understood something that suited his pretensions of transcendence.

When the gray sky changed to blue and the sunlight illuminated the world, I considered that my mission was over and, at the same time, my stay in the village. Then I took my gear and returned by the same way I had arrived, crossing the same torrent and heading towards the grasslands, all the way accompanied by a group of villagers.

Hours later I arrived at a town that had a stone church and many adobe houses with baked clay tile roofs. There the driver of the organization's van was waiting for me.

"That was it!" I said to myself.

Chapter 12
Repeated Delusions

Leafing through the *New York Times* I found a story tucked away in the police pages. The story reported that the body of a drag queen had been found in one of the side seats of a subway car. The discovery had occurred at the Bronx station near the zoo.

The man had been left shrunken as if he had been taken out of a cold chamber. Everything pointed to his death being due to a disease, either viral or non-infectious causes. In this pandemic, deaths due to coronavirus or AIDS were common, although an overdose was still not ruled out.

Then I remembered Harry, my high school classmate, the only drag queen I ever heard of, at least the only one in my high school graduating class. We called him Harry because of his resemblance to the musician Harry Belafonte in his performance of *Hava Nagila* at Carnegie Hall. Harry was the son of a Bolivian businessman; his mother was a woman of extraordinary beauty even in middle age. They had migrated after the National Revolution, one of many revolts in the Altiplano country. This took place when Siles Zuazo, Paz Estenssoro, Juan Lechín and Walter Guevara expropriated the tin barons, Simón Patiño, Mauricio Hochschild and Carlos Víctor Aramayo, of their mines in Potosí and Oruro. I never understood what went wrong in Harry's upbringing, how they got to the precipice.

This day I am introduced to places in the outskirts of that city: St. Patrick's Cathedral, Rockefeller Center, the Empire

State Building and the Wall Street financial district. I take walks along the Brooklyn Bridge, from Cadman Plaza Park to City Hall Park and have lunch at a Vietnamese restaurant in Chinatown, continue through Little Italy and on through SoHo to Greenwich Village to find a lonely restaurant like the legendary Cafe Wha?.

Later I went back to the hotel room and lay down to reflect on my anguish. I imagined a path of begonias and ants through which I entered a moor with a dense forest that I identified as a rainforest. Maybe it was a ravine in the cloud forest or simply a place in an inter-Andean valley along the banks of a river. The village was an old two-story kind of place, with wooden paths that time had warped and a courtyard paved with boulders. To the north and south, along the only street, stood adobe houses. The group of buildings, which included a chapel with a bell tower, was part of a community that had dedicated itself to the cultivation of a variety of potatoes and to the raising of sheep.

In one of the courtyards of the main house, which was accessed through a mysterious hallway, a carpet had been spread out to hide the floor paved with feldspar slabs. At the sides they had placed metal benches with maguey boards that had the traces of the children's pinching in the soft part of the xylem.

In that place I pondered on my readiness to face whatever would follow the coming shipwreck of feelings. I smoked tobacco mixed with nostalgia and watched a child pass by, handicapped by some rare disease that I identified as infantile polyneuritis that had left its mark in the form of muscular atrophy of the lower limbs. The child had been placed in a wooden cart that his father had probably made and was being pulled by two healthy children using two esparto grass ropes. It brought to mind another child riding in a cart made from a fruit crate to which two axles had been attached, each with a metal washer with a ring on the inside.

Then I thought about my life. Maybe I was like that little boy who was being dragged by two other little boys. I suspected that the little boy was asking to be taken to the top of the slope. The boys pulling the cart were exhausted by the weight; nevertheless, they pushed all the way to the top.

"What is happiness?" I asked myself. I knew I wouldn't get an answer because no one was sure they knew.

Evaluating possible options for the pursuit of happiness, I remembered reading about a black mass in an Italian city, a ceremony that turned into an open orgy for those who wanted to participate in a different experience. The event was intended to parody the Catholic and Russian Orthodox masses, with constant and improvised elements. The sacrifice that was immolated during the rite was a subject of extraordinary beauty; he had to be very white, with very clear eyes and without an ounce of excess fat. The moment of greatest emotion took place when the man was totally naked and enormous individuals, with their bodies painted black, carried him on their shoulders as if he were a recumbent figure while the rest of the attendants tried to caress him. The body of the sacrifice floated at a certain height as it moved through a crowd eager to feel its skin.

The ceremony reached the orgasmic climax as a manifestation of collective madness. The cult was repeated every year with a connotation of a secret Dionysian rite that attracted individuals with a different sensuality. Perhaps it was not only a matter of exotic pleasures, but something more: a hedonistic way of facing existence. I imagined that the attendees were young men and women from the upper class of society: "From what society?" I asked myself. Perhaps they were members of a secret lodge that met annually in order to participate in the orgiastic celebration for which pilgrimages were organized from different parts of the world. What I was not sure about was whether this type of rites was confined to the post World War II years, during the second half of the last century, or whether they continued to be organized in the present times. Nor did I know which city had been chosen for this year.

The ceremonies became traditions over time. Just like that of the Neapolitan people who observe every year the liquefaction of the blood of San Gennaro, which takes place unfailingly on September 19, except for some circumstances related to bad omens, such as the occurrence of plagues, wars, mass impoverishment due to the economic crisis and corruption.

If the blood of San Gennaro does not liquefy and bubble like geysers before the eyes of the Neapolitans, the faithful interpret it as a warning of a catastrophe. To avoid bad times, the believers kneel before the saint and beg for mercy. Entire families, young children, old hunchbacks and the handicapped do this. It is then that they understand that this year will be bad, like the cycles of time or like the punishments for a sin committed by a sector of the population or by an important person that could have brought the wrath of heaven.

The orgiastic ceremony and the rite of the liquefaction of the blood of San Genaro are absolutely alien to my genetics. As someone said to me, "You may be a neighborhood boy, a boardwalk or a barracks boy, but you will never become a city boy." I could answer that this was not my intention, not even for a moment. Nothing could be further from my childhood of old shoes, hollowed out soles, overalls and shirts made of denim or devil's leather than the costumes worn by pedestrians on the rich streets and by those who rode through the tourist neighborhoods on carts pulled by percheron horses. I didn't fit in, not even after walking around the Champs Elysées and the streets near the Milan Cathedral. Nothing could be further from my aspirations than fashionable clothes and crocodile-skin shoes with suede jackets from the Alps. The suites of the Waldorf Astoria and the rooms of the Ritz will never be part of my life, even if I have stayed in them and slept in their beds

Later I saw in the streets of Buenos Aires and Madrid the loneliness of those who walk among a crowd that wants to reach the train station in Retiro or Atocha. It is the same feeling of loneliness that is felt in the cars of the subway trains, trying to squeeze in with a crowd of anonymous people each struggling to reach their destination. It is the same loneliness of those of us who travel in an empty car in the early hours of a sleepless night. The next day I looked for someone in a cafeteria, where I asked for a coffee with two croissants, to talk about the cold that comes from the delta of the river or about the humidity of the early morning, which is felt more in the Plaza Cibeles. And I was answered by an old man with a beanie covering his baldness or his gray hair.

"Yes, my boy, autumn is raw."

Perhaps I remembered a narrow street with two-story houses painted white with blue balconies. The road was so narrow that the balconies that protruded from the wall were close together and you could jump to the one in front of you without difficulty.

Somehow, I had avoided walking down the street during my youth, where pizzerias were dens selling marijuana and cocaine and bars dispensed absinthe. Street fights would break out there, sometimes involving knives and bottle picks. I avoided that street for fear that I might become part of that world.

There was no time for romance. The sidewalks were invaded by men in jackets or coats with many pockets in which they hid demerol and methamphetamines. Guys were getting high on anti-flu tablets, eye drops, or turning pseudoephedrine into ecstasy or gamma hydroxybutyrate, which they called liquid ecstasy. People who, in order to hallucinate, resorted to prescription drugs such as pentazocine, tramadol and ketamine, or intoxicated themselves with ivy such as stramonium or chamico until they went into psychosis and ended up in a state similar to decerebration. Some inhaled alcohol known as *oxy shot* or used paint solvents, carpentry glues such as terokal, with which the poor children of the big cities were drugged.

Faced with such a bleak outlook, I felt the isolation of the innocent. I considered myself a fool who did not know the name of the street or where I intended to go. Like a Cro-Magnon from the Paleolithic era, a stranger walking along roads where you came across rats more than thirty centimeters long from snout to tail. The prehensile tail allowed them to balance using the pipes of the drains. Along the way I saw mange-ridden stray dogs vying for food from the garbage cans with the rooftop cats and rats. On the same street, homeless people burned the garbage from the dumpsters to warm their bodies, which were chilled by the cold of the bay.

I was totally at odds with the graffiti painted on the German metro cars and with the shiny-plated motorcycles that cruised the superhighways of the United States or parked on Madrid's Gran Via. I didn't think those bikers could be world champions or muscle-armed, tattooed thugs. Worse, the Central Park rappers were performing something I didn't feel or, at least, didn't understand even if I paid full attention to it. I seemed to fit in with the music of Nirvana and Sid Vicious and his Sex Pistols, but these new musicians I didn't understand.

I had to stop running away. I had to face every detail of my existence. For example, I had to talk for the umpteenth time to the person I loved to explain what happened that time. Then she answered me with a sentence that remains engraved in my memory, together with hundreds of thousands of pyramidal cells and a tangled bundle of nerve fibers. I can remember the exact sentence, "When you don't have an argument, you look for an explanation." I interpreted the sentence as a categorical end and did not insist.

I tried to remember at what point the relationship got screwed up. As I was thinking, I was walking down a cobblestone street that was lined by the rails of a streetcar that had stopped running years before. Surely the screeching of the steel wheels rubbing would be unbearable, equal to the sound of the rockets that were produced in the windlass hoisted on the roof, when it received the electric current from medium voltage cables that extended along the street and three meters high.

She had desisted from continuing with our business when she heard the string of jokes I had spouted about the plumage of the birds and the colors of the butterflies, when I told her about the funny things about the St. Bernard dogs I had the idea of taking care of, when I told her details of my travels chasing emerging diseases. I tried to explain to her how the water of the marshes boils due to the chemical processes of decomposition of the eutrophic algae. I had also told her that the meanders of the great jungle rivers had temperatures in excess of thirty-eight degrees Celsius. Suddenly, at some point, her diskette changed and she was no longer the same.

I cried in her lap and she told me to go to hell. I told her that I was lonely and that my life was a tango in the suburbs of Buenos Aires, but instead of understanding, she just dug her heels in at the news. Then I grew to hate her for her insistent anger and the stubbornness with which she refused my pleas. I emailed her a hundred times and commissioned our friends to tell her that she suffered from chronic melancholy. I wanted to paint a picture that had a single motif: a blue tear on a fuchsia background. I could think of nothing more pathetic than a painting with a dilettante's tear. Then came oblivion.

The last time I saw her was during a visit to San Sebastian, where one of my children lives. He greeted me with a warmth that I did not expect. After a string of explanations on my part, he kissed me on the forehead and said, "I'm sorry. I would have liked to have the good fortune of your company. I am proud to be your son. We all feel the same way." He was referring to my other children.

At that moment I let out something like a sigh that released the tightness in my chest. It took me a while to identify whether it was angina pectoris or a spasm of the esophagus due to achalasia caused by Chagas disease, which I had contracted in Chaco from the bite of a vinchuca bug that had inoculated me with *Trypanosoma cruzi*. "Collateral damage of the war", I said to myself, thinking that I had gotten off lightly.

I had won the consolation prize: I didn't have the affection of their mother, but at least I had the affection of my children. I had to accept I couldn't win her back. I was carrying a heavily laden backpack. She seemed to be waiting on the platform of the train station. I remembered her from the period of running her restaurants in a tourist town by the ocean. Then I saw her in a dream in which she was traveling on a trans-Andean railroad linking Antofagasta and Salta. At the last station of Socompa we had to walk panting at four thousand meters of altitude to find the other station, which was across the border, after immigration and customs control. Our companions were Gypsies, Argentinean backpackers and Chilean beggars who moved from one country to another for a few pesos.

"Do you know how much it costs?" The Gypsies had a giant cheese that they cut with galvanized wires. The beggars had bread fresh from the oven and the Argentinians carried cans of canned picadillo. Nadia had sausages and empanadas and I brought beers.

The train climbed panting, as if it too was affected by the altitude. The whistle announced the arrival in the villages on the slope, like an echo that excited us, as if from the other side a convoy was arriving in the opposite direction. We traveled second class, with the benches against the wall and a space between them as a corridor. As the train struggled against the rails, we travelers danced to cuecas, Catalan rumba, Romanian music. Nadia and I had something difficult to classify. Perhaps it was the vision of colors superimposed on a range of grays.

Thinking about these contrasts brings to mind an episode in my life that I often confuse with the fragment of a nightmare during a feverish period. The plot places me in the main square of a very old city. I was walking around its perimeter holding Nadia's hand. Suddenly she asked me to sit on one of the benches in the square to listen to a retreat or maybe it was the music of a group accompanying the procession of some image. With that in mind, we walked through the gardens and the accesses that converged in the center, where they had erected a monument to a pre-Hispanic warrior. But we did not find a single empty bench where she could rest and I could sit next to her. The place had been invaded by ragged beggars who rested on the stone seats without caring about the time of day or the people passing by. Their faces were haggard and their bodies covered with ragged clothes. I sensed that their skin and scalps were covered with lice. The stench they gave off came from far away and their alcoholic breath was noticeable despite the open field. The males had overgrown beards and matted hair. The women had their hair braids sticky with dirt.

To get away, I suggested we go to a coffee shop downtown. I figured it might be similar to the one Wagner used in St. Mark's Square in Venice. I guessed that the people on the benches in the square were people in misery.

I don't know at what point Nadia started giving handouts to the elderly. As a result, an avalanche of homeless people surrounded us to receive the coins. At first, I found it an annoying situation, but one with no risk. When I observed the cavernous faces with scars, the toothless smiles, the eyes with palpebral ecchymosis, I realized the danger we were in of being savagely assaulted. Then, after shouting and shoving those closest to us away, we got into a cab that was driving along one of the perimeter streets of the square.

The beggars were pushing to open the door of the vehicle, we were struggling to keep it closed. It was a fight for survival. The cab driver pulled out abruptly and left several beggars scattered on the floor. In that way we were able to get rid of what seemed to have ended up being an assault by grim-faced pariahs with shapeless faces, handicapped people with spinal deformities and people with paunches.

When I recall the episode, it seems to me that I have experienced similar situations. I remembered being in a hut with several sick people. When I was trying to examine them, I noticed that in a corner, almost hidden by the darkness, there was an individual who was clapping his rifle. The fellow did not say a word, but in his attitude I could guess a feeling akin to hatred, to the censure of the old judges. "You heal my people or you die!" It was the veiled threat he intended to convey to me as he greased the gun. When I conversed with those who seemed to lead the command, I received the same offer, "You have to fix them or we'll see." There was no alternative.

They were all very young; they were at the age when you are not afraid of anything. I tried to look them in the eyes to find answers to my questions. I tried to string together a prayer I had learned with my mother. I prayed that the combination of antibiotics and corticosteroids, plus electrolyte replacement, would work and save the lives of the sick and also my own life. I used my therapeutic arsenal to lower the fever and reduce the agitation.

As I struggled to heal even one of them, the young men took turns watching my every move. Some covered their faces with red scarves; others wore scout hats. I estimated that the younger ones were between twelve and fifteen years old and the older ones were no more than twenty-five or thirty. I would have liked to explain to them that the healing of the sick did not depend on me. We had to wait for the reaction of their bodies. When I looked into their eyes, I could see the futility of any explanation.

"What I need is several days for the medicine to take effect on the disease," I told a boy in a Basque cap.

"We don't have much time, you bastard. You fix them up or you die," he replied. He could have added "Hurry up, arsehole!" although he didn't say it. Still, I understood.

I remembered other similar circumstances, surrounded by trigger-happy guys with different faces. They also had no idea what my work consisted of and suspected that my presence in their territory obeyed other interests.

Some nights I had nightmares in which I saw myself bound hand and foot after being captured and taken to a village of huts with high ceilings. In one of the huts I remained a prisoner, until my fate was decided by unknown leaders. In other huts the Massaco natives, who had ambushed us in the jungle, shot arrows with poisoned tips at us. They even hit their targets and wounded several comrades. In these dreams I saw the women being captured and dragged along the bank upstream while the bodies of the men lay on the ground, mortally wounded. Possibly, the nightmare was related to an episode in which I had to remove an arrowhead from the body of one of the reservation rangers. The segment, which was approximately twenty-five centimeters long, had dissected the pectoral muscles at its insertion into the ribs and lodged in the axillary hollow. In the dream I saw myself in an emergency room, or maybe an intensive care unit, with endotracheal tube and ventilator support to prevent respiratory arrest. In addition, he received a load of antibiotics centrally for septicemia. Afterwards, I always woke up anxious, as if I was living the dream.

I thought again of the girl who accompanied me to the hotel lobby. That time she did it in a dream. She looked like the girl I took to my friends' guitar party. Maybe it was even her. The same fine face and the same shape of the eyes. I would say she had an exotic and natural beauty that had me spellbound.

She was coming back from a very long trip that she would not tell anyone present about. I did not ask any questions about the place from which she was returning, nor did I ask any other impertinent questions that were not relevant. I kept quiet waiting for the twists and turns of the conversation to elucidate some of my doubts. What was her country of origin? I wanted to know if she was a descendant of an immigrant family. I looked into her eyes and told her they were the most beautiful I had ever seen. One of the attendees at the meeting commented that she had a special beauty.

She settled into an armchair near the musicians, leaned her head on mine and whispered in my ear a few words that I did not understand, but which I interpreted as points in my favor in a relationship that I expected to be much longer than normal for a tireless traveler or a quarter-hour visitor to that place.

The next day she called me on my cell phone from another room in the residence, which highlighted the columns of its façade that supported a veranda that, at the same time, was a terrace with a balustrade molded in stone. "In my dream we were riding in the bed of an old pickup truck driven by a mean guy," she said. "You covered your feet with a brown wool blanket. I was covered up to my neck with another light blue blanket. We were in each other's arms and we both swore to love each other until the end of our days.

During this dream I felt an immense happiness. I looked into your eyes and hallucinated, because you spoke to me in a language that only I understood. At every bend in the road the inertia brought our bodies closer and closer together. There seemed to be an end to any fear. I prayed that the trip would not end and that the van would not stop anywhere.

"Suddenly, in my dream a guy explained to us that we had to get off at that place, on the edge of a megalithic archaeological site. I was very sad; however, you kissed me on the forehead and asked me not to be afraid because you were by my side to protect me. Among the stone constructions we found a path bordered by green grass. Along that path we walked hand in hand. I saw your smile and you seemed very happy to walk beside me. At that moment I asked you,

'Are you happy, honey?'

"You answered me that you were not only blissfully happy, but that you were thrilled to be in a wonderful place together with the person you loved. I too was experiencing indescribable happiness."

It was her voice on the cell phone that told me her dream. It was her image in my mind that filled my senses.

I explained that I had visited ports with infamous canteens and traveled through swamps with three-meter crocodiles. I told her that I had walked along a path where the branches of trees hid poisonous snakes that slithered down to inject venom into travelers. I had been in places where children carry heavy machine guns and stare at you as if you were from another planet. I confessed that all those times I had been very afraid.

"I love you, honey!" she blurted out.

I thought we would end up in a restaurant in Barcelona eating a seafood paella.

I saw my companion standing in the main square watching the dance of the Collas and the Chunchos. The Collas wore a scarf to cover part of their faces. I imagined that they were hiding a face deformed by the spundia. Perhaps it was not spundia, but scars from smallpox or sputum with hemoptysis from pulmonary tuberculosis. I thought the black shawl was a hallmark of the sick. What was not clear to me was whether they wore the badge voluntarily or whether there was a higher authority forcing them to wear it.

The little men of the rocks and the natives in loincloths who came from the high jungles had all fought for the melt water that gushed from the ground among the weeds and then became a sonorous and foamy pipe that irrigated the pastures and fed the wild and domestic animals. It was the water of human life. Without water, everything would be dead. The rocks would be dark dens and the grasslands would run dry. The earth would shrivel and deep crevices would furrow it.

The procession continued with the image going through the main streets and the square. On the roofs of the houses the demons were placed, with their masks and multicolored clothes. The masks had deformed profiles and horns. The seven horned devils represented the forces of evil. Some already carried these evils in their bodies: ambition, pride, crime. Others represented external forces: epidemics, wars, droughts, earthquakes.

It was time to pray for people, for the children, I would pray for survival. I would pray for an outbreak of good fortune that would allow me to find companionship and affection. Perhaps I would pray for the natives of Madeira, for the Tuaregs, for the Bedouins, for the Collas, for the settlers of the leper village, for the Islamic Burmese, for the slaves sold in Libya and southern Algeria. I would pray for refugees and for the end of wars. I would also pray for scientific advances to eliminate diseases. And for utopias and new times.

Nearby were the places I had frequented in the past including the huts built on the slopes of the mountains, close to the streams that descend from the snow-capped mountains. As I climbed up the path, my shoes sank into the wet grass and slipped on the ice of the rhizomes. I noticed the smell of wet earth and the scent of trees that the humid forests give off. From afar I was watched by the natives, highwaymen, with tiny arrows and galena stone *boleadoras*. Nobody attacked me because I was part of their ethnic group.

"It is the returning traveler," reported an old woman who seemed to be an expert.

"I came to say goodbye," I said, "I won't be able to come back for them." They were sad. Then I continued, "Others will come, younger and, therefore, with more energy and much more knowledge."

They will be left with doubt and sorrow. In this way, I felt the affection of those people he had helped in the past. Some sighed; others cried with anguish. One intoned a nostalgic melody with a flute and drum.

Then I realized that I was not in that place, but in the jungle of a navigable river in Southeast Asia. My group intended to reach a port near the Chinese border. We sailed in a twenty-meter sampan, with canvas sails supported by bamboo poles at every turn. I thought our voyage was being watched by the descendants of the Khmer Rouge or by some opium smugglers. I needed to climb Angkor Wat to find the Khmer Buddhist temples that had been built in honor of the Hindu god Vishnu and later became Buddhist temples. I had it in mind since the day of my psychiatry exam, when Fracassi referred me to the beauty and solemnity of the place. For me it had the same beauty, exotic and permanent, as Machu Picchu.

The pagodas were elevated on atriums accessed by steep stairways. The tops of the towers, shaped like an ogive or cone, pointed to the sky. The complex was surrounded by a well, a lagoon that showed a tongue of land as a dike. The walls of the temples, built in stone, had carvings worked in slate, brick and laterite. The high reliefs represented faces of monarchs, scenes of daily life, such as cockfights, crocodiles in the river and canoes full of fishermen.

Angkor Thom, the city of the Khmer Empire, home to more than seven hundred thousand inhabitants between the ninth and fifteenth centuries, had its heyday during the reign of Jayavarman VII, between 1181 and 1215. It was the most populous and lavish city of the tenth century, when its enemies, the kingdom of Champa to the east and Ayutthaya to the west, besieged it episodically.

I found the ruins of Ta Prohm overrun by giant strangler fig trees and lichen on the walls. Hundreds of Buddhist monks were housed there in its heyday. Now the monastery is abandoned.

The doorway of the Kbal Spean marked the sacred place where the highest-ranking monks prayed. It seemed to me that the entrance to the sanctuary was similar to the Maya and Tiahuanaco doorways, with those vertical stones supporting the horizontal slab, where the high reliefs representing the tutelary gods were engraved.

At that moment I realized that the world was bigger, immensely bigger than the one I had known before. The circles became wider and wider and the atriums steeper and steeper. The journey continued through places that looked to me like puddles with rice fields and wells where naked children played. The swamps and puddles were swarming with mosquitoes. Someone suggested that we should take quinine to avoid malaria. For me, malaria could be avoided with doxycycline capsules because my heart was fucked up and I was afraid of cinchonism and blood dyscrasias.

Then I became aware of what I was: a subject made to the measure of the moment. Neither good nor bad, which was much closer to the non-dualist philosophy, antipode of Cartesianism. Neither extensive nor thinking. My body was a set of structures that came from the evolution of centuries, which left behind the fins of the pterygotes, and my brain derived from the cells of the ectoderm, specialized in maintaining interconnections, but at a distance, with extensions that infiltrated the rest of the tissues.

I was classified among a group of bumblers who pretended to be assholes in order to have company in the moments when the hand was heavy. At the same time, I oscillated in my decision making, but I was always attentive to those who asked me for something I could give them, especially if they were sick or weak. That was my primary compulsion. All it took was for someone to say they were screwed up to get me involved to the core.

I had been created by the dreams of a father, when the man was a lonely immigrant who felt the chill of the wind coming off Lake Michigan as he performed his duties as an elevator operator in any of the buildings during the era of the cut-faced gangsters. Over time I became a stylite who worked miracles when his robe brushed against the lepers of villages that clung to rocky outcrops.

At night, lying on the bunk of a tent in a camp, I was reading Malcolm Lowry's novel *Under the Volcano,* where the author explored "the search for the highest human ideal in degradation, the strange ties that bind grace to guilt, and the representation by symbols of the most pressing reality," just as the author himself symbolizes his creation. In the plot, the British consul in Mexico, an alcoholic named Firmin who was struggling with his addiction, loses his life in a brothel as a result of a gun attack carried out by fascist thugs. I felt I was in the same boat: I was struggling to get out of my depression and to find a life with other goals. I was anguished by the lost hours and days. I believed that I was like an aromo tree whose roots creep through the cracks in the stones, or that I belonged to the papilionaceae that grow in the tropical rainforests. Nothing would be easy and nothing would be given to me for free. I had to find the track, the trail, the path and then trudge, stumble, with wounded knees.

In the end, I understood that not everything was perfect. There were the ethnic differences, the confessional hiatuses, the clashing languages, the struggles for survival. There was exploitation, slavery, extreme conditions, starving children, deaths of innocents crossing the front lines; all of this was already there, even if I did not know when the fighting started.

I sat on the bank of a river, on top of a smooth rock, and looked into the water, which was dragging branches and mud in its path. Then I tried to come up with an answer: "I had no choice but to use what I had to try to get what I so needed". It was as simple as that.

I looked for feldspar rocks and asked the stonecutters to cut them, taking advantage of their cleavage planes, and then polish the fragments, as they would be the basis of a dwelling. The result could be a hut or a residence.

I understood it when I found the group of health workers shivering at the border. I asked them if it was the cold shivers of fever or the fear of the mercenaries of the task force. They answered me, "We are looking for yellow fever cases."

I realized that we were in the Mekong jungle. I was trembling like a soldier in a war where the enemy was nowhere to be seen.

I could only hear the roar of the guns in the line of fire three hundred meters away, behind a hillock. I discovered that the soldiers had the tremors of beriberi and damaged necks.

Then I became aware that I was sick. I was not suffering from fevers caused by an infection or wheezing due to respiratory failure. It was something deeper. Something of the mind. A dementia with many fantasies and little coherence. I was a sick person who had pretended to cure other sick people.

Epilogue

"Who would think of moving New York City, no matter that many more than fifty thousand people had died with SARS-CoV-2, no matter that as many as two million had been infected?" I asked myself. No one; at least, none of the New Yorkers. I imagine the empty buildings, the streets without cars, Times Square without neon lights, without commercials; Seventh Avenue without a person on Broadway trying to get a seat for the theater season. I imagined Brooklyn Bridge with no traffic even at rush hour, Wall Street with no stock market movement and SoHo with hospitals closed or full of overcrowded sick people.

Daniel and his streetwalkers would have gone south, perhaps to Baltimore, or further south, where the climate was more favorable. Littmann had left classes at Columbia University. Perhaps Stiglitz was still meeting with other Nobel prize winners to interpret the post-pandemic economic crisis. The war was almost over; perhaps it was still raging in the suburbs or in the countryside. But the war itself really was dying out, leaving more than three million dead, more than one hundred and fifty million sick, more than three hundred million confirmed, many of them asymptomatic and oligosymptomatic. More than two hundred million workers had been laid off, and more than five hundred million jobs were lost forever. More than one hundred million fell into extreme poverty, swelling the twenty percent of the needy that existed before the pandemic. The cities continued with their caravans of beings moving to the suburbs, and when they got tired, they sat. I imagined the lights and the sirens of ambulances going through the city at all hours. At night you would hear the whistling sound and see the reflection of their lights on the windowpanes of the buildings.

The coronavirus did not come out of nowhere. Those of us who were in the business knew it as SARS-CoV, in the case of China, and MERS-CoV, in the case of the Middle East. I imagined it could be one of many diseases that emerged after the Iraq-Iran war, the intifadas, the secessionist wars in Syria, or the invasions of foreign troops in Iraq and Afghanistan. Perhaps the winds and typhoons had washed away the pollutants. Perhaps the bad wind had come out of Turkestan or the sandy terrains of Uzbekistan and Kazakhstan, such as the Kyzyl Kum, to reach the Arabian desert and, in the east, the Thar desert between Pakistan and India. The wind carried tangles of dry scrub that rolled across the surface of the arid land. It formed swirls of sand that could be seen from fifty kilometers away.

With the branches moved bugs stuck to the veins, fungi that entered the lungs of dromedaries and the nostrils of goats in the Afghan mountains, pulmonary bacteria that penetrated the alveoli of shepherds and travelers who traveled the route of traders between the East and the cities of the Black Sea and reached the ports of the Mediterranean. At some point SARS-CoV reached the Altai Mountains after having traveled through the Gobi Desert. The microorganisms traveled in the nostrils of dwarf horses or in the fleeces of camels. Finally, they found their way into the jaws of the vampire bats that sucked the blood of the animals carrying the viruses. There, in the vessels that irrigated the respiratory tract of the chiroptera, the mutation occurred that turned the virus into a deleterious germ, with the possibility of being transmitted to other mammals, including pangolins.

Most of the animals that became sick from the epizootic died from infection or from the oversized response of the organisms' defenses. This was known as a cytokine storm. I imagine thousands of bats rotting in the caves while the pangolins dried out inside their scaly cover, under the aerial roots of the reeds. The natives of the jungle near the Altai Mountain range found the pangolins outside their natural habitats, afflicted with a deep languor. And the bats moved in flocks that darkened the sky like gloomy nimbuses.

Rural people hunted pangolins to use their meat and scales as food and as an aphrodisiac for urban populations. They sold their catch to traders in the Wuhan meat market. No one imagined that the virus could enter humans by handling or eating contaminated food and produce systemic infections that later became a zoonosis that traveled from person to person through Flügge droplets expelled by the sick in sneezing, coughing and breathing; even through hands that had touched contaminated objects.

Cities reproduced the queues of the Great Depression of 1929. The New York Stock Exchange once again had its Black Thursday and five days later its Black Tuesday, with shares passing from hand to hand and a fall of more than fifty percent of the nominal value of the quotations. Stockbrokers were going bankrupt and banks were trying to help companies on the brink of crisis. Billions of dollars, perhaps trillions of dollars, went up in smoke.

The price of oil plummeted, causing the oil-producing countries to feel the crisis as well. Millions of jobs were lost because markets had vanished. Agriculture changed its model, seeking greater industrialization and rationalization of agricultural production, with a consequent reduction in the workforce. The result was obvious: millions of unemployed, especially the migrant populations from neighboring countries, who were used as cheap labor in restaurants, civil and public construction, harvesting, land clearing and livestock care.

The first country to suffer from the crisis was the United States, which until then had led the world economy. The economic war with China had no clear winner because of the co-dependence of the economies. There was no chance of avoiding the economic collapse. The countries dependent on the giants succumbed to the disaster of the metropolises. The small countries were dragged down by the global collapse and the medium-sized countries tried bilateral negotiations to find a balance, in addition to seeking greater industrialization to avoid importing consumer goods. Against this backdrop, political and economic ideas were born. Ideologies that were thought to have been overcome, such as Nazism, ultra-nationalism, Stalinism and nihilism, resurfaced. Racial persecutions and ethnic wars increased. Fundamentalist religions led a rebellion against secular states and against traditional religious doctrines. Thousands of unemployed were on the move in an exodus for food.

There was an increase in the activities of groups that seemed to have been defeated, such as Daesh, the Kurds in Iraq and Turkey, the Maghrebis, the Tuaregs and Berbers, the dissident groups in Sierra Leone and those in Sudan. Terrorist groups were activated in several countries in Europe, Latin America, Africa and Asia, taking advantage of the discontent of the population.

Ten times more lethal than H1N1 influenza and more lethal than H3N2. The viral load sneaked into the cells and these lent it the messenger RNA so that it could replicate, sending the message to the DNA of the nucleus of the target cells by means of reverse transcriptase. Viral proteins competed with interferon, alpha and beta importins, to penetrate the nuclear membrane. The crown-like lipoprotein coatings were the surface antigens, which generated a first line of antibodies that destroyed the viral capsids and exposed their genetic material.

Next, macrophages and lymphocytes prepared a second and even third line of defense: macrophage cytokines alerted T helper lymphocytes, which support B lymphocytes to produce interleukin-1, tumor necrosis factor, TNF alpha and beta, platelet growth factors, and endothelial cell growth factors. The cytokine cascade produced an uncontrolled inflammatory process, with intravascular thrombosis, destruction of the arteriolar and capillary endothelium, total and partial obstruction of coronary, cerebral, renal and mesenteric vessels. They destroyed the basal membrane of the alveolar epithelium with exudation of fluid into the pulmonary parenchyma.

The second line corresponded to cellular defense with *natural killer cells*, giant lymphocytes that attach themselves to cells invaded by the virus and inject them with cytolytic enzymes that kill them. It was similar to what happened with the cells of neoplasms. The *natural killer* did not distinguish which cells were necessary for the survival of the individual, either part of the renal glomerulus or the pulmonary alveoli, the pancreas or the endocrine glands. The disproportionate cytokine cascade resulted in the destruction of vital tissues and the concentration of proinflammatory cells: macrophages, lymphocytes, neutrophils. This caused greater damage than that caused by the viral invasion itself; in severe cases, it resulted in the death of the patient.

No one was spared from suffering an amplified reaction of resistance to viral infection; however, statistics showed a greater vulnerability in older adults, carriers of chronic lung diseases, cancers, diabetes mellitus, morbid obesity, hypertension. Lethality did not exclude young people with no pathological history. This circumstance could be attributed to the viral load of the inoculum or to wild viruses of the most aggressive strains.

The pandemic spread throughout the world without respect for borders, race, age or economic conditions. Developed countries paid their share and then it was the turn of poor countries, which showed the world that we were not prepared to sustain a generalized onslaught. Hospitals were overwhelmed; intensive care unit wards, in particular. There was a lack of ventilators, monitors, secretion aspirators, infusion pumps; oxygen supplies failed. Doctors and nurses could not cope with the demand for hospitalization. Some of these professionals proved to be unprepared for the management of critical patients.

Eventually the disease became better understood. Not all exposed humans contracted it, as it was found that some of people in contact with the sick did not become infected; they did not even test positive in the rapid and molecular tests, as if they did not have cellular receptors. Those positive were, for the most part, asymptomatic and generated IgM antibodies at the beginning and then IgG at the end, as memory antibodies.

The SARS-CoV-2 pandemic, called COVID-19 because of its onset in 2019, was giving curves with acmesis between thirty and fifty days after its entry into the regions. Then the curves decreased due to the new cases reported and the number of supposed or proven deaths. The behavior of the pandemic followed the curves of other pandemics, epidemics and infectious diseases, with a rise in the curve, an acme after weeks, a dome for several more weeks, then a de-escalation to levels of a minimum number of new cases and, after several months, a second escalation or peak, with the contamination of sectors of the population that had not been exposed to the first onslaught of the virus.

I seemed to have experienced *déjà vu*. The quarantines, the confinements, the search for new cases, the tentative treatment, the follow-up of the cases, the tomographic studies, the pathological studies and the cytochemical studies of the sick and the dead.

It was not the first time that vampire bats had transmitted diseases. The Ebola virus had been proven to be a zoonosis originating from bats. Rats and their vectors spread the typhus and hantavirus rickettsiae. Yellow fever was transmitted by jungle monkeys. All of them were transmitted by Flügge droplets and caused pandemics with a higher mortality than coronavirus. The smallpox virus spread very rapidly and killed between two and five hundred million people before the twentieth century before Edward Jenner's vaccine was widely used. According to Professor Uriel Garcia, in agreement with Jared Diamond, the population of pre-Columbian America was decimated by the *Variola virus*. It started with the Mexica at the siege of Tenochtitlan and caused the death of Cuitlahuac and thousands of his warriors. During the conquest of the Inca empire, it preceded the conquerors, as it arrived through the Central American tribes that traded with the Incas. This provoked the death of Sapa Huayna Capac and, as a consequence, the secessionist war between the brothers Huáscar and Atahualpa; a confrontation that facilitated the conquest of an empire with more than fifteen million subjects.

Smallpox had a lethality ranging from thirty to fifty percent. Its first symptoms could be confused with any viral disease: fever, headache, chills, cough, myalgia, arthralgia. This was before the appearance of pustules all over the body, with a great deterioration of the general condition that led to the death of half of the people who contracted the disease.

Smallpox has been eradicated from the earth, for which purpose mass vaccination was instituted, as advocated by the World Health Assembly in Resolution WHA11.54. The last reported sickness from the wild virus was Rahima Banu, in Bangladesh, in 1975. The last officially reported death was that of medical photographer Janet Parker, in November 1978, due to a handling accident in a laboratory in Great Britain. The eradication of smallpox is considered mankind's greatest triumph in the control of infectious diseases.

Another disease that devastated mankind, with epidemic and pandemic outbreaks that caused the death of millions of victims, was the bubonic plague or Black Death. It took its name from the two most frequent manifestations: the appearance of buboes or infarcted and purulent lymph nodes in different parts of the body and the pneumonic plague variant, with hemoptoic sputum and darkening of the skin due to renal and adrenal damage. This disease was caused by the bacterium *Yersinia pestis,* named after its co-discoverer, the Swiss-French scientist Alexandre Yersin, who described the etiological agent together with the Japanese Kitasato Shibsaburö.

Yersin was sent by the French Government and the Pasteur Institute to Hong Kong to investigate an outbreak of bubonic plague in Manchuria in 1890. He also discovered that the bacillus initially attacked black rats in the countryside and was then transmitted to humans by the bite of the vectors: body lice.

After a short stay in France, he returned to Southeast Asia and settled in Nha Trang, where he pioneered the massive cultivation of rubber in Vietnam and the Andean cinchona tree, which he used to cure another of Asia's endemic diseases: malaria. He founded the Faculty of Medicine in Hanoi and the branch of the Pasteur Institute in Nha Trang. He died there in 1943, being recognized by the post-war governments as an Öng Näm (Mr. Näm Quinto) and as one of the founders of the Hanoi Medical School.

The same disease, known in its time, between 540 and 550, as the Justinian plague, devastated the Byzantine Empire and caused the death of half the population of Constantinople. It spread to the Balkan countries, the Danube, Greece, North Africa (Carthage), today's Italy and elsewhere. However, it is important to study the economic impact of the disease in order to know how the current coronavirus pandemic will affect society.

The Byzantine Empire was at war with the Vandals in the region of Carthage, with the Ostrogoths in the Italian peninsula and with the Sassanid Empire. Before the epidemic, great churches had been built, such as the basilica of Hagia Sophia. The plague had catastrophic effects on the economy, decreasing tax revenues, paralyzing commercial activities and affecting large settlements and rural centers dedicated to agriculture. The rats infested silos and food warehouses. The inhabitants of the countryside fled from the invaders and carried the disease to the outskirts of the cities, abandoning the countryside, which led to a great plague of locusts that attacked Hispania, Syria and Iraq and the Visigothic kingdom. Those cities dependent on agricultural production, such as Dougga and Carthage, lost between fifty and seventy percent of their populations. The cities of the Byzantine Empire themselves ceased to be a focus of resistance and security, since they did not have the economic resources to supply the troops and pay the mercenaries.

The economic crisis of the empire allowed the invasions of Avars from Mongolia, who took eastern Europe, such as the Balkans and Greece. In 568 the Avars had already conquered Hungary, western Romania, Slovenia, Moravia, Bohemia, eastern Germany and western Ukraine. The Slavs, vassals of the Avar peoples, completed the invasions of eastern Europe and settled in the region. Later, the Lombards from Germania, the present-day Czech Republic and Slovakia, allied with the Avars and the Slavs to invade the imperial territories of northern Italy and Tuscany.

The outbreaks of the epidemic created a climate of social instability that gave rise to revolutions such as that of Flavius

Nicephorus Phocas Augustus against Emperor Mauritius in 602. The revolution began with the insurrection of the troops cantoned on the Danube, which contained the advance of the Avars in the northwest of the Byzantine Empire. Commanded by Phocas and supported by the green faction, they fought and defeated the emperor and imposed a reign of terror. In turn, Phocas was defeated by the exarchs of Carthage, Heraclius and his son, which led to an upsurge of violence against the rulers of the day.

It seems that history repeats every now and then the same pages with different protagonists, but with the same plot. In each of them we find the invisible enemies, which are hiding somewhere. Can we be prepared for the silent attacks and for the devastating consequences that wars will leave behind?

This story took place in the past and mankind survived. Men will continue their long march between avenues and deserts, between places of crops, mines and oil wells. They will always wear a cloak over their bodies, laurel leaves in their hands and will drag their children and the elderly with them. There will be no room for despondency; on the contrary, they will have their heads raised and their eyes fixed on the celestial horizons.